EDGE OF ALLEGIANCE

A Cold War Spy Novel

By

Thomas F. Murphy

Copyright © 2005 by Thomas F. Murphy

ISBN 0-7414-2737-0

Published by:

INFINITY
PUBLISHING.COM

1094 New DeHaven Street, Suite 100
West Conshohocken, PA 19428-2713
Info@buybooksontheweb.com
www.buybooksontheweb.com
Toll-free (877) BUY BOOK
Local Phone (610) 941-9999
Fax (610) 941-9959

Printed in the United States of America

Printed on Recycled Paper

Published September 2007

Acknowledgments

There are many people who became involved in one way or another in the creation of this book and to whom I want to express my gratitude. I want to thank Joyce F. for her early comments and encouragement. Bob F. (no relation) provided research material on Moscow and talked about the bad old days there. Doug S., my friend of thirty-eight years, read the first half of the manuscript and made several helpful suggestions. Bob Baer and Brad Thor tried to connect me with an agent (not the secret variety). My half-sister Claire Smylie and her friend Judy Paul put me in touch with an editor. Leigh Platt Rogers gave me sound guidance that got me through the twists and turns of the publishing process.

My half-brother Jack Mulholland took time from a busy schedule at the Mayfair Diner to look through this manuscript. He proved to be a diligent and surprisingly analytical reader.

Brian P. generously agreed to buy a copy for each of his employees long before the book was finished. Thank you, Brian. J.M. and his wife, M.M., introduced me to the Middle Eastern dishes I describe in the book. That research was not only easy, but tasty. And my appreciation is extended to Col. Dick Friedman, who briefed me on NATO operations in Brussels.

Thanks, too, to my younger daughter Sarah, whose intelligent comments and suggestions were so helpful. Our tuition money was well spent.

Most especially, I would like to thank my wife Sandy, who read various versions of this book countless times and whose unflinching criticism kept me from cutting corners. Her praise when it came was all the more appreciated because I knew that it, too, was given honestly.

Prologue

Last summer I meandered through my professional past. Some friends from out of town came to visit and wanted to see the International Spy Museum. I had heard it was the second most popular museum in town after the Air and Space Museum and tickets were hard to come by. But I called a friend who had a friend. That's the way things work in Washington. Once inside I came across many of the espionage cases I had worked on or known about in my career with the Central Intelligence Agency. My friends seemed fascinated by them. But one old case, perhaps the most intriguing of all and the one I knew best, was missing from the exhibit. That's when I decided to tell this story.

My name is Mike Deemer, but that's not important. What is important in terms of this book is that from 1981 until 1994 I was a counter-intelligence analyst in what used to be called the Soviet and East European Division at the CIA and that makes me uniquely qualified to tell you about the Bagatelle case.

Within the walls at Langley, or at least within the Directorate of Operations, the agency's spy component, the case was famous. As you can imagine, it was difficult to acquire productive Soviet assets, Russians who were willing to risk capture and execution in order to provide us with secrets. We tried to spot those who were flawed and somehow vulnerable, then we approached them, but always on our guard against provocateurs. That was certainly true when we came across Vladimir Sergeyevich Shurin. We gave him the code name Bagatelle.

Every tale of espionage has its twists and turns, the Bagatelle case more than most. This is not a boom and bang thriller. Rather it's a classic spy story and a people story and I give you fair warning that it ended badly and when it did I was charged with discovering how it had gone wrong. That was in 1983. It took me another eleven years to put all the pieces together. At first I considered it just another job to be done. But gradually the search became an obsession. It was like a Greek tragedy. By the time I completed my work the Berlin wall had come down and the Soviet Union had collapsed. It was too late to

1

restore reputations and I couldn't raise the dead. But at the main entrance to the CIA you will see a quotation from the gospel according to John: "And you shall know the truth, and the truth shall make you free." I wanted to know the truth.

Because I have laid this out in the chronology in which it came to me, you may be confused and you will doubtless have questions. Rest assured things will become clear and your questions will be answered in the end. Also, in what follows I've been forced to take license with atmospherics, conversations, intimate thoughts, settings and so on, but in its essentials this story is the truth as I know it and I know it all too well.

Many people in the agency believe that the Bagatelle case started in 1981, when we first became aware of what he was doing in the West. Not true. It really began in 1968. On August 20 of that year, the Soviet Union led five armies of the Warsaw Pact into Prague, Czechoslovakia to quash the liberal government of President Alexander Dubcek. The international outcry was deafening. There were even small protests within the eastern bloc countries. One such demonstration took place on September 6 outside the Soviet Embassy in Budapest, Hungary. It was led by a young Hungarian Air Force officer named Istvan Pinter. He and his fellow dissidents were quickly surrounded and bundled off to jail. In the closed trial that followed, Pinter was sentenced to eight years in prison. He would never serve that sentence.

Chapter 1

In 1968, Istvan Pinter was twenty-five years old. He was exceptionally tall for a Hungarian, almost six feet four and gangly. At seven o'clock on Monday, December 16, before a drizzly dawn in Central Europe, he gazed through the windshield of a black BMW 2002 at the water reflected in the lights of a bobbing ferry. The Danube River, which slapped and trickled off the stone embankment ten meters from the car, was slicked with oil patches and turbid in the slow winter flow.

"Strange," said Pinter. "I never thought of this before. The Danube isn't blue. You can't tell that in the dark, of course. But it's true all the same. Johann Strauss must have been a sentimental sod."

The leather-jacketed, thuggish man in the passenger seat appeared to take some time to digest this remark.

"Either you're thick as concrete, or you're in shock, or...," and here he hesitated, "you're one cheeky bastard." The man wore one of those strangely popular black plastic fedoras. He reached in the pocket of his jacket and took out a mostly crumpled pack of *Cigány* cigarettes and a yellow plastic *Bic* lighter. "When were you sentenced?" Leather-jacket flicked the *Bic* and took his first deep puff, tilting his head back slightly. As he exhaled, he offered the pack to Pinter, who waved it away.

"In September," Pinter said as he leaned toward the rear view mirror.

"You were in for only three months?"

"That was enough. You try spending three months in that rat hole." Pinter reached up behind him and switched on the ceiling light. In a glance he saw that his black hair was speckled with white powder that made him look five years older. It was less noticeable on his waxen forehead. He just had time to run his hand through his hair before his passenger turned off the light.

"Now I know. You are crazy. Or dumb. No lights. Just because we helped break you out doesn't mean you can't go back in. This isn't over."

Pinter moved slightly to his left to create an angle in the side mirror that allowed him to study the lighted southwest tower of the Vac prison two hundred meters behind them on the Liszt Ferenc Sétány. Even in the darkness and pre-dawn mist he could see things were normal.

"You just lit a cigarette. That was a light. I have flour in my hair from that bakery truck. I know the risks. It's my plan, remember? You may have gotten me out, but it was you who put me in there in the first place." He straightened in his seat. "The machine is ready?"

3

Most people would not have trifled with the bull-necked man in the leather jacket. Once again he studied Pinter, narrowing his dull porcine eyes until they were barely slits. Then he shrugged and took another drag on his cigarette.

"Gassed up and waiting for you. This morning's report from Férihegy was that visibility is seven kilometers and the cloud cover is at three hundred meters."

"Férihegy is a hundred thirty kilometers from Fertöszentmiklos," Pinter countered.

"So you're not so cool. Don't worry. If you stick to the plan, your plan," and here leather-jacket smiled derisively, "this will work. Just don't take unnecessary risks. The Austrian forecast calls for low clouds, but no storm front."

The car sat at the end of a park that ran parallel to the embankment. Even in darkness, several people were walking, some with dogs, in the grassy area between the rows of stark winter chestnut trees. Pinter noticed that despite the suggestion to relax, his passenger's own hand trembled as he raised his cigarette to his mouth.

"Since you seem to know the plan, how are we on time?" Pinter asked.

"Perfect. Look." The passenger pointed ahead and Pinter saw a ferry sailor lowering the chain that blocked access to the boat. The ferryman waved the BMW, first in the queue, to come forward. "This is where I leave you." Leather-jacket opened the door and twisted his bulk out to the cobblestone ramp. "Happy journey, my friend," he flexed and snapped his forefinger and the cigarette, like an out of season firefly, spun off and sputtered out in a shallow puddle.

Pinter watched in the side mirror as the fellow lumbered up toward Esterházi Street, then he put the BMW in gear and rolled forward. By the time he stopped at the bow of the boat, another glimpse in the mirror showed a yellow Lada that turned off the Sétány and pulled beside his former passenger, who got in. The car sped off in the direction of Budapest.

Pinter almost jumped in his seat when he heard the tapping of metal on glass next to his ear. It was the toll collector using the back of his ring finger. Pinter rolled down the window and handed the man a ticket. As the fellow moved down the row of cars behind, Pinter got out stretching his long frame. The BMW was in line to be the first off on the far shore. He was on the cusp of freedom. Looking back toward the stern, he saw there were three rows of cars, about twenty-five in all, and most of the drivers had elected to sit where they were. To Pinter's left was an elevated wheelhouse. He climbed the metal steps and leaned on the rail gazing out in the darkness as the diesel engines revved and the boat cast off. The chill wind washed over him and for an instant he forgot that he was now a sitting duck until the boat reached the opposite bank.

4

The same toll collector came up the steps and passed behind him. "Good morning," the man said.

Pinter only nodded and the fellow continued along the gangway into the wheelhouse. They were already one third of the way across the river before Pinter looked back at the lights atop each corner of the prison. So far, he saw no sign of unusual activity.

The crossing took ten minutes. The ferry tied up on the northeast side of Szentendre Island, which was barely higher than the water line. Pinter angled his way into the driver's seat as the same ferryman came to lower the chain. Suddenly out of the corner of his eye Pinter saw a flash of light back across the river. He wriggled to get the car keys from his pocket, but dropped them on the floor. Once again he had to turn on the light, and then had difficulty getting the key into the ignition. Finally, he started the motor and turned to look back. The corner tower lights of the prison were now augmented by searchlights that were sweeping the interior yard and the immediate area outside the walls. Even with the windows closed Pinter heard the sirens and looked at the ferryman, who was standing with his mouth open. Pinter honked his horn and the man seemed undecided. He honked again and the fellow lowered the barrier slowly, looking first at Pinter and then at the license of the BMW. The car's wheels slipped and churned on the cleats of the wet metal decking as it rolled forward onto and up the cobblestone ramp.

The single road extended almost due west across the mid-river island. Pinter got the car up to ninety kilometers an hour even around the curves and left the other drivers behind. On either side of him, still hardy in early winter, stands of rushes and high water grass blocked much of his view. The few cottages he passed had uninhabited storks' nests on the chimney tops. He recalled that this was an island populated mostly by gypsies, narrow, flat and sandy and now he reached and crossed the low bridge that connected the western side to the far bank of the river. Once off the island he turned northwest on Route Eleven and breathed a sigh of relief.

He reminded himself that if things went as he had anticipated, the searchers would concentrate initially on the northern and eastern banks where the Danube flowed south toward Budapest. They would suspect he had driven toward the capital. Even if the ferryman reported him, by the time they realized he had crossed over, he would have at least an hour's head start in the opposite direction.

He stayed along the river roads almost as far as Györ, where he connected with Route Eighty-Five and headed toward Sopron. With first light, the December mist was clearing. In the fields among the stubble he saw countless pheasants, the hens and colorful cocks stuffing themselves to their content on the grain left behind after harvest. The trees had shed their leaves and now only the muted rusts and burgundies and flat browns

5

of Central Europe showed in the woods. It was approaching nine-thirty in the morning when he got to Fertöszentmiklos. Skirting the town, he drove along a dirt road into the low rolling hills. He parked on a rise at the edge of a grove of gray birch trees and returned the keys to the visor over his seat.

At this point he was east of Sopron, where the Austro-Hungarian border extended into Lake Fertő, or what the Austrians called the Neusiedler See. He had selected this spot because he had come here as a boy to hunt with his father and knew the area well.

He made his way over the clear knoll to a centuries-old oak and a mound of brush and briars about the size of a haystack at the edge of the tree line. He noticed matted grass and tire tracks about ten meters long leading from the clearing to this spot so he knew he was in the right place. Circling the pile of dead branches he spotted the opening he was searching for. On all fours he burrowed beneath the stack and lifted the edge of an olive green tarpaulin. Underneath, he saw what he had been told would be waiting for him. He crawled back out, satisfied himself that no one was in sight, then set to work throwing off the sticks and desiccated branches that camouflaged the canvas. He thought he had worked quickly, but worried that the cleaning had probably taken longer than he had anticipated. He then had to move back and forth several times to cach side of the tarp, throwing it back as hard as he could over the propeller blades. Despite the cold, he found he was sweat-beaded, his shirt glued to his back and his upper lip tangy with salt, but he was pleased and excited that everything had gone so well.

With the tarpaulin removed, he stood looking at a nineteen-forty-one Nagler-Rolz 54V-2 one-man helicopter. Draped over the open levers was a beige canvas windbreaker, leather cap and goggles, a watch and a wrist compass. Pinter put them on, stretching the goggle strap and mounting the lenses above his forehead. He tugged the eighty-pound craft forward along the same tire tracks to the spot where it was obvious from the wheel marks that it had landed. Now the machine was completely clear of overhanging branches and surrounding bushes but he checked the propellers carefully to be sure no brush had tangled in the mechanism. He was satisfied that the little ship was airworthy.

The copter was antiquated and primitive, three beams with a low pressure wheel at the end of each and a thin metal seat that remained open to the elements. There were two blades, each powered by an eight horsepower Argus motor. Pinter straddled the seat and lowered his goggles. As he settled in place, he figured that Bruno Nagler, the inventor, must have been shorter than six feet. Pinter had to bend his knees at a sharp angle. With the thick leather safety belt fastened, he turned the ignition. Both engines kicked in immediately and the blades rotated, slowly at first, then faster. He tested the two levers, the first to control engine speed, and the second to regulate blade pitch. Despite the cold, he continued to sweat under the leather cap. He crooked his arm and glanced at the compass. Finally, he revved the engines and tensed as the craft rose, again slowly at first, then steadily higher until he was well above the tree line.

He felt a surge of sheer joy. He could see the road along which he had driven and he shifted to lateral flight. Although the copter's maximum speed was only eighty kilometers an hour, at sixty-five meters with a December wind in his face and no covering to protect him that seemed considerable. But he paid little heed to discomfort. Rather it was the giddiness of flight and the ecstasy of freedom that now swept over and through him.

Pinter twisted his right wrist and looked once again at the compass and headed west-northwest. He continued to climb, and in less than five minutes spotted the water. Much of the lake was shallow, reedy, and brackish, home to herons, spoonbills, storks and egrets. Cruising down one bank was a patrol car.

When the border guards spotted him, the car stopped and both occupants got out. He made out one man pointing at him and a second who raised a pistol. Though he couldn't hear the shots over the din of the engines, he knew they had been fired as he saw the man's hand recoil several times. Pinter canted twenty degrees to starboard and could feel the pressure on his right buttock. Like all good pilots, he really did fly by the seat of his pants. Now he increased his speed to the maximum. Someone had miscalculated. He had been assured that those guards would be at the far northern end of the lake. He glanced at the watch. No wonder. He was almost ninety minutes behind schedule. Still, the shots were not even close and he righted the little machine and sped toward the far bank. As he passed over the barbed wire electrified fence just east of the border he experienced an elation that came to him only with flying and sex. The feeling stayed with him up to the instant he saw the Soviet MI-4 helicopter with the Hungarian border guard insignia.

At first Pinter was indignant. They had no right to be there. They were clearly on the Austrian side of the lake, but had positioned themselves between him and dry land. The gun ship swung lazily from side to side like a venomous spider dangling from an invisible strand. Pinter knew it had air-to-surface rockets, but they were not his concern. It was the machine gun turret that could spray the air and cut him to pieces that he feared. He understood immediately that his only chance to survive would come before the craft steadied itself and fired. He banked hard left and dove. The twelve point five caliber guns opened up. The firing was audible even over the din of his two motors. The bullets whizzed overhead. Although he couldn't hear them passing, he could almost see the air moving above him. He tilted again, this time sharply to the right and still down toward the water. He struggled to maintain control and at the same time tug on the safety belt. There was a sudden crack above his head then everything seemed to come apart at once. He was twisted almost out of his seat from a stunning blow to his left side. Somehow, he slipped the notch on the belt and tumbled out, cart-wheeling twenty feet down, as limp and uncomprehending as a shotgunned water bird. He belly-flopped on the lake surface and felt his nose flatten and his cheeks crack. The collision knocked the remaining air out of his lungs. He went under quickly and his final sensation came from the fingers and palm of his right hand as it slipped into the bottom mud. Crazily, his last thought was to wonder whether the watch he had been given was waterproof.

Chapter 2

Colonel Imre Galos sat studying the Hungarian translations his staff had compiled from the Thursday edition of the western newspapers he had spread across his desk. Galos was not a brilliant man. He was a plodder, a forty-eight year old former policeman who had made his way through the security ranks by dint of determination and hard work. He wore a civilian suit with broad lapels. It was gray like Galos himself and it needed pressing. Though it was not yet eight o'clock in the morning, smoke curled upward from a lighted cigarette on the ashtray to his right. Galos gritted his tobacco-stained teeth as he went from one translation to the next underlining certain paragraphs. When he had put the last paper on the pile, he pressed the buzzer that connected his desk with the outer office. A young lieutenant in the uniform of the AVH, the Hungarian security service, entered the room.

"Is General Acs able to see me yet?"

"Yes, sir, the general said you can join him at your convenience."

"Good." Galos rose from his desk, folded the papers under his arm and walked through the ante-room and down a red-carpeted hallway. Entering a door on the left, he spoke to the buxom peroxide-blonde secretary, who ushered him into the inner office of his superior, General Peter Acs. The general, in his service uniform, silver-haired, slim and straight-backed and in his mid-fifties, looked up.

"You have news I take it?" For an instant Galos glanced through the window behind the desk. There was a misty view of the still lighted Chain Bridge over the Danube and he could just make out the Fisherman's Bastion in the Buda hills.

"Yes, General. The Austrian papers gave it the most coverage."

"What do they say?" Acs held a black fountain pen with small gold bands near the tip and wrote something on the top sheet of a pile of papers in front of him.

"Somehow they got his name. 'Attempted escape of twenty-five year old Hungarian, Istvan Pinter, the youngest commissioned pilot in the Hungarian Air Force and son of the former Hungarian ambassador to the United Nations, who lived for five years in the United States.' They give some details, that he was part of an opposition group connected to the Czech dissidents, the Prague Spring, all of that. A chauvinistic mention that," and here Galos read from the translated article, "'The helicopter was built in Vienna and taken to Hungary after World War II.' They say, 'It was one of only four produced as Hungary and Austria collaborated with Germany...'"

9

"Yes. Yes." The general looked up from his papers and waved his pen in the air. "What about the rest?" Galos reminded himself that Acs had little patience for non-essentials.

"The Austrian government has protested the incident, which clearly took place over their territory."

"They say nothing about the body?"

"No."

"And no one other than the prisoner was hurt in the escape?"

"No. From that standpoint, it was all planned very well. Pinter is dead. I doubt anyone will make another such attempt. Still, we'll have to tighten security in the prison. What will you tell the minister? I guess there will be hell to pay."

Acs put down his pen and swiveled in his chair slightly to his left. He, too, took a moment to admire the view.

"Imre, what I've learned over the years is that in a situation like this it's best to tell the minister as little as possible. He'll be angry and complain about the bad press, but it will pass, although you may be sitting in this chair by the time it does."

Chapter 3

Orphans are generally wary and have a singular detachment from the world. Those few who are not overcome by a sense of rejection and are able to stand on their own often develop ambition and determination. Such was the case with Francis Xavier Manion. At age five he had lost his parents and was placed in St. Vincent's Orphanage in Philadelphia. The following year he was moved, through the intervention of a family doctor, to Stephen Girard College for fatherless white males. The college, really an elementary, middle and high school, prided itself on instilling integrity, honesty and character and in Frank's case they had succeeded nobly. Through a series of subsequent adventures, all compressed into the ten years that followed his graduation from Stephen Girard, Frank became a singular man, experienced beyond his years and totally self-reliant. By serendipity he found his way to an organization where such qualities were highly valued coins of the realm.

On March 15, 1981, Frank Manion stood in a sun-dappled corner of the arrival hall of Rio de Janeiro's Galeão International Airport. At twenty-eight years of age, he was a newly-minted CIA case officer on his first assignment. For over forty minutes, he fixed his attention on the corridor from the customs area. Finally, passengers from the Eastern Airlines plane from Miami began coming through the double doors. Still, about fifty people passed him before young Manion spotted his man.

"Mr. Rzepnicki?"

"Yes."

"I'm Frank Manion. Welcome to Rio."

"It was long trip. Longer than I was told."

"Yes. This flight is long. The one back to Miami is even longer. It goes through Brasilia. It makes a triangle. Be sure to keep your immigration form. You'll need to turn it in when you leave. Did you sleep on the plane?"

"No. Government pays only for economy class and seats are too narrow. I wanted to be on aisle to get up for toilet, but then I couldn't sleep. Goddamn people always were climbing over me."

"Let me help you with your bags. I have a car outside." Frank pointed in the direction of the exit and they began walking.

They were a Mutt and Jeff pair. Frank was five feet eleven inches tall, dark-haired, with eyes that were the blue of stonewashed denim. He was tan and very fit and his walk fluid and steady. Boguslav Rzepnicki was in his early sixties, squat at five feet four inches, one hundred eighty pounds, balding with a gray toothbrush moustache. His skin was sallow and his lips the dulled red and rough texture of beets. His dark eyes were furtive and his gait was labored. He took a graying handkerchief from the pocket of his wrinkled khaki pants and wiped his forehead.

"You stationed here?" Rzepnicki asked.

"No. I came down from Washington as you did. You were still out on assignment so we didn't have a chance to meet up there. I've been here for only a few days."

"I was in Athens. I got back day before yesterday and I have to go back there when I finish here. Is too much goddamn travel." Frank continued to carry the heavier of the little man's two suitcases, a tan canvas bag with leather straps that had seen better days like its owner.

"It's so hot here," Rzepnicki grumbled.

"This is the end of their summer, but I understand it never gets really cold." Once outside the terminal, Rzepnicki seemed to wilt before Frank's eyes. "The apartment stays cool," Frank assured him. "There are fans and you can take a rest before we get started. I assume headquarters told you what this is about." When Rzepnicki didn't reply, Frank spoke again. "Maybe I assume too much."

"No. They told me, but not very much. We are just contract employees so they don't permit us to read complete files, just summary." Rzepnicki suddenly pointed a stubby finger at Frank and shook it. "But you better understand that I don't want to be stuck in one-room flat to work all goddamned day and have you come out to get tapes once in a week. That's how most case officers do teltap operations. And I don't want my per diem cut just because you picked out expensive place."

Manion looked with curiosity at the little fellow. In the library at Stephen Girard he had read voraciously, relentlessly, everything from nursery rhymes to Shakespeare. Rzepnicki reminded Frank of the pictures in donated fairy tale books of Rumpelstiltskin about to stamp his foot. He had long ago discounted age as a guarantee of maturity and had been warned in Washington that this man had a prickly personality.

"Boguslav, I think the apartment's okay. It's got several bedrooms. The base picked it out. You'll have to work out your per diem money when you get back home. For my part, I'll come at least twice a day. I don't want just transcriptions. I want to talk to you about what this guy that you're listening to is like. I don't think you'll be hard pressed to do this job. It's only one man we're interested in, one teltap, one audio op, and the apartment is paid for out of operational funds."

Frank muscled the bag into the trunk of the blue Ford and unlocked the front door on the passenger side. Rzepnicki stood by the rear passenger door, obviously intending to put his second bag on the back seat. Frank reached in and pulled up the inside lock.

"We should stop for something to eat," Rzepnicki told him as he swung his bag in the back.

Frank understood full well that the transcriber's care and feeding were now part of his job.

"I went shopping yesterday. You have groceries at the apartment."

"What if I don't like what you got? I shouldn't have to pay for that." Rzepnicki seemed to have a permanent snarl on his face.

Frank walked to the driver's side holding himself in check. He looked over the top of the car. Only the bald pate and the upper half of Rzepnicki's face with its thick gray brows and tired, shifting eyes showed. Frank kept his voice even.

"You don't have to eat it and you don't have to pay for it. But why don't you take a look first? Eating in the apartment is probably cheaper than eating out."

When Frank opened the driver's side door he immediately rolled down the window.

"This car don't have air conditioning?" Rzepnicki lowered his own window.

"I'm afraid not." Frank twisted in the seat to back out of the parking space.

"You speak Portuguese?" Rzepnicki asked.

"Yes." Frank accelerated and pulled out of the lot onto the service road and rolled toward the highway.

"You look too young to be doing such work."

"I feel myself aging by the minute." Frank glanced over at his passenger, but Rzepnicki didn't appear to catch his meaning. Frank turned on the radio and the blare of samba music filled the car.

"Why did they pick you for this case?" the older man asked.

"I've asked myself that question a number of times. They pulled me out of Portuguese class to come down here. I still had a couple of months to go. Maybe if I finish here soon enough, I can get back in the class." Frank rested his left elbow on the window frame. "I think the real reason is that I speak Russian."

"Where did you learn that?"

"In California in the army."

"*Tak. Vy govorite po russkiy?*" ("So, you speak Russian?")

"*Da. svobodno.* ("Yes, fluently.) This case isn't one of the more important ones the Soviet Division is working on otherwise they would have turned it over to a more experienced officer. But there are only a handful of Russian speakers. I guess you know that."

"Yeah," Rzepnicki pulled down the sun visor, took the same handkerchief from his pocket and wiped his beaded brow again. This time he kept the cloth in his hand rather than return it to his pants.

"And most have bigger fish to fry. This fellow we're after has only ten weeks to go before he goes back to Moscow, and they think we might be able to recruit him. Headquarters wants someone to get to him before he leaves Brazil. So I'm the one."

"What if he turns you down? Most of them do."

"I'm using an alias and if I'm able to meet him somehow, I'll do it in disguise." Frank rolled slowly behind a diesel truck. With the exhaust spewing from the truck's pipe, he decided to pull in his arm and raise the window. Better to sweat than to be asphyxiated.

"Why were you studying Portuguese?" Rzepnicki asked.

"I'm supposed to go to Brasilia this summer."

"If this guy talks Portuguese on tapes, you gonna have to do those."

"Yes, I know." Now Frank felt perspiration forming on his own forehead and had to wipe his hand across his hair line. "How about you, where are you from in Russia?"

"I'm not Russian. I'm Polish, but I learned Russian language when I was very young. My village was on Soviet border. Sometimes I got mixed up and we spoke both Russian and Polish."

"Great," Frank thought. This really was the second team. Like the car company they would just have to try harder if the operation was to succeed.

The trip in took almost an hour mostly on the heavily traveled industrial road. By the time Frank turned into a small back street in the Leme district, it was lunch time and Rzepnicki said his stomach was growling. This time Frank opened the trunk of the car and stood there. Rzepnicki, with the bag he had taken from the back seat hanging almost to the ground on a shoulder strap, looked at him then grudgingly tugged on the handle of the bigger suitcase and tilted and wobbled along the sidewalk like a decelerating top and entered the hall of the apartment building.

"The elevator is out of order," Frank announced.

"What?"

"Here." Before Rzepnicki could complain, Frank took the larger bag out of his hand. He thought the little man might have a heart attack carrying two bags upstairs even though it was only one flight. That would not be an auspicious beginning to the operation. Frank pictured himself writing the cable home saying that his transcriber had arrived safely then died before listening to even one tape.

The apartment was modest, but clean and well provisioned. It had been leased by a base officer under a false name. Frank immediately turned on the radio and the television. Actors were reciting their lines in a Brazilian soap opera, but he wasn't interested. He wanted only background noise to overcome any audio bugs. He stood beside Rzepnicki and spoke in a low voice.

"I'll let you unpack. You can look in the refrigerator and see about lunch. If you decide to go out, there are three little *feijoada* places right on this street. I exchanged fifty dollars for you. The *cruzeiros* are in that envelope on the table. After lunch you can take a nap. I've got to go and get the first bunch of tapes and I'll be back around five o'clock. I'll let myself in with the key in case you're still asleep, so don't put the chain on the door." Before Rzepnicki could grumble about that arrangement, Frank moved to the small foyer. "I'm leaving a key for you on the table."

Frank had arranged the rendezvous site by cable before he left Washington and now he spent the next hour driving and walking the back streets checking for surveillance. He stopped in a Jumbo Supermarket, where he bought an umbrella, and at several newsstands for magazines and a copy of the other major Brazilian paper, "*O Globo*". He had chosen this route because it would force any surveillance team to move from crowded areas into empty streets and shops where they would be easier to spot. Satisfied that he was clean, he headed for Leblon.

Six tiny tables under colorful *Cinzano* umbrellas were positioned on the sidewalk outside a small café on the rua Ramos, but Frank went inside where he would be less conspicuous. He ordered a *chope*, a Brazilian draft beer, and practiced his Portuguese reading the newspaper. For another twenty minutes he kept one eye on the paper and the other on the entrance.

A stunning dark-haired woman came in. Her green high-heeled shoes clicked on the black and white tiled floor and she took off her sunglasses and tried to focus as she moved out of the sun. Every male in the place including Frank stopped what he was doing and stared. Her legs climbed to heights most of them surely dreamed of scaling. But Frank saw she had more than physical beauty. There was almost an aura about her. She must have known they were all gawking, but she seemed indifferent to the stir she had created. Most women would have made some self-conscious gesture, running their hands back through their hair, or smoothing their skirt, but this one was statuesque, unruffled. Frank thought she was probably accustomed to the attention. He took her for Brazilian until he spotted the international edition of that week's Time Magazine in her left hand and realized she was holding the sunglasses in her right. Those were the recognition signals. She was his contact.

When her eyes fixed on him, Frank folded the *Globo* and held it where she could see it. He put on his own sunglasses and immediately removed them. She moved between the tables with an athletic grace. Frank rose to slide the cane-bottomed chair out from the table, but she raised her hand to show her palm.

"No need."

In the instant he was standing, Frank figured she was about five feet nine, a hundred thirty very shapely pounds. As she sat down she stuck her sunglasses in her small white purse and slipped the leather strap from her wrist.

"You're Pushteau?" Frank used the pseudonym he had seen in cable traffic.

"Yes, I'm Julie d'Andrade, nice to meet you. I see you have an umbrella. You'll probably need it. The clouds are gathering. And you got the shopping bag. Good."

"I'm Frank Manion."

"Yes." She gave him a sympathetic look he suspected she normally reserved for the infirm. Unlike the Rio Base cable, his true name had been in the headquarters cable.

"I'm sorry. I wasn't expecting..." For an instant Frank's voice trailed off. "I mean the cable I saw in headquarters gave this café, but it said a Dale T. Pushteau would meet me."

"So you weren't expecting a female. Is there a problem?" The smile had disappeared and Frank realized it was not the way to start things off.

"None, other than the fact that every guy in the place is looking at you and after they look at you they look at me. But I guess you can't help being...," Frank stopped short again.

"A woman?"

"No. Actually, I was going to say you can't help being attractive. Are you a secretary?" As soon as the words were out of his mouth he realized he had committed blunder number two. Julie tilted her head back and this time she did run her hand through her hair. Her eyes were emerald green with the tiniest flecks of hazel. For an instant they flashed.

"No. I'm a case officer." She had a disgusted, heard-this-too-many-times-before tone. "I'm on my second tour. The first was in Paris. Three years. You on the other hand have yet to work overseas, right?"

Frank figured he had to lighten things up.

"Yes. Is that a problem?" He smiled, but she didn't react to the prompt. Instead, she took a pack of Marlboros from her purse, lit up and inhaled. The smoke came out as she talked.

"Let's start over," she said. Once again she smiled what Frank already realized was her perfunctory smile. "I assume you have all the time I need. As for me, I have about forty minutes max. They sent me for two reasons, first, if the Brazilian security people should see us together, their machismo leads them to only one conclusion: We're romantically involved, to put it nicely. That's our cover story." She paused and took a second puff. "And the answer is no. We won't live our cover."

She had read his mind, at least partly. He was instantly attracted to this woman. But even though he would have enjoyed a romantic fling, technically he was still married. At least he was when he left Washington. And he was the kind that would always be faithful to his wife.

"Here is my home phone number. Use it only in an emergency." She passed him a slip of paper. "When you call, say you've seen an apartment you want to rent. Tell me the floor. That will indicate day of the week. First floor is Sunday, second Monday and so on. The price will be the time, twenty-four hour clock: eight hundred a month is eight o'clock; thirteen hundred, one o'clock. Got it?"

"Yes."

"This will be our rendezvous point. Take a table outside or in here by a window. I'll come by in my car and you come out."

"What kind of car do you drive?"

"You'll see it when we leave here."

"When do you usually get home from work?" he asked.

"That's hard to say. I guess since you haven't been in the field yet you don't know how things are. The work goes round the clock and you do, too." She glanced at his left hand. "I see you're married. I hope your wife trusts you implicitly because you'll be out almost every night and when she asks where you've been, you're going to have to say, 'Darling, I love you, but I can't tell you.' Your personal life will revolve around your operations, all that is by way of saying that I don't keep regular hours."

That touched a nerve and Frank didn't know whether his discomfort showed through. His marriage was rocky, but that wasn't something he was about to bring up now. The operation was complicated enough.

"So in an emergency you may not be there?" He picked up his glass to take a swallow, but he thought it would be impolite before Julie had her drink, so he put it back on the table.

"Between the base number you called and my number, you should be able to stay in touch." Julie twisted sideways and leaned down from the table to adjust one of the straps on her shoes. "You're from the Soviet Division, right?"

"Yes."

"They sent an officer down here about three months ago to pitch another Soviet, Bunin." She sat up again. "The fellow turned down the pitch and reported it to his ambassador. Do you know about that case?"

"Yes."

"There was a protest. Our ambassador was called in to the Foreign Ministry. The chief of base told me to tell you he doesn't want that to happen again. So first, if you find this guy doesn't look good, don't invite him to the dance. Understand?"

"Yes." It struck Frank that she had taken charge of the meeting fairly quickly and he was impressed by that. He didn't surrender his independence easily. But he wanted to hear her out, to see how good she really was.

"Second, since we first got the lead on this fellow Shurin, I've been assigned to try to get in touch with his girl friend, the Brazilian woman. So I'm not just your inside contact. I'll be working with you on the case."

The waiter in an open-necked, short-sleeved white guanabara shirt finally came to the table. Julie looked at Frank's glass.

17

"*Eu tambem, eu terei um Brahma chope.*" In perfect Portuguese, she ordered a Brahma beer.

"*Mais um para mim.*" Frank ordered another. "So, you speak Portuguese?"

"Yes. That was Portuguese."

Frank began to wonder if the recruitment itself might not be the easiest part of the operation. So far, the two people he was to work with seemed less than amiable. He knew that just as he did with men, he would let her go only so far before he reacted, and he decided now that she had reached that point.

"With a Portuguese accent, not Brazilian, you sound as if you learned it from a Portuguese fisherman in New Bedford. You didn't bring the tapes?" Frank saw no package.

She looked at him with an expression that seemed to border on amazement. Now she spoke slowly and stared at him. Her tone wasn't hostile, but it was measured.

"I left them in the car." She took another puff of her cigarette and looked slowly around the room. It was several seconds before she turned to him again. "You come with me when I leave. We sit in the car. That way you can put the tapes in the grocery bag without anybody seeing you. We'll do it that way when I come out. Otherwise, I'll send a secretary and she'll carry a Jumbo bag just like the one you have and you'll do a switch."

"Sounds okay to me," Frank finished the beer in his first glass. He saw less need to be polite.

"By the way, I see you're wearing a watch." She had switched back to her game face and her take-charge manner. "I wouldn't if I were you. And you might even take off your wedding ring. Bands of kids roam the streets looking for gringos. They'll have that watch quicker than," she paused, "grain goes through a goose."

"I'll consider it."

"Suit yourself."

"So you don't think of yourself as a gringo? Actually, you look Brazilian." Frank added quickly, "That's a compliment."

"My family is Portuguese, from Brooklyn. We're originally from New Bedford. My father was a fisherman."

At first, Frank thought she was joking, but then he saw in those hazel green eyes that she was serious.

"Sorry. There's nothing wrong with New Bedford." Frank felt the way he had when he was an altar boy at St. Vincent's and had knocked over the chalice of consecrated wine in front of the Sunday congregation. Julie didn't change her expression.

"We were always taken for Puerto Ricans, but we were Portuguese."

The waiter brought Julie's beer and gave Frank his second. Frank raised his glass as a gesture.

"Thank you for coming. I know you must be busy."

"It's what I get paid for. Just like you." Julie took off her linen navy blazer. Underneath, she was wearing a short-sleeved pastel green ribbed cotton blouse and as she crooked her arm and sipped her beer, Frank looked at her elbows. He judged a woman's age by her hands, her elbows and the corners of her eyes, and figured Julie for about thirty-one or two, three or four years older than he was. He took a deep swallow of his own beer.

"Any word from headquarters?"

Julie pulled a small white hankie from her purse and dabbed at her lips. There were no cocktail napkins.

"They sent an updated bio sketch of Shurin. I don't think you should get too excited. They aren't treating it like a big time case. He's an administrative officer in the consulate."

"Yes. I know."

"He's definitely not KGB or GRU and he doesn't seem to have great access to anything. He's straight foreign ministry. I'm not sure why they're interested in him. That's probably why I got assigned to the case. They usually dump the trash on me. Maybe they're not interested in him at all. Maybe they're just trying to give you some experience." She inhaled deeply on her cigarette and turned her head as she exhaled.

"What makes you think they're not really interested in him? Did they say something in the cable?" Frank pushed the copper ashtray across the table closer to her.

"It's the cryptonym they assigned." Julie took a glance around the room. By now the men had long since gone back to their drinks, though every once in a while one would look her way and shake his head in admiration. "They're calling him 'Bagatelle.' Do you know what that means?"

"It's a trifle, something without importance."

He could see she was trying to conceal surprise. He didn't know if the impression he might have made was good or bad.

"Yes. Well, that's what tipped me off."

Against the light from the doorway and small windows, Frank watched the smoke from her cigarette curl and rise slowly to the ceiling fan. Suddenly he got a sense of where he was. This was like a Bogart movie, "Key Largo," or "Casablanca." And he realized that he looked at her differently. When she came into the café and stood at a distance she was remote and unattainable, possibly an object of some later fantasy. But now that she was close at hand and accessible he realized that he had begun to wonder and maybe even hope uncharacteristically that something would come of their meeting besides a professional collaboration.

"Still, Rio is lovely, the tropics. It has to be fun," he said.

She shrugged her shoulders.

"It's a lot less fun when you're trying to operate here. I run two safe house-keepers. I pick up mail from three accommodation addresses and I run a couple, Russian émigrés, access-agents to the Soviet Consulate. They were the ones who got us the keys to Shurin's apartment so we could put in the audio device. They were able to get close to his wife."

"I saw that in the file. That was a good little operation." Frank immediately regretted having used the adjective little, but she appeared to ignore it.

"I do have one press placement fellow, another older White Russian. He's sweet and he does good work. I have a couple of developmental cases. It took me almost a year to get them this far. One is the Polish first secretary, but I'm convinced that he only wants to get into my shorts." Frank didn't comment on the Pole's ambition, which seemed reasonable to him.

"Well, since they sent me here, I'll do what I can. They still believe Shurin's recruitable, right?" He took another sip of his beer.

"I suppose. And it's true that he's different. He's still on the phone a lot with the Brazilian girlfriend. A lot of the Sovs run with the local ladies of the evening and for the first year he was here Shurin did, too. But none of them calls a Brazilian woman and says he loves her and talks about their future together. If his boss found out, Shurin would be out of here. The girl's from a prominent family and he sounds as if he's really in love. I doubt the family knows about it. They would stop her from seeing him, but they haven't so far. Plus, he has unusual freedom to move around. But I guess you know all that." Frank just nodded. "Anyway, that's why headquarters figures you can get next to him." Julie drank again.

"Do you have any suggestions as to how I might do that?"

"No. We really know very little about him and that's why you're down here, to figure out what he's like, see where he goes and how you can meet him. I'll be concentrating on the girl. Her name is Justinha Marques."

"Have you made any progress going after her?"

"Some. Her family belongs to the Joquei Clube. I think I may be able to meet her there."

"You're a member?"

"Yes. Did Rzepnicki get in on time?"

"Yes. He's back in the apartment."

"He's not going to be a problem? A couple of the fellows in the office said they've dealt with him and that he's pretty crotchety and difficult to work with."

"It will be all right. I think he likes to feel he's important."

"If you do have a problem, let me know right away. We don't want any flaps. The Brazilians don't know about you or him. And I want to finish my two years here. If I get PNG'D for something I screw up, fine. But I don't want it to be over this case." Julie took another deep puff on her cigarette and a swallow of beer almost at the same time.

"I'll watch him."

"Let's see the bag."

"Right here," Frank lifted the blue plastic bag with the orange logo of the Jumbo Supermarket from under the table. He carried the magazines in it to give it bulk.

"Okay. That's big enough. Are you ready to go?"

"Are you in a hurry? You said you had forty minutes."

"I think we've covered everything for now. And I have to meet an asset. This will give me a little more time to check for surveillance."

"Let me pay for your drink," Frank offered.

"I'll take care of it."

"Suit yourself." Frank waved to the waiter, who took his time coming from behind the bar.

"How long have you been with the agency, Manion?"

"Two years."

"Why haven't you been overseas yet?" Julie said this with what Frank took to be feigned surprise and perhaps to remind him once again of the pecking order.

"I finished the ops course and paramilitary training a year ago and now I'm in language school. I'm supposed to go to Brasilia, to the new embassy."

"Not very much happening there." Now there was another look. This time she seemed to want to convey knowledge of something he had yet to learn, but perhaps he was reading too much into it.

"Maybe I'll be able to get something started." The conversation had been almost all business, but he couldn't help being aware of how beautiful she was. He had to keep reminding himself to act professionally.

"Maybe," Julie took her own watch from her purse and drained her glass. "What is wrong with this guy?" She raised her hand to the waiter, who was only five feet to her right. She paid for the drinks and Frank left half of his beer on the table. Outside Julie pointed to her left. "After my meeting I still have three contact reports to write up. Come on. I'll give you the tape." Up the side street, Julie unlocked the passenger door of a beige-colored Peugeot then stepped toward the trunk. "You get in the passenger side. I'll get the package." Frank did as she instructed and leaned over to unlock the other door. She closed the trunk lid and slid into the driver's seat, her skirt riding up her thighs. They were slightly separated and awfully inviting. Frank couldn't help but glance, something she noticed immediately. She scowled. "Here." She handed Frank a single thin box, six inches square.

"Just one?" He was surprised.

"Yes. Don't worry. It's LP. It has several days of conversation on it. That will keep Rzepnicki busy. Meet me on Thursday, same time. When he finishes this tape, bring it back and I'll give you another. Take this." She handed him a guide book to Rio de Janeiro.

"That's nice of you. Thanks."

"I didn't bring it to be nice. In the section on restaurants and cafés, I've underlined four places. They're numbered one, two, three, and four. The place we were just in is number one. We'll keep rotating for as long as you're here. Next meet is at number two." Frank put the box and the book in the shopping bag among the magazines.

"Thanks."

"Manion."

"Yes?"

"Try to stay out of trouble." She looked straight ahead as he got out and he was barely on the sidewalk when she pulled away.

For the next hour Frank walked and drove again. While he was confident he hadn't attracted any attention and he didn't doubt Julie's word that she watched for surveillance, he had to take his own precautions. At this stage he wasn't sure how good she really was and he suspected the Brazilians might be following her and would be interested in anyone she might meet.

Back at the apartment Frank unlocked the dead bolt and turned the doorknob. But as he pushed, the wood grated against the chain and stopped. He knocked softly and called through the slit.

"It's me. Open up." There was no response. Once again, he feared Boguslav might have had a heart attack. But he thought it more likely the fellow was asleep. He called louder and with still no reply, was forced to knock harder.

The chain rattled and Rzepnicki opened the door.

"I was asleep. I'm exhausted."

"Yes, and I wouldn't have woken you if you hadn't put the chain on the door." Frank was losing patience. "I told you I would come in with the key." Frank held it in front of him almost in the little man's face. "Did you eat lunch?"

"Yes. I took from what was in fridge."

"Okay." Frank raised his index finger as a sign of caution. He walked to the television and turned it on. Once again, the program was one of the almost constant soap-operas. He turned up the volume then returned to his chair and spoke in a low voice. "I got the tape. You don't have to start on it tonight, but I want to talk about what I need from it."

22

"Okay. But I got to get some sleep." The older man leaned back on the sofa and spread his stubby arms over the top of the cushions and tilted his head back. This forced Frank to lean forward in order to be heard.

"They did a personality assessment of Shurin at headquarters. But I'm still interested in your impression of what the guy's got in his head. Then, above all, I want to know about his movements, where he goes, who he sees. Focus on appointments he makes. I'll need at least a day of lead time if I'm going to be able to run into him."

"I know all that. I been doing this work for over thirty years, but no work tonight."

"Right, I'll be here first thing in the morning."

"Where am I going to get supper?"

"That's up to you, Boguslav. We start tomorrow. I'll be here bright and early."

"Not too early."

As the mid-March sun set around eight o'clock, Boguslav Rzepnicki sat uncomprehending before the TV. What kept him interested were the breasts and bottom of the female star. The evening soap opera was followed by a U.S. western with dialogue dubbed in Portuguese. Rzepnicki lost interest. Unable to sleep again so soon after his siesta and not quite hungry enough for a cooked meal, he wandered out of the apartment. Two blocks over he saw a sign for the "Lone Star Bar."

Inside, he discovered it was obviously a hangout for a mixed crowd of Brazilians and gringos. The dumpy little man sat alone on a stool and had several vodkas with tonic. He didn't usually take tonic, but he reasoned that it would ward off malaria. The medics had assured him that was not a problem in Brazil, but you could never count on the medics. He also asked the bartender for some information. The fellow spoke some English and directed Boguslav to an intersection close by, where, with a few words of Portuguese and by counting on his fingers, Rzepnicki contracted for the services of a dark-skinned prostitute in a shiny red mini-skirt.

Boguslav followed the dusky young lady as she turned into the doorway of a cheap hotel a few doors down from the intersection. The night clerk, a wizened, cigarette-puffing mulatto, tossed her a key and she preceded Boguslav up the steps to the second floor. She seemed to exaggerate her movement, sacheting her bottom back and forth and he figured it was for his benefit. He reached up and put his hand between her legs.

"*Espere, homen.*" ("Wait, man.") She jerked forward, smacked at his hand but kept climbing. At the top of the stairs, Boguslav was breathing hard, but not in anticipation of the sex. Fortunately for him, rooms on this floor were reserved for in-and-out clients and he didn't have to struggle further.

In the room, the girl, who was probably nineteen or twenty, immediately held out her hand. When Boguslav forked over the two hundred *cruzeiros*, she lifted her thin, white cotton top over her head, undid her stiff-cupped brassiere, and slipped out of her skirt and thong panties. Her breasts were full and still firm with dark nipples and she sat on the bed with the small black triangle between her legs beckoning to him.

"*Nos vamos ter um bom programa.*" (We're going to have a good program.") She smiled, showing crooked front teeth, and stuck her tongue over her lips and moved it from side to side. The only thing Boguslav understood was "a good program." He approached her and she quickly undid his belt and the button and fly of his trousers, which fell to his ankles. He turned away and duck-walked to a solitary, plastic covered chair and sat to untie his shoelaces. The legs of the chair were uneven and he rocked a bit as he shifted from side to side. The whore slapped her palm on the bed several times motioning for him to join her quickly. He knew she wanted to do this trick fast and get back out on the street, but he intended to get his money's worth.

"No. You come here. Down on your knees." Boguslav said this aloud in English, but added the necessary gestures so she would know what was expected of her. For the next thirty-five minutes, the whore worked her wiles. After the first five minutes they moved to the bed, with Boguslav flat on his back, his belly rounded like a scoop of vanilla ice cream, and the girl kneeling over him. At several points she almost gave up as he went flaccid, but each time, Boguslav grabbed her thick black hair with both hands and forced her mouth back to him. He began to moan, then growl and pull her head harder to himself. Finally, he started to thrust and lift his bottom from the mattress, where his skin had grown sweaty. He arched back and grunted as his head struck the bed board and he reached his orgasm at the same instant. It was a feeble climax, but the girl had more than earned her money.

The vodka had some effect and outside on the street it took the little man some time to reorient himself. He got back to the apartment by eleven. The work would begin the next day and he wasn't looking forward to it. And now he cursed himself for having already spent what he might have saved from his first day's per diem. What would he tell his wife? She counted every penny he earned. He would say that the base had cheated him out of it, forcing him to stay in an expensive apartment. That should convince her. Still, things were off to a bad start. He didn't like this smart-aleck kid and for some reason he had a bad feeling about this case. But then Boguslav Rzepnicki had bad feelings about most things.

Chapter 4

The beach resort of Armaçao dos Buzios, which the Brazilians call simply Buzios, sits on a spit of land about a hundred fifteen kilometers northeast of Rio de Janeiro and by late March the summer crowds had returned reluctantly to the city. The stucco-walled villas, white-washed, orange tile-roofed and sumptuous by local standards were owned mostly by Brazilians and the left-over beach-goers were predominantly Brazilian, many of them couples married to other people. They came to escape Rio's congested reality, and often their spouses.

On the same day that Frank Manion and Julie d'Andrade were meeting in Leblon, a pasty-faced man in his late thirties walked up the gradual slope of the Buzios beach away from the sea. He was obviously not Brazilian. His hair was dark enough, but he was squinting through light blue heavy-lidded eyes, and the skin on his trunk was pale, "*creme de leite*" ("cream of milk") as the Brazilians would say. He was bull-necked, with a thick-torso and rough appearance. His nose, the most prominent of his facial features, was rubbery and bulbous. He went by different names at different times, never using the same name twice. On this assignment, he was documented as a Canadian named Paul Loest.

Off the beach Loest stood beside a rented red Volkswagen manufactured in Sao Paolo and pulled a pair of baggy khaki shorts over his swimsuit. Now he sat sideways in the driver's seat and stuck his legs out the open door, leaning over to brush the sand from his bare feet. He put on beige canvas-topped athletic shoes, tied them then stood to pull a T-shirt over his head and his ample belly. Once dressed, he studied his face in the rear-view mirror and used a pocket comb to tidy his hair.

Groomed and ready, he turned the key in the ignition and pulled from between the cars that had sandwiched him in and steered in the direction of the Ilha do Cabo Frio. At the sign that marked the southern limit of Buzios, he checked his car odometer then continued down the coastal road. At precisely seven and three tenths kilometers from the Buzios town limits sign, he turned onto the left shoulder of the road and parked. The lone car behind him moved past and for several minutes he sat alone at that spot.

Satisfied that no one else was about, he took a canvas bag stuffed with straw from the back seat and got out of the car. He made his way for just short of a kilometer along a sand-encrusted trail and finally clambered over flat granite rocks down to a secluded inlet. It was high tide. Almost at water level he carefully examined the larger rocks in the late afternoon light. He walked ten paces to his left, then came back to his starting point and moved several paces to his right. There he spotted what he was searching for. Higher up the bank on one rock were two parallel eggshell-colored streaks, which might possibly be mistaken for tidal marks, except the tide never got that high. Wedged in at the base of the marked boulder were several smaller rocks each about a meter long. Loest raised the side of three of them, one at a time, the first two causing him to grunt with the strain, but the third coming loose and up with ease. Though it looked in its texture and coloration like all the surrounding rocks, the object he now held in his arms was man-made of a rough Styrofoam.

Glancing up the slope to satisfy himself that he was still alone, Loest took a Swiss Army knife from the pocket of his shorts. With the thickest blade he cut along a seam of the molded package and succeeded quickly in separating it into two halves. In the hollowed out inside were several items: two packets of one hundred cruzeiro notes secured with thick rubber bands; a set of Northern Irish identity documents; a vial containing six white tablets. It was topped with cotton and secured with a cork. There were two yellowish glass ampoules, and two black metal tubes about nineteen centimeters long that were joined together like soda straws with a knobbed plunger on the end. Loest took a white handkerchief and wrapped the double tubes in it and carefully placed the remaining items in the straw-filled canvas bag. Back in his car, he put the bag on the front passenger seat beside him and transferred the new documents to a concealed space in the inside lining of a scuffed leather briefcase. He then pried open the side panel of the Volkswagen and taped the tubular instrument to the door metal, then pressed the panel back into the clips. Satisfied that he had everything he needed, he headed into the lake region and west toward Rio de Janeiro. By nightfall, he was walking up the steps of the Ambassador Hotel.

"The key for six eleven."

"There you are *Senhor* Loest."

"Has my passport been returned by the police?"

"I can check." The desk clerk opened a drawer behind the counter. "What is your nationality?"

"Canadian."

"Yes, here it is."

"I need a wake-up call at six-thirty."

"Without fail. *Boa noite, Senhor* Loest."

As he rode up in the elevator, Loest went over a mental checklist. This operation had originally been scheduled for carnival week and he had looked forward to moving through the streets with coffee-colored, almost-naked willing women, but the man he was to deal with had left town so he had to postpone his arrival by three weeks. Bad luck. But now he had done his casing and was as ready as he would ever be. All he needed to finish the business was that combination of timing and luck that he always hoped for, but could never predict. Waiting was always the hardest part.

Chapter 5

Frank Manion felt guilty. Boguslav Rzepnicki had been at it for almost two weeks and so far, aside from translating a few snippets of phone conversations from Portuguese to English, Frank had done nothing more than act as a courier. Every morning he had come from his room at the Gloria Hotel to the apartment and sat for hours in silence, or walked and drove the streets to study the layout of the city. The transcriber was doing all the work.

The apartment building was in a narrow street and being on the second floor the windows got only oblique or reflected sunlight most of the day. Whatever light did angle its way down was filtered by sheer curtains that they kept drawn. As a consequence, and because of what Frank saw were Boguslav's less than tidy habits, the place had already taken on a dusty look. The older man invariably sat at a corner L-shaped table and the surrounding floor was littered with lined yellow sheets of scribbled notes. But they were indecipherable to Frank even though he read Russian. The times he had been present while Rzepnicki worked, the latter paid him little heed. A set of adjustable earphones slightly too large for the little man's head even at their narrowest position cut off the noise of his surroundings. He would lean his stubby neck over the Uher reel-to-reel tape recorder, his right hand on the start-stop-rewind control going back innumerable times over the same snippets of tape, straining every sense to catch sound and nuance. He may have been physically in the room with Frank, but his mind was wherever Shurin, the Russian speaking on the tape, happened to be.

Today, as soon as Frank walked through the door, Rzepnicki took off the headset and gathered several papers from the desk and the floor. Frank was ready for some kind of confrontation. Instead, the little man spoke evenly and to the point.

"If you want to talk, I can talk. I now have idea about this guy."

"You have my full attention." Frank turned on the TV for background noise and the transcriber came to the sofa, twice dropping and picking up yellow sheets of paper on his way across the living room. He spoke in a low voice.

"Shurin is unusual if compared to other Soviets I worked on."

"In what way?" Frank had to lean closer to hear over the noise of the television. He noticed Rzepnicki's head was the shade and consistency of kneaded flour with deep creases across his forehead, like the fissures between tectonic plates. At this distance he could smell the man's acrid breath and at the ends of his bristled moustache was the

27

unmistakable sheen of cooking grease. Still, Frank tried to concentrate, to picture Vladimir Shurin's face, the one he had seen in the file photos.

"He's risk taker," Rzepnicki went on. "Maybe he has some protector in Moscow who looks out for him. Or maybe he knows how to work Soviet system, but whatever reason, he does things other Soviets would never think to do."

"Like the affair with the Brazilian woman?"

""Yes. And from phone talking you translated I think for both of them it is serious situation."

"Is that the only way he's unusual?"

"No. He has ability to get things done even in this foreign situation. He seems able to go from point A to point B without going around to C, D, E. Most Soviets can't do that. They are too used to inefficiencies of Soviet Union. They think things are done that way everywhere."

"So Shurin is a fixer?"

"Yes. He handles orders for diplomatic functions, receptions. Soviet ambassador in Brasilia has his own chef, but for big parties it is Shurin who arranges things even up there. He also takes care of maintenance of their buildings here in Rio. He's administrative officer, but not usual kind. He wheels and deals."

"And you're certain that he's not KGB?"

"Only one indication he might be."

"What's that?" As the older man skimmed through his notes trying to answer the question, Frank noticed that Rzepnicki's fingernails were long and dirty. Boguslav separated several sheets from the pile of paper.

"Here." Rzepnicki pointed to entries he had made on each of the sheets. "He hangs around with several known KGB types in consulate, especially Barchuk. But I think that's because they use him. They are all well trained to speak local language, but Shurin not only speaks Portuguese, but, like I said, he has good feel for how to get things done here and he got contacts everywhere."

"What about where he goes, what he does?"

"No pattern yet, but I'm working on it."

Frank continued the routine. In his wanderings through the city, the problem of how to get to Shurin securely was never far from his mind. So far, he had no idea how he could pull it off. Then, early on Saturday morning of that third week he got the break he had been waiting for. As he came in the door, he saw immediately that Rzepnicki didn't have the headset on and wasn't at his worktable. The little man had already let it be known that he had no intention of working over the weekend. Instead, he was sitting on the sofa watching the TV.

"Why don't you go down to the beach, Boguslav? The rain has stopped and it's turning into a beautiful morning. I'll go with you. I haven't even been there yet." Here Rzepnicki surprised him. He had a wry smile on his lips, the first one Frank had seen. It vanished so quickly, Frank wondered if he was hallucinating.

"I think you should go instead to Copacabana Palace Hotel."

Frank walked to the side table and turned on the radio for added noise then came back to the sofa.

"That's where Shurin goes?"

"Yes." Rzepnicki didn't refer to any notes.

"For what?"

"He has contact there, fellow named Paulo. This Paulo talks Russian. He does catering on side for Soviet Consulate and there is to be reception for big shot visitor who is coming."

"When?"

"On Monday."

"Day after tomorrow? Who's the visitor?"

"Deputy Minister of Foreign Trade." Rzepnicki turned away from Frank to look at the TV, seemingly disconnected. Frank thought the older man must be enjoying the moment when he was in control.

"This was on the telephone?" Frank asked. Rzepnicki took his time answering. Finally he turned.

"What? Yes, part of it. Consulate called embassy in Brasilia to set up meetings there for next week. But I found out about what Shurin will do through that audio device in his apartment, not on phone. He told his wife they will have to go to reception. He said he's going to have to set that up, arrange for catering. He already began, but still he'll be busy as hell over weekend. They had fight."

"Why? She's complaining?"

"She said they never do anything. He's always out. And in this fight I learned three things."

"What?"

"First is why he seems free to move about like he does. They do have protector, her father. I don't know what's his position, but from what I heard, he must be big shot in party or maybe Politburo."

"What are the other things?"

"Difference in their social standing. That is reason they fight so much. She throws in his face that his father was only taxi driver, while her family is in *nomenklatura*."

"The privileged people."

"Yes."

"But they'll go together to the reception on Monday?"

"Yes at consulate. And then later on phone he told his girl friend something you got to translate, something about Pinocchio."

"Pinocchio?"

"Come. Listen." Boguslav got up and walked to the table. Frank followed him. The little man handed him the earphones. "I stopped at that spot." Rzepnicki put his finger on the reel.

Frank flipped the switch on the Uher and heard the ring of a telephone. A woman said hello. Shurin spoke.

"Hello, love. I have bad news."

"What happened, another fight?"

"No. Well, yes, but it's not that. I can't come on Monday night, or Tuesday."

"What's going on?"

"A visitor in town, there's a reception for him on Monday then I have to take him shopping. Tuesday night he wants to go out for some night life. I have to take him to Pinocchio's."

Frank had a pen and wrote on one of the yellow pads. As the conversation flowed, he was unable to translate it verbatim and wrote only the gist of what he heard. There was silence for several moments and that gave him a chance to catch up.

"And what do you think you'll do there?" the woman asked.

"Nothing for me, I promise. I'll have a drink. If he wants something special, he'll do that himself. I can't hold it up for him."

She laughed.

"You promise?"

"I swear. Now I have to go."

Frank listened to their goodbyes then switched off the machine. He continued to hold the pen and he looked at what he had written.

"What is Pinocchio's?" He got up and walked behind Rzepnicki back to the sofa.

"How would I know?" Rzepnicki grumbled as if he couldn't be expected to know everything. "You better check with base. Sounds like sex bar or whorehouse."

"You said there was something else you learned?"

"Shurin's wife was screwed by Barchuk, KGB guy. Shurin knows it and always curses her."

Frank went to an empty bench in a tiny park three blocks from the apartment. Still standing, he took from his leather briefcase the Rio guidebook Julie had given him then he put the briefcase on the wet wooden planks and sat down on top of it. The wood was cracked and still sopping from that morning's downpour, but typically after the rain the sun had reappeared. Puffy white clouds scudded across the rectangle of azure sky visible above the surrounding buildings. For a moment, he tilted his head and stared marveling at the strangeness of his situation. Who did this kind of thing for a living? In a way, he was a bounty hunter but without a weapon and if he succeeded in bringing in his man, no one could know about it but the people who had sent him. He lowered his head. Better not to wonder.

He went through the guide book to confirm the location of the next café on their list then he went to the back of the book where there was a map of the city. He checked the route he had chosen to get there. Then, with time to kill before he tried to call Julie's home number he leafed through the rest of the book and got another break. There was a section on historical sites, shops, restaurants, and, in the club and disco pages, several ads devoted to adult entertainment. His eye fixed on the one for Pinocchio's and the small black and white photo of long-limbed girls with pasties hanging from their nipples and G-strings covering their crotches.

From the little park Frank walked for over a mile before he reached a pay phone. He stood in the shelter of the yellow and blue plastic bubble that protected callers from the worst of the rainstorms and dialed Julie's number. There was no answer. He decided he would have to tell her whatever happened after the fact. Now he headed back to the rented Ford and wove his way through narrow side streets to the Avenida Atlantica. He drove past the pastel stucco entrance to the Copacabana Palace Hotel pool, made a u-turn and parked on rua Duvier. He looked up and down the street, then took the dopp kit out of the glove compartment, unzipped it and removed a plastic bottle of actor's glue. He unscrewed the cap, which had a small applicator attached to it, and was about to begin putting on the sticky stuff when he saw in the rear view mirror that his upper lip was beaded with perspiration. He pulled his shirt from his pants and wiped away the sweat. Now he tilted his head below the top of the steering wheel and daubed the glue evenly under his nose. Within seconds it had become tacky to the touch. From a small plastic case, he took one of three moustaches. Each had very dark hair matched to his own threaded through nylon netting. Looking in the mirror he pressured both sides with his index fingers then used the thin teeth of a comb to press the netting against the glue and his skin. He pomaded his hair and slicked it straight back, exposing more of his forehead. Finally, he hooked wire rims of the clear lens glasses over his ears. His name would now be Richard Boland.

For a few seconds he sat there studying his new look and for the first time he realized the extent to which his physical appearance determined his identity. For most of his life his face had been the only thing he had that was his own. He felt like a clock that was still calibrated, but with the numbers on the front scrambled and out of order. Still, he knew this was necessary as so many deceptions were in the spy business.

He got out of the car and headed for the hotel. When he reached the Avenida Atlantica he walked past the main doorway to the small arched entry to the pool, where he sat at a glass-topped table under an aquamarine and white umbrella. He ordered an orange juice.

The upper floors of the hotel looked out on Copacabana Beach. The girls in Rio had just begun wearing thong bathing suits. One young woman, her *café-au-lait* body stretched out on the aquamarine cushion of a white wrought iron lounge chair was wearing one, if wearing was the right verb. It was a yellow one, which covered her pubic area and, when she turned over, the crack of her bottom. The hedonism of the place didn't do much for Frank's spirits and even if the disguise was effective, he felt uncomfortable in it. But he forced himself to stay put for almost thirty minutes.

Unfortunately, that gave him plenty of time to think. He looked often at the girl, who must have been in her late teens and he felt himself getting aroused. Up to now in his marriage he had been a straight shooter. But his absence from home during the long training course and Beth's own career as an attorney had combined to keep them from enjoying time together, time they needed to fill if only to keep from being idle. So far in Rio that was all he had been. Now his worry combined with nervousness and he wanted to finish with this case and get back home.

He got edgier. Every five minutes he stood and walked into the hotel lobby through the pool entrance. About eleven-thirty, as he came back out to the pool, two kids were tossing a ball and splashing about in the shallow end. Frank headed around to the far side, but as he passed the opening from the street, he almost collided with Vladimir Shurin. It was that simple.

Frank felt a surge of adrenaline. It was definitely his man. He recognized the Russian from the file photos and the description. Shurin was six feet two, three inches taller than he, but sinewy and not so muscular. He had light blue eyes and flaxen hair. His features were sharp and typically Slavic. The file said he was thirty-five and he looked it, but the question was how to meet him? Frank had struggled with that problem since his arrival and had come to no firm answer.

Shurin walked the length of the pool past the snack bar and into the rear area that housed the hotel kitchen. On impulse, Frank went out on the street. He walked to the intersection of the Avenida Atlantica and rua Rodolfo Dantas checking the license plates of each car he passed. Nothing. He walked the long block to rua Duvier, the side street where he had parked. Still no luck. He went up Duvier and looked at every plate on the left side of the street. He passed his own car, the blue Ford. Finally, as he approached the intersection with Avenida Nossa Senhora de Copacabana, he spotted Shurin's car two places in from the corner, a navy blue Mercedes. The tag was CD 32-947. The CD stood for Corpo Diplomatico and 32 was the indicator for the Soviet Consulate.

Frank started the Ford and drove around the block. He was hoping that his parking space would stay empty. When he made his turn back into rua Duvier, he saw up ahead that his luck had held. With a hard pull to the right and an immediate spin of the wheel he scraped the navy blue Mercedes. He continued to his space and parked once again. Now he walked back and surveyed the damage. Not much of a dent, but the paint on the driver's door was scraped. Now he went back to the Ford and sat.

It was another thirty minutes before Shurin turned the corner. All the while, Frank kept pressing against the moustache. He was sweating heavily and hoped it would hold. He waited until just before the Russian passed by on the sidewalk before he opened his door and got out to stand in the street. Shurin never noticed him. Now Frank waited beside the Ford while Shurin kept walking toward the Mercedes. As the Russian stepped from the curb and was taking the keys from his pocket, Frank moved toward him.

"*Chort vozmi.*" ("The Devil take it.") By now Frank was only ten feet away and heard the curse. Shurin reached down to rub the scratched surface.

"I'm very sorry," Frank called in Portuguese. He stood looking down at the Russian, who turned immediately. "I did that." Now Shurin straightened and looked directly at him, but he kept silent. "When I turned the corner, I held the wheel too long." Frank held up the palms of his hands and shrugged his shoulders. He tilted his head to one side. Shurin seemed to look at him more intently. Frank had a lot of self-confidence, but he had never worn a disguise before and it made him very uneasy. Had his moustache slipped from the perspiration?

"So what can you do about it?" Shurin finally asked.

"It doesn't look too bad, but I don't know what it would take to repair it. This is my first time in Rio."

Shurin just shook his head. His face had a disgusted look and he put his hands in the back pockets of the gray linen slacks he was wearing.

"It's bad enough." They both stood looking at the dent and the scrape.

"I'm driving a rental car. I'd really like to avoid all the problem of insurance," Frank said. "Can we settle it right here?"

"How can we do that?" Shurin asked.

"I'd like to do it with cash. Do you live here?"

"Yes."

"You don't look Brazilian, that's why I asked. But if you live here, you must have some idea of what it would cost to fix this. I would guess about fifteen hundred *cruzeiros*. What do you think?" Frank saw the briefest change of expression. The fifteen hundred would do it, but he knew what would come next.

"More like two thousand."

"Okay, two thousand." Frank looked both ways, then took out his wallet and counted out the money, but still held it in his left hand. "I'd like to get some kind of receipt to show I paid for it." He took a small note pad from his shirt pocket. "Can I borrow that pen?" Shurin reluctantly handed over the gold ballpoint from his own breast pocket. Frank wrote out two sentences and drew a straight line beneath them. Shurin studied it briefly then hesitated. "I didn't have to stop at all, you know? Nobody saw it happen." Frank continued to hold out the receipt. Finally Shurin took the outstretched pen and signed.

"There."

When Frank looked at the paper he saw the name on the line was Eugenio Fontes.

"Again, I'm sorry. Maybe I could buy you a drink?"

"I'm in a hurry."

Frank extended his hand, but Shurin had already unlocked the door and was getting into the driver's seat. Frank moved to the sidewalk and the Russian backed up, then cleared the car in front of him and drove off. Frank had said his name was Boland. Shurin used the name Fontes. It occurred to him that Pinocchio's might be an appropriate place for both of them to start telling the truth.

Chapter 6

The Guanabara Bay and the surrounding mountains that rise defiantly against the sea divide Rio de Janeiro into three major parts, north, central and south. The southern section is home to the famous beaches and the chic and luxurious clubs and apartments of the Leme, Copacabana, Ipanema, Leblon and Barra da Tijuca sections, while the northern area consists mostly of industrial buildings and the working class neighborhoods. The center is the historic heart of old Rio. On the cliffs, smudged against the pastel blue sky, are the *favelas*, the slums.

The man known as Paul Loest checked out of the Ambassador Hotel in the city center at six in the morning and drove his VW along the Avenida Beira Mar through the series of tunnels and bridges toward the southern half of town. Just before entering the final tunnel he turned into the Parque do Flamengo, a verdant crescent at bayside immediately south of Santos-Dumont Airport. Orchids and oleander and impatiens were in riotous blossom irrigated by the still frequent, heavy downpours of the ebbing rainy season. Loest wore a beige cotton jacket. With a large navy and white Varig travel bag on his shoulder he walked a gravel pathway to a wooden planked bench and sat studying the traffic that careened around the park on the landward side. From his jacket pocket, he took the Canadian identity documents. He tore them methodically into strips and then into tiny squares. At water's edge, he sprinkled the paper into the lagoon. In doing so, he ended the brief life of Paul Loest of Ottawa, Canada and instead became Seamus Duffy of Belfast, Ireland.

Back in the car, Duffy unscrewed the cap from a small plastic bottle and took out one sodium thiosulfate tablet. He swallowed it then looked at his watch. He had timed himself before and knew he would have to give the tablet thirty minutes to be absorbed into his system. Now he removed the black tubular device from inside the door liner, stuck it in the blue canvas bag, then drove to the Interlocadora car rental office on Avenida Princesa Isabel, parked and dropped the keys in the night box. He walked west to Rua Barata Ribeiro, where he hopped a bus to the Botafogo section.

By now, Duffy knew this part of the city almost as well as he knew the streets of Minsk, the city of his birth and upbringing. He approached the doorway of the building at 158 Rua Mariana and checked his watch again. He was on schedule. Just inside the door he stood perfectly still and listened. He could hear no movement on the upper stories or anywhere inside the building. Outside, a car moved down the narrow street, but it did not stop.

Duffy set his bag on the tiled floor of the entrance, took off his jacket and bent over to remove the small black metal instrument. Opening two cotton-stuffed boxes, he took out one of the clear glass ampoules. It contained an aerosol mixture of hydrocyanic acid. He inserted the glass in the open end of the top tube, pulled back the spring-tension piston and snapped the ends of a steel clip that held the piston in its extended position. He tore several pages from the previous day's newspaper and wrapped them carefully around the small tubes without putting any pressure on the two clips that held the piston in place. The gauze face mask he stuck in his left jacket pocket along with a small ampoule of amyl nitrate. He put everything he didn't need back in the Varig bag. Now he waited.

The morning was still cool, but the humidity was oppressive and he was perspiring heavily even without the jacket.

Suddenly, he heard a door open on an upper landing and he took a step toward the staircase. But the noise of the door was followed immediately by a child's voice and the reply of a woman. Seconds later, an orange rubber ball came bouncing down the tiled steps, higher and farther with each bounce. Duffy got the impression that all this was happening in slow-motion. The child, a tow-headed Brazilian boy of light complexion, laughed then held the railing and descended one step at a time in pursuit of his ball. The woman, a bony dark-skinned nanny, held his other hand. Duffy withdrew quickly into the shadows behind the staircase.

In all of his earlier casing this had never happened. If his man came out now, he would have to postpone the action. But the boy and the woman got to the bottom of the steps, retrieved the ball and continued out the door. She was carrying a net shopping bag. Duffy stuck his head out after them to see the direction they took. The instant he stepped back into the entrance hall he heard another door close and someone inserting a key in a lock. Duffy checked one last time to be sure the newspaper still concealed the tubes. He put his left hand in the jacket pocket. He had practiced this maneuver countless times, still he was nervous.

With the left hand fingering the gauze and wire mask and his right hand gripping the newspaper, he started up the stairs. An older, white-haired man in a cheap dark suit, white shirt and dark narrow tie moved toward the top of the landing. He had papers in one hand and was struggling to fit them into his briefcase. Duffy avoided eye contact until the last moment.

"*Bom dia.*" Duffy smiled as he greeted the older man. At the same time, he raised the newspaper and tubes until they were only centimeters from the man's face and he took out the gauze mask and covered his own nose and mouth. The newspaper slipped off and fell to the steps and the tubes were exposed. When Duffy squeezed the clips, the piston snapped forward forcing air pressure from the top tube and cracking the glass

36

ampoule. The hydrocyanic gas was expelled in a small cloud before the startled victim's face. This was the moment Duffy enjoyed. He was always curious to see the eyes of his prey at that last instant of recognition that time and act would end. There was confusion, then understanding and, above all, terror. The old man clutched his chest, then immediately slumped with the lower half of his body on the landing, and his midriff, chest, arms and head down the top steps. The loose papers fluttered, then settled on the stairs and a couple of cheap pens fell out of the briefcase.

Duffy took the glass ampoule from his pocket. He held his own breath as he took away the gauze mask and brought the ampoule close to his nose and crushed it. He inhaled the amyl nitrate, then turned and started down the stairs. When he looked back up at the body, he saw that the gas cloud had already dissipated.

At the bottom of the steps he retrieved the Varig bag from behind the steps. Suddenly he experienced a sharp pain in his chest. His perspiration streaked the sides of his face. What was happening? He had been assured that the medications would protect him, but what if that was simply a way of luring him into a false sense of security and dispatching him along with his target? He knew the KGB was perfectly capable of devouring its own. But why would they bother to do it that way when they could simply wait for his return to Dzerzhinsky Square and put a bullet in his brainpan?

He picked up the Varig bag and put in the tubular gun. Certain of his work, he walked outside. The street was empty with the exception of the black woman and the boy, who were coming back toward the door. Her shopping bag was still empty. They must have forgotten something. Duffy turned in the opposite direction and walked to the corner. Several blocks from the scene of the murder, he caught a taxi on the fly. Once in the cab, the pain in his chest subsided.

"*Aonde va, senhor?*" ("Where are you going, sir?") the driver asked.

"*A Santos-Dumont, o aeroporto.*" ("To Santos-Dumont, the airport.") Duffy answered. He checked the rear view mirror. Below the driver's line of vision Duffy looked in the canvas bag at the gas gun. At the airport he threw it into a trash can and made his way to the bank of lockers, where he retrieved his packed suitcase. Then he walked to the Varig counter.

"Checking in for Brasilia," he handed his ticket to the desk clerk. He drummed his fingers on the counter then reminded himself to relax. This one was over. The chest pain was gone. Apparently, he thought, his bosses still required his services. That need and his own wits were the only things that kept him alive.

Chapter 7

Street urchins hung from the outside of the pale yellow tram like soiled ribbons on a kite. Out there they paid no fare. But it could be dangerous. The trolley crossed the Arcos da Lapa, a Roman-style aqueduct eighty feet above ground. The panoramic scene of Guanabara Bay drifted in and out of view through the plane trees. When the car stopped, Frank Manion, who had sat inside on a wooden-slatted seat, stepped down into another world and time. Here in the Santa Teresa section Brazil's colonial legacy was untarnished. Pastel stuccoed houses with brightly painted shutters lined the labyrinthine cobblestone streets. It was an unusual day, with dark clouds hanging stagnantly over the hillside, but the street colors made their own glow.

Along the Rua Almirante Alexandrino Frank found the Bar do Amaudo, the third meeting site on the list, and went inside. The interior light was almost as bright as the light on the street and he spotted Julie sitting against the rear wall. Only two of the other yellow metal tables with the Skol logo were occupied.

"You're late." She made no gesture and barely looked at Frank.

"Five minutes. I didn't realize how long the streetcar took."

"I was in the middle of a pretty important cable. I really don't have a lot of time." She was sipping an espresso. The single waiter came and Frank ordered an orange juice. "So what is it, why the call?"

"I tried to get you on Saturday and most of the day yesterday."

"On Saturday I was teaching."

"Teaching?"

"I teach reading, writing to the kids in the slums, the *favelas*."

Frank looked at her for a moment. It occurred to him that in addition to being beautiful, this was a very interesting woman. It was a shame she wasn't friendlier.

"What got you into that?"

"I was a teacher when the agency recruited me. I think it's worth doing."

"That's pretty generous of you considering you don't have a lot of free time."

She looked at him without any particular expression. Frank got the feeling she measured everything he said, but did it quickly. She took a little more time sizing up his compliments.

"Yesterday I was out sailing," she said. "I met Shurin's girl friend."

"Justinha Marques?"

"Yes. I got to play tennis with her mother last week and she invited me along on the family boat yesterday. Justinha and I have a tennis date on Wednesday. I didn't even have to propose it. Her mother said I was too good for her and Justinha would give me a better match."

"Great. That's good work, Julie." He smiled. It was the first time he had spoken her name and for an instant she looked at him differently. There was softness there in the mouth and eyes. "Did you have any time alone with her?"

"A bit, but I'll have more when we play. I'll invite her for a drink in the club afterward."

"Did she mention Shurin?" Frank asked.

"No. But she's not exactly a kid. She's divorced and has two daughters. She works for the Banco do Brasil. That's what the cable is about. I'm suggesting that if you have no luck contacting Shurin, I may be able to meet him through her." Frank could see she was watching for his reaction. She had to know it was really his case and he had been sent to do the job and what she was suggesting was slightly out of bounds, but he never changed expression. "Again, why the call?" she asked.

"I ran into Shurin." Frank smiled more broadly. "Actually, you can take that literally."

"What do you mean?" He could see she was surprised. He wondered if she might not even be a bit disappointed, but his impression of her, despite her reluctance to personalize things so far, was that she was competitive, but also too intelligent to be petty. They were both working toward the same goal.

"I found out he goes to the Copacabana Palace. I went there on Saturday morning. That's why I was trying to call you. He came by the pool. So I found his car on the street and scraped the door with my fender. I waited until he came back and paid him for the damage."

Julie was about to take another swallow of her coffee, but she only held the cup at her lips, then put it back on the saucer. She had a half-smile and this one seemed to come from inside. He noticed how white her teeth were against that lovely tan of her cheeks and the pink of her lips and for a few seconds she said nothing. Again, Frank wondered if she saw this as a contest and was pleased that now he might have tripped over himself, or if she thought his little ploy was funny, or that it showed he had some moxie. He found himself hoping that she had a sense of humor. Women without one were a lot less interesting; men, too. The waiter brought Frank's glass of orange juice.

"Did anybody tell you to do that?" Julie tilted her head to one side and the smile continued to play on her lips.

"Not that I remember."

"How much did you give him?"

"Two thousand *cruzeiros*."

"You may be out of pocket there, fella." She shook her head from side to side. "I can just about guarantee you that the base won't pay for it, so unless the Soviet Division does, your next paycheck will be a little light."

"I need a thousand dollars by Wednesday morning, five hundred in dollars and five hundred in *cruzeiros*."

"You're really full of surprises aren't you? You ought to talk to the fellow who owns this bar. Have you ever heard of Ronnie Biggs?" She reached up, tilted back her head and ran her hand through her thick, brunette hair.

"The name sounds familiar. Who is he?"

"In Brazil he's known as the Wizard of Odds. He helped pull off the great train robbery in England. He escaped from jail and as they say in England, 'he did a runner.' He came here about ten years ago and bought this place. He comes in often. Maybe you should hang around and ask him for a loan."

"Look. It's more than possible that I won't spend a cent of it, but I want to have it with me just in case."

"In case what? You decide to run over Shurin's wife?"

Frank smiled again.

"That's good. I like that. Shurin is accompanying a deputy minister."

"Yes. I know. The Brazilians almost shot him over the weekend." Julie sipped again from her demitasse.

"Shurin? What do you mean?"

"Just what I said, not Shurin, the deputy-minister. We told them there was a visitor in town and he might be up to something. Shurin took him out for a stroll and the fellow jay-walked and one of the young surveillants drew his gun and was going to shoot him. Fortunately, the team leader stopped him."

"The best laid plans."

"So, were you able to line up another meeting with Shurin?" she asked.

"No. But he's supposed to go to a club, Pinocchio's, tomorrow night and I plan to be there."

"Isn't that a sex bar?" Her eyebrows lowered slightly and her eyes narrowed. "I know prices in Rio are high, but I think you two ought to be able to reach a happy ending for less than a thousand. Or do you need some special treatment?"

Frank chuckled.

"You are funny. I love funny women. I mean people. I love funny people." He raised his palm in submission. "I don't intend to give him money there. But maybe I can line up a meeting. If I do, I want to show him I'm serious."

"That's it?"

"No. I'd like two bottles of Stolichnaya vodka and a fifth of Johnny Walker Black Label. Also, there's a cable in here." Frank slid a copy of the *Manchete* magazine across the table. "It brings headquarters up to date. I also bought these two pens at H. Stern. They're Cartiers. They have to go to headquarters by immediate pouch. The techs know what to do. It's all in the cable. I'll need the pens back right away with the one-time pads and the secret writing material. I'm also asking Tony Valletta for authorization for the base to give me the money."

"You know Tony Valletta? What's he got to do with this case?" She seemed surprised.

"He's the branch chief for the division, External Soviet ops for Latin America."

"SE/X/LA, since when? He wasn't in that job when I left headquarters. He was in EUR Division. He was chief of the French desk while I was in Paris."

"I think he moved over about four months ago."

"He's one of my favorite people, a first generation immigrant from Italy. My father talks the way Tony does, not as grandiose as Tony, but formal."

"He's a great guy." Frank liked Tony, but he wanted to get back to business. "The cable has immediate precedence. If Tony approves, I'd like to get the money as soon as possible, but no later than Wednesday morning."

"Okay. Is that all you need?"

"Yes."

"If headquarters signs off, I'll get it to you. Write out a receipt and sign it and have it ready when we make the pass. I've got to go. My car is down the street. I'll give you the latest tape."

"Fine," he finished his orange juice. "I notice you didn't smoke at all today."

"I've given it up. For the third time, but this time I'm going to make it. Listen." She sat for a moment looking out toward the street. "If I seem a bit harsh, I apologize. Frankly, you surprised me. I didn't think you would get this far so quickly. That's good work, too."

"I appreciate that." Frank wondered if his mention of Tony Valletta had helped. Or maybe she was softening a bit.

"Do you know the Maracana Stadium?" Julie reached in her purse and left change on the table.

"In the Zona Norte? Yes."

"I've written the instructions here." She showed him a five-by-eight white card. "Slide over." Frank pulled his chair to the corner of the table. Now he could smell her perfume, a flowered scent, and her dark hair almost brushed his cheek as he studied the directions. "Take the four-sixty-four bus from Flamengo. Stand on Avenida Osvaldo Aranha at the corner with Rua Prof Eurico Rabelo. I'll drive toward you on Osvaldo

Aranha. I'll watch for surveillance all the way and if I'm clean, I'll blink my lights. You walk around the corner. I'll turn right on Eurico Rabelo and have the passenger side window down. I'll hand you the package with the material, an envelope with the money. You throw in the receipt."

"I'll be there."

They both turned at the same instant to face each other and each was surprised by their propinquity. For several seconds, neither spoke. It was Julie who broke the brief silence.

"I hope you enjoy the show at Pinocchio's. Don't let your nose grow, or anything else."

"You're funny."

Chapter 8

On Tuesday evening, Frank stood on the narrow sidewalk outside Pinocchio's. He wore white duck trousers and a black T-shirt that gave him a sculpted look. His disguise was unnatural. Like blinders on a stallion it didn't seem to fit with the rest of him. That made him uneasy. Each time someone approached, he had to step off the curb into the gutter to let them pass. Most of the male pedestrians stopped to take a look at the glass-enclosed cases with colored photos of scantily clad showgirls. He had arrived early in case Shurin and his visitor should show up when the place opened. But he wasn't waiting only for Shurin. Julie had telephoned and double-talked clearly enough to let him know she would meet him at the door. He didn't know which prospect made him more nervous, dealing in disguise with the Soviet, or watching a sex show with a lady case officer.

At nine, when the club opened, he saw her walking down the street toward him. When she got close enough, apparently she couldn't resist.

"I like your moustache. Is it mink?" Julie was dressed for the part. She wore a white halter over an electric blue vinyl mini-skirt that showcased her gorgeous legs. Her blonde wig was waved and blown dry and combined with black stiletto heels to make her appear taller than Frank. She was wearing Sophia Loren sunglasses, the ones with the black plastic frames and violet lenses. She looked like a hooker. She held up her arms and spun around to show off her new persona.

"I don't think this is such a good idea," he said. "I've been out here for a while and I haven't seen one other woman go in. And what's the point of having Shurin see us both together?"

"Believe me. It wasn't something I thought up. The chief of base didn't want you in there alone. Maybe he thought you would be distracted by the little wooden man." Frank shook his head. "I think the real reason, and I'm not being glib, is that the boys in the office want to keep me as the butt of their jokes for the rest of the time I'm here and whenever they run out of ammunition, they can fall back on my visit to Pinocchio's."

"The woman thing," Frank shook his head again.

"Try being a female case officer sometime. You'll get the picture fast." She didn't sound petulant, just matter-of-fact.

"Okay. But if Shurin shows up with surveillance, I won't be able to get at him."

"We called off the hounds. We told the Brazilians that if this official is up to something, it won't happen until he gets to Brasilia. Now are you happy?"

"I'm not sure. But there's something else. When I was a kid, I walked a girl home from a skating rink once. For four blocks neither of us said a word. We were both too shy and it was embarrassing. The farther we walked, the worse it got. So if we're doing this, let's agree ahead of time that whatever happens and however raunchy this gets, we won't be embarrassed. It's just the job. Okay?"

"That's considerate of you. Yes." Even through the makeup and the glasses he thought her look was one of appreciation.

At the door, Frank paid the cover charge for two. The Brazilian who took the money eyed Julie from top to bottom. He appeared to show special appreciation for her bottom. They sat in the left corner of the room on a lounge sofa that extended almost all the way across the back of the club. Julie didn't take off her tinted glasses.

"Can I serve you something?" The waitress was in net stockings, a thong and a push up bra. She had a white French maid's cap.

"*Duas caipirinhas, por favor.*" Julie ordered for both.

"What makes you think I want a *caipirinha*?"

"You don't have to drink it." She spoke with just a hint of agitation. Frank chalked it up to nervousness now that they were getting closer to the action.

At the front of the room, which was painted in peach and cream and had a black and white tiled floor, there was a low stage. Only four or five of the tables were occupied. The music was loud with a lot of percussion. It came from speakers hanging along the side walls. An announcer all in black was prattling on about the evening's entertainment. With a wave of his right arm, two scantily dressed girls, lithe and buxom, bounced out on the stage. Each carried a basket of fruit. They were followed by two young men dressed like the announcer in black, but with red satin vests. One sat on a raised platform behind an elevated set of drums. The other picked up a tenor saxophone from its stand on the stage.

"Is this a Brazilian version of the French chef?" Julie asked.

"Have you ever been to one of these places?"

"No, of course not," she frowned, "have you?"

"It's not my kind of thing."

"Then I guess we'll have to wait to see what happens next."

"I'm sure they won't leave anything to the imagination."

Julie said nothing more. She had slipped her glasses down low on her nose and was watching the stage with a look of wonder on her face. And Frank was watching her. He had an urge to protect her, to put his hand on her cheek and brush the blonde hair back from her bare shoulders. Above all, he wanted to give a gentle squeeze to her breasts. He felt that too familiar stirring in his loins. Right away he reminded himself why he was there. He didn't want to be embarrassed if he should have to stand.

The waitress brought their drinks. Julie immediately downed half of the mixture of cane liquor and fruit juice. Up front, the women were toying with their own fruit, licking it and each other. The musicians had replaced the recorded music with a thumping, blaring repetitive melody. Frank kept checking the door. From the back, another two customers came in and sat over on the right side of the room. Neither was Shurin. Girls paraded past the tables and stopped to chat. When a man was interested, he invited them to sit and join him. One girl came to Frank's table. She spoke to both of them. Frank heard what she said, but didn't understand it all.

"What's that about?"

"She wants to know if we're interested in a...," Julie looked away, but said the last word loud enough for him to hear, "threesome." Now she glanced from the girl to Frank and back to the stage. He shook his head and motioned with the back of his hand and the girl started to drift off, but Julie held up her glass. "*Mais uma caipirinha.*" Frank looked at her.

"You're playing your role pretty convincingly," he said. The showgirls writhed and contorted up front. In no time, their waitress brought the second drink.

Suddenly, accompanied by a loud drum roll and clash of cymbals, a young man came on stage. He was wearing a chef's hat and a red and white striped kitchen apron. Julie was about to take a sip from her new glass, but now she set it down on the table and watched intently.

"You called it," Frank told her. "The guy is a chef. Are you sure you haven't been here before?"

"I'm sure." She nodded.

"And it looks as if he has a baguette under that apron."

Julie was speechless. The two girls began to caress the chef and fondle him under the cloth, which began to rise like a French loaf. One of them untied the lace from his neck and it dropped off uncovering his most noticeable feature.

"Oh, my God," Julie looked away and Frank could tell she was embarrassed. He tried again to ease the tension with humor.

"I'm not sure he has a license to carry that thing. It looks like a bazooka." Frank's first thought was to describe this scene for Beth, his wife, but he quickly dismissed the idea. First, he got depressed thinking about her, however briefly, and second, even if things had been going well between them, he wasn't sure she would understand his being at a sex show with another woman even in a professional capacity. Julie just sat there, her glasses now on the table, her hand against her cheek and her mouth open. At that moment, Frank spotted Shurin and the man he took to be the deputy-minister. Both were chatting and laughing and the deputy-minister was pointing at the young man on stage as they walked toward one of the front tables. Neither man glanced at Frank or Julie. "There's our man," Frank told her.

"What?"

"Not up on the stage. Over there, the tall one."

Julie turned to the right.

"What now?" she asked.

"Don't worry. Nothing will happen for a while. You can go on watching the show." By now the sex chef and the women were intertwined.

"No, really," Julie turned to him. "Don't tell me you had us both come here without having any plan. Are you going out and run into his car again?" She sounded annoyed.

"I'm hoping for a chance to talk to him alone. Let's see what happens."

Girls approached the table of the newcomers. Five passed by before the deputy-minister, dressed in a white open-necked shirt, asked one of them to sit. Shurin motioned to another to join them. On stage, the sexual gymnastics continued. Julie finished her glass and ordered another.

"Hey," Frank took Julie's hand. "You may be the senior officer here, but maybe you ought to go easy on the alcohol. Remember, you've got a tennis match tomorrow."

"I'm in control and if I weren't, I wouldn't need you to watch over me." After another few minutes, the deputy-minister and the lady of his choosing got up from the table and headed for the door.

"That's what I thought," Frank said.

"What?"

"They were negotiating. Now they've agreed on a price and they won't be back for a while. I just hope Shurin keeps his promise to Justinha and doesn't leave, too. I want to get to him before the other one comes back. Wait here. I'll be right back."

Frank got up and followed the couple as far as the door. The deputy-minister had his arm around the girl's waist and she was leaning on his shoulder. Frank watched from the doorway as they went down the street and into a nearby hotel. When he came back in, he looked over at Julie. A man was standing at the table talking down at her. Frank didn't have time to handle that. He figured she would have to fend for herself. Instead, he went straight to the front of the room and stood a few feet behind Shurin's table.

"*Senhor Fontes*?" Shurin never looked back. Frank called a little louder. It was the girl who turned first, but then Shurin twisted in his chair. For a second he showed no sign of recognition. "Do you remember me?" Frank spoke in Russian now, but with an intentional American accent. The Soviets may have been suspicious of Americans, but they were even more concerned about one of their own, someone from the KGB, staging some kind of provocation, testing their loyalty. But the KGB men would speak English, or perfect Russian. Shurin smiled at him and Frank could see he was trying to make the connection. "I hit your car on Saturday."

"Yes, you, but now you are speaking Russian."

"So the girl won't understand. You were in a hurry the other day and didn't have time for a drink. Can I buy you one now?" Frank sat down without being asked in the chair the Russian official had vacated.

"I already have one." Shurin held the glass in his hand and raised it toward Frank. He still seemed pleasant.

"I think each of us has a confession to make. You're not *Senhor Fontes*, and I hit your car intentionally. I wanted to meet you."

If it was all going to hit the fan, this was where it would happen. But Shurin sat calmly. He did take a Kool Light cigarette from the cardboard pack he carried in his shirt pocket and he was no longer smiling, but neither did he show emotion.

"And why would you want to meet me?" Shurin glanced back at the club entrance and lit the cigarette with a blue plastic lighter. The girl, with a cheap red fall that contrasted with her dark skin and heavy makeup, looked bored now. She spent most of the time looking at the stage.

"Your colleague won't be back for some time, but I won't take more than a few minutes. I've come down from the United States. I know that you've gotten involved with a Brazilian lady. I won't say the name, but the initials are J.M."

"What has this to do with her?" Shurin's tone changed abruptly. He sounded aggressive now.

"I don't know her and I don't have to know her. Believe me, I'm not here to make trouble for you. You may be able to help me. But maybe you won't. That will be your choice. I don't want to put any pressure on you. But I know that if you're serious about the lady, and I think you are, I am certainly in a position to help you if you decide to come back to Brazil someday."

"Help me, how?" Shurin took two quick drags on his cigarette. He pinched it between his forefinger and thumb in the European way and as the smoke rose he squinted.

"I said I didn't want to cause any problem for you, so I think we could talk more securely someplace else. I saw you at the Copacabana Palace. If you pass by there again and you're interested to know what I can do for you, look for me by the pool, or if it's raining, in the lobby. I'll have a room there and we can talk. I'll be there every day between noon and two o'clock, the lunch hour. If you come, I'll start up to the room. You can follow me."

"I don't believe I need your help."

"Just think about it. If you want to talk more, I'll be here for two more weeks. See how things go."

"And what if I should report your attempt to my ambassador?"

"Vladimir Sergeyevich, you're certainly free to do that. But then people would wonder why I approached you and not someone else? They might begin to watch you, or they might want to know about Justinha." That certainly got Shurin's attention. He looked as if he had been punched in the gut. He pressed his cigarette into the copper ashtray and twisted it several times to extinguish it. "Whether you come or not," Frank said, "I wish you all the best."

Frank got up and on his way to the back motioned to Julie that they were ready to go. Several couples were on stage and at least half the tables were full. The man who had been talking to Julie was now sitting beside her. She seemed to be doing her best to ignore him. Frank walked over and dropped two one hundred *cruzeiro* notes on the table and signaled to the waitress that he had paid. The man had obviously taken a fancy to Julie, who was the most beautiful woman in the room even in her silly blonde wig and when she stood the fellow put his hand on her arm and tried to hold her back. Frank smiled and spoke to the man in Portuguese.

"Pardon me, my friend. This lady and I have already made our arrangements. I already paid for her services. I just had to step away for a minute." Frank took Julie's other hand and tugged. The Brazilian let go.

"What are you pulling me for?" she asked.

"Keep walking. Is he getting up from the table?"

"No."

"That's why I didn't want you along. I told you to stay out of trouble. I should have punched the son-of-a-bitch."

"Oh, my God, a Neanderthal. Listen, junior. I told you I can take care of myself." He slowed to let her get beside him.

"Sorry. He shouldn't have tried to pull you down."

The man who had taken their money on the way in held the door for them. When they got outside, Julie pointed to the left. There was a wind and with the Bernulli effect it blew down the artificial gullies between the buildings. Frank took off his glasses.

"Well?" she asked.

"Well, what?"

"What did he say?"

"Not much. I did most of the talking. He knows where to meet me if he's interested. I'll put it all in the cable to headquarters. But I'm going to need that money."

"I have it in the car."

"You left a thousand dollars in the car?"

"I wasn't going to carry it on me. It's in a concealment device. A litter bag with trash in it. It has a false bottom."

"Dressed like that you're like a neon sign."

"Manion just hold up your end. Now tell me exactly what you said to Shurin and what he said to you." Frank went on to recount the exchange almost verbatim. "You mean you pitched him?" She stopped in her tracks.

"Yes, of course."

"What do you mean, 'of course'? And he turned you down?"

If he had any doubts before about her sobriety she now seemed perfectly clear-headed.

"I told him to think about it. We won't know if he really turned me down until he shows up or he leaves for Moscow."

"Or he reports it to his ambassador and there's another protest."

"Could be."

"Frank, why did you do it?" She looked directly at him. It was the first time she had called him by his first name. "I told you the chief of base doesn't want another flap."

"The way I presented it, he can't report it. I talked about Justinha and he's not about to admit to his boss that he's involved with her. Besides, this is a business of risks."

"But not foolish ones, you were supposed to just meet the guy and assess him."

"There isn't time. He leaves in seven weeks."

"I don't know what they taught you in training, but this is the real thing. Cold pitches don't work. You should have eased into it."

"How?"

"That was what you were sent here to work out. Invent some ploy. Use your imagination. If you don't have imagination, you're in the wrong business. Size him up. Assess, develop, recruit, not just recruit. As a last resort, we might have gotten to him through Justinha. Now the Soviets can embarrass us again."

"If there's a problem, I'll take the hit."

"And I'm sure you'll get away with it just because you're a guy."

"What's that got to do with it?"

"Just that you guys are a club, and you can't be a member of the club if you don't have a member." Frank smiled at that, but looked into the street to keep her from seeing his reaction. Then he turned back to her.

"I don't know, Julie. I've had to work hard all my life to convince people that I'm not just another pretty face...," He paused then for a hoped for comic effect. "an outstanding body, brilliant mind, sparkling personality. Shall I go on?"

"I don't see the humor in any of this. What a night. Could anything else go wrong?" She threw up her left arm.

"Come on. Things aren't that bad. And you haven't told me what you thought of the show."

"That," and again she used her left arm to point back at the sex club, "was pathetic, disgusting and a disgrace." Frank didn't know if by

49

"that" she was referring to the whole experience, or the most prominent part of it.

"I admit it's an acquired taste."

"I'm not a prude. What I'm talking about is that they were just kids. Somebody brought them down from the *favelas* and they're paying them a pittance to go out and expose themselves for the delight of a bunch of degenerates."

"You're right. I'm not defending porno shows. But look at it this way. When we're old and the kids are grown and they bring the grandkids over, we won't remember much, but we'll never forget our first date." She looked at him as if he had just been released from bedlam and she couldn't be sure he had been cured. "Besides, if this guy accepts my pitch, you'll get credit, too."

"I won't hold my breath," she said. "I don't think they're going to be giving me any medal. I won't be the one who made the recruitment, but at this stage I don't think they'll be giving you one either."

"But you're working on Justinha and I think that could be important if Shurin cooperates."

"I'm not sure headquarters is going to let me recruit her. They'll probably want me just to stay in touch." They reached Julie's Peugeot. Frank stood in the street at the passenger door. "Now, even my best agent has missed his last two meetings. Manion, you're a disappointment." Inside, she reached over and unlocked his door. It was now completely dark. The Brazilian winter was on its way. They sat silent for a minute. "What the hell. It's too late to do anything about it. Here's the money." She removed the cloth litter bag, turned it upside down and unzipped a cavity underneath. "Sign this receipt. There's a pen in the glove compartment."

"I'm not as pessimistic as you. I think there's a good chance he'll show up." Frank handed her the slip of paper.

"Let's hope so. I'll drive you to your car so you won't have to carry that much cash. The vodka and whiskey are in that brown bag on the back seat." They rode through side streets. Julie was turning at every other corner and stops at red lights seemed optional. "I have to admit tonight was memorable, even if I only got to watch."

"You didn't fool me. I saw you were watching a lot." When he looked over at her, she was smiling and shaking her head.

"I'm sure that's what you'll tell all the boys when you get back to headquarters."

"You're wrong. I know how to keep secrets." He rocked from side to side with her turns. "But tonight was my first taste of the real thing. I'm talking about operations."

"Take my word for it. I don't think you ever know the real thing." She looked almost sad as she said this.

"What do you mean?"

"In this work, everything you see is distorted. I know this is a cliché, but it's the best simile I can think of. It's like those mirrors in the fun house on Coney Island that make fat people look thin and short people look tall."

"It's up here on the right." Frank shifted in his seat. Julie slowed and pulled close to the line of parked cars.

"Well, if Shurin does show up, you'll have your first recruitment." She stopped next to the driver's door of the Ford. "You'll have lost your virginity. I think that's an appropriate metaphor for this evening."

"Similes and metaphors, you must have been an English major." He opened the door.

"I was."

"By the way, I lost my virginity when I was nineteen."

"Is that supposed to impress me?"

Frank got out. She drove off and turned right at the end of the block.

"You're not easy to impress," he said, half out loud.

Chapter 9

In the 1930s and '40s, the Copacabana Palace was the most lustrous diamond in the tiara of beach hotels on Rio's Atlantic coast. Hollywood stars, foreign heads of state, business tycoons, anyone of consequence who came to Rio stayed there. By 1981 it had fallen into neglect. Its art-deco walls were faded and in some places peeling. When Frank checked in, he had to pass under wooden scaffolding set up to repair cracks in the exterior walls.

After a week, he was tired of the place. He resented having to wear the flimsy disguise every day. It prevented him from using the pool, or even swimming in the ocean early in the morning. Sitting around was the hardest. The snack bar was made of jacaranda, a Brazilian hardwood. Frank had counted all the ribs in its fluted base. He had counted the windows he could see at pool side. He stretched on a lounge chair and watched for any movement in the rooms above. There was virtually none. Each morning he read the International Herald Tribune from front to back, but that took only twenty minutes. He was burnt out on Portuguese paperbacks and horny from girl watching. And what upset him above all else was the likelihood that he was accomplishing nothing while his marriage was collapsing. That last part was definite. He had called home on Thursday night. Beth's words and one sickening sound kept playing in his head.

"I'm moving out," she had said.

"What are you talking about?"

"I thought it was succinct and easily understood."

"Why?"

"I told you I was tired of sitting alone waiting for you to come home. If this comes as a surprise to you, you're probably in the wrong business."

"Somebody else said that to me recently. But it's the only business I want to be in."

"We all make choices."

It was then that he heard it, a cough, definitely a male sound. He had pictured her in the kitchen talking on the wall phone, but when he asked she said she was in the third floor bedroom. His stomach sank, then rose and turned cold. He thought he might vomit. It brought back that nightmarish most frightening, gut-twisting talk he'd ever had. The time he learned his parents had been killed.

On the phone he figured he could confront her, but how would that play out when they were separated by fifteen hundred miles? Instead, after the slightest pause he forced himself to pick up the thread of the conversation.

"Yeah, I chose to put you through law school. Three years when you studied all day and every night. I never complained. I just paid the bill and the way I paid it was by working in that insurance company and doing what I'm doing now. So now that you're set up, you walk?"

"I'll pay you back, Frank. Listen. I don't want to hurt you, but living overseas isn't for me. I do have a career and it's here. Let's talk when you get back. I'll let you know where I am."

And that was it.

As for Shurin, time was running out with him, too. Frank clung to one tenuous and uncertain clue as to what the Soviet might do. The day after he took his room at the hotel, Frank went to pick up Thursday's tape and he pressured Rzepnicki to transcribe it immediately despite the curmudgeon's inevitable resistance. As soon as Rzepnicki had done the work, Frank was after him.

"Was there anything unusual in his behavior?"

"Yes. It's good this is sound-activated system. On Tuesday night he and wife argued. That's not unusual. She went to bed about ten. But he stayed up. He never said one word. All he did was pace floor until about one a.m. Then he called his lady friend."

"At one in the morning?"

"Just after. Come listen. I don't know what they said. You will have to translate."

Again Frank put on the headset. This time, the voice he heard was familiar.

"Have you met any Americans lately?" Shurin asked Justinha.

"One, she's a friend of my parents. I met her at the Jockey Club. We play tennis together." This time Frank stopped the machine long enough so he could copy every word. He turned it on again.

"What is she doing in Brazil?"

"She's a diplomat at their consulate here."

"I have to talk to you, but not on the phone. Come on Friday. The same place."

"What time?"

"I'll be there at noon."

Rzepnicki looked over his shoulder and read the translation.

"This means you have seen him?"

"I don't know what it means." Frank was not about to tell Rzepnicki about the contact. The older man didn't need to know about it.

Frank called for an emergency meeting with Julie. They talked in the car as she drove along the coast east of the city.

"Can you pull over somewhere?" he asked. "There's something you have to see." She slowed to the right and stopped near the sea grass on the edge of the road. He passed her the transcript and gave her several minutes to read it. "What do you think?"

"Not much."

"Have you seen Justinha?"

"Yes, for tennis. We play again next week. But obviously, it means I'm not about to break cover and try to recruit her. I told you I would get screwed in this case."

"I'm sorry, Julie. I don't see anything else to do but wait. Maybe after he leaves you can recruit her. You can be his means of staying in touch."

"And if frogs grew wings, they wouldn't bump their ass on the rocks. I used to think a woman's worst enemy was cellulite, but that was before I met you, Manion."

Frank's only consolation was that the rains were less frequent and he was able to walk. And he could sit outside to watch for Shurin to show up. Yet when it happened, Frank almost missed him. On Saturday morning the hotel pool was crowded with youngsters and their parents occupied most of the chairs. Frank looked up as one kid dropped his bathing suit and began to pee in the pool. His mother ran over to stop him. When Frank happened to glance at the snack bar, there was Shurin. He must have come in the back. He was talking to a Brazilian employee of the hotel, maybe the Paulo heard on the teltap. Frank got up from his chair, took his towel and tossed it in the laundry basket as he approached the bar.

"An orange juice, please," he told the counterman.

"*Sim, senhor.*"

"And put it on my bill. I'm in room four-twelve." Frank never looked at Shurin, but spoke loud enough for him to hear. He repeated the number in Portuguese, signed the bill then drank the glass without stopping and walked into the lobby and across to the elevators. An older couple got out as he was getting in, but he brushed by them in his excitement. Up in the room he checked his disguise in the mirror. There was a shred of orange pulp in his moustache. He was getting like Rzepnicki. Frank barely had time to open his briefcase, turn on the tape recorder, snap the bag shut and position it under the table before he heard the knock at the door. On the way across the room, one last time he pressed each side of the moustache with the back of each hand.

"Please." Frank said it in Russian and motioned with his arm for Shurin to come in. When the Russian passed by, Frank followed. At first they were like two tropical fish dropped in a bowl, both swimming in seemingly random directions, but each keenly aware of what the other was doing. Frank turned on the TV, but kept the volume low. As always he wanted to create enough ambient noise to defeat any audio device, but now he had to be sure not to interfere with his own attempt to record the

54

meeting up close. "Please sit down. Can I offer you a drink?" Frank went to the tiny refrigerator and took out one of the Stolichnaya bottles. But Shurin didn't sit. He went first to the window and looked across the balcony at Copacabana Beach and the ocean.

"You say you know a lady who knows me?" Shurin started off in Russian. Frank held the chilled bottle in his right hand and two glasses in his left. He stood to one side of the Soviet, who still faced the window.

"I've never met her. I do know you seem to be serious about her." Suddenly, Shurin turned and spoke in English. It was heavily accented, slightly incorrect, but perfectly comprehensible.

"You want for me to be spy. Is that it?"

Frank, too, switched to English.

"I want you to see, I want us both to see if you can provide information."

"You can say what you want, paint it in such pretty picture, but I would still be traitor."

"You would betray a system that has already betrayed your country."

"How did you say you are called?" Shurin asked, still in English.

"Richard Boland."

"You have identity document?"

"Yes, but it probably wouldn't prove anything. Anyone in my position could get documents."

"You are right. So how do I know even you are American?"

"I can prove that if you really require proof."

"And how would you do that?"

"Well, let's say that you might pass by the American Consulate General at 165 avenida Presidente Wilson."

"I know where is found American Consulate."

"They're doing some construction on the second floor. There is a big plate glass window. If you stand on rua Virato at two-fifteen, I can have someone, a marine guard let's say, walk to the window, remove his cap, run his hand over his head and replace his cap. We can do it next Tuesday and Wednesday."

"And if this happened, then what?"

"Then you'll know I am really an American who can make such things happen and you can decide whether you want to meet again." Frank set the bottle and glasses on the stone-topped table. He unscrewed the tin cap and poured a full glass and held it out to his guest. "How much time do you have today?" Shurin didn't answer and he didn't take the drink. "Vladimir Sergeyevich, I told you I didn't want to cause problems for you."

"How considerate."

"You say that sarcastically, but it's true. I could have tried to talk to you anywhere, but instead I waited until the circumstances would be safe for you. Why don't you sit, have a drink and hear what I have to say? If you're not interested, you can leave and I promise I won't bother you again." Shurin, who had been standing with his arms folded across his chest, slowly pulled the striped satin-upholstered chair from the table and sat, but only on the edge of the seat. He took the vodka glass in his hand, but stopped just short of his first swallow.

"Now you have my fingerprints on this glass." Frank got up and walked to the bathroom. He came back with a wet washcloth.

"Here. Wipe them off after you use the glass if that makes you feel better." Frank took the second glass from the table and poured from the bottle. Now he sat across from the Russian. "Believe me, I'm not here to blackmail you. On the contrary, I'm in a position to be helpful to you if you're interested."

"Go on." Shurin leaned forward with his forearms on the table. Frank saw that those arms were slim, but sinewy, with that Slavic toughness that had beaten off waves of Turkic tribal invaders. Shurin had pointed hawk-like features and pale blue eyes that stared accusingly at Frank.

"I know enough about you to understand that you're not in a sensitive position at your embassy. But you may go back to Moscow and find that you have access to information which might be important to the United States."

"Who knows that you are here today? Who knows of me?"

"Three, four people at most." Frank paused, raised his glass and glanced at his watch at the same time.

"Why me, there are many others in my embassy who would be of more interest to you?"

Since Shurin had set down his glass, Frank put down his own without drinking.

"As I said, I know a lot about you and I think that you are someone who will at least be willing to consider what I have to say."

"And what is that?"

"I know that you are not happy with your wife."

"I could tell you names of many men who are not happy with their wives. But they do not become spies." Here, Frank decided to take a chance.

"You're right. I'm having my own problems." Shurin, who had remained rigid and expressionless up to that point, gave a hint of a smile, just the slightest rise at the corners of his lips. "You're tired of your wife, but in my case it's my wife who is tired of me and the profession I've chosen."

"So, we are somewhat same. Why do you not spy for me?"

"One difference between us is that in your case you're doing something about it. You're involved with a young Brazilian woman."

"But you say you are not trying to blackmail me?"

"Not at all. In fact, if you're serious about her, maybe I can help."

"Did your employer pay for that woman you left with that night?" The question came out of the blue. Frank thought for a second of Julie and her blue vinyl, blonde-wigged disguise.

"Yes. But she was just an escort for one night."

"You have good taste. I went back there and found her. She hangs around there. I fucked her, too."

Instantly, some internal engine no one ever mentioned in training started up. Frank understood the fellow was lying and without the least hesitation he began to operate on two levels.

"Did you enjoy it?"

"Of course. You know in Russian we say that makes us 'milk brothers.'"

"Well then, you know I wouldn't try to threaten you, my brother." Actually, Frank said, "*moi brat*," thinking the Russian words would convey just the right note of levity.

"Cain killed Abel. But what you are asking is serious. What makes you think I would be someone who would cooperate?"

"Your father fought in the Second World War. Stalin cost the lives of countless Russian soldiers in that war because of his purges of the officer corps and his blunders with Hitler before the war started. He killed millions more over the years, in the camps, through starvation. That system that he put in place continues today. The party can't be wrong. It will tell you how you can live your life. But it is wrong, and when it is, it's the people who suffer, you who suffer. Why shouldn't you be free to live in Brazil if that's what you want? Why shouldn't you be able to marry a Brazilian?"

"Let me tell you something of Stalin." Shurin pushed his glass to one side and leaned farther forward across the table. He put his palms flat against the stone top. Frank noticed the fellow had long hands structured on prominent carpal bones. His fingernails, like Rzepnicki's, were dirty. "Before he died in 1953, women in building where was our flat went outside each evening in March. They used to read sky like ancient Romans for signs and omens. For almost one week, perhaps more, women, everyone saw violent portent. Red daggers and blood in sky. America would invade, they said, drop bombs. You can imagine as seven-year-old what impression that made on me. Then Stalin died and we knew what these signs meant. People were crying in streets. Women were all dressed in black as procession passed by. I was there. I saw it. I remember. But my father pulled me back from this crowd and said to me, 'Listen to what I tell you. Thank God tyrant is dead.'"

"Your father was right. But the system is the same. I think you want to stay in Brazil to be with Justinha. But your government won't allow it. They're making the decision for you, but I think you are someone who wants to decide for himself."

"Whether they allow it or not, I could defect. Then we could talk all you want."

"As we both agreed, there wouldn't be much to talk about. A little bit, but not much. You aren't in the KGB or the GRU. You really don't have much information that would be of interest."

"Then why are we talking?" Finally, Shurin sat back in the chair, glass in hand and took his first swallow. "You said you could help me. Now I say I might defect, but you say you will not help at all."

Suddenly Frank understood that things had taken a turn. They were no longer talking about whether or not Shurin would do the deed, but about terms. And it dawned on him, too, that he had a knack for reading the sub-text, not what this man was saying, but what he was thinking.

"We're not an agency that handles refugees. We deal in information. If you return to Moscow, you could probably gain access to the kind of information we need from the foreign ministry. I could pay you well for that. Then if you're assigned abroad again, you could defect next time with a good deal of money and our assistance in resettlement."

Shurin now took several more swallows of the vodka then sat for a moment before he replied.

"How much money?" He appeared more relaxed as they negotiated. He lit a cigarette, this time a Marlboro, and tilted his head back to exhale the smoke toward the high ceiling.

"That's something we can talk about. If you agree to do what I'm proposing, I would have to teach you, train you to communicate securely. You leave in six weeks, so we don't have a lot of time to do that. I would have to know quickly whether you are interested."

"I know you were prepared to offer that idiot Bunin five thousand each month. For me it must be ten thousand or it is none such thing."

Bunin was the Soviet the agency had pitched three months earlier. The thought that went through Frank's head was that capitalism was right again. It pays to advertise.

"So you knew about Bunin?"

"Of course, how do you think? Everyone did when ambassador made protest."

"How do I know you are worth that kind of money or anything at all?"

"You must be interested in what I can give you otherwise you would not have followed me." Shurin extended his hand and turned it over to show his palm with spread fingers as he made his point.

"I said you knew some things even here," Frank said. "You can show me, give me a sample of the kind of information I need."

"What is interesting to you?" Shurin tapped his cigarette on the edge of the thick malachite ashtray at the center of the table and the ash fell away.

"Something to establish your bona fides, let's say the identities of the KGB people in the consulate." Frank knew this was the first big hurdle and for Russians it was a frightening one. If you screwed with the KGB, you died. Shurin sat for a moment, took another long swallow of vodka and put the glass down. It clinked on the stone tabletop.

"I don't know those people."

"You must know some of them. And you have a pretty good idea about the others."

"I know only two, Barchuk, Anatoliy Vassiliyevich and Stepashin."

"Where is the referentura?"

"What?"

"The referentura, the office where the KGB people all work."

Shurin shifted in his chair. Then he looked out the window. Frank knew that from that angle, the Russian couldn't see the beach or the sea. Because of the cement balcony and railing, the only thing visible was the sky. Shurin took one more swallow. The glass was almost empty.

"Special office is on third floor."

"The referentura?"

"Maybe, they never say name of it."

"And whom do you know who works there?"

"They don't work there all day. People come and go. But I know best Anatoliy Barchuk. He is from Ukraine. He sometimes asks me to do things."

"Like what?"

"To get things for him, whiskey, chocolates, to give as gifts and he asked me to use a contact I have at airport to stamp passport."

"Whose passport?"

For the first time, Shurin smiled a full smile. Frank saw his teeth were yellowing and uneven.

"Yes. Okay. I will give you one chestnut. You can roast it if you want. I think you will find it tasty." The Russian raised his glass and finished off the vodka in two more gulps. Frank refilled the glass. "He gave me passport of man named Seamus Duffy." Shurin pronounced the name "See-mus Doo-fie."

"Who is he?"

"Well, at first Barchuk told me this was man from Belfast, Ireland. Eugenio, my man at airport, never saw name, but I did. Eugenio put stamp in that said Duffy arrived that morning at Galeão. There was Aer Lingus flight morning of murder. He had to turn numbers on his stamp. That way, Duffy could prove he could not have had time to kill that old man. But it was false passport."

"He killed somebody? What are you talking about? How do you know?"

"Because later, Barchuk and I went out for drinks. Barchuk had already been drinking and he said one thing he should not."

"What?" Now Shurin started on his new glass.

"He said that Duffy was here for some 'wet work'."

"You mean to assassinate somebody?"

"Yes." Shurin looked at his watch. Frank checked his own. It was one thirty. "I will have to go soon."

"Who? Whom did he kill?"

"Barchuk said it was some old czarist." Shurin waved his left hand back and forth as if to dismiss the significance of the victim. "He said to me, 'Can you imagine, those people are still around?' This man, this one Duffy killed, was writer who attacked Soviet government."

"So he shot him?"

"Yes, but with special gun, gas gun. It looked like heart attack."

"Here in Rio?"

"Yes. Just back here in Botafogo section." Shurin gestured with his thumb toward the rear of the hotel. Frank may have looked skeptical, or surprised. "Barchuk said special gun came in our diplomatic bag. He hid it in Buzios for Duffy to pick up. If you don't believe me, check with that little boy or his nanny. They were coming back to building when Duffy went out front door. Barchuk said it was bad luck that anybody saw assassin, but he doubted things would come of it. Then he saw obituary in paper here and in those Russian émigré papers, *Russkaya Misl'* and *Novoye Russkoye Slovo*. Some of old man's articles were published in them. Both said old guy died of heart attack." Shurin took another swallow. He looked satisfied with himself now. For most people, the effect of the alcohol would have become apparent, but Shurin's look was the same. "That is how you can find name. Check list of death. It was about two weeks ago only. Now what about you show me something?"

"What do you mean?"

"You said money."

"You're right. I'll give you five hundred dollars for each time you come here." Frank reached under the table and unsnapped the brass clip on the briefcase. He reached into one of the small compartments taking care not to jostle the recorder. He pulled out a white envelope and counted out five one hundred dollar bills. He also withdrew the bundle of *cruzeiro* notes. "As for your time in Moscow, I will ask for authorization to pay you ten thousand dollars a month for as long as you keep communicating with us. I can't guarantee that Washington will approve it, but I'll try. If you come abroad again, we will work out a resettlement package that will enable you to live well."

"I need one thousand for today."

That was it, the real reason Shurin had shown up. Frank figured the fellow was somehow in debt. Maybe he was skimming funds for catering arrangements he made, or maybe he had spent money on Justinha and with his transfer coming up, he had to repay it.

"That's a lot for just one hour."

"And what would it cost me if I am caught?"

"Okay. I'll have to give it to you in both *cruzeiros* and dollars."

"All *cruzeiros* would be more easy."

"Sorry. This is all I have. And I have to have a receipt." Before Shurin could object, Frank explained, "I don't mean you have to sign your real name. Sign it Fontes the way you did when I scratched your car." Frank wrote one sentence and drew a line beneath it. He handed the pen to Shurin.

"If I do this, if I go back to Moscow and send you messages, how will it work?"

"That's what we'll talk about next time. When can you come again?"

"I don't know. In one week is possible. I can leave message for you in box downstairs."

"Boland, room four-twelve. I'll be here every day. I'll start to put the plan together. Also, when you come to the door next time, as a last safety signal, so you'll know I'm here in the room and no one is with me, I'll put this envelope under the door. If you see it there, that means it's okay to knock."

"Yes. I understand. And there is one thing more."

"What's that?"

"When I go back to Moscow, I want poison pills that will work instantly. I will not allow KGB to take me alive."

Julie had abandoned the list of cafés. She had switched to car meetings. That night she picked Frank up in Barra da Tijuca and headed along the shore. He told her about Shurin.

"It's still early. Why don't we get something to eat? To celebrate." She seemed genuinely pleased.

"You've gone native," he said. "It's ten o'clock."

"You haven't figured it out yet? Nothing starts around here until ten. There's a place called the Garota da Urca with a great view of the water."

"Whatever you say, you're the senior officer."

"Before I forget, that package on the back seat is for you. The pens are in there with the one-time pads, SW materials, the whole deal. And headquarters approved the money." Julie took the beach road, Avenida Viera Souto, and continued along the Copacabana stretch and in toward Botafogo. She raced behind, beside and ahead of the nocturnal Brazilian drivers. Once again, she stopped at some traffic signals, but not others. The scene reminded Frank of photos made by leaving the lens open to

61

create streaks of light. Along the Avenida Portugal, he looked up to his right at Sugarloaf.

"You know, when he agreed, the adrenaline kicked in. I was flying. But that last part, when he asked for the pills, sobered me up fast."

"I don't know if headquarters will go for that." Julie shook her head.

"Maybe I can talk him out of it. The other thing I thought was that the first person I wanted to tell was you." She turned toward him and stared. Frank thought surely she would crash the car, but she seemed able to maneuver with only peripheral vision or some female sense.

"That's sweet." If she had smiled, that would have said one thing. But she didn't, and to him that meant more. "Maybe it's just that you have nobody else to talk to except Bogey."

"Bogey?"

"Yes. That's what we call him in the office. Isn't that his first name, Boguslav?"

"Oh, Rzepnicki, in Washington they call him Bugs. He thinks it's because of the work, but Tony Valletta told me it's really his colleagues making fun of him."

"Have you talked to him about the meeting?"

"No. Believe me, he's not very much of a conversationalist. More than that, he's a strange bird. But he doesn't need to know what happened. In fact, I would be surprised if headquarters doesn't call him back to Washington now that they know that I'm in touch with Shurin."

"Anyway, congratulations." By now she was looking again at the road ahead. "I mean it. We don't know how it's going to turn out, but you did a great job just getting him this far."

"I'm not sure they're in order." Frank looked out his side window.

"Is that false modesty, or do you think he might not go through with it?"

He turned back to her.

"I think he will. It's true that this is my first field experience. But while I've been in headquarters I've read a lot of case files and I have yet to see an unqualified success, so maybe congratulations are premature."

"I told you this business is never what it seems."

"So you did. Fun house mirrors."

Julie curved further to the right along the water.

"Did he give you anything to establish his bona fides?"

"Yes. It's in the cable. He told me about Barchuk and Stepashin."

"Just those two names?"

"No. Listen to this. I put it in the cable, but I didn't tell you." Frank smacked his hand on his forehead. "He told me about an assassin. The guy is still here in Brazil. He's up in Brasilia."

"And that's in your cable?"

"Yes. He killed a Russian émigré here in Rio with a gas gun. He made it look like a heart attack. It was an old man, a writer who was opposed to the Soviets."

Julie sat still and silent. Only her hands and forearms moved with the wheel. This time she continued to look ahead, but for several moments Frank thought she had switched to auto-pilot. Even in the fleeting reflections as they passed street lights he could see her face lose its color.

"Did he give the man's name?"

"No. But he said I could look it up in the obituaries. It was about two weeks ago. There was also a little blurb in the Russian émigré papers, *Novoye Russkoye Slovo* and *Russkaya Misl'*."

"The man lived in Rio?"

"Yes, in Botafogo."

"I feel sick." She slowed suddenly, pulled over onto the tiled sidewalk at the edge of the beach and stopped.

"What's the matter?" he asked. She sat for several moments staring ahead without answering. "What is it?" he asked again. She just held up her hand to keep him silent.

"I need some air." Julie got out of the car. She stood on the mosaic swirls of tile that covered the sidewalk, lifted one foot and took off her shoe, then did the same with the other and walked out onto the sand. Frank put his feet out the door. By the time he had removed his shoes and socks she was almost at the water's edge. He had to run to catch up.

"What's going on?" He was breathing heavily in the sultry night air. The moon was silver and low and its rippled reflection on the undulating sea looked like a blowing ribbon on an old navy cap.

"You remember I said that I had one good asset, a press placement man?"

"Yes."

"And that he hasn't shown up for the past couple of meetings?"

"Yes."

"I just found out he died of a heart attack."

"A Russian émigré you said?"

"Yes. He used to write articles and get them in the Brazilian press and we had them picked up in Argentina, Chile, Mexico City."

"And he lived in Botafogo?"

"Yes. He knew a lot of Brazilian senators and military officers. He fed them horror stories about the Soviets, reasons why Brazil should break off diplomatic relations. But he was such a sweet old man. He had that old European charm, clean white hankie, kissing my hand, all that."

"Oh, no."

"I just pray to God I had nothing to do with them finding him."

"From what you say, he wouldn't have been hard to find. I doubt it had anything to do with you. Shurin never said they thought the man was

63

working for us." They walked on then without saying anything. Frank wanted to put his arm around her, but the shoes interfered. He switched them to his left hand. Suddenly, she stopped and began to cry, wrenching, convulsive sobs that shook her upper body. Frank took hold of her arm and turned her. Then he dropped his shoes and socks, put both hands on her shoulders and drew her to him. While his urge to comfort her was genuine, he had to admit to himself that the first thing he noticed when she was up against him was the firmness of her breasts and how her legs and belly pressed against him perfectly. He was not sure she would let him kiss her, at least not romantically. He looked over her shoulder up at the enormous illuminated statue of Christ the Redeemer on Corcovado. Jesus seemed to be watching to see what he would do next. He chose to do nothing but pat her on the back and whisper what he thought were consoling words.

"Bagatelle is going to make them pay."

Chapter 10

On the fourth floor of the CIA headquarters building in Langley, Virginia, Tony Valletta, the chief of Soviet operations for Latin America, leaned back in his chair until his head almost touched the window. He was in his white shirt sleeves. A wrinkled black and green striped tie was loose around his neck and his collar was unbuttoned. At his waist, several worn curves by the holes on his belt indicated he'd had to let it out a few notches. In the past several years, his early fifties, his swarthy skin had turned puffy and was marked by one prominent mole between his cheek and his nose. His eyes were glossy and dark, magnified by thick glasses and his red pepper lips protruded a bit. What little long black hair remained to him was combed flat from the crown over his bald pate. All those features combined to make him resemble a swamp frog. Behind him out on the grounds, the budding crocus and forsythia promised that the annual cycle of renewal would begin again. But he never looked back. Instead, he rocked forward to do battle with Harry O'Meara, better known in the agency as the Raven.

"I don't know why you're pooh-poohing this, Harry. I realize that you have the experience and I know we have to wait a few more meetings. But so far it looks like a genuine recruitment to me. Splendid work, I'd say."

Harry puffed rhythmically on a cigarette. He put his head down almost to his chest and hesitated before he looked up and answered.

"With Soviets, they're only as good as their last meeting. If they produce today, they're good today." Now he tilted his head back and stretched his long frame. His eyes had a wild look under thick, black brows and the Coke-bottle lenses of his glasses. His nose was curved and could have passed for a beak. Tony recalled someone telling him that the fellow had two identical suits, both perpetually rumpled. Both were black. As far as anyone could remember, Harry had never worn anything else, thus the nickname. "This guy hasn't really given us anything," the Raven said.

"Aren't you overlooking the assassin? Have you seen this cable? The Brazilians found the chap in the Hotel Nacional in Brasilia. It corroborated Bagatelle's story. They now have the villain in jail."

"Sure. I saw that. The Soviets wouldn't mind giving away that kind of information. In fact, they would benefit from it. I'm not trying to rub your nose in it, but here's where it's important to have some institutional memory. You came over from EUR, what, four, five months ago?"

"Yes."

"I've been here a while. Twenty-nine years. The KGB cut out the wet work about twenty-five years ago in the fifties when a guy named Karpovich defected to the West Germans. Seems he had a crisis of conscience and confessed. He said he had been sent to kill a couple of Ukrainian dissidents. The Krauts didn't believe him, but he took them to a river down in Munich where he said he threw away the gas gun. It was still there. The killing in Rio would put out the word to all the émigrés that the assassins are back in business. Scare the bejesus out of them all over again." Tony had no ashtray on his desk. Harry flicked his ashes toward the gray government-issue trash can just out of arm's length in the corner of the room. They didn't quite reach it.

"And the names, Stepashin and Barchuk, known KGB? We've confirmed them," Tony said.

"Normally they wouldn't give them away. But maybe they figure it's a small price to pay to get us to feed Shurin requirements and find out how we're operating these days in Moscow. The killer might give Barchuk up anyway when the Brazilians squeeze him."

"So what do you recommend?"

"I would cut the whole thing off. Bagatelle is an admin guy. He's never going to be in a position to give us anything even if he's straight. But that's not management's philosophy these days. They'll probably tell you to keep it going. Put another pin up on the board. Take it over and show it to Congress."

"And what's to be done with the transcriber, Mister Rzepnicki?"

"Bring him home. Have the kid tell him he's no longer needed, that Shurin turned down the pitch. You know, don't you, that you've got to create a bigot list?"

"Forgive an itinerant ignorant EUR body, but what exactly is that?"

"It's the names of everybody who's aware of the case and the fact that Bagatelle has been recruited. If there's a leak and the case goes bad, it gives us a starting point for a damage assessment."

"But I thought you said this should not be considered a good recruitment?"

"Who knows what it will turn out to be? But in the meantime, we start the list."

"Shall I include the transcriber on it?"

"No. Not if the kid handles it right. Find out which people in Rio base know about the case. The woman case officer certainly knows, the chief of base, the commo boys. But the recruitment cable was in restricted channels, so it shouldn't be widely known there. Send a cable to the chief of base telling him that from this point on, he's not to discuss it with anyone other than the girl. What's her name?"

"Julie d'Andrade. Pushteau is her pseudonym. And the kid, as you call him, is Francis Manion."

"Yeah, have the chief of base brief the woman and the commo officers to make sure they don't assume everybody knows about it. This is probably the first bigoted case they've had to deal with. The last recruitment we tried down there blew up in our faces and everybody knew about it. We never needed a bigot list."

"Yes. That was right after I got here. Anything else?"

"A lot. We don't want to give this guy anything. Have the kid train him in a throwaway commo system, something very simple, SW, secret writing. We don't give Bagatelle any commo gear we want to protect. Teach him one-way voice link with one-time pads for frequencies and messages. We load a dead drop, tell him by radio where it is, and let him go find our packages. That protects our people in Moscow."

"And for his communications to us?"

"Give him an accommodation address. Maybe the case officer in Brazil, the woman, Pushteau, can handle it. Set up a postal box in Rio. He uses the SW to write his letters, just good enough to get past the censors. That way we don't contaminate anybody else. If he should start to produce, which I doubt, we can always change it around."

"In this situation you're right. I am at a loss."

"What the case officer has to do is debrief Bagatelle on his routine in Moscow. I mean everything. If the guy develops a bunion on his ass, we need to know about it because he may have to go to a pharmacy and that may offer us a place to put a drop where he can get it. Get it?"

"Yes."

"I'll tell somebody on the USSR desk to come over and help you. Normally, we would send a trainer down there to work with the kid. But with a simple plan, he can do the training himself. That way we don't expose another officer. With the instructions in the cable, he just follows the bouncing ball." Harry took his rumpled pack of Camels from his shirt pocket and lit a new cigarette as he rose to leave.

"Just as you say, I'll work with the USSR desk and get the cable out today. I'll route it through you just to be sure." Tony smiled. But when his visitor had gone, he opened the office window to remove all sensory traces of the Raven. He didn't appreciate Harry's attitude toward the case and Frank Manion. He doubted that Harry had ever made a recruitment in his career. Many of these Soviet Division officers had not. But they ran the agents and took credit for what others had done. Without the Manions of the agency, people like Harry O'Meara would have little to do. That struck Tony as metaphoric. Ravens, after all, were scavengers.

Chapter 11

Once again, Frank found himself waiting in the hotel room. He had waited every day for a week and only on Friday did Shurin leave a message saying he would arrive on Saturday at the same hour as last time. For the hundredth time Frank studied the scene on the wallpaper, balmy, tropical, dark green palm fronds and pastel beaches and water. Now he stood, papers in hand, and walked to the window to look across the avenida Atlantica at the real thing. Nature disappointed. Only a few sun worshipers today. There was little sun to be worshiped. They lay under a between-season, undecided sky with occasional steely clouds transforming the light. Turning again, he checked the refrigerator. He had stocked up on vodka and Brahma beer and had written out on water-soluble paper a sanitized version of headquarters requirements for his debriefing and training of Shurin. But the fellow was ten minutes late. Frank had just started re-reading the instructions when he heard the knock.

"Show time," he muttered as he pushed the button on the tape recorder, set his briefcase under the table and went to the door.

"Have you heard the last news?" were Shurin's first words. Beads of perspiration stood out on his high forehead. "The ambassador sank."

"Your ambassador?"

"Yes."

"He was on a ship?"

"No. Maybe this is not right word. *Utopilsya.*"

"He drowned?"

"Yes."

"In Brasilia?"

"No. He was here. He was swimming off Barra da Tijuca. He came down here to see off Deputy Minister of Foreign Trade. That man you saw with me at Pinocchio's." Shurin paced the room. "He and two assistants, first secretary and attaché, all three were good swimmers and all three sank. *Utopilis.* That is why I was able to get out today. I have to make arrangements to send bodies home."

"Was he a good man?"

"He was decent chap, but I didn't deal with him much."

"I'm sorry. As I told you, I think your system is lousy, but there are good people stuck in it. Please, sit down." Shurin took the same seat as last time. Frank had noticed that it was something people usually did when they came into a room they had been in before. "Look, I don't want to be insensitive, but how much time do you have today?"

"Perhaps one hour, perhaps little more." Shurin squirmed in the chair, apparently not ready to concentrate.

"Okay. Let's take a couple of deep breaths. I know you're upset about the ambassador and it stinks to have to go right to business, but we have a lot to cover. Still, before we begin, if anyone interrupts our meeting, our explanation for your being here is that you went to get your car repaired, but my payment did not cover the full cost of the damages and you've come to get more money."

"Yes. Okay."

"And let me ask you one question."

"That is why I am here." Shurin raised and waved his right hand almost dismissively.

"No. This is personal. You asked for poison. So you know you're risking your life in what you're going to do."

"Of course." Now Shurin seemed to try to focus.

"Why, for Justinha?"

The Russian hesitated. He was handsome. His bone structure reminded Frank of a taller Kirk Douglas, with those chiseled features and blue eyes. His gaze turned to the window.

"Life can end any moment. Look at ambassador. But while I am living, I want good life. Better than those others. I told you of my father. He was good man, but only taxi driver. Fuck that and these bastards who have tried to keep me down. I won't let them. I like it here. But I know that it takes lot of money to live well here. Justinha says her parents probably would not help. In such case I want to get money my way and get out." Shurin now looked directly at Frank. "Did man in Washington tell you to ask me that?"

"No. I had to know for myself. I can't ask anybody to do this work without being sure they know the risks." Frank stood and moved to the small refrigerator and withdrew the frost-covered bottle of Stolichnaya. He picked up two glasses from the jacaranda chest and poured a short glass of vodka for Shurin and one for himself. "Let's stick to one glass today. What I'm going to show you may save your life, so I want you to be clear headed."

"Since we are talking from our souls, I will tell you something else. I knew from first moment that you were American agent." He smiled. "When you were at my car, it did not surprise me. At ministry before we left Moscow, they warned us that Americans might try such tricks. But in my case, I was looking for way out. When I heard that you had tried to recruit Bunin, that idiot, I cursed. I said to myself, 'Why could that not be me?'"

"But you weren't very encouraging at the car."

"I was sure we would meet again and I wanted to see how you did it. When I saw that you were careful not to put me in danger, I decided I would risk it."

"Good. Let's get started."

"Not yet." Shurin held up his arm. The flat of his palm was extended toward Frank. "You have asked your question, now I must ask mine. What about money?"

"Yes. It's approved. We'll give you ten thousand U.S. dollars a month. We will put it in an escrow account in Switzerland."

"Why not here in Banco do Brasil? Justinha could help."

"She can't know anything about this. Besides, they wouldn't handle a numbered account. In Switzerland your name won't be associated with the account. If you communicate with us for three years before you come abroad again, we will give you a bonus of one hundred thousand dollars in addition to the monthly amount." Shurin came back almost immediately.

"So that would be four hundred sixty thousand dollars all together."

"I thought you were a language student at the university. That's pretty quick math. Yes."

"Why not make it five hundred thousand? That's easier number to remember."

He took the pack of Kool Lights from his shirt pocket and lit up. One perk for diplomats from the East when they came to the West was that they got to smoke American cigarettes. Frank had never been tempted to take up what he thought was a self-destructive habit.

"Jesus, Volodya," Frank slipped into the familiar form for the Russian first name. "Are you sure you don't have a carpet to sell me?" Shurin just smiled, but more broadly this time. Again, Frank thought, his teeth were not his best feature. They were slightly yellow and the bottom row was crooked from crowding together in his pointed jaw. "Look. So far we can't even be sure you'll be in a position to provide good information. Let's agree to this. If you accept what I just offered but you come up with something really important, I'll do my best to get Washington to increase the bonus, but no promise other than that."

"Yes. Okay."

"I want to keep this as simple as possible. We'll work on two areas, our messages to you and yours to us. Today we'll start with us to you. I want you to buy a radio, one capable of receiving short wave transmissions, like that one." Frank pointed at the night stand by the bed, then got up and brought back a black and gray Grundig Ocean Boy radio with a stainless steel speaker grill and put it on the stone top of the round table in front of Shurin.

"This kind?" Shurin turned the radio to look at its face.

"I leave it to you, this, or something similar. They sell them in the dollar stores in Moscow, but I want you to buy it here and have your wife get accustomed to seeing it. That's how we'll send messages to you. Turn it on. Try tuning it to these frequencies." Frank pushed a paper across the table with two sets of numbers. Shurin smiled and leaned forward. He balanced his cigarette on the edge of the thick ashtray and pressed the power button.

"This wheel?" He held the edge of the grooved knob with his forefinger and thumb.

"Yes. The big knob is for tuning."

Shurin turned quickly at first and the pointed indicator on the radio band moved down the numbered strip. There was the crackle of static and the rise and fall of Morse code signals. They made Frank think for an instant of all the ships beyond the window tapping away on electrified keys. Then, as Shurin got close to the first number combination, he slowed.

"That's it," Frank said. "This radio has an automatic feature. It tunes in to the best reception for any given frequency." Shurin went through the two sets of numbers.

"So, what will I hear?" He took up his cigarette again.

"You'll hear a voice giving numbers, zero through nine. It may be a man's voice or a woman's. They'll be spoken numbers, not beeps. They may be in Russian or English. And you'll use a list like this to know which set of numbers will be your message."

Frank positioned a pad of paper turned halfway between himself and Shurin. On it were lines of figures divided into five-digit groups.

"You'll know it's our message to you when the group of five numbers you hear is exactly the same as this first group on the list. Then you copy everything after that. The groups that follow will not match those on your list, but you keep copying by group until you hear another group that does match." Frank gave Shurin the list and started reading from his own list. He gave the first five digits that matched then a series of five digit groups, and finally another matching group. "That second matching group indicates that it's the end of the message. Do you understand?"

"Yes. And how will I know what it means?"

"Okay. First, are you comfortable with what I've said?"

"Yes."

"Right, now you take the second group of five from your list and you subtract them from the second group you heard on the broadcast." Frank began lining up the radio groups above those on the pad and drew a line beneath each set. He then showed Shurin how to carry out false subtraction. "And you do this with each group. You carry no numbers. Every two numbers will match up with a letter on this list." Frank showed Shurin a card with the alphabet and a row of corresponding double digits from one to twenty-six. "You see? Zero one is the letter a, zero two is b, and so on." Again, Frank demonstrated. "Now you try it." It took Shurin almost no time to pick up the technique, but over the Russian's objections, Frank insisted on practicing for fifteen minutes.

71

"We're not going to be sending the first message for some time after you get back and I don't want you to forget how to do this."

"I will not forget." Shurin took the vodka in four swallows and continued to hold the empty glass and looked expectantly at Frank. Frank did not offer to refill it. "You are not very generous today."

"We've still got more to do. Now I want you to think about your routine at home in Moscow. Where will you be able to listen to these messages without your wife becoming suspicious?"

"Our flat is on top floor of building. There is kind of small attic that we use as storing place. It has window in roof which we can open. I go there sometimes to read, especially in summer."

"And when can you do it regularly?"

"Best would be at weekend. My wife often goes to her parents' dacha in countryside. I don't go much. I don't contact well with her family."

"Saturday?"

"Yes, Saturday morning."

"Okay. Then we agree. Every Saturday morning you will hear a broadcast. It will be between ten-thirty and ten-forty in the morning Moscow time."

"Yes, fine."

"Today I'll give you your list of numbers." Frank stretched out a tightly rolled plastic strip no thicker than a cigarette, but six inches long.

"They are small." Shurin took the strip from the table and held it to the light.

"You'll have to use a magnifying glass to read it at home. And we'll conceal it. You'll be able to take it securely past customs."

"How?"

"First things first. So, you'll take it back with you. And if you have nothing else, this list will let us communicate. It has the radio frequencies on which we'll broadcast and the code groups and the coded alphabet. And you know when to listen. Saturday morning."

"I see. I understand, even when you say it only once." Frank sensed Shurin's boredom. This was a guy accustomed to wheeling and dealing rather than detailed systems.

"Volodya, I'm not insulting your intelligence. People have different ways of learning. With some, things have to be repeated again and again. Others get it the first time. But remember what I said. This is something you won't use for a long time and when you try to do it, you may not remember."

"You have not lifted your glass." Shurin gestured toward Frank's vodka, sitting untouched on the table. Frank was always reluctant to drink. He had no ambition to control others, but he strove always to control himself and he didn't want to omit any details in the training. He had not exaggerated when he told Shurin that one slip could cost him his

72

life. Still, there was the human element. Russians bonded better with someone over vodka, so Frank took a small swallow.

"Now, when you listen to the radio and you copy the coded message, it will give you instructions on getting to a place where you will find a package. In the package will be a paper, but it's special paper." Frank took out several pieces of what appeared to be plain sheets of good quality bond. "This is important. You must do this exactly as I show you. We'll put a sheet of instructions in the package in case you forget the technique. First, you put down a regular sheet of paper on a clean, even surface. Then you put the sheet on which you will write an ordinary letter, to a friend, let's say."

"Which friend?"

"Not to an actual friend. Just someone whose name I'll give you, a Brazilian friend. We'll call him Eugenio Fontes." Shurin smiled at the reference to the name he had used on the day of the accident. Frank continued. "So, you write 'Dear Eugenio.' And you leave a bit of extra space between the lines, like this." Frank started a letter and filled in ten lines or so on the paper. "Now, you put this sheet, this coated sheet on top of the letter. Finally, you put this plain sheet on top of that. So all together there are four sheets, but you have to put them in that order: plain sheet on the bottom, letter sheet next, chemical sheet next, plain sheet on top. Now you begin your secret message to us on the top sheet, but writing so that the lines of the secret message are between the lines of the visible letter." Frank wrote a few words to demonstrate. "You see? Go ahead. Try it."

In spite of his earlier impatience, Shurin seemed interested in this part of the training. He stubbed out his cigarette, took the pencil and wrote carefully on the top sheet. He wrote in Russian and Frank was unable to read it upside down. It was a long message.

"There."

"Something I forgot to mention. Please print rather than write in longhand. But you've got the knack. Now you take away the top sheet and the second sheet and you examine the letter sheet like this." Frank extended the paper toward the window at an angle and Shurin leaned closer to study the paper. He took it in his hand. Frank took it back and changed the angle. "Hold it like this, in glancing light. Look for impressions, because that's what they will do at the post office when they check mail going abroad." He handed the paper back to Shurin, who did the same.

"I see nothing."

"Good. Now we'll develop it." Frank reached again into the briefcase and took out a small bottle of clear liquid. He unscrewed the black top. "You won't have to worry about this part. We'll do the developing when we get your messages, but I want you to see how it works." There was a brush attached to the metal top and Frank applied the liquid between the lines of the visible message Shurin had written. "It will take a couple of minutes." Shurin kept eyeing Frank's vodka glass.

"You know, in Russian we have saying. One is lonely number." Shurin pushed his empty glass across the table.

"Okay, one more." Frank poured reluctantly, slowly from the bottle, which was covered now with water droplets. "Do you still go out with Barchuk?" Again, Shurin downed his drink in gulps.

"Sometimes, I helped him find martial arts lessons, Tae-kwan-do and *capoeira*."

"What's that?"

"It is Brazilian martial arts. African, how do you say it, *rabiy*?"

"Slaves."

"Slaves, yes, they told Portuguese that they were doing dances, but it was really to learn to fight."

"I see. Okay. Look. It's starting to come up." They looked now at the paper and Shurin's message was becoming visible in a brown ink. It was a Russian poem.

"Do you know it?" Shurin asked with a half smile.

"It's from Pushkin."

"Yes. Can you translate?"

"I think so." Frank scanned the lines.

"So, my mid-day has begun,
I have to confess that, I see.
So be it: Let's say a friendly farewell,
Oh my light-hearted youth
Enough. With a clear soul
I set out now on a new path
To rest from my past life.'

"Very appropriate." Frank laid the paper on the table.

"That is very good. Do you know this work?" Shurin asked.

The only one of Pushkin's works Frank had read was "Pikovaya Dama," and he suspected this was an excerpt from something else.

"Yevgeniy Onegin."

"That is right."

Frank could tell from the nod of Shurin's head and his steady look that he had scored points. Russians loved their poets and none more than Pushkin.

"It was a guess, Volodya."

"No. You are too modest." Shurin shook his head. Frank wondered if the vodka was taking over. "You know Russian well. How did you learn?"

"At the university and I read a lot of Tolstoy." Frank was not about to admit he had learned the language in the army. That seemed to arouse animosity among Soviets.

"We say that man who reads Tolstoy usually speaks good Russian. So, then you also must know Russian saying, 'It takes three horses to pull troika.'" Shurin held out his glass yet again.

"Yes. Okay. We're finished for today and the time is getting short. You said you had one hour."

"Yes. After this I must go." He took the glass and finished only half before setting it down.

"I have one last thing to show you." Frank reached down in the briefcase and withdrew a gold Cartier pen. Shurin glanced at his shirt pocket. His own pen was still there.

"It is like mine." He held his pen to compare the two.

"I noticed it when you signed the receipt for me at your car," Frank said. "But this one is slightly different from yours. See if you can spot the difference."

Shurin examined both pens carefully. Frank could see the wheels turning. The Russian realized immediately that if there was a difference, it had to be inside the new pen and he unscrewed the tip of his own and the tip of the pen Frank had given him. He laid both ink cartridges on the table. He looked in the liquid-filled shells.

"They look same."

"Here's the difference." Frank took a tiny cap off the end of the ink holder of the modified pen and slipped a clear plastic sleeve up and off the cartridge. Then he unrolled the plastic inside just as he had done earlier with the list of numbered groups. "That's your one-time pad. It has all the numbers you will need to decrypt our message. It also has the two radio frequencies at the top in case you can't remember them."

"*Ochen' khitriy.*" (Very clever) Shurin reverted to Russian.

"It's clever enough to get past customs. Do you feel comfortable with it?"

"Yes."

"Good." Frank re-rolled the plastic strip around the ink holder, slid the sleeve back in place, and replaced the tiny plastic cap. He put the pen back together and handed it to Shurin. The Russian took two more swallows of his drink. "Now, when you're settled and ready to receive our message, I want you to go here." Frank unfolded a map of Moscow and pointed to a location. "The Ostankino public park, do you know it?"

"Of course," Shurin nodded.

"Here." Frank spread out another large paper. It was a sketch of the park's interior along with two black and white photos. "As you face the front of the palace, this bench is on the left. I want you, when you're ready for our message, to put a mark on the left support of the bench like this one. See?"

"Yes, I see."

"Wait until at least six months after you get back. Settle in. I won't give you any note to remind you. You'll have to remember this on your own. It will set everything in motion. Will you remember?"

"Yes."

"Good. But I'll still go over this each time you come here until you leave for home just to be sure."

"As you like, Boland, but I will remember."

"Do you think there's any possibility that you'll be assigned abroad again in less than three years?"

"No, but after that perhaps. It will depend on sponsor. That is why I will shop for gifts before I go back."

"For whom?"

"For anyone who can help me get new assignment."

"What do they expect you to give them?"

"I plan to buy several of those knock-off Seiko watches."

"So aside from your official postings you're never able to travel outside the Soviet Union?"

"Well, once each year there is international Tae-kwan-do tournament. It is held in Warsaw Pact countries, different one each year, this year in Moscow, next year in Prague, and so on."

"And you go to those?"

"Yes."

"So you're really into martial arts?"

"It is good exercise, good condition activity. Also it gives confidence. I am able to defend myself." Shurin took up a defensive position, both arms bent with one extended in front of the other. "Do they not teach you in your service?"

"Only how to get people by the balls."

Shurin chuckled.

"Yes. That works."

"I need one other thing, photos," Frank said. "I want to take a couple of pictures of you."

"For what?"

"If I'm hit by a bus or for some other reason someone else has to meet you, they will have to know what you look like."

While headquarters had file photos of Shurin, they were shots of him taken by a Brazilian news photographer with Barchuk at social functions. Rio Base had bought the negatives from the photographer. But Frank needed straight on pictures. He positioned Vladimir against the door and took several snapshots. Vladimir stood there, grim-faced holding his glass out of the frame.

"So you acted on information I gave you." Vladimir put his glass down on the table.

"What information are you talking about?"

"Don't be silly, that assassin, Duffy."

Frank felt blind-sided. Julie had said nothing and Frank didn't know how to answer.

"*Chestno govorya.*" ("Honestly speaking") Frank decided to tell the truth and thought it might be more convincing in Russian. "Really, I haven't heard anything. What happened?" He cradled the camera between his forearm and chest.

"Barchuk told me. Again he was drunk. Brazilians arrested this guy in Brasilia. They did not tell you?"

"No. Maybe the arrest was something they did on their own."

"Boland, Richard, I don't believe fairy tales."

"I just don't know what happened. If I find out, I'll tell you if I can."

"Okay. I must go take care of transport of bodies. But with all your instruction, you forgot one thing."

"What is that?"

"Money for today. You said each time."

"Sorry, here." Frank took an envelope from his briefcase. "Once again, sign only Eugenio Fontes." The signature was a scrawl. The Russian stuck the envelope with the cash in the inside pocket of his jacket. "Aren't you going to count it?" Frank asked.

"I trust you already with my life. I am not worried about some few *cruzeiros.*"

Frank accompanied him to the door, where Shurin turned. He squeezed Frank's hand a little harder than the last time.

"I'll see you next week. Good luck Volodya."

"You know, you in the West think we are all unbelievers, but we keep God in our sayings. We say, 'Only God knows.'"

Two days later, Frank passed the reception desk in the lobby.

"*Senhor* Boland, there is a message for you."

"Thank you." Frank thought it might simply be some hotel notice of a bill due. He was surprised when he realized the message was from Shurin.

"I must accompany packages back home. Since I was so close to return anyway, they will not send me back here. My wife is left to bring back our things. I leave tomorrow. I count on you to keep our agreement and I shall make mark in O. park then wait to hear from you."

There was no signature of any kind. Frank realized the word packages must refer to the corpses. He held the note in front of him and re-read it as he walked slowly across the lobby to sit on a plush chair where he read it yet again. Immediately he tried to figure out what this meant for the future of the case. He went over in his mind the rudiments of the communications plan he had given the Russian and asked himself whether it would be enough to re-establish contact. Shurin's last words came to mind. "Only God knows."

Chapter 12

Betty Cooper swung the black Saab GLE hatchback smoothly to her right off the George Washington Parkway and approached the checkpoint into the CIA compound.

"I'm here to pick up my husband for lunch." She produced her driver's license and the guard gave a cursory look at her name and photo then waved her through the barrier. Where the road forked, she went left and then turned right in front of the headquarters building. It was late March, too chilly to slide back the sunroof, but the season when the agency's flowerbeds were blanketed with daffodils. Up ahead she immediately spotted her husband Steve on the broad steps under the concrete canopy of the main entrance. He stood head and shoulders over most of the others who were waiting to be met and with his prematurely white hair and light complexion he was remarkable even from a distance.

"You're right on time." Steve angled into the passenger's seat, fitting his stiff left leg into place and buckling his seat belt.

"Where are we going?" Betty asked.

"To Mr. Smith's."

"The one in the District?"

"No, the one out on Leesburg Pike." Betty put the car in gear and peeled away from the curb.

"So how has your day been? Learn anything interesting?" She asked.

"If I told you, I'd have to kill you." Steve waved his right hand in front of him as if to dismiss his own comment. "It's what everyone says these days."

"I take it that means nothing interesting." Betty asked him the same question every day and got no meaningful reply. Steve just shrugged his shoulders.

"I'm an admin officer. In administration, things are always the same. We write the checks, do the accounting, arrange for housing, over and over."

"Even spies have to have roofs over their heads."

"Listen. I may not have had an exciting morning, but you can make up for it over the lunch hour." Betty watched with a noncommittal look as he placed her hand on his crotch.

"Oh, bugger, I can't do that now. This is a stick shift and that stick doesn't change gears. Don't be a prat. The guard will see you." But Steve had a firm grip on her wrist and would not release her. Betty rolled forward past the guard shack. The man only glanced over and she saw that after she passed he didn't check her license. Apparently he hadn't seen what was happening, or chose to ignore it. "Why would you do that? Why do you take such sophomoric chances?"

"Adds a little spice to life. Besides, haven't I done all right so far? Who would have thought I'd be working for the CIA? Just applying was a risk. You know what people say. You can't argue with success."

"There's something else people say. Don't put your hand in the cookie jar too often. One of these days you're going to get caught in some silly prank and everything will come crashing down."

"But cookies taste so good." She looked over and he was smiling, an unusual expression for him. Betty had turned right on Route 123 and stopped at the light at Potomac School Road.

"Relax. You'll live longer. Listen. Before we eat I want to stop in Night Dreams, the sex store. That's why I picked Mr. Smith's. It's right around the corner. I want to get some of those candies for the party on Saturday night." The light changed and she started off faster this time.

"What are you talking about?"

"You know those taffies that are shaped like cocks. Harold will appreciate it and the other people will get a kick out of them."

"But we're going to have lunch afterward, right?" Betty looked over at him quickly then turned ahead to the traffic.

"Yeah, that, too."

"Did you make a reservation?" she asked.

"They don't take reservations for lunch." Twenty minutes later, they pulled into the lot of the Pike Seven Plaza. "Park all the way over on the side and back in." He took her hand and put it once again on his crotch. "After we eat and go to the store, you're going to do something for me."

"Here in the car park? That's what I mean. We can find a better place."

"Okay, then, in the park at Turkey Run." Betty just shook her head, reached for her purse and got out of the car. It took Steve a bit longer as it always did, but he limped at her side, leaning on his silver-knobbed walking stick as they headed down the row of cars toward the sidewalk. Suddenly, he bent over and spoke in a low voice. "You see that guy?" Betty saw that Steve was looking to his right into the next lane. As they walked on between cars she could see the person he was talking about the way one saw old time flickers, a frame at a time. They were moving in the same direction.

"That little man?"

"Yes."

"What about him?"

"I've seen him in the halls at the agency. I don't know his name, but I think he's in the operations directorate." Once on the sidewalk, they fell in behind the fellow. From behind, Betty made out that he was short, portly, bald, and, she guessed, in his mid-sixties. He was wearing a beige raincoat and she noticed that his shoes were down at the heels. He turned left into the short arcade just as they passed Mr. Smith's. Steve stopped her at the corner of the building. "Wait a minute. That's interesting. He's going into Night Dreams. Listen. I don't want him to see me in the store. You go in alone and get the candy and try to chat him up. See if you can persuade him to come to the party on Saturday night."

"Steven, are you sure? We're not the host. What will Harold say about inviting somebody he doesn't know?"

"I'll call him ahead of time and straighten it out. Turn on some charm and see what you can do. Try to find out this guy's name. Invite him for a drink back at Mr. Smith's. I'll be at a table, but you stay with him at the bar and don't let on that you know me. Go ahead." He put his hand in the small of her back and gave her a slight push.

"Another of his pranks," she thought. She looked at him and tried to show her reluctance by tilting her head to one side and pursing her lips, but she knew he had his mind made up and when that was the case, he brooked no opposition.

"Just do it," he said. "I'll wait for you back at the car."

Betty continued into the arcade and stopped for a minute in front of the plate glass show window of the sex shop. There were two mannequins, each one showing intimate apparel. She looked at the red bustier, red lace pants and black garter belt on the doll on the left. The one on the right had the same attire, but with the colors reversed. The garter belt was red and the upper pieces black. Then she saw her reflection. She was a thirty-one year old Brigitte Bardot look-alike at the peak of her beauty. Her cheekbones were high and she had that full-lipped pouting expression and pneumatic body that turned men's heads. She was well aware of the effect she produced. At times she enjoyed that, but there were also times when she found it silly. For now she moistened her finger with the tip of her tongue and rubbed it across her eyebrows from the bridge of her nose to her temples then smoothed her blonde hair to one side and opened the door.

The shop was small and the little man, the only other customer, was in the back on the right examining sex toys. The sales lady, a buxom redhead, looked up and smiled. Betty had been in the store before, and the woman obviously recognized her. That was not extraordinary. Betty was sure that most of the customers would be men and an unaccompanied female would be memorable.

"Hi. Could I have a bag? I'd like to get some of the candy."

"Of course," the lady handed Betty a brown paper lunch sack. Betty took it and approached the man and stood just to his left. The phallic-shaped lollipops were clustered in a container on the shelf and she leaned forward to gather in a dozen. She knew the man was watching her and she turned to face him.

"They're for a party." She smiled, but the fellow only looked grim. "It turns the men on to see women sucking on these." Again, he did not respond. "Are you shopping, or just looking?"

"Looking," was all he answered.

"These are fun." Betty took hold of one of the rubber dildos on display next to the candy. "Are you married? I see your ring."

"Yes."

"Your wife would enjoy this."

"Do you work here?" he asked.

"No." Now she could see him study her more closely. She twisted the base of the toy and it began to vibrate and hum. "Mmmm. Gets me excited just thinking about it."

"So why don't you buy it?" His tone was almost sarcastic, but she kept her poise.

"I already have one."

"What about all people at party? You could pass it around. After candy." Again, she listened to his intonation. He still sounded antagonistic.

"They bring their own."

"What kind of party is this?" There was the slightest change in his voice, a hint of curiosity.

"Couples come who want some variety."

"Swapping party?"

"Yes."

"And you do it, too?"

"Sure." She watched him look her over and for the first time he smiled. He had bad teeth, tobacco and coffee stained to a dull yellow. In spite of his moustache, she could make out two tufts of prominent white nose hair like abbreviated walrus whiskers. Betty wondered why Steve would be interested in this man.

"How does one get invited to such parties?" The little fellow kept his hands in the pockets of his raincoat. Betty saw no movement, but he looked like someone who would play with himself.

"Are you interested?"

"I'd just like to know how it works."

"Are you going to buy something here?"

"I don't know."

"I came just for these." Betty held up the bag. "I'll pay for them and why don't you come with me. We can have a drink around the corner at Mr. Smith's. I'm buying and I can tell you about it. No strings attached. I'm not a prostitute. It won't cost you anything. You can decide if you'd like to come." Betty knew he was hooked now. She was sure the fellow had never had an offer this good in his life. She went to the counter and paid with a fifty-dollar bill. He stood just behind her and followed her out the door. "So, what's your name?" she asked. Betty caught the fellow's

81

hesitation and figured he would lie. Instead, he turned the question around.

"What's yours?"

"I'm Betty." She said nothing for a moment, but he never introduced himself.

"You from England? You talk like that."

"London, actually, I came here five years ago."

"I never been there."

"Do you think your wife will be willing? Sometimes the husband is, but the wife won't go along. Occasionally it's vice-versa."

"My wife would never come." They walked in silence out of the arcade and turned the corner. The fellow seemed to be going over this opportunity in his mind. "Is it possible for man alone?"

"Maybe." Betty had to open the door to the restaurant. The man never made a move to hold it. She figured then he was not only unattractive and dull, but lacking in basic manners. Inside, it took her a moment to adjust to the darkness. Then she spotted Steve seated at one of the back tables. He gave only the slightest smile as she moved to the bar with her new friend. Again she wondered what this guy could possibly do for her husband. But she, herself, knew she had to do just about anything he wanted, although it would be more difficult with this man. "My husband might be able to arrange it. If he can, how can I get in touch with you?"

"Better you should give me number. I can call you." The bartender approached from Betty's side.

"I'll have a Campari and soda." She opened her purse and took out a navy blue ballpoint pen and a business card. The bartender looked at the little man.

"Vodka, no ice."

"Pay no attention to this side. It's from a sales lady at Hecht's. Here's my number." Betty crossed out the name and information printed on the face of the card and wrote on the blank side. "Call me before Friday and I'll let you know."

"What if your husband answers?"

"Just tell him you want to talk to me. He doesn't mind."

"How long does it last? Party, I mean."

"It starts at eight and goes on all night. But you don't have to stay that long. Do you live close by?"

"Not too far."

"And do you work around here?" Betty watched the fellow's reaction. He hesitated, then brought the glass of vodka to his lips, but didn't drink. Still, he didn't answer. "Cheers." Betty raised her glass and glanced over the slumped shoulder of her new friend back at her husband, who lifted his own glass in salute. Steve already had his lunch in front of him. She knew he wouldn't be happy if she couldn't find out more about this man.

"I work here and there." Finally, he sipped his drink.

"You're a traveling salesman?"

"I do technical work."

"Okay. So far what have you told me? I don't know your name or what you do. If you call me, how am I even going to know who I'm talking to?"

"My colleagues have given me nickname. It's because of my work. As I said, I am technician. I do work for company. You could call it exterminating company." Knowing the fellow worked for the agency, Betty almost smiled.

"So what's the nickname?"

"My name is George, but you can just call me Bugs."

Chapter 13

Of the twenty-four guests on the first floor of the estate house on Leigh Mill Road in Great Falls, Virginia, Steve Cooper was the only one naked under a navy blue silk robe. The eleven other males may have been as anxious as Steve in anticipation of what was to come, but no one else was so obvious. He moved with a stiff-legged, ungainly gait from the buffet table in the dining room, back across the ballroom-sized living room. His silver-knobbed walking stick, his pale, almost diaphanous skin and the protrusion under his robe made him look like an egret with a third leg and one ruffled feather. He extended his bony right arm and the two Waterford crystal flutes of champagne to Betty, who sat at the far end of an L-shaped pink chintz sofa.

Steve slumped into his seat and surveyed the room. The house belonged to Harold Blaney, who owned several restaurants, appropriately named Harold's, and some commercial buildings in and around Washington, D.C., and it was he who had sent out the invitations. Three of the couples had flown down from New York on the Eastern shuttle and two couples had come all the way from Palm Beach. While a number of the guests glanced back at Steve, most ignored him. He was not, after all, going by the rules. These parties were not orgies. Everyone normally took off their clothes only when they had been assigned a new partner using a blind selection of keys and found an empty bed in which to have sex. A number of the men did, however, look admiringly at Betty, and apparently hoped that their key would fit in her lock.

Betty took a sip from her glass.

"It's getting late. What if he doesn't come?" She was wearing a beige short-sleeved silk blouse and brown cotton skirt. Though she was full-breasted, she could still get away with no bra and did so out of neglect, while she intentionally wore no panties for convenience.

"Then we'll just have to carry on by ourselves, won't we? Count on the luck of the draw."

"I hope he doesn't show up," she said.

"Why?"

"He's a peasant."

"You British, you're so class conscious."

"I can tell by looking at him that his skin is clammy, amphibian, like he just crawled out from under a rock."

"Just count sheep or something. This is important to me."

"I knew you'd say that."

"So why bother to complain? This is what we do." He faced the great room, the walls of which were covered with frescoes of naked Roman prostitutes and patrons in various positions. "Harold tells me there are people here from Florida. They must be the ones over there."

"Which ones?" Betty looked across the room and studied the guests who were seated on a white leather sofa that ran the length of the opposite wall.

"The tan ones." Harold, the host, approached them. "That's some collection, Harold." Steve raised his champagne glass in the general direction of the art work.

Harold Blaney was a heavyset man who managed to carry his girth without appearing fat. He was wearing a claret-colored linen shirt open at the neck that revealed thick white chest hair over which hung a gold chain and lion's medallion. He was a Leo.

"They were discovered in the whorehouses of Pompeii. Archaeologists say they were the billboards of the day. I believe in advertising." Harold drank from a small cocktail glass. Betty knew it was fruit juice. Harold never touched alcohol. He thought it diminished his sex drive. She could testify personally from earlier parties that he had that in abundance. "So what should I know about the fellow you invited?"

"He's her friend." Steve twisted his head slightly in Betty's direction. "She met him at the sex shop where she got the candy." Betty realized that for an instant she might have looked surprised, but she changed her expression immediately. She knew Steve figured that Harold would not object to the breach of rules if she were the guilty party. Harold liked her. He had even asked her how she wound up with such a loser. If he only knew!

"Sorry. I don't know much about him. I'm not even sure he'll come," Betty said. She took a sip of her champagne.

"Well, Steve, if he does, you'll have to sit this one out tonight. Your new friend will get your partner."

Betty could tell that Harold was not fooled by Steve's disclaimer.

"I'll just have to make up for it later on." Steve looked unconcerned.

"Maybe next time," Harold said. "The couple from Palm Beach is scheduling the next party. I talked to Norman, the husband. He told me they have a fucking palace on the Intra-coastal Waterway with an Olympic-sized pool. We'll all go skinny-dipping before we pair off. That should suit you." The husky Harold turned at the sound of the doorbell. "Excuse me."

Steve nudged Betty.

"That's probably our guy. Go and introduce him to Harold. And try to get a look at his car keys."

"So you still want me to match up with him?"

"Of course, I told you. Didn't you listen?"

"I guess I was in denial." Betty got up with a resigned look and followed their host toward the oaken front door at the end of the tiled hall. She knew she would go along as she always did. On the way, she looked at Harold's ass. The man was an unusual character, wealthy, uninhibited, hung like a bull. His restaurants were renowned not for their food, but for the murals of frolicking, big-breasted women being chased and accosted by muscular, obviously vigorous satyrs. Unlike the whores depicted on the walls of his home, the women in the restaurant paintings had a modern look and the rumor was that Harold had engaged models, some of them prominent women in Washington, to pose for the works. Diners spent their lunches in a guessing game of who was who. Now he opened the door and there, in a drab sport coat over a nondescript gray shirt open at the neck stood Boguslav Rzepnicki, the man Betty knew as George.

"And you are?" Harold extended his hand, but had a diffident expression on his face. Betty stepped forward.

"Harold, this is George. George and I share an interest in candy." Rzepnicki's hand disappeared in Harold's meaty paw.

"Well, Betty has vouched for you, so you're welcome. Come in. I would show you around, but I've got to get back and start the projector. You're in good hands with Betty. She'll be your escort for the time being." Harold turned and walked away. Betty stopped Boguslav from moving further into the hall.

"So you made it after all."

"It was hard to find. I don't get out this way much."

"But you said you live close by?"

"Right."

"Let me see your car keys."

"Why?"

"So I'll know what they look like." Boguslav seemed reluctant, but pulled the key chain out of his right pocket. Betty turned it over in the light. There was a medallion from the American Embassy in Paris. "They should be easy to spot."

"What do you mean?"

"You'll see." When she got back into the great room, Betty saw that Steve was nowhere in sight. Harold stood behind the projector. The unmistakably tinny music of a sex film blared from the speakers and on the screen a cheaply dressed couple was entering a motel. Harold turned down the volume and moved to the center of the room.

"Can I have everyone's attention? I hope you've all gotten drinks and food aplenty. Sex may be my avocation, but by profession I'm a restaurateur, and I always want people to be satisfied in both the things I do." People laughed. Harold was always a clever host, able to put his guests at ease. "Now that we've all arrived, though we haven't all come yet," he paused meaningfully and again there was laughter, "I think we should get to the reason for being here. Would all the women gather on this side of the room and all the men on this side?" Harold stretched his arm to indicate directions and people got up from their seats, stepped around the glass-topped thick mahogany coffee tables and around each other to get to their proper place. "Now the women should turn their backs and I want all the men to put their car keys on the round table in the corner. You know the drill."

Betty was second to pick and she held up Boguslav's keys. He did not change his deadpan expression, but other men looked disappointed. Betty held the keys over her head.

"So, who's my partner?" she asked. Bugs stepped forward. He kept his eyes fixed on Betty and didn't look to either side as she led him into the hall and back to the first bedroom on the left and closed the door.

Steve had been watching from the corner. Now he got up and came to sit on the white leather sofa. The others paired off in turn and disappeared. He was left alone across from the movie screen. The couple in the grainy black and white film took up different positions over the next thirty minutes and Steve's bottom grew sweaty. At that point he decided to get dressed. But just as he stood, he heard shoes clicking on the hardwood and he spotted his quarry headed for the front door. Now he moved like a trotter who had broken stride.

"Glad you could join us. Hope to see you again." Even with his bad leg, Steve had managed to make it across the great room and into the foyer just as Bugs reached the door. The little fellow turned, but obviously did not recognize him, said nothing, and was out the door into the night.

Steve dressed and Betty joined him. They said their goodbyes to Harold. In the Saab, she drove.

"Well, are you going to tell me what happened? What did he say?" Steve asked.

"Nothing."

"Nothing? You were with him for a half hour."

"Forty minutes. It took me that long to get him off."

She had the car up to fifty miles an hour and still managed the curves along the Georgetown Pike. But she was occasionally straying to the left.

"You've been here five years and you still drive on the wrong side of the road."

"Bloody hell, I do it when I'm upset."

"But you found out nothing at all about him, where he lives, his last name?"

"He told me he lives in Bethesda. He said he didn't know if he would come to another party."

"Pangs of conscience?"

"Who knows? Men lose interest after they've come."

"Yes. But he'll get horny again, especially after he thinks about how easy this was. Then he'll be back. If I see him first, I don't plan to give him any choice."

"Knowing you, I'm sure you have a plan with a lot of imagination."

"That I do, my dear. That I do."

Chapter 14

Julie lay on her back on a red and beige striped cotton blanket on Copacabana beach. It was Sunday, Frank's last day in Rio, and she had suggested they spend the afternoon the way the Brazilians did, on the sand by the sea worshiping the sun.

"I can't believe that in all the time you've been here you haven't been to Copacabana beach," she told him. "It's Rio's front porch."

"Things just took off and I never got around to it. But you look like a real Carioca."

It was an overstatement. Julie had not gone entirely native. She was not wearing the thong bathing suit, but her Kelly green bikini showed every advantageous angle of her marvelous tawny body and several times in the course of the afternoon, Frank had gotten aroused. He hoped she hadn't noticed.

They went over the case twice and Julie would have continued talking about it, but Frank changed the subject.

"You told me your family is Portuguese."

"Yes," Julie said.

"Are your parents still living?"

"Yes. And I have three brothers. They're married. I have nieces and nephews."

"You're the only girl?" Frank took a handful of sugary sand and let it slip slowly through his fingers.

"Yes, the youngest. What about you? Any brothers or sisters?"

"No. I was an only child."

"Funny, you don't act like one. I was a tomboy. My brothers were my bodyguards. I tagged along with them a lot. They didn't appreciate that, but whenever they didn't have enough for a team they would let me play baseball with them and basketball. My mother put a stop to it. She made me take ballet lessons."

"That's how you got such beautiful legs?"

Julie took a moment to consider his compliment. She didn't frown, but neither did she smile. In the end she seemed to dismiss it.

"I had a great jump shot."

"So, you play tennis, baseball, basketball. What else?"

"I love to ski."

"So do I," Frank smiled. It was easier without the disguise.

It had been a golden-toasted, royal blue day that lazily slipped away with the waltz and sweep of the emerald sea. Frank couldn't remember a day like it. Julie rolled over toward him and propped herself on her elbow. That only exposed more of her breasts. He tried not to look.

"I noticed you haven't lit a cigarette today."

"So far, so good," she raised her hand to show her fingers were crossed. "So, you actually saw Shurin get on the plane?"

"Again? Yes, I was on the observation deck. They loaded the coffins and he was right there while they did it."

"No one saw him off?"

"Oh, sure, Barchuk was there. I recognized him from the file photo. And there were a couple of others who came all the way to the plane. I didn't see the wife, but she was probably with him in the terminal." Frank took another handful of sand and lightly threw it downwind. "You never told me that the Brazilians arrested the killer."

Julie rolled onto her back but kept herself propped on two elbows and looked at the water. Frank followed her gaze. He knew by now that this was an unpredictable sea, mild and caressing one day, fitful and violent the next with twisting rip tides that carried off and devoured countless souls including the three Soviets that Bagatelle was taking home. Today it was subdued with slow, low breakers against the gentle slope of the sand.

"The base chief said you didn't need to know that. He didn't want Shurin to know whether we had passed on his information, or if the assassin screwed up and got caught on his own."

"I see. Did you agree with that? I mean did you think I would slip up and talk about it to Shurin?"

"No."

"I looked pretty silly when he was the one who told me and I didn't know anything about it."

"That's the way it is in this business. The sooner you understand that, the better off you'll be."

"So I can't trust even you?"

"Frank, it's not a question of trust. Or, yes, there has to be trust. We trust each other to do what protects our agents best. But there's something else. And this is not my question, okay? But it's something they may ask you when you get back to headquarters. Did you really meet this guy just as you said and did he really agree to the recruitment?" Frank was speechless at first, then confused, then angry in turn. But before he could answer, Julie added something. "I know how the system works. I've had bad things happen to me. I know how they think at home and that's what you'll have to be prepared for. Why are you looking at me that way?" Frank knew his expression showed annoyance. "It's happened before." She leaned over on one elbow again, closer as if to emphasize the point. "There have been case officers who invented agents just to get credit. I know you didn't do that, but I just want to let you know that others may doubt your story. And there are always people who want to show that

90

they're smarter than you, more important than you, and they'll try to pick the case apart."

"It all happened just as I said and just the way I reported it. The ambassador drowned. Come on. That was in the papers, right?"

"Yes."

"And there was an assassin."

"Yes."

"And doesn't it make sense that somebody would have to take the bodies back to Moscow?"

"Yes."

"And wouldn't Shurin be a likely candidate to do that?"

"Probably, but you said you recorded the meetings, then the tapes turned out to be useless."

"I set the machine up exactly as they told me to do it in headquarters. At the same time, I had to create background noise. I'm not a sound engineer. You kept his note, right, and his receipts?"

"Of course."

"When you pouch them to headquarters, they can check to see that it's his handwriting if they don't believe me."

Julie turned away. A man passed in front of them carrying metal skewers of barbecued meat. He extended one toward them, but Julie waved him off and turned back to Frank.

"We don't have samples of his handwriting. I'm just trying to be helpful. I want you to be ready if they start quizzing you. Keep your cool."

"But you believe I'm telling the truth?"

"You said that you know Tony Valletta."

"Right."

"If he's the branch chief now, I'm sure he'll help you." She shifted back to her previous position. Her stomach was almost flat with only a slight rise just below the navel. Frank found it almost irresistible. "You know his wife is an invalid?"

"No. I didn't know that. What's that got to do with the case?"

"Nothing. I just think it's good to know all you can about somebody."

"Yeah, so?"

"They were in Rome in the fifties when the polio vaccine came out. The embassy was giving the shots or the oral vaccine, but Tony was on a trip up north and in the two weeks he was away, his wife contracted polio. She's been in a wheelchair ever since."

"Terrible." Frank shook his head.

"Tony blamed himself. He knows what's important in life. He'll understand your predicament."

"I don't believe I have a predicament, at least as far as this case goes, but I'll keep that in mind. But you still haven't answered my question. Do you believe me? It's important to me to know."

"Yes. I do. I said I did."

"Funny, I didn't hear that."

"It's not me you have to worry about, believe me." She looked at him with those clear, dark emerald eyes and he lost whatever annoyance he felt. All afternoon he had suppressed raging hormones, pheromones and all other moans. Now he decided to speak his mind.

"I leave tomorrow and since you're asking about what's real, there's something else I should say." Julie looked concerned. Frank thought she might still have doubts. "It's not about the case." He shook his head and looked down for a moment then decided to come out with it. "I just want to tell you that I've enjoyed working with you. More than that, I can't help finding you really attractive."

Julie suddenly sat up straight and held her palm between them like a traffic cop.

"Oh, no, stop right there. Despite what you may have heard, I don't get involved with married men."

"I'm married, but I don't know for how long. You were right. My wife can't take this life. She said she was moving out. For all I know, she's gone already. There's no answer at home."

"I'm sorry to hear that, but it really has nothing to do with me."

"Wait. I'm not talking about a lifetime commitment here. I just thought we might see each other again if you come up to Washington. We could go out to dinner or something."

She stood, brushed off her long legs, ran her fingers under the shoulder straps of her bikini top, then reached behind her thighs and stretched the bottom straight. Frank continued to sit.

"It's the 'or something' that concerns me. Listen, Frank, in spite of what you might think, I like you. What you did that night on the beach, just holding me trying to console me that was sweet. But let's leave it there. We were together to do a job and you just assured me that we've done what we were supposed to do."

"You're tough. No wonder your brothers didn't want you along. I'll bet you slid into second base with your spikes up, a female Ty Cobb."

"Yes. And between innings I sat on the bench and sharpened them."

"Did I tell you that Shurin told me he had sex with you?"

"What?" She put her hands on her hips and leaned over him. "What are you talking about?"

"He figured you for a whore that night at Pinocchio's. I took it for braggadocio."

"That was big of you." Now she knelt on the blanket facing him. "I've seen him twice, once at Pinocchio's and once when he came to talk to Justinha just before he left."

"Wait a minute. Where was that and when were you going to tell me about it?" Now it was Frank's turn to be annoyed.

"He came to the tennis court at the Joquei Clube."

"Did he see you? Did you talk to him?"

"He saw me from a distance. I was sitting on the bench beside the court and they were standing at the gate. She never introduced me."

"Did he recognize you?"

"I doubt it. The disguise I had on that night wasn't the greatest, but it was distracting. But I certainly didn't sleep with him. And if the guy lied about that, what else would he lie about?"

"This has been an education in itself. Is this the way everybody in this outfit deals with everybody else?"

"I would have told you if I thought it meant anything. But as I said, I never got to talk to him and Justinha said nothing."

"Okay. Have it your way. I still think it's a good case."

"And I doubt we'll ever hear from him again or that Justinha will either. Believe me. I know how it is. These guys make all sorts of promises, but when they get back under big brother's control, they have second thoughts. I wouldn't go thinking you've made a firm recruitment. You're still a shallow water swimmer until he starts reporting something worthwhile from Moscow, and I don't believe that's going to happen." Julie took her towel and folded it. Now she stood again on the sand and picked up the blanket. She walked around him and began shaking it. The sand blew off in the light breeze that had begun to move in from the sea. "I think it was another example of a guy stringing a woman along just to get in her pants. That happens a lot to Brazilian women."

"Well, if you told me the truth, you didn't get to talk to him. I did." Frank got up, too, and took one end of the blanket. They shook it together. "And I can tell you he's an unusual guy."

"He's full of crap." Frank could tell that Shurin's claim of sexual conquest had angered her. "And I'm beginning to think that you're after the glory."

"I'm not after the glory. I'm after you." Frank smiled, but Julie did not.

"I told you. Forget the rumors. I don't get involved with married men and I can tell you from personal experience that if you are a glory chaser, you'd better be prepared to take what goes along with it."

"What does that mean?"

"Sooner or later, you'll find out."

Chapter 15

At CIA headquarters, Frank rode the elevator to the fourth floor and walked the halls to the D corridor and the door marked SE/X/LA. The secretary looked up as he came in.

"I'm here to see Mr. Valletta."

"And what is your name?"

"Frank Manion."

"Can you wait a minute? I'll tell him you're here." The woman, around forty-five or so, attractive but Rubenesque, leaned on the door frame and stuck her head in the branch chief's office. "A Mr. Manion is here. Do you want him to wait?" Frank heard Tony's familiar baritone.

"Wait? He who is my brother? Who fought with me upon Saint Crispin's Day? Never." The woman backed out the door. She had a half-smile of resignation on her face as she motioned to Frank to go in.

"Francis, delighted to see you, a conquering gladiator." Tony half rose from his chair and extended his chubby hand. "Please come and sit down and tell me about your adventure, all the things you couldn't put on paper." He gestured toward one of the two gray steel chairs by the desk.

"Henry the Fifth," Frank said.

"I beg your pardon? Oh, yes, of course, you clever fellow." Tony dropped back into his armchair. "How was your flight back?"

"Fine, I connected in Miami. No problem."

"And I suppose your wife was delighted to see you."

"She wasn't at home when I stopped. Then I came right to the building."

"You could have gone on to her office. We can always wait. Our spouses put up with so much." In light of what Julie had told Frank about Tony's wife, the comment had more than passing meaning.

"She's probably busy anyway." Frank had decided on the drive in to say nothing about his marital problem for the time being. When he walked in the door of his town house two hours earlier, nothing looked different until he noticed a bare space on the living room wall. That was where Beth's favorite water color of a country scene had been hanging when he left for Brazil. She was gone. He remembered Julie's admonition about private life and the spy business. It was always difficult to know where to draw the line between the two.

"Well, I must say you had everyone's attention. A bit of bad luck at the end, but you did a splendid job." Tony leaned forward, his forearms on the desk. Frank wondered if he had spun the swivel chair to its top position in order to be comfortable. He was a short, rotund man.

"Thanks. I appreciate it."

Tony reached up and scratched his mostly bald pate, but with just the tip of his index finger, then he smoothed the sparse hairs of his comb-over back into place.

"Don't lose heart about the case. There's always the chance that if Comrade Shurin behaves himself, he'll come abroad again and we'll have another go at him."

Frank hesitated and his expression must have shown his surprise.

"You mean people are giving up on the case? Julie d'Andrade said that might happen."

"Ah, the glamorous, the incomparable Miss d'Andrade, how is she?"

"Fine." Tony had slipped off the topic of discussion. Frank sensed that something was going on.

"You two got along well? From this end it appeared that you worked well together."

"Does a goose take a gander? We did. She did a great job. But we kept it professional." Frank paused and watched Tony's expression. He hoped he had not protested too much. Tony's look was non-committal.

"A lot of men have difficulty dealing with Julie. Naturally, they find her very attractive, but she really is a fine case officer and that can be intimidating. I believe it's a carapace. She's so sweet once you get past that gruff exterior. And she has a Hungarian connection you may be interested in."

Frank wondered for a second about that comment. He didn't know what that had to do with the Bagatelle case. He wasn't about to ask.

"Yes, but what about Shurin? The guy is recruited and I believe he'll do what he said he would do. Unfortunately, I just didn't have time to tell him very much about what we're interested in or how to get the intelligence to us. But he agreed to try. Does anybody doubt that?"

Tony turned away and glanced for a second at the window, then looked back.

"Francis, people are divided about how to interpret Shurin's behavior. But you have to understand that with a hostile case that's always the reaction here, a bit of double-think, or maybe quadruple-think, or ad infinitum-think." Tony pushed off the desktop with his hands and leaned back. "We're set up for a meeting this afternoon with Bill Marshall, the Division Chief, and Harry O'Meara, the CI chap. We'll sort through it then."

"Well, right now can you give me an idea of how things look? I can see there might be questions about where we go from here, but does everybody share your impression that I did my best with the guy?" Frank saw immediately that the question forced Tony to pause again. That didn't look good. "I'm not asking so I'll see my name in lights." Now it was Frank who leaned forward. "I just want to know where I stand."

"All I can tell you is that in a situation like this there will be a lot of questions. It's possible that we'll need a lot of time to get just a few answers, or that the answers may never come. I just want you to know that I firmly believe you did an outstanding job and I have stated that opinion at every opportunity."

"I take it from the way you phrased your answer that other people have doubts."

"And they always will, dear boy. That's the nature of the business. What I'm really saying is you're not to worry. Now sit tight." Tony leaned to his left, picked up his phone and dialed a four-digit extension. "Hello, Grace, Tony here. I just want to confirm that we're on with Bill at two." Tony looked at Frank with a knowing smile then he winked, "Perfecto." He gave a thumbs-up sign. "Thank you, dear." He hung up. "Two o'clock in the division chief's office. We'll hash it out there. In the meantime, welcome back. Skulk about a bit." Tony rose and came around the desk and put one hand on Frank's shoulder. "Have lunch. Call your wife. Just remember to be in Marshall's office by two."

Frank walked to the men's room in the C corridor. Of the three urinals, two were being used. Frank stood at the middle one. The men on either side bracketed him like bookends. The man to Frank's right zipped his trousers, flushed, and went to the nearest sink, where he rinsed his hands. The man on Frank's left was about six feet two, slender, lanky with carrot-colored, tightly curled hair and fair freckled skin. He had a flaming moustache and goatee. Neither Frank nor the redhead spoke until the door closed behind the first man.

"Have you ever noticed the pissing protocol here?" the redhead asked. "Nobody stands next to anybody else at the toilet unless they have to."

"You know in the time of Ramses II Egyptians stoned people like you," Frank said. "I thought you were in London. What are you doing back here? You didn't like their urinals?"

Carrot-top flushed, zipped and went to the sink.

"The weather didn't suit me." After he rinsed his hands, he reached for a paper towel.

"So something happened?" Now Frank stepped away and went through the ritual. At the sink he pushed the plunger and the viscous green soap splattered in his palm.

"Yeah, something happened." Patrick Kerrane worked his palm, his forefinger and his thumb in a smoothing motion several times down his goatee and looked in the mirror as he spoke. "I was in touch with a couple of fellas from the movement."

"I.R.A.?"

"Sinn Fein. They were lads I knew when I was just a tike. School chums. The station chief screwed me."

96

"That was it?" Frank, who was leaning over the sink, looked over his shoulder. Kerrane was just standing there, his head half turned toward the door.

"Yeah, listen, boyo, have you stuffed you pie hole yet?"

"No. I was just about to go down." Frank pulled two brown paper towels from the stainless steel container on the wall. "I have to kill some time until two."

"Come on then. I'll tell you about it."

"Are you still playing the ponies?"

"Yeah, at least the London bookies were sorry to see me go even if MI-5 wasn't."

Patrick Kerrane was born in Belfast, Ireland and had come to America when he was eight. His family had settled in Boston, but his father was an alcoholic who couldn't hold a job and abandoned the family within two years of their arrival. Despite his best efforts, Patrick had never gotten over it. Whereas Frank took great pains to dress well, maybe a reaction to all the cast-off clothes he'd had as a boy, Patrick never wore a suit. Instead, he dressed in sport jackets and trousers that never matched, spotted neck ties and scuffed shoes. Now he walked half a step ahead of Frank down the hall. Several people passed them going in the other direction, but the two men didn't speak again until they were in an empty elevator and Frank had pushed the button for the ground floor.

"So you weren't supposed to be dealing with the I.R.A., right?"

"The Brits shit pineapples. The COS thinks he's got a polyp on his vocal chords. It's not a bloody polyp. That's just how far MI-5 and MI-6 have gotten up his ass. We roll over for them every time."

"Maybe they were a little concerned since you're an Irishman."

"One wanker said to me 'With that name there won't be a problem, will there?' They had run their traces on me, of course. I had all I could do to keep from smashing his maw."

"I'm proud of you for controlling yourself and keeping Anglo-American relations from going down the toilet."

"You're Irish, too, X a few times removed. You're a black sheep, but you'll return to the fold one day."

The letter X was not a CIA contrivance like James Bond's M and Q. Kerrane simply used the first initial of Frank's middle name. He had done that since their days together at the Defense Language Institute in Monterey. Patrick just had his ways.

They exited the elevator and walked past the bulletin boards on the ground floor toward the cafeteria.

"No. I'm American. My people came over on the coffin ships. If there was ever anything Irish in my family's genes, it got killed off by all the whiskey." No one had ever told him, but Frank had always believed that his father had been drunk the night of the fire.

"Suit yourself, boyo." Kerrane walked with the disjointed stride of a fellow who had never really adjusted to his growth. It was not a spastic walk, but one that progressed in segments. "So when I got back they told me you were in Brazil. What were you doing down there?"

"I was in Rio. The base had leads to a couple of guys. They didn't want to use their own people to follow up, so they asked for a Portuguese speaker."

"Not a Russian speaker?" Patrick gave Frank a knowing glance.

"Portuguese." Frank kept looking ahead and tried to keep his tone even.

"But you haven't finished the course, right? I heard that they'd never pull people out of language class to do that kind of thing. I heard you couldn't get a day off unless it was for your ma's funeral and then only if you brought in her ring finger with the diamond still on it to prove she was dead."

"They did this time. It gave me a chance to see what I could do." They entered the cafeteria and slowed behind the group that had formed to pick up trays.

"Did you succeed?"

"I'll tell you later. Let's sit by the window." They split up. Frank went to the line at the steam table. He figured that with Beth gone this might be his only hot meal of the day. He carried the molded plastic tray with his plate of meat loaf, mashed potatoes and green beans to the cashier. When he paid, he spotted Patrick standing by a table next to the floor to ceiling window motioning to him.

"So were you able to recruit those people?" Patrick was seated as Frank approached the table.

"No, but I set it up so I can see them again when I go down there this summer."

Though they were friends, Frank was not about to discuss the Shurin case with Kerrane. Patrick didn't have the need to know. Frank remembered Julie on the beach. She was right. This had nothing to do with friendship.

"You haven't said anything about my beard." Patrick fluffed his new growth with the back of his hand. Frank noticed that the Irishman had his tray turned the wrong way. They were designed to fit together on a table. Patrick was just one of those people who never seemed to figure out how to adapt.

"A priest I knew, Father Daniel, always told me that if you don't have anything good to say about something, it's better to say nothing at all."

"Manion, up Munster, up Ulster, up Leinster, up yours."

"You look like Beelzebub, or maybe Mephistopheles. I could never keep the two straight."

Kerrane had two hamburgers on sesame buns and an enormous pile, probably a double order of French fries. He had sloshed most of his plate with ketchup and added pickles and onions to both sandwiches and the mixture leaked out the bottom as he pressured the roll with his first bite.

"I guess the missus was glad to see you. Back in the saddle again?" Patrick didn't stop chewing as he talked.

"No." Frank kept silent for a while, cutting his meat loaf carefully, deliberately with his fork. Now he stopped. "The fact is she's gone."

"Gone? What do you mean? Gone where?" Kerrane stopped his own chewing and wiped his lips and moustache with his paper napkin.

"When I called from Brazil, she told me she was moving out. I think by now she may be living with another guy. No. I should correct that. I know she's with another guy."

"Shit." (Patrick pronounced it shite.) "The woman left you? She must be daft, and not very smart for a lawyer. You'll be able to charge her with adultery."

"I don't think she cares. She told me she doesn't want anything. No money. Not the house."

"Ah, the shame of it; I'm sorry, X. Did you not see it coming?"

"Does a fornicating leopard see spots?"

"Manion, do you lie awake at night concocting these rhetorical gymnastics? From now on I guess you'll be doing it while you stroke the bloke."

"I can only handle one thing at a time."

"So how does this affect your plans? Does LA division know about it?" Kerrane raised his sandwich to his mouth again. "The Brazil assignment is still on?"

"I don't see why not. I haven't told anybody yet. You're the first, so keep it to yourself. I was only certain of it myself this morning when I stopped at the house on my way in."

"Check around. I heard they've put out a call for a Portuguese speaker to go to Brasilia in June or July. Wasn't that when you were supposed to go?" Frank stopped eating again. He put both his knife and fork on the plate.

"Yes. But nobody said anything to make me think it's not still firm."

"An old Mormon, Henry Carpenter, is interested. He's made a career out of jobs in Brazil." Frank sat there wondering what else could go wrong. Patrick had always been good about ferreting out news, maybe because he was conspiratorial by nature.

"Maybe they've added another slot," Frank said hopefully.

"I don't know, lad. That's why I asked you how things had gone on your trip. It wasn't just my normal nosiness. If you screwed up somehow, they'll want to find out why. That's what they're doing to me."

"What do you mean?"

"They want me to think they're throwing me a bone. They said I'm being considered for the deputy's job in Prague."

"No kidding?" Frank smiled. His approval was genuine. "That's a move up. And it makes sense. That was Czech you were studying in Monterey, remember?"

"It's got nothing to do with language. It's all because of my London adventures. They think I might get pissed if they confront me and try to put me on the box. Nobody wants to risk having us jump ship and spill our guts to the press, or the enemy. But this way I have to take the polygraph even if it's out of the five-year cycle. When they give you a denied area assignment, you have to take the poly before you go in and after you come back. That's the real reason behind it. If I pass, they'll send me back for a Czech refresher course at FSI and I'll go. If not, they'll have me making wigs, or stocking safe-houses with whiskey. This way it's all very well oiled and inoffensive."

"I think this business has made you even more paranoid than you always were. It's a step up, right, deputy chief of station?"

"Oh, for fuck's sake, X, it's only a two man station. And there's no such thing as paranoid here. Here they call it a counter-intelligence mentality. It's bloody respectable."

They both continued to eat then without speaking. But finally, Frank had to satisfy his curiosity. He knew he was taking a chance. Patrick was terribly clever at seeing through ploys.

"I worked with a woman in Brazil. You were in EUR Division. Maybe you knew her. Julie d'Andrade?" From the puckish gleam in Kerrane's eye, Frank knew immediately that he had made a mistake.

"There wouldn't be any connection of course between the pending demise of your marriage and the fact that you're now in touch with prime trim?" The Irishman pushed his ketchup-smeared dish forward on the tray. He could eat faster than anyone Frank had ever known. Now Patrick pulled a pack of Chesterfield cigarettes from the pocket of his rumpled tweed jacket.

"For God's sake, I saw her half a dozen times."

"And had carnal relations on five occasions? Say five rosaries and a good act of contrition. I know you otherwise I'd say sin no more."

"What do you mean you know me? I never cheated on Beth. In this case I was tempted, but nothing happened."

"You had all those girls in Monterey."

"I was single then."

"D'Andrade's a real fox. You know about her, right?"

"No. That's why I asked you."

"You know her pseudonym?"

"Pushteau."

"Here they call her Push-Pull. She was getting it on with Peter Halley." Kerrane blew his first puff of smoke toward the window.

"The chief of station in Brazil, the guy who died?" Frank asked. Now he was getting somewhere. Banter aside it would be Patrick who would have the scuttlebutt on anybody.

"Himself. He was the deputy in Paris. She worked for him there. He got her on the fast track, got her promoted. When he was sent to Brazil, he took her along. But she was in Rio and the station had moved up to Brasilia. He liked it that way. He thought people wouldn't talk. But he went down to Rio every other weekend and people talked anyway. They said she was riding Halley's Comet."

"But Halley was married?" Frank was a deliberate eater, but by now he had finished and he, too, pushed his plate forward on the tray.

"Yes. He had a heart attack. His family packed out and came back here. The fox stayed in Rio. Is that why you're so concerned that your Brazil assignment might be in jeopardy?"

"What a sick mind you have, Kerrane. And this time I think you're off the mark. I could be wrong, but I don't believe she would have been involved with a married man."

"Well, laddie buck, I'm just human. I only tell what I hear."

"Whatever slops your hog, brother."

At ten minutes to two, Frank was sitting in the outer office of Bill Marshall, the Soviet Division chief. There were three secretaries in a row, one for Marshall, one for the deputy chief and the third for the chief of operations. The deputy's secretary was taking a late lunch, eating a sandwich and reading that day's copy of the Washington Post that was spread across her desk. A tall, thin, somewhat stooped man in a black suit walked by and went right in to Bill Marshall's office. Frank thought that was probably Harry O'Meara. Even Frank, who had not been long in headquarters, knew him as the Raven. Then Tony came in.

"You made it? Good." Tony turned to the first secretary in the row. "Is his honor ready to receive us, Grace?"

"Yes. Go ahead in. Harry's already in there."

Tony motioned sideways with his balding head and Frank got up and followed him into the large office. Frank took the instant before he greeted Marshall to admire the view. There was an L-shaped corner window that looked out to the trees, which were now budding and opening up. He was sure the Japanese cherries must be in blossom on that side of the building.

"So you're Frank Manion?" Marshall stood up from his chair and Frank extended his arm across the desk. Frank saw Marshall was six feet one or two, an inch or two taller than he was. "Good to meet you. We didn't have a chance to talk before you went down there. You had us going back here. We really thought you were on to something. Please, sit down."

"Thanks." Frank joined Tony on the sofa. Harry O'Meara sat to the right on a single chair. Frank noticed the government-issue prints of exotic plants on two walls. Behind him over the sofa hung a winter scene of a troika driver passing St. Basil's. It reminded Frank of Shurin's plea for a third vodka. On a long credenza in back of Marshall's desk was a collection of what appeared to be thick white ropes tied in different shapes. They were mounted on varnished boards and each rope had a different designation painted in white above it. Frank couldn't make out the words from that distance, but he thought they were probably nautical knots and wondered if Marshall had served in the navy. In the corner formed by the solid walls he spotted a green-bordered graph on a white background with blue lines. There were orange, red and green pins in different columns. He had heard that Marshall kept track of cases under development, now he saw that the rumor was true. He wondered which pin represented the Bagatelle case.

"So, tell us what happened. Is this guy for real?" Marshall asked. All three looked at Frank, a moment for truth. He knew the question was coming, but on the way up in the elevator, he had decided to answer politically.

"If you're asking whether it's a good case, that's not a question I can answer. I spent a lot of time on the desk reading old files before I went to language training. Among the things that struck me was that several case officers said the same thing after they came back from meeting Soviets. They said 'If this guy isn't telling me the truth, he's got to be the best actor in the world.' But we had since found out that there were a lot of great actors."

No one said anything. Frank could almost feel Tony's approval wafting his way from the other end of the sofa. Even the Raven seemed nonplused. Marshall swiveled half-way in his chair, looked briefly at the trees, then turned again to Frank.

"That's a healthy way to approach the case. Look, Frank, this isn't a star chamber. We're not going to come to any conclusions just based on your gut feeling. But it does help to have impressions from the only case officer who talked to the fellow. Those impressions are what we want to hear."

Frank put his right hand palm down on the sofa cushion and paused a second before he answered.

"I thought his comment about Stalin rang true. He gave us the name of the assassin and that checked out. When he did that, he seemed pleased that he was able to tell me something I might find of value. We also know that the affair with the Brazilian woman seems pretty serious."

For the first time, O'Meara spoke.

"You were right the first time. Those are just impressions. The Soviets wouldn't mind giving up the killer." O'Meara had been sitting with his elbow bent and one hand holding his chin and had not changed position or expression since the meeting had started.

"I don't think it's fair to ask Francis for his impressions then challenge him because, with a logical caveat, he gives them to us," Tony said.

"Shurin probably reported the contact," O'Meara said. "Most of them do."

"If that were the case, wouldn't they have protested to the Foreign Ministry as they did with Bunin?" Frank asked. O'Meara skipped right over Frank's rebuttal.

"It's also possible the Soviets found out about you being in touch and yanked him back home." The Raven kept watching Frank. He seemed energized as he came up with each new impediment. Frank couldn't resist the opening.

"So they had the ambassador and his two aides swim out and drown themselves so Bagatelle would have to take the bodies home?"

The Raven's face darkened. He glared at Frank for a moment then turned toward Marshall as if his place were on the side of the angels. He took his hand from its supporting position and leaned forward, both elbows on his knees.

"Bill, we could talk about impressions all day. The question now is where to go from here. I don't think we're going to decide that based on a CT's impressions."

Everyone in the room except O'Meara knew that remark was uncalled for. Frank had been a career trainee, but now he was a fully certified case officer even if he had not yet served overseas. He decided to turn the tables, at least halfway. He, too, looked at Marshall.

"I agree. I already said my impressions shouldn't be decisive. It's up to you, Mr. Marshall, but I think that if we're going to continue with the case, it should be because we have a reasonable expectation of getting intelligence out of it without taking real risks and only Bagatelle can show us that."

Again, Frank knew he had gotten a solid hit, perhaps not a home run, but maybe a double. Marshall saw the tit-for-tat going on and intervened.

"You're learning fast, Frank. One thing you have to learn right now is to call me Bill." Marshall leaned forward on the desk. "So, do you have any idea how we could get Bagatelle to do that?" The division chief seemed to be straddling the fence. But Frank believed that Bagatelle's pin was already on that board somewhere and that Marshall would not be the kind who would take it off without an overwhelming reason to do so.

"You've all had a lot more experience at this than I have," Frank said. "But assuming Bagatelle gives the sign of life I instructed him to give, I believe we might just go ahead and make the first broadcast and see where things go from there. I would have to leave it to the people on the Soviet desk to figure out how to do that."

"But you gave him only what we told you to give him, right?" O'Meara tried once again to corner Frank. The Raven was still sniffing for blood, but Frank knew he was far from dead. Not even wounded.

"I didn't even give him all of that. As I said in my last cable, I didn't have time. But he has enough to get messages from us. I gave him the one-time pads in the pen. He has the radio frequencies. He knows he can still get a receiver in the dollar stores if he wasn't able to get it before he left Rio, and he knows where to go and what to do to let us know he's ready to receive our message."

"What about his communications to us? None of that will help if he can't send us any intel." O'Meara tilted his head down and looked at Frank over the rim of his wire-rimmed glasses with their thick lenses. Frank was surprised that the Raven had gone out on such a flimsy limb.

"Again, I would have to defer to you. But I did show him the essentials of an SW message. If we broadcast to him and just give him a dead-drop site, we can put all the instructions in a package. The package can go down before we tell him where to find it. That way no station officers will be compromised if he's under control. We can give him an accommodation address in Brazil and he writes SW messages to it."

"Exactly what you outlined when you and I talked, Harry." Tony looked as if he had put a final nail in the Raven's coffin. Frank watched Marshall. A slight hint of a smile told Frank the question was just about decided.

"I'm for that approach," Marshall said. "While we all question whether we'll ever get anything out of this case, I agree that if he makes the mark, we can take it another step as long as there's no risk involved. Tony, you work it out with the Soviet desk." Marshall looked at all three then stood. That was the signal that the meeting was over, or so Frank thought. Everyone got up, but Marshall spoke again. "You two go ahead. I have something I have to raise with this young man." Marshall came from behind his desk as Tony and O'Meara left the office. He took Tony's still warm seat at the other end of the sofa and stretched his legs, crossing them at the ankles. He motioned to Frank to sit again then put his hands behind his head, looking all the while at Frank. "I wanted you to know that I think you've done a superb job with this case."

"Thanks."

"Tony has been complimentary of your work all along."

"But Harry O'Meara has doubts." Frank lifted the edges of his lips. It wasn't quite a smile, nor was it a smirk. He felt resigned to the game and that in-between mind set was what he intended to show.

"Harry is paid to have doubts. But I have a big favor to ask." Marshall leaned forward and flattened his feet on the carpet. He put his hands on his knees. Frank saw that his hands were rough, age-spotted and a bit wrinkled. He figured Marshall was probably in his mid-fifties. Frank kept silent, waiting for whatever was to come. Given his luck lately, he didn't expect anything good. "I have a feeling about this case. It gives a lot of indications that it will go nowhere, but over the years I've seen that just when you expect nothing, something important happens. I wasn't going to say that in front of the others. No need. But given the work you've done so far, I want you to stay involved."

"Thank you." Frank said nothing more for a few seconds until it dawned on him that it would be hard to be connected to an agent in the Soviet Union if he was in Brazil. "Does this mean my assignment to Brasilia is still on?"

"That's where I need your help. I saw in one of your cables that Bagatelle usually travels to these martial arts competitions. He hasn't been there for the past few years while he's been in Brazil, but now he's in Moscow again. Next year the matches are in Prague. I went back over the rotation. The thing has been going on for several years and if the organizers follow the schedule they've stuck to so far, the year after that it will be in Budapest. So I want you to go where they drink bull's blood and their national hero is Attila the Hun."

"You mean on assignment?" This time Frank made no effort to conceal his surprise.

"Yes. You'll be deputy chief of station."

Frank recalled Patrick Kerrane's remark about Prague.

"It's a two-man station."

"Yes. There are two communicators, an intercept fellow, and a part-time secretary."

"But I don't speak Hungarian."

"We'll send you through FSI for a year."

"I haven't even finished the Portuguese course there."

"No problem. I had a look at your file. You have a very high aptitude for languages. Hungarian is a bear of a language, so we need someone with your talent anyway. You'll go through denied area ops training. You'll work under surveillance over there and learn to deal with it. After a year, if Bagatelle shows up, you'll be able to lose them and make a meeting with him up in Prague. And if anything should go wrong with the case and Moscow needs help, we could send you in and out. You already have Russian. It's a good match."

"Why not send me right to Moscow?"

"We don't know if Bagatelle is clean yet. But by the time he comes to Prague and Budapest we should have a better idea of where he stands."

"You mean if he comes to Budapest," Frank interrupted.

"Yes. There are a lot of ifs. There always are in this business. But if nothing comes of it, you will still have had an operational tour that will hold you in good stead for the remainder of your career. What do you think?"

Frank sat in silence for several moments. He wondered if Patrick Kerrane's paranoia had some basis. But in the end, he felt he had little choice but to go along.

"If that's what you need, you call, I haul."

"That's the spirit." Bill Marshall clapped his hands as he rose from the sofa. "One last thing that may make this a bit more attractive, Tony Valletta is going as the chief of station."

"To Budapest?"

"Yes. Within the Warsaw Pact, the Hungarians are responsible for defense against Italy. Tony knows a lot about Italy. He won't speak Hungarian, but you will."

"Where do I sit in the meantime?" Frank stood up. Marshall was between him and the door, but he started moving aside.

"Finish up with Portuguese. You never know. It might still come in handy someday, maybe when you're chief of station in Lisbon, or Brasilia." Marshall smiled. "Then as I said we'll have you set up for the denied area ops course in June and you'll go back to FSI in August. If you have any down time, you can spend it on the Hungarian desk reading in."

Marshall appeared delighted with himself and Frank saw no reason to argue. Another year in Washington would give him time to straighten out his personal affairs. He was not about to explain that to the division chief at this point. Instead, he shook hands, left the front office, and went down the elevator and out the south entrance. As he walked to the distant row of the west parking lot where he had left his car, he recalled that Tony had certainly known about the job in Budapest, but had said nothing. Marshall must have wanted to raise it first. DCOS wouldn't be a bad job, especially if he worked for Tony. In fact, as he went over it in his mind, the only thing that disappointed him in the new equation was that Budapest was awfully far from Rio and Julie d'Andrade.

Chapter 16

Steve Cooper had kept his eyes open, but three months went by before he spotted the little fellow he was looking for. Steve was at the end of a line of four people at the blind man's stand. He held a pack of peanut butter crackers in one hand and had his cash, a five-dollar bill ready in the other. He looked over the heads of the two people, a man and a woman, immediately in front of him and it was a moment before he realized that the balding head at the front of the line was that of the man Betty knew as Bugs. The short fellow paid and passed Steve on his way out without recognizing him. Steve put his crackers back in the rack and followed quickly. He didn't want to lose the guy again. He could see Bugs in the lunchtime crowd moving down the hall past the credit union. The little man turned right toward the cafeteria, but stopped on the right to look at the bulletin board where they posted new books about intelligence. Steve stood to the left and slightly behind his man.

"That looks interesting, a new Le Carré." Steve kept his eyes on the cover displayed behind glass. "He's rabidly anti-American, you know." Bugs turned and looked up, but still without recognition. He said nothing. "You don't remember me, I see." Steve smiled. For appearance sake, he intended to make it a friendly smile, but, in fact, he was smiling because he felt he already dominated this little guy. Now Bugs looked again, this time with some concentration. "I should hope you would recognize me. You got a better look at my wife, of course, Betty, in the house on Leigh Mill Road?"

Boguslav looked as if he had been struck by lightning. His eyes widened as his normally oyster-gray cheeks turned crimson. He looked at the passersby to see if anyone had taken notice. No one had.

"I didn't know it was your wife." His look now was one of embarrassment and confusion.

"Well, we try to be discreet. But sometimes that's hard to do when you get so intimate with someone." Steve extended his hand. "I'm Steve Cooper. I said good-bye to you that night at the door, but I don't suppose you remember. I work in SE support. Betty said she knew you only by a nickname. But seeing that we're agency colleagues, I think you can confide in me. What's your real name?"

Rzepnicki appeared stymied. He stood there saying nothing and Steve could tell he was weighing the risk of giving his name against the likelihood that Steve would find it out anyway.

"I don't work in this building. I come in only once in while. I don't think you need to know who I am." With that he turned and started down the hall toward the cafeteria. Steve hadn't anticipated having the fellow bolt, and his limp was more pronounced as he hurried to catch up with the quick short steps of his new acquaintance.

"That's not a very friendly reaction from somebody who enjoyed my wife's favors." Steve said this out loud as he closed the gap and came up from behind. Bugs looked around again to see if anyone else had heard Steve's remark.

"That was one time. Like I said, I didn't know whose wife she was. She invited me. I didn't ask her." He spoke over his shoulder in a tone just above a whisper still walking toward the exit beyond the cafeteria doors. Steve allowed him to move outside. Bugs didn't hold the door and Steve was forced to shift his silver-topped cane to his right hand as he pushed against the glass door with his left. The day was overcast and still muggy as early September days could be in Washington. This time Steve moved beside the man and saw that Bugs was beginning to perspire already. Steve figured it was not from the heat. Steve had extended a carrot without the desired result, so he decided to use a stick.

"I don't understand why you won't even shake my hand and tell me your name. I told you. I'm in support, so I'll find out anyway one way or another. I was hoping you'd be coming to another party. When I find out more about you I can call your home to invite you. If you're not there, I'll just give the information to your wife. Next time we can invite her, too, of course."

Boguslav had turned to his left and headed toward the parking area. Now he stopped in his tracks.

"My wife don't know nothing about it. She would not come to such thing."

"I understand. Wives can be like that. But there's no reason you shouldn't. In fact, we were hoping you could come over to our place and we could get to know you. Betty enjoyed her time with you. I agree there's no reason to be indiscreet. Your wife doesn't have to know about the parties and I would be the last to tell her anything if we're civil to each other, you and I." Steve towered over the little man and shifted back and forth from his bad leg to his good. He had been smiling earlier in the exchange. His eyes now were blank and cold. In fact, with his prematurely white hair and pale complexion, he looked glacial even in the steamy air of Langley. And he wore a beige pin-striped suit with a brown and white polka dot tie and a tobacco brown pocket kerchief that accented his lighter skin. His shoes, the color of light bourbon, were polished to a glow. Boguslav stared at him then looked down at his own shoes, which were scuffed and unpolished. He looked up again.

"My name is Boguslav Rzepnicki."

"There. That makes things easier all around. Where do you work, Bugs?" This time it was Steve who started to walk, but at a slower pace. Rzepnicki hesitated for an instant then fell in beside him. "You know, I call you by your nickname because I feel we already know each other. And, after all, we shared the intimacies of the same woman."

"I work in transcription branch of Soviet Division."

"So, we're both in SE. Funny I haven't noticed you before. But then our circumstances were a bit different." The sidewalk curved along the chain link fence and the walk was now up a slight incline. Neither man looked athletic, but it was Rzepnicki who began to breathe heavily. "Is this where you park?" Steve raised his cane toward the rows of cars in the visitors' lot.

"No. I have space in front. Like I said, I don't come in every day."

"I notice you speak with an accent. Where are you from originally?"

"Poland."

"Really? So you do translations from Polish?"

"Mostly from Russian. Listen. We're walking wrong way. I have to get back to my car. It's in front of building." Rzepnicki stopped and turned, but didn't move until Steve did.

"That must be interesting work. I do nothing but administrative things, as I said. Do you travel much?"

"A lot. I just got back from Greece."

"Oh, that's why I haven't seen you around. I've probably even processed your accounting. In fact, now that you told me your name, it rings a bell. What were you doing out there? They needed you for Russian translation in Greece?"

"Yes."

"Listen, Bugs. I wasn't exaggerating that Betty would like to see you again. I don't mind leaving you two alone if that's what you prefer. We live off River Road. I have to be away for the next two weekends. She could use some company. Why don't you give her a call? She said you live close by, where?"

"In Bethesda."

"So, that's not far at all for you to come." Steve thought of adding that from what Betty had told him of Rzepnicki's lack of sexual prowess, it might be long, but not far to come, but he was not about to put the fellow off at this point.

"I don't know. My wife..." Rzepnicki's voice trailed off.

"It doesn't have to be at night. That might be harder to explain. How about Saturday, maybe in the afternoon?"

"Maybe."

"Here. I'll give you our address. Do you still have the phone number?"

"Yes."

"What if your wife were to find it? It has Betty's name, right?"

"I put it in my sock drawer in one of rolled up pairs of socks."

Steve laughed. He took out a business card.

"There. Now you have both the phone number and address and it has my name on it in case your wife asks. You can tell her I'm just a colleague. You can destroy the old card. Why don't you write your number on the back of this one?" Steve handed Rzepnicki a second card. The little man turned it over and took a ballpoint from his shirt pocket. Steve noticed the pen had left an ink stain on the cotton.

"In kind of work I do, I know how people can get in trouble talking on phone." Rzepnicki held the card flat in the palm of his left hand and wrote his number with his right and gave it to Steve, who looked at it. It had the three-zero-one area code, so it was probably the real number. This little guy didn't appear to be mentally agile enough to invent a number on the spot.

"Why don't you give me your work extension as well?" Steve gave the card back.

"I don't think we should discuss anything at work."

"Don't worry. We're just two colleagues talking about getting together. This can all go smoothly. You'll see."

Boguslav wrote the full seven-digit phone number.

"Since we're out of building, you have to dial this number."

"I understand. I know you're in a hurry. I won't keep you." Again, Steve smiled in that non-revealing Cheshire way. "We'll talk again soon. Betty will be happy to hear I ran into you. Stay in touch. Or we will." He stared at Rzepnicki then and was sure the little man got his meaning.

Chapter 17

In November, the Moscow sun didn't rise fully until almost nine o'clock. By the time its rays angled through the dusty panes and sheer curtains and crept across the imitation oriental carpet to reach Vladimir Shurin's pillow, it was close to ten. When he opened his eyes, the first thing he noticed was the connected procession of small clay figures, a brown-robed priest, a cotton-clad boy on a burro, a gaucho with a wide sombrero on a spotted pony and a honey-shaded mulatto girl with a polka dot dress and a red bundle balanced perfectly on her raven black hair. The little parade was making its way across his bureau. Their vibrant colors contrasted sharply with the drabness of the rest of the room. They were his final remnant from Rio.

Ever since his return from Brazil, he had the impression he was seeing everything in a half-light. He missed the sun on Copacabana. He missed Justinha. When he thought of her he became aware of his erection.

He lifted his head slightly. High on the opposite wall was a photo of Yuriy Gagarin in his cosmonaut's helmet, visor raised, his broad Slavic features conveying sincerity, modest heroism. And there, at the foot of the bed below Yuriy's friendly look was Irina's face. She did not appear friendly at all.

"You're finally awake? For the last time, are you going with me or not?" Irina held the metal bed rail and shifted her weight to her other foot.

"How many times do I have to say it before it fixes itself in your perma-frosted head? I am not going with you. Do you hear me?" He hated starting off the day having to put this woman in her place.

"There is no need to shout." She crossed her arms over the printed polyester dress. Her heavy leather coat was already draped over her shoulders. "I can hear you. What I can't understand is how you can keep refusing to see my parents after everything my father has done for you."

"It's easy."

"And what do you intend to do while I am there? What is it you do each time I go? What is her name, the latest one?"

"Who? What are you talking about?"

"You know what I'm talking about. I thought all that would stop when we left Brazil. You're already sticking your pike in some tart's ass. I know it."

"The only tart I know is you. You're a whore, but not a capitalist whore. At least they make money at it. You're a whore of the people, so you just give it away."

"You foul bastard. I have never had to tolerate such talk until I married you. You belong in the gutter."

"Not even from Barchuk? He used language that would make a randy monkey cover his ears. But I guess he didn't have to say much to get you to roll on your back."

"You're nothing but shit." She turned and went out the door into the outer room.

"Give my best to the *nomenklatura*," he yelled at her retreating back. He sat up now and swung his legs over the bed to the carpet. He heard Irina's heels clicking on the hardwood then softened by carpet then more clicks. Finally, the outer door of the flat opened, a few more clicks, then a slam. He was alone. He checked his watch on the bedside table: Ten-fifteen.

An hour later, Vladimir got off the metro at Theater Square near Red Square. The platform was crowded, but on a Saturday the pace of the travelers was more leisurely than during the work week. He spotted his new friend, Natasha, standing next to one of the black-speckled labradorite columns. She was wearing a red rain slicker and a red and white kerchief in the country maid's way on her head. Under the cloth, her brunette hair, dark as a beaver's pelt, was done in a bouffant style that was passé in the West. She carried a black purse and the ever-present *avoska*, the bag Muscovites took along on the chance that they might spot something available that was worth buying.

"That's a nice leather jacket. Did you get it in a *beryozka*, or did you bring it back with you from Brazil?" Natasha was referring to Vladimir's coffee brown rough suede coat.

"Brazil." He kissed her on each cheek then looked her up and down. "So, we're both dressed for the outdoors. Let's start." Vladimir took her by the arm and they caught the train to Chistiye Prudi and walked the corridors toward Turgenevskaya and the connecting line to Ostankino. "What did you learn about the room? Did you talk to the widow?"

Natasha Osipovna Chernenko was twenty-six. She had come to Moscow from Perm eight years earlier to attend Moscow State University, graduated when she was twenty-two, and went to work in the foreign ministry, but still lived with a married cousin and the girl's husband. Vladimir had given her a lead on a spare room in an apartment, a rare commodity in the Union.

"Yes. I went to see the place. It will be perfect." She squeezed his arm and pulled it to touch his triceps to her breast.

"And she will take two-fifty?"

"Yes, if it is in hard currency."

"And there is the separate entrance through the back stair?"

"It's just as you said. She spends most of her time at her dacha in the country. If we take it, we will have complete privacy." They maneuvered their way through the crowd in the chandeliered corridor at Turgenevskaya. The Moscow metro was one of the few architectural achievements Stalin had done right. There was no other system like it in the world. Khruschev had overseen much of the work. At the end of the corridor, they came out on the platform for Ostankino.

"Is your wife at home?" Natasha asked.

"She went out to Peredelkino to her parents' dacha. She won't be back until tomorrow. She sends her greetings." He smiled sarcastically.

"I doubt that. But if you don't have to go home tonight, then later I may give you a surprise." Again, Natasha pulled his arm tight against her breast.

"I like surprises." They both smiled as the rubber-wheeled train pulled up almost silently. In the crowded car they found themselves standing pressed against each other. Vladimir unzipped his jacket and Natasha put her hand against his chest to steady herself.

"You've been back for six months. Are you happy, or do you miss Brazil?" The train started off smoothly, but with the acceleration, they both felt their weight shift to their back foot.

"I miss the colors, and the sun. They're connected, of course."

"And the color of the women, do you miss that, too?"

"In the dark you can't see what color they are." They rocked a bit and she pushed harder against his chest.

"And since you are a man of the world, I suppose you didn't care."

"Right, we all belong to the international proletariat."

They got off at VDNKh and followed the crowd. To their right was the skyscraping TV tower.

"You were away for the Olympics. The games were broadcast from here," Natasha told him. "Did you see them in Brazil?"

"Yes, along with our brave lads invading Afghanistan and putting explosives in toys for the kids." Natasha ignored his criticism.

"We should have a meal up there sometime." She pointed to the Seventh Heaven restaurant more that three hundred meters above them.

"Sure. They won't even have to toss the salad just let it go round and round." He twirled his finger in circles. He was referring to the fact that the dining room rotated slowly as people had their meals.

The great cast iron gates of the public park stood open and they passed in with everyone else. Men held balloons in one hand and the hand of their child in the other. Just next to the entrance was an ice-cream vendor, unusual this late in the year. Women seemed to relish the outing the most and rightly so, since the majority of them held jobs and still kept the family going. Weekends provided their only real relief.

"I'll bet Count Sheremetiev must have had his gilded family crest on those gates before the revolution," Vladimir said. "Some things were better then. For the rich, of course," he hastened to add.

The broad alley that stretched out from the entrance was covered with the golden and russet leaves from the surrounding oak wood. They turned left and passed a large, brackish pond on their right and walked past the palace as far as the Church of the Life Giving Trinity with its five cupolas before turning back. Now children were tossing breadcrumbs to swans.

"Do you smell the mushrooms?" Natasha tilted her head back slightly and inhaled.

"Yes. That sharpness is unmistakable even for a city boy."

"This was the season when we would gather them when I was a little girl, when we lived on the collective, before I came to Moscow."

The wind picked up in sudden gusts. Vladimir looked off into the trees.

"Look at the leaves. They rise like frightened water birds, first in ones and twos then a whole flock. They circle and flutter, then settle again after the disturbance is past."

"Who do you think posed for these statues?" Natasha nodded toward the white marble, aristocratically-coiffed busts of ladies of long ago.

"The *nomenklatura* of their day. We've traded one group of aristocrats for another." Vladimir pointed to a green, wooden-slatted bench on the right. "Let's sit."

From that vantage point, they could see the steps at the main entrance to the palace and the Museum of Serf Art. Vladimir noticed that like the leaves, people rose and descended in bunches.

"The room will be perfect." Natasha took his arm again, his right arm. "But it needs some things, a good bed, a table, two chairs, a rug."

"Do you have paper and a pen?" Natasha rummaged through her purse.

"Only paper," she held out a small pad of block-lined paper.

Vladimir had a piece of charcoal in his jacket pocket, but he suddenly got an idea.

"What about lipstick?"

"Yes. Here." She handed him a brassy metal tube. He removed the cap and turned the base. He freed his right arm and wrote.

"Go see this guy. His name is Yakov Voronsky. He works in this shop on Kalinin Prospekt. He's the only guy in the Union who can get things done. He was in the Gulag, in the same camp as Solzhenitsyn. Now the KGB guys who arrested him and did the interrogation have to kiss his ass in front of Lenin's Tomb to get him to move their names up on the list to get furniture." She laughed. "Tell him you're my 'special friend.' He'll get you everything you need right away. Did you go to the *beryozka*?"

"Yes."

"And you got the radio?"

"Yes. But that was a lot to spend on a radio, more than seventy-five Deutschmarks."

"It's the one I said, the Grundig Ocean Boy?"

"Yes. What do you need such a radio for? We should have gotten a TV."

"We will. But if I go abroad again, it might be to London. I want to listen to the BBC to practice my English. And you're sure the rear entrance is private?"

"As I said, it's up the back stairs."

"The widow knows my wife's parents. The dacha she told you about is in Peredelkino, where my in-laws have theirs. I don't want to run into her."

"She told me that she'll spend most of her time out there now. I don't think she'll even be around when you come. Have you told your wife you plan to work at night?"

"Not yet. I wanted to wait to be sure it's arranged."

"I talked to my boss. If he approves, you and I can be on the midnight to eight shift. I think he was happy to have a volunteer. No one else in the ministry wants to do it, so I think he will accept you. If you get it, after work we can have tea with bread and jam in the room before you go home. Then you can come again in early evening before we have to go again."

"You have it all set up. That's good. You can be my manager. Those are handsome children." He gestured with his right hand, lifting it from Natasha's grip and pointing toward the palace steps. She followed his look and having distracted her he dangled his left arm over the cast iron stanchion of the bench and looked to his left. The few people who were approaching paid no attention to him. He scraped the lipstick tube up the side of the metal to seat level, back down and up again, then he replaced the cap and passed the tube back to her. "Shall we go in?"

They both rose and made their way across the broad path to the steps. Inside, they wandered on the polished, multi-patterned parquet floors through gilded connecting doors, past statuary, sky-blue drapery and under glistening chandeliers. They stared at the portraits of the Sheremetiev family members.

"What were they thinking? Can you guess?" Natasha asked.

"They look a bit arrogant as if they thought it could go on forever."

"You and I will." She squeezed his arm once again. He did not reply. They wandered more, but Vladimir found the rest boring.

"It's a surprise the place hasn't burned to the ground by now." He looked around him.

"But it's made of stone," Natasha said.

"No. It just looks to be so. That was the skill of the builders. It's all wood. Even the pillars and mantels that look to be marble and bronze are wood." He led her to one of the faux-marble columns. "Touch it." She flattened her palm against the pillar. "Knock on it." Natasha tapped on the column with her knuckles. "You see?"

"I never realized."

"That's why it's so cold in here and dark. There is no electricity because they are afraid of fire."

"You're a clever fellow. And so was the count. Did you know that he married a serf actress?"

"No."

"Her name was Praskovya Kovalyova. She called herself Zhemchugova. It is said she was a remarkable actress."

Outside, the day was darkening and the wind was more humid and a bit colder. Vladimir zipped his jacket all the way up.

"It's been three years since I went through this kind of weather." He hunched his shoulders to protect his neck.

"You've grown soft. But only in some places." Natasha looked down at the front of his trousers and smiled. She continued to smile as they strolled back the way they came. He thought she seemed content. He was not about to disappoint her now. But later on he would have to dampen her expectations. Passing the bench where they had sat, Vladimir looked back over his left shoulder and beyond Natasha's kerchief. He could make out the mark, but only by knowing it was there and by looking carefully. The Americans could see it. But he had made it not just for them, but so they would reassure Justinha that he would escape one day and return to her. As they got to the top of the metro steps at VDNKh, the first snowflakes landed on Natasha's red and white kerchief. A dark thought went through Vladimir's mind. Russia's snows had defeated Napoleon and Hitler. He hoped the Americans had learned from history.

Chapter 18

At eight o'clock on the drizzly evening of the first Thursday of December 1981, Steve Cooper limped along the tarmac footpath laid out at the edge of his River Road condominium complex. Cars passed him, mostly in groups of three and four carrying ambitious late workers or executives headed west from the District of Columbia toward their suburban homes. Just beyond the corner of the rail fence that marked the end of the property, the path turned to the right downhill toward the total darkness of the woods that bordered the clearing. Steve had taken only three or four steps in that direction when suddenly, in fractions of a second, he saw two beads of light, reflections from the halogen street lamps, undulating but headed straight for him. Instinctively he raised his cane. He barely had time to extend it and brace the silver knob against his hip before a pit bull leaped for his chest and the thud came.

"What the hell?" Steve's exclamation came at the same instant as the dog's loud yelp when the rubber tip of the cane caught the animal square in the sternum and he flipped over backward. The dog rolled and scrambled to his feet and went whining and slinking off in the direction from which he came. Then Steve saw the owner running uphill.

"Oh, God, I'm so sorry. He's never done that before."

"Whether he has or not, you'd better keep him on a goddamned leash. He was trying for my throat." Steve stood motionless and obviously shaken and angry.

"I don't know what got into him." The man turned now to the dog, "Max, bad dog, bad dog." Steve was barely able to make out the man's features, but could see he was five feet nine or ten and was wearing a dark jacket and a Redskins cap. The man fumbled a bit looking up at Steve and back at the dog as he knelt and attached a leather leash to the animal's collar. The pit bull stood still breathing heavily, but apparently chastened and subdued.

"I should call the animal control people," Steve threatened.

"That won't be necessary, really. I won't let him off the leash until we get home and I guess I'll just have to get a muzzle for him."

"You do that. But he could still knock people over."

"I'll get one of those expandable leashes."

"Sure."

"It won't happen again. I promise."

"That dog's a goddamned menace," were Steve's parting words as he resumed his walk downhill from the road.

Farther along he shined a pen flashlight ahead of him from side to side across the path like a blind man with a cane and looked back to be sure no one and nothing was behind him. He saw no silhouettes against the light, no dogs or dog walkers, and heard nothing except the hum of wet tires on the blacktop up the hill. He stopped to regain his composure and for several moments he enjoyed the solitude. Fifty yards downhill at the far end of the fence he turned right again and his flashlight caught the reflection of a yellow happy face sticker near the top of the corner fence post. It made him smile in spite of his earlier mishap. He continued in the same direction and at the end of that leg of his route he went uphill back to the rear of the parking area outside his condo. He had completed a rectangle of over a mile and was pleased that he felt no pain in his hip.

"You'll never guess what a scare I just had." Steve pulled his key from the door and began unbuttoning his raincoat as he entered the apartment.

"What happened?" Betty asked, putting her hand to her mouth. He told her about the near attack.

"Those two eyes were coming at me like a rifle shot. I just had time to raise my cane and brace it against my hip. It knocked the wind right out of him."

"Did he bite you at all?" Betty reached out and helped him slide the coat from his other arm.

"No. He never got that close."

"I think I've seen that dog." She hung his coat on a hanger and left it to dry over the tiles in the foyer. "What about New York?"

"I'm going up this weekend." He winked at her.

"What about me?" She nodded and smiled back.

"I want you to stay here. I'm going to call the Bug. He should be back from his travels by now. I'm going to tell him to come over. If he knows I'm not going to be here, I'm sure he'll come up and you can show him a good time." Betty said nothing. Her smile now disappeared. Steve was shaking his head as he went into the bedroom. "Unbelievable, scared the hell out of me. That dog was completely wild. Like a wolf."

That weekend, the first Saturday of December at two-thirty in the afternoon, Betty looked down from her balcony windows and saw Boguslav Rzepnicki pull into the parking lot two stories below. He was driving a faded red Honda hatchback. She watched him twist out of the driver's seat, stand, then lock the car door and pull up the collar of his tan jacket to shield his stubby neck from the chill wind and light drizzle. He tugged twice on the peak of the blue woolen cap he wore to cover his head as he made his way between other parked cars toward the downstairs entrance. She waited a bit then went to stand behind the door to her apartment. But after several minutes there was no ring. When she looked through the peephole, she saw the back of Bugs's bald head, with its narrow ring of white hair. The head seemed to bob up and down like a tiny inflated life raft on an invisible sea. She wondered what he was waiting for then realized he must be trying to catch his breath. Finally, she heard the chime.

"Hello, again, so nice to see you. I'm glad you could make it." Betty had one hand on the doorknob and extended the other to take him by the arm. She was wearing a satin lime green top that showed significant cleavage, and matching lounging pants. The clothes were from Victoria's Secret and Steve had chosen them for her to wear today. Her mid-heeled mules, which made her several inches taller than Boguslav, were beige and had those little tufts of feathers on top that swayed as she walked him in.

"Your husband is not here?"

Betty almost laughed. Bugs asked the question even before he took off his coat. Steve had the knack of sensing vulnerability in people. He seemed to have put the fear of God into this grotty little man.

"No. Like he told you on the phone, he had to go away. He's up in New York for the weekend. But he was happy that you wanted to come. And we can get to know each other better than we did over in Great Falls." Betty helped him off with his jacket. It was tan cotton with a taupe synthetic lining. Cheap like the man, she thought. "Please, sit." She motioned to a pale yellow chintz sofa that sat parallel to the balcony windows that constituted most of the far wall. As he maneuvered around the glass-topped coffee table, she went into the guest bedroom, folded the jacket wet side in, and left it on the bed with the cap on top. When she got back to the living room, Bugs had moved to the polished mahogany bookcases. His head was tilted back and his eyes were squinting to give whatever focus they could muster.

"Your husband has lot of spy books."

"He's a spy thriller junkie." Again, she headed him toward the sofa. "And he loves to write himself. The problem is he's never actually done the spying, so he has a hard time getting it right. Anyway, how have you been?"

"Okay." She noticed that his feet barely touched the floor when he sat.

"What a coincidence that my husband saw you in the hall at the agency. We couldn't believe it. I told him you said you worked for an exterminator and we both thought that was so funny." She sat at the other end of the three-seat sofa and put her arm up on the back. The satin top draped over her breast and gave it greater definition. She knew the move was not lost on her visitor.

"It surprised me also," Bugs said.

"I'll bet. But still, it's been a few months since I saw you. We thought you would come right after Steve ran into you in the building."

"I was traveling."

"That's what my husband said. Can I get you something to drink?"

"Vodka, plain."

Betty got up again. She knew he would be watching her bottom, so she exaggerated her swing a bit as she crossed to the cooking island that separated the living room from the kitchen. She reached into a cabinet above the counter and took down a bottle of Smirnoff.

"This isn't cold. Are you sure you won't take ice?"

"No ice." He shook his head vigorously. This was a man who could easily become agitated she thought.

"So, Steve says you do translations from Russian?"

"Yes."

"That must be terribly exciting, going out on secret missions like a real-life James Bond." She reached to another cabinet and took down a wine glass and poured from a bottle of Sauvignon Blanc.

"Yes, but not easy, I tell you."

"I can imagine. He said you have to travel a lot." This time she was more controlled as she came across the room, balancing the two glasses without spilling a drop. She set her guest's vodka on the table. "Here's a coaster." She picked up his glass and placed it on a round ceramic replica of the Danish Little Mermaid.

"That becomes harder, too."

"I'm sure. Here's to our friendship, chin-chin." Betty reached across the middle cushion and clinked her glass against his. They both drank. "How did you learn Russian?"

"I spoke it where I grew up. Polish was first language, but I was boy in town next to Soviet border, Bialystok."

"And then the Russians came?"

"First Germans. When war came, I was sent west to fight them, but I was taken prisoner almost immediately. Russians occupied eastern part until Germans drove them out. Then Russians came back and chased Germans to Berlin."

"How terrible, did you have to spend those war years in some kind of camp?" Betty took another sip from her glass. Up to that point he had been fidgeting. Now she sensed that he was starting to relax. He took a deep swallow of the vodka, leaned to the table to replace his glass then stretched as he leaned back against the cushion. She wanted to get him talking now since she couldn't be sure how long he would stay around after the sex.

"Only at first, for few months. You Americans don't know how easy you had it."

"If you recall, I'm British. Actually I wasn't born until after the war."

"In Germany war years was tough time. But then they sent me to work for family who had small hotel. It was also tavern and also restaurant."

"That must have been better than mucking about in a concentration camp or as some kind of slave labor." Betty crooked her right leg and brought it to rest on the cushion that separated them. She caught him looking at her crotch and knew he was trying to discern the rise of her vulva.

"In some way, yes, but was still hard. But I met daughter of owner. After three years, we married."

"So you weren't married when the war started?"

"No. Then after war, my wife made law suit against her family for all years she and I worked without pay. She is tough woman. Court ruled for her. We went into DP camp. Then Catholic Charities sponsored us to come to States. We got here in 1948 and we had little money from what my wife received. We went to Pittsburgh. I worked in steel factory. But in 1950, I saw in Polish club on bulletin board flyer from Washington asking for people who could speak Russian. My wife told me to send in letter. I did that and I came here to work."

"Let's see. That means you've worked for the agency for thirty-one years?"

"Yes. My wife wanted me to come. I would have been happy to go back to Bialystok."

"But life is better for you both here, isn't it?" She realized that she had yet to hear this man say one thing that was entirely positive and now he held true to form.

"Maybe, maybe not. I could retire. I am sixty-one now. But I think I will wait until sixty-five. Most of them get forced out at sixty, but I am civil service, so they can't push me out."

"Don't you find the work interesting? I think it must be fascinating. Are you a case officer?"

"I do technical work for them. They can't do what I do." He took two more swallows of the alcohol.

"Steve wanted to become a case officer, but because of his handicap, he couldn't pass the physical for overseas duty."

"I saw he don't walk good. What happened to him?" Bugs had an expression that looked to her like a sneer.

"It was a hunting accident. He was shot. His hair turned white overnight from the shock. He doesn't talk about it, but that's the reason he had to settle for the job in administration. He has a master's degree in accounting from SUNY at Binghamton. He came down here six years ago. We married the following year."

"You have nice place. What did it cost?" Betty wasn't surprised by the question. Most visitors would be too polite or discreet to ask it, but this man was crude. She watched him look around the room. He seemed to be calculating the worth of each thick, hand-made oriental carpet. They were mostly Persian in ruby and navy blue. They covered dark-stained maple hardwood floors. The furniture was polished hard wood

121

with fine inlaid veneers covered in expensive fabrics. On one Baker table, there was a collection of Herend figurines. She suspected that Bugs would believe that she and Steve were living well and she had to admit to herself that he was right.

"The apartment itself cost us ninety-two thousand dollars. That was five years ago."

"Lot of money." He finished off his glass, put it back on the coaster and moved across the cushion. He put his hand on the inside of Betty's thigh.

"Ooh, you're after that already?" She took another swallow of her wine then twisted away to put her glass, still half-full, on the table.

"This is why I came."

"Sure. We missed you in Palm Beach."

"I was traveling."

"Will you come to the next party?"

"Why should I come to party when I can come here?" Now he put her hand on his trousers.

"Well, for some variety. That's why."

"You were best last time. Would be same again." She pulled her hand away and stood.

"Let's move to the bedroom."

"Why? I want to do same as last time. You can do it here. Just get on your knees."

"It's easier for me on the bed." She moved quickly only glancing back to be sure he would react. He got up, somewhat reluctantly she thought, and followed her across the carpet down the hall and into the master bedroom. Betty had already turned back the flowered bedspread and propped up the pillows. "I'll be right there. Why don't you take your clothes off?" She walked to the louvered doors of the closets that filled one wall. She opened the left door and took a half-step in. Behind the right unopened door was a tripod with Steve's newest gadget, a Polaroid movie camera. It was part of a new system called Polavision. He had adjusted the slats of the louvers to allow filming of the bed and had taped the little red light on the front of the camera to prevent his subject from seeing it when filming was going on. Betty pushed the button on top as Steve had instructed. But it had no sound system, so she also pressed the start button on a tape recorder on the shelf. The whole thing took her two seconds then she lifted her green satin top and slipped out of the pants. When she turned to Bugs, she was bare-breasted and wore only a thong. "There, is that better?"

"Come here." Boguslav had his shoes and trousers and shorts off and had thrown the clothes on the carpet, but left his white shirt and his socks on. When Betty moved down on the bed, he grabbed her head and pulled it to him. She worked him as she had the first time. Several times she wanted to twist her head to be sure the angle to the camera was right.

Right or wrong, she hoped it was a long tape because, just like the first time, Bugs was awfully slow in coming and the result was insignificant. Afterward, she moved up onto the pillow. Boguslav was breathing hard. She hoped he wouldn't have a coronary.

"I think your wife doesn't do this for you as much as she should." Betty ran her finger gently along the hairs of his forearm. She wanted him to stay so she could get him to talk more. Steve had insisted that she try.

"My wife never does what you did."

"I do whatever my husband wants. Your wife doesn't do that?"

"She works night and day. She sells houses. She is in million dollar club at her office every month. She is German, after all."

"Maybe she should pay less attention to the mortgage and more attention to what you need." She could see that after his climax, he was totally disinterested in any physical stimulation. She took her hand away, crooked her elbow on the pillow and propped her head on her hand.

"Maybe, but at least she wants to keep me at home. Your husband lets you fuck anybody. If you were my wife, I would keep you at home."

"Steve and I have an agreement. We both like the sex. I guess your wife doesn't."

"I told you. She works. Germans are like that. And she is right at home in bloody America. Which do you think is largest ethnic group here?"

"Irish, I suppose. That's what we British think anyway."

"No, Germans."

"You sound as if you don't like America. So you would have gone back to jolly old Poland?" Betty twisted one ringlet of her blonde hair next to her ear around her index finger.

"I would have been happy there. And all Jews are gone. It would have been good. My family was always there."

"Is your family still living in, where was it?"

"Bialystok. Now no. My father was in first war. He was in Russian army, with Samsonov at Masurian Lakes. Millions died. But he lived and went back to Bialystok, and I was born."

"Is he still alive?" She saw that his stomach under the shirt was an ample mound rising and falling slower now than it had before. She figured he would live through the experience.

"No. My grandfather also was conscript in Czar's army. He was in Kamchatka and fought Japanese. One night he was on patrol with another soldier. Next morning, new patrol found them both almost frozen to death in tree. Those others thought they had hid from Japanese, but really they were chased there by wolves."

"Oh, my!" That reminded Betty of Steve's experience. "My husband was attacked by a pit bull the other night. He stuck it with his cane." Bugs turned his head and looked at her. She realized it was the first time he had done so since the sex. But he said nothing. He didn't seem to understand what she had said, or was incredulous. "So now you've been in Washington all these years. And your work must be so interesting. Tell me about it."

"I can't talk about that."

"Why not? Steve tells me what goes on in his office."

"He does admin. I do operations. On polygraph they ask me if I tell unauthorized people."

"Do you tell your wife?"

"No. She don't want to know anyway."

"It doesn't sound as if you're very happy with her."

"She takes my pay check."

"So if your wife is not interested in sex, what were you doing in the sex shop that day?"

"I wanted to see what they had. I thought they had movies."

"Porno films?"

"Yes, but they don't."

"We have some. I can lend you whichever ones you like."

"I couldn't take them home. My wife could find them."

"We could watch one here."

"I don't got time."

"You don't sound like a happy man. If you could do it again, would you marry her?"

"No. I would go back home." Suddenly he sat up in the bed. "I got to go."

"Oh, no, already, you took so long to come and now you have to go so soon?" She saw his offended look and understood the implication of what she had said. "I meant to come to our flat." But Bugs was already stepping into his pants and quickly fitted his feet into his shoes. At this point, Betty didn't really care. If the camera had worked properly, she believed she had everything Steve wanted from the afternoon. "Well, if you have to, you have to. But I hope you'll come sooner next time." Again, she understood the double meaning only after she had spoken. This time she almost laughed. And once again, he seemed to take offense. But she figured he would get over it and come back for more. Men always did.

Steve came home the following day. Even before he took off his coat, he asked about the film.

"Have you watched it? How did it turn out? Can you see that it's him?"

"Oh, yes," Betty answered. "And I even got him talking about his wife. He says he wouldn't marry her if he could choose today. It's obvious she wears the pants in the family. I think he's terrified of her."

"Great. Is it still in the machine?"

124

"Just switch it on." She had left the cartridge in the Polavision viewer because she knew this would be her husband's reaction. Steve leaned down to watch the tiny screen. Betty hunched over beside him on the sofa.

"Look at that. It was focused perfectly. Look at that little pecker. That's really good." Steve clapped his hands once.

"It's not good for me. All bloody awful."

"It will be worth it this time."

"But he wouldn't tell me anything about his trips, or about his work."

"He'll tell me."

"I'm not so sure."

"Listen. Right now we've got the Bug just where we want him, under my foot. When he sees it might come down and squash him, he'll do whatever I tell him to."

"Shall we invite him to the next party?" she asked.

"No. No more parties for the Bug. And no more sex. You did your job. No one will remember him from Harold's, and no one has seen us together at work. From now on he's going to come here. He'll be our little collector's item. We've got him stuck on a pin like a little beetle. Look, he's wiggling like one." Sure enough, Boguslav was twisting his head back and forth on the pillow.

"I couldn't see that from where I was," Betty said.

"Don't worry. You really came out tip-top, as the British say."

Chapter 19

On the Friday before Christmas, Frank Manion and Patrick Kerrane rode a crowded headquarters elevator to the fourth floor. Everyone was celebrating at the annual Christmas party. But Frank hadn't visited the desk the previous week and was anxious to get caught up on what was happening before he joined the festivities. He stepped out as the door opened and Patrick pressed the button to keep it from closing, to the annoyance of the other passengers. Patrick's only concession to the season was that he was wearing a dark green shirt and an exceedingly bright red tie.

"Meet me on the fifth floor in the B corridor. That's where NE Division has their party. That's always the best."

"Don't you have to be invited?" Frank asked.

"X, you must know by now no one would invite me anywhere. But I'm a citizen of the world. I go where I please."

Only when Frank walked off did Patrick allow the elevator door to close. The halls were crowded. As Frank turned into the D corridor he saw most people had drinks and food in hand. He turned into the door opposite the walk-in vault. No one was in the outer offices so he just stuck his head in Tony's door.

Tony had the phone in his right hand. He held up his left hand, thumb and fingers together, and flexed his hand back and forth in his Italian wave. He reminded Frank of the Pope. Frank moved in and sat. Tony now covered the phone speaker with the hand he had used to wave.

"Francis, it's lovely to see you. I'll be just one second." He removed his hand and talked again. "I understand. That's splendid news, Bill. Francis Manion is here and I'll tell him. Then we're going to talk about it all with our visitor. I'll get back to you within the hour." He hung up and turned to Frank. "You weren't here last week. Things have happened, earth-rending things."

"I wanted to get some shopping done. I'm going up to Philadelphia over the holidays. What's up?"

"I'm sorry. I don't mean to be churlish, but I'm very tied up right now and I'm expecting an important visitor. The one bit of news I can give you right away is that the DDO and Marshall have signed off on our assignments, yours and mine. Congratulations."

"That's great, Tony," Frank raised his arms as if he had scored a soccer goal, "a nice Christmas present. I was beginning to think I would spend my career in headquarters." While his initial reaction to Marshall's proposal that he go to Hungary had been lukewarm, he had come to count on the idea and was relieved that it now looked likely that he would get there.

"What are your plans?" Tony asked. "Can you come back in thirty minutes?"

"Sure. I'll just hang around."

"Don't be diverted. All three of us must talk. It's about Bagatelle and the future."

"Who's coming?"

"Don't concern yourself. You'll find out what happened when you get here."

Frank wondered at the mystery, but the welcome news of his assignment was enough for now and he didn't pursue things. Instead, he went out and wove his way through the merry-makers. Several young women, strangers, possibly emboldened by the drinks they held and by the season, said hello to him. He nodded, but kept moving. One stepped in his way.

"I've seen you around. I'm Carole." She was blonde, thin-faced and willowy. She had a tiny sprig of mistletoe in her hair.

"Have you been good this year, Carole?"

"Yes, but all that could change right here, right now. Just say the word."

"Merry Christmas, I hope Santa brings you what you wished for." Frank stepped around her.

"I thought he just did," she said pouting as he walked away.

Up on the fifth floor, Frank could see that once again Patrick had scoped things out. Everyone seemed to be one step farther along toward abandon than the people on the fourth floor with drinks for all, though no one seemed to have any food. Middle Eastern music was playing over the speaker system and undulating down the hall was a bare-footed belly dancer in a gold gauzy tasseled skirt, a sequined bodice that showed her full midriff, and a long white head veil that swayed from side to side with her gyrations. The crowd parted like the Red Sea before Moses as she advanced. Frank caught a glimpse of red hair just inside the NE front office and moved along behind her in that direction. At the entrance he noticed that the Near East Division's decoration covered the entire door. Fittingly, it was a beige paper camel with palm trees, silver stars and a crescent moon on a shiny green Christmas paper background.

"X, welcome, this is Helen." Patrick loomed over a short, dark-haired, slightly chunky lady who looked to be in her mid-forties. "Helen is an analyst. She has served in the Middle East, right?" Patrick looked at the woman for confirmation. "Helen escaped from a harem. She's already invited me into the vault for some undercover business." Patrick's new friend just smiled. She was dark-skinned and clearly had more than a few Arabic genes. She wore a tailored gray worsted woolen suit with a white blouse and, like Patrick she had a narrow red tie, though hers was more subdued. Her face had taken the first slide toward puffiness, but she seemed friendly and at first glance likable. "This is X," Patrick said to her. "He and I studied together in California in our army years. Now we're spooks."

"What is your last name, Helen? Patrick sometimes forgets his manners."

"Helen Hassan."

"Okay. I'm not just X. My name is Frank Manion. Francis Xavier Manion. Patrick likes to be dramatic. It's the Irish in him. So, what's it like to work in NE Division?" Frank had to raise his voice to make himself heard over the din.

"I don't work in NE now. When I got divorced, I moved over to Soviet operations in the Middle East. I didn't want to be in the same division as my ex. But my friends invite me back for the parties."

"SE/X/NE?" Frank asked.

"Yes. Then I transferred to SE/CI."

"Counter-intelligence? Harry O'Meara's office?"

"He's my boss."

"I met him for the first time last spring." Frank was not about to tell this woman what he thought of the Raven. Let her open up first.

"I kept the house in Chevy Chase. The O'Mearas are neighbors. Harry blamed Uthman for the break-up and he felt sorry for me, so he gave me a job."

"That was nice of him."

"Harry and Linda helped me a lot. They're great people. They lost a son in Vietnam. Their younger son is on a tennis scholarship to Stanford." Helen took a couple of swallows of her wine. "The drinks are back there." She pointed over her shoulder toward the middle of the open area.

Suddenly there was a commotion as the door to the conference room opened. For Patrick, it was like a starting gun.

"That's where the food is," Patrick announced. He maneuvered his way, all bony elbows and forearms, to the front of the line that had formed almost immediately. Frank was left to go around the table with Helen.

"I guess you've never seen Patrick eat. You're in for a surprise. And you'll have to help me out here. What's what?" Frank pointed with his fork.

"That's an appetizer. It's eggplant stuffed with rice, onions and tomatoes. It's called Imam Bayildi. It's a Turkish dish. This is mishmishiya from Morocco. It's a tagine of lamb with apricot. It has onions, cinnamon and chickpeas. Mishmish is Arabic for apricot."

"I'll take some of that. Do you speak Arabic?"

"Yes. My ex-husband was Lebanese. We served in Jordan and Beirut and Damascus, the sandbox."

128

"Is this a meat dish?" Frank pointed to brown, torpedo-shaped pieces on lettuce leaves.

"That's kibbeh, from Syria and Lebanon. It's ground lamb with tamarind, paprika and chopped scallions. It's served cold."

"You're an expert. Was your husband foolish enough to give you up, or was it the other way around?"

"He found somebody else, some fresh young thing, a mishmish." Helen looked at him without much expression.

"I know the story. I was on tdy in Rio. My wife is a lawyer. When I got back, I found that she left me for another lawyer."

"Did she take you to the cleaner?"

"No. She didn't take much more than her clothes. And her favorite painting, but I didn't like that picture anyway." They continued along the line selecting dishes.

"You were in Rio?" Helen asked. "You didn't happen to run into a case officer there, Julie d'Andrade?" Frank perked up.

"Yes. We worked together."

"She's a great person. She did her interim assignment with me about four years ago before she went out to the field."

"I liked her." Frank smiled. Helen returned the smile and it transformed her face. Frank could see that in her younger days she must have been a beauty.

"She's easy to like. She had a great tour in Paris right up to the end, but she got a bum deal and she's the target of a lot of rumors. Don't believe them," Helen said over her shoulder.

"Someone else told me the same thing."

"A woman on the French desk started the one about her and Peter Halley. Have you heard that one?"

"A friend of mine passed it on."

"Malicious and false," Helen said.

"Julie told me to be careful of the gossip mongers back here. I guess women have to worry not just about men giving them a hard time."

"Women can be savage to other women." Someone had turned off the Middle Eastern music and switched to traditional carols. "And you'll get over the divorce. When the word gets around that you're single, the girls will be all over you."

"I'm only now beginning to realize what a mistake it was to have married Beth in the first place."

"They were both nuts, my husband and your wife. And speaking of nuts, these are the desserts. This is sholezard. It's an Iranian dish. Those are almond balls and this is baklawa. It's fillo pastry with pistachio nuts with syrup."

Having made their choices, they rejoined Patrick just outside the door.

"See? I told you he had no shame," Frank said to Helen. "He's positioned himself to get back in for seconds." Frank spoke to Patrick. "I saw your plate was piled on a scale with Mount Everest, but you've already gotten it down to Kilimanjaro size."

"I had no lunch."

"Well, now you've had two."

"I've known people like you," Helen said. "They can eat all day and never put on an ounce."

Frank spoke first to Patrick. "I doubt that you know this, Patty." Then he turned to Helen. "He hates it when I call him Patty." Now he looked at Kerrane again. "That statue they have out front of Nathan Hale?"

"What about it?" Patrick asked between bites.

"He looked just like you. He was six feet three with flaming red hair. He didn't have the goatee, of course."

"Manion, you're so full of shit."

"It's true. And you know what happened to Nathan Hale. You may be in the wrong business." Frank turned again to Helen. "I love to toss his salad." All three concentrated on eating then Frank looked at his watch. "Sorry. This is great, but I have to go downstairs. I have a meeting with Tony Valletta." He looked at Helen. "Do you know Tony?"

"A very nice man."

"He's going to be my boss in Hungary. I just heard that Bill Marshall approved my assignment and the DDO signed off. Maybe things are looking up."

"Why the hell didn't you say so?" Patrick balanced his plate in his left hand and extended his right. "Congratulations, boyo. If they approve mine, we'll be neighbors."

"Thanks. I probably won't see you, Helen. Happy holidays. Please excuse us for a second." Frank tugged on Patrick's arm to pull him aside and spoke just loud enough for Patrick to hear him over the din. "What are you going to do for a ride home?"

"I think that's taken care of, X." Patrick glanced back at Helen. "She wants to get stoked. Most divorcees miss that. The last divorcee I had couldn't get enough of it. She could do more things than a Swiss Army Knife."

"Helen strikes me as a mumblety-peg kind of person."

"You've heard of the old-boy network?"

"Sure."

"Well she's in the old-girl network, the divorcees, the old maids, little women in tennis shoes. That's real, X. They run the place, black widows."

"I saw a bumper sticker the other day that said 'Divorce is the screwing you get for the screwing you got.' If it doesn't work out, don't take it personally."

"You're the philosopher-king, X."

"I am, yes. What are you doing over the holidays?"

"I'm going up to New York. I've got a lot of money riding on the tournament. I've picked La Salle to win it."

"My alma mater."

"Two of the St. John's starters are coming down with the flu. That's inside information. By game time tomorrow night they should be sick as rabid curs and won't suit up."

"Patrick, have you ever thought you might have a problem with your gambling?"

"I know I have a problem, chum. It's called losing. But this will be a turning point for me."

"The luck o' the Irish to ya."

"Don't wish that on me, Manion. Don't you know anything about your history? When were we ever lucky?"

"Well, in keeping with the season I'll say whatever trims your tree."

"I have a pretty good idea of what's going to be sitting on the old Yule log in a couple of hours." Patrick gave him a knowing glance and Frank turned to snake his way down the hall.

Down on the fourth floor, the inner offices were relatively quiet with everyone still out making merry in the hall. As Frank approached Tony's door, he could hear the Italian's baritone voice. The other was that of a woman and it sounded awfully familiar. When Frank stepped into the doorway, he was almost speechless.

"Francis, I believe you know Miss d'Andrade."

At such moments, the craziest thoughts come into one's head. It suddenly occurred to Frank that these offices were a standard size, probably ten by twelve feet and that was extremely small for three people. Then he saw that Tony was watchful and apparently enjoying himself. He had set this up.

"Hello," she said. "I guess headquarters has relaxed the dress code since I left." She was looking at his royal blue v-neck sweater and open collared shirt.

Frank smiled warmly in spite of her jibe.

"I'm not working in headquarters. I'm coming from the language school."

"You're still studying Portuguese? Did you get left back? You could learn it better in New Bedford. I heard you never made it to Brasilia."

"Now I'm studying Hungarian." Frank continued to stand beside the only other chair in the room.

"I haven't told our guest yet," Tony said to Frank. "Sit." Now he turned to Julie. "Francis and I are going to shake off all these Washington barnacles and encrustations and head across the great salt sea to Budapest. I'm to be Achilles and Francis will be my myrmidon."

"Without a Greek interpreter I would guess that means he'll be chief and you're going to be the deputy?" Julie asked Frank.

"Looks that way." Frank smiled. Julie was clearly surprised and maybe, he thought, impressed.

"Congratulations. You have a wonderful chief to work for."

"I agree," Frank said. Tony just smiled. "So what brings you back here?"

"Sorry, Francis," Tony interrupted. "That's what we're here to discuss. I told you a lot has happened. You can congratulate Julie. She recruited Justinha Marques, Bagatelle's lady friend."

"Good work." Frank extended his hand. He knew it was an unnecessary gesture, somewhat affected, but he simply wanted to touch her. Her own hand was soft skinned and smooth, but she still had her usual firm grip. "Was there a reason for doing it now?"

"Justinha got a postcard from Shurin," Julie said.

"He wasn't supposed to write to her," Frank said.

"He was forced to, Francis, by our incompetence, more particularly by the incompetence of Moscow Station. We were on tenterhooks waiting for his signal." Tony had his stubby forearms on the desk and leaned forward. "Now we know why it was delayed. It seems the outdoor site they selected is now covered in snow. Here. You can read the note he sent." Tony extended a Xerox copy of the message side of a postcard. "Very innovative I would say."

"Did you learn enough Portuguese to read it?" Julie asked, a half-smile playing on her lips.

"Let's see."

Frank studied the short note. In English it said,

"Dear Justinha,

"We are having a grand time. Please tell your tennis partner that we went to the Ostankino Park and the Serfs' Museum as she suggested. Our Inturist guide did a wonderful job of giving us the history of the palace. We had a picnic lunch on the benches in the park. It was a good thing we went that day since it snowed heavily right after we left. Hope to see you soon in the sun.

"Fondly,

"Eugenio Fontes."

"So he knew who you were on the tennis court?"

"Apparently so," Julie admitted. "Or he made an educated guess."

"What did the people on the Soviet desk say?" Frank asked Tony.

"I think they were guilty of complicity in covering up the inappropriate choice of a site. But now they have agreed we should go ahead with the first broadcast. Bill Marshall is very pleased. That was he I was talking to on the phone when you came in earlier. In addition to conveying the good news about our assignments, he wanted me to congratulate both of you on your splendid work. You'll both continue to be involved in the Bagatelle case in one way or another."

Frank turned to Julie.

"What's your understanding with Justinha?"

"I told her I can act as a go-between, that we'll get in touch with Shurin discreetly and he can send his messages to her through the diplomatic bag. I have no doubt that he told her about his cooperation with us before he went back to Moscow. She hasn't said anything, but she knows."

"So you got your recruitment after all." Frank watched her. Each time he looked at her he wanted to take her in his arms as he had that night on Copacabana.

"Yes." Her expression didn't reveal just how she felt about that.

"You were a bit skeptical that it would happen, if I remember." Frank didn't want to say he had told her so.

"And you got your recruitment if he's really on the level." She had to add that qualification, Frank thought. Tony got up and came around his desk.

"Listen, you two, I'm sure Harry O'Meara is not at his desk, but I want to check in the hall to see if I can find him. He might be able to contribute something to this conversation. I'll leave you to get reacquainted."

Frank wasn't sure of Tony's reason for leaving. He thought it might be to give them both time to move their personal relationship along. But what Tony didn't understand was that there was no personal relationship to start with. For Julie, it was all professional.

"You came up smelling like roses," she said. "I hope it lasts." She had no distinct expression on her face, so Frank didn't know how to interpret that remark. And he knew he was heading into dangerous territory, but he had to know more than she had told him.

"I'm curious. You said you never met Shurin. Then how did he know you?"

"What do you mean? Oh, I get it. You're going back to that lie he told you about screwing me, right?"

"Wrong. I never believed that for a second."

"Then why are you asking? Go ahead. Get it off your chest. Let's clear the air here."

"Don't tell me," Frank said. "You're working for the Environmental Protection Agency now?" Frank knew he had pushed her too far even before she reacted.

"Screw you." She started to stand up.

"Okay. Here's my question. Why the hell would Shurin be sending that message to you? You said you never talked to him, that all he knew was that you were an American and you played tennis."

133

"You've been hanging around headquarters too long, Manion. I told you this was the way they thought here. If you got out in the field and did some work, you would begin to think in operational terms."

"You said something once about frogs growing wings, so here's one. If cows could fly, there'd be pie in the sky. You didn't answer my question. He must have known something more about you. What?"

"I asked Justinha that. I said, 'Did you tell him anything other than that I was an American?'"

"And what did she say?"

"That she had said I was an American diplomat. I thought right away that Shurin was taking a chance that diplomat meant agency." Her tone was not at all apologetic and to Frank it did make sense. Shurin was always looking behind the veil. More often than not there was nothing there, but this time he had found the truth and it had probably saved the operation. When Frank realized that, he sat for a moment and said nothing and Julie didn't either. Finally, he tried to make peace.

"Well, if they broadcast to him, I guess we'll just have to see where it goes from here." He thought it was a pretty lame approach and Julie was having none of it.

"You know, Manion, for a while I thought you were decent. I actually enjoyed working with you a lot. And I even thought...well, I thought about what you had said about seeing each other again. And if you hadn't been married, I might have been willing. But you're just like all the rest. I did something worthwhile, something that made sense. Now you're trying to turn it around."

Suddenly, Tony came back in the room. Behind him was a rheumy-eyed Raven.

"I found Harry in the hall." Tony looked at their faces and seemed to recognize the stalemate. "I promised him we wouldn't take up any more time than needed, but that we could all benefit from his operational erudition."

O'Meara did not appear happy to be there. His eyes were bloodshot and his cheeks flushed from alcohol. He still held a half-empty glass of whiskey in his right hand. Frank stood and surrendered his chair. There were no others in the room.

"I'm Julie d'Andrade." Julie extended her arm, but didn't get up. O'Meara shifted his glass to his left hand, but took only her fingers with his right and barely moved them before letting go. He said nothing and didn't sit.

"Harry, I suppose the matter at issue is where we go from here." Tony had made his way around the desk and sat in his tilt-back chair.

"If it were up to me, we'd go right to the toilet and flush this down with all the other crap." The Raven looked from Tony to Frank as he said this. His look conveyed anger and Frank had the strong impression that

134

O'Meara's emotion was directed at him. It was a look of barely contained hatred.

"I know you have invaluable experience in such cases," Tony said. "Can you share your reasoning with me and these young people?"

The word young seemed to set the Raven off. He careened to his left and bumped his shoulder against the wall. His right hand jerked a bit and he spilled some of his drink.

"The only thing young people have to look forward to is getting old...or not." He directed his remark at Frank. "Either way, you lose." Now he looked at Tony. "Who the hell knows what game they're playing here?" he bellowed. "This guy may have been a dangle from the beginning after we pitched Bunin. And he went back either willingly or unwillingly before he was supposed to. Either way he's under KGB control." Now O'Meara shifted his foggy gaze back to Frank once again. "I remember you never included that possibility in your impressions." He emphasized that last word, and it came out scornfully and a bit slurred.

Suddenly, it struck Frank. This guy really did not like him, but Frank didn't think it was a case of jealousy so much as resentment. He remembered Helen Hassan's revelation that O'Meara had lost a son in Vietnam. There were fates worse than being an orphan. Was it possible that the man was blaming Frank just for being alive? Frank felt sorry for him. As bad as it was for a child to lose his parents, it has to be worse for parents to lose a child.

"I spoke with Bill Marshall. He wants to go ahead with the broadcast," Tony said. "We lose nothing by doing so, wouldn't you agree?"

"I wouldn't touch this with a ten foot pole. Now Bill wants to go ahead and have Moscow officers pick up this guy's drops. We're not even going to have him use the accommodation address in Brazil. That's just dumb."

"I believe Bill has decided to have tdy'ers and Moscow Station officers who are coming to the end of their tours make the pick-ups," Tony said. "If anyone is spotted, they will be asked to leave the country, but we won't have lost much."

"Suit yourself. You seem to know it all after only six months. There, folks, you asked for my opinion, my 'operational erudition' (Again, the words were scornful and O'Meara pronounced the last one "errordition".) and you got it." The Raven simply walked out, a bit unsteadily in his first two steps. During his brief stay, other than shaking hands with Julie, he had never bothered to acknowledge her at all. For a moment, the three who remained said nothing. Finally, Tony broke the silence.

"Well, that was enlightening." Tony looked at them both. "We now know, if we didn't already, where Mr. O. stands in regard to Mr. Bagatelle." He paused. Neither Frank nor Julie said anything. "Anyway,

Francis, beyond what Harry had to say, you're now *au courant* on the case."

"Yes. Thanks."

"And you said you were going to visit your family in Philadelphia over the holidays?"

"I'm going to Philadelphia, yes." Frank was careful not to elaborate.

"Well, I hope you find them all well. I don't want to keep you from the frolicking. I just wanted you to know that matters are proceeding apace. I'll continue to keep you informed and pretty soon we'll have to begin discussing things Hungarian. On one thing in particular our lovely visitor is an expert, but that will have to wait. For now I beg you to excuse us. I still have some things to discuss with Julie whose time, as you can appreciate, is limited."

"Sure," was all Frank could muster. He turned to Julie. "You need a ride anywhere?"

"I have a rental," she said then she turned away from him and sat looking at Tony.

"Well, Merry Christmas to you both and Happy New Year." Frank got up. "It's good news about the postcard. You saved the case, Julie." She still said nothing and for once, neither did Tony. Frank knew he was odd man out and he just left the office. The elevator took him down to the ground floor and he got out, but his spirits went far lower.

Chapter 20

On the first Saturday of January 1982, Vladimir Shurin carefully removed dishes, pots, spices and a potted geranium from the wide-stepped ladder that served as shelves in his kitchen. He steadied the two side supports against the panel in the ceiling and climbed up into the cramped attic under the eaves of his apartment building. The space was supposed to be one of the added features he got for the extra rent he paid. He and Irina stored a few non-perishables there, empty trunks and suitcases, an old, but still serviceable mattress, and that was where he kept the Grundig Ocean Boy radio wrapped in burlap and concealed beneath one of the many loose floor boards.

The area may have been sheltered from the elements, but it was totally lacking in any comforts. There was no light and no heat so he had to carry a flashlight and wear his great coat, which made the climb more difficult. Now he sat and shivered on the uneven floor as he had each Saturday morning since he made the mark on the bench in November.

As a first step, he extended the receiver's chrome antenna as far as it would go then switched the set to battery operation. He shined the flashlight on the radio face and turned the dial slowly to the frequency he had memorized. When the setup was complete, he resigned himself to listening to the crackle and static coming from who knew where. By now he was questioning whether this would work at all. But in his lap he balanced a note pad and the Mylar strip with the code groups he had brought from Rio concealed in his pen and took a small magnifying glass from his pocket.

At ten-thirty a voice came from the speaker. In Russian it announced numbers in groups of five. Vladimir dutifully followed the sequences growing accustomed to the cadence and balancing the flashlight to check constantly what he heard with the first number group on his list. Suddenly, just as he was blowing into his hands to warm his fingers and less than a minute into the broadcast there it was. "Five, two, eight, one, zero." He blinked and looked directly at the lighted face of the radio as if for confirmation and in his astonishment almost failed to hear the start of the next group, but he recovered and for the next six minutes copied down everything he heard until a number group corresponded with a second one on his own list. End of message.

He couldn't believe it. It really happened. The Americans were talking to him. In his excitement he realized that he had even forgotten about the penetrating cold. He turned off the power, lowered the antenna and re-wrapped the radio and put it in its space between the floor beams.

Stuffing the note pad and magnifying glass in one pocket of his coat and the flashlight in the other, he duck-walked under the low roof to the opening. He climbed several steps down the ladder, replaced the ceiling panel, and jumped the last three rungs into his kitchen.

Immediately, without even taking off his coat, he sat at the kitchen table and began to line up the groups on his pad with those he had heard on the radio. He didn't have to worry about any interruption. Irina had gone again to Peredelkino to her parents' dacha. Still, he worked quickly, anxious to know what they were telling him. When he had finished the false subtraction, he divided the numbers into sets of two and matched each two-digit group to a letter on his list and finally he had his answer.

"Dear Friend,

"Warmest greetings. Take a shopping bag. Go to the University of Moscow. From the main entrance, walk straight toward the octagonal planted area in front of the building. On the left side you will see a row of six juniper trees. On the ground between the third and fourth junipers will be an object. It will be covered in juniper needles. Put it in your bag. Take it home and crack it open. Remove the contents and save the plastic wrappings and the thick rubber band.

"To let us know you have succeeded, go on the Saturday after you have picked up the package to the Yaroslavl Railway Station. As you face the main entrance, look to your left. At the end of the adjacent building are six columns. Counting the columns as you walk from the main entrance to the building, on the inside of the third column nearest the building (not the street side) make a mark with dark crayon. Make it about ten centimeters long and about at the height of your waist. We will see the mark and know you have the package.

"When you have a message for us, use the special paper you will find in our package and follow the instructions we will include to write it. Wrap your message in the plastic bags from our package and put it in an old sock. Roll up the sock and secure it with the rubber band. Then go to Krymskiy Val and enter Gorkiy Park. Continue from that entrance on the path to the embankment. At the embankment, turn right on Pushkinskaya Naberezhnaya. Count the benches on your right hand side. Sit very briefly on the fourth bench you come to. It is in front of the light stanchion and the sixth tree in the row. When you are able to do so securely, toss your sock with your message in it over the hedge so it lands close to the base of the light stanchion. Leave the area.

"After your have done this, go to the Moscow Workers' Publishing House across from the Moscow Soviet of Working People's Deputies. Go there any evening except Saturday or Sunday. Wear a hat. Between 1930 and 1940 hours stand at the bus stop for the number twenty bus. Do not get on the bus, but when it arrives, take off your hat and scratch your head. No one will contact you, but we will see you and know your package is ready for us and we will go get it.

"Your loving friend from the south sends her regards.

"Best wishes from us."

When he had read the message, he jumped with elation, twirled with outstretched arms in his great coat, gave one of his tae-kwan-do kicks and knocked a pot from its hook. It bounced off the far wall, clattered off the stove and onto the linoleum floor.

He knew the best time to make the pick-up would be that evening. Irina would not be back until Sunday night and he was energized, almost manic now that it had all really begun. He had planned to spend the evening and the night with Natasha. That would have to change.

At noon, Vladimir walked along Kalinin Prospekt. At the intersection with Markovsky street, Natasha was waiting for him.

"*Ciao*, beauty," Vladimir kissed her on both cheeks.

"You look happy." Her breath came out in visible puffs as she stamped her feet on the hard-packed snowy sidewalk.

"The sun is shining for a change." He was right. There was a double sparkle off the white banks pushed up against the trees and it wasn't just he who seemed invigorated. Everyone appeared to be out to take advantage of the gold and blue and white day. "Come along. We have to talk a bit." He took her by the hand. "I thought we would go to the Arbat Restaurant and have a bite."

"But we're still going to the cinema?"

"Yes, of course. But first let's eat something."

They strolled along the recently finished boulevard. The broad sidewalk was crowded and cars were competing for parking spaces on each side of the roadway where the snow was piled up. Fifty meters along, they saw a large crowd. As they approached, Natasha pulled him over to see what was happening. People were jostling for position and Natasha, at five feet two, was unable to see to the center, but Vladimir saw a man with one good eye standing next to a stack of already empty crates.

"It's an Armenian. He's selling oranges."

"Do you think we can get some?" Natasha asked. She held up her ever-ready net bag.

"Too late, they're already gone."

"Pity, an orange would have been awfully nice. We could have saved it until after our meal."

"Yes. It's hard to find fresh fruit in winter."

"When I was on the collective, we had several plum trees on our private plot. They were Italian plums, good for prunes. In early fall we would spread out willow wicker trays over a big smoking fire pit behind the house and smoke the plums into prunes."

"Funny, your face doesn't have any wrinkles that I can see."

She squeezed his arm and smiled. That prompted him to look at her closely. Her hair was as dark as a sable's pelt. He thought of the

Brazilian women, their blend of African, Indian and European bloodlines that had produced tawny beauties. In Natasha's case, with her clear dark slightly narrowed eyes, her black brows and lashes and her full, firm body, he could see a touch of Tartar and an overlay of European and he realized that the Union had its own stunning mixture. But he still missed Justinha.

At the Arbat, there was a midday crowd. When they finally got a table, they ordered hot borscht with sour cream, *shashlik* and tea. Natasha asked for a small side dish of dilled cucumbers. The lunchtime tables had no cloths. Natasha took a handkerchief from her purse and wiped away crumbs.

"This is the time of the year for preserving fruits. We used to put them in jars out in our shed. It was wonderful to take them in later in January and February."

"You seem to have fond memories of the farm. Why didn't you stay there?"

"I had greater ambitions. Perm was a backwater. There was industry and mining and a big hydroelectric station. In summer, you could take a cruise through the locks and out on the reservoir. It's enormous. That was pleasant. But I wanted to come to Moscow, the bright lights."

"Not many make it from the countryside to the university. Usually one has to have some party connection."

"I did. My mother's two brothers are chairmen. My uncle Timofei is chairman of the miners' collective and my uncle Alexander is chairman of the farm."

"And who is the cousin you were living with?"

"My uncle Timofei's daughter, Tatyana."

Their beet soup came.

"I won't be able to come to the room until later tonight," Vladimir told her.

"Why not? Your wife is away. What else would you have to do? Or maybe I should ask who else would you have to do?"

"Hush. You're beginning to sound like her." He waved his finger back and forth in front of her lips. "She's coming back to town. She called this morning. Her parents have tickets for a concert and I have to go with her and them. But afterward, she will spend the night at their flat, so I will come then."

"That's some story. What concert?"

"It's Mussorgsky, at the Moscow Conservatory. Don't be a shrew. It doesn't suit you."

"Then what time can I expect you?"

"Toward midnight, I will let myself in with the key."

They went to the Borodino cinema. There was a retrospective of the works of Eisenstein and they watched Ivan the Terrible. Vladimir had seen it at least four times, the first time as a boy. He'd had several nightmares because of it. This time the air in the theater was musty from wet boots and the floor under his own seat was sticky and as his morning's exhilaration wore off and his midday meal settled, he fell asleep. He was awakened by the battle scene at Kazan.

At four o'clock, he left Natasha at the intersection where they had met earlier and went home. He heated a pot of kasha and brewed himself some coffee. That was the extent of his culinary skills. And he kept looking at the clock. At seven-thirty he left his flat. Three blocks away he caught the metro to Leninsky Prospekt Station and connected to the number seven trolleybus from Gagarin Square along Kosygin Street up into the Lenin Hills. As he made his connections and when he got off at his final stop, he watched carefully to see if anyone looked like a tail, but even though the train and the trolleybus were crowded, he spotted no one who showed any interest in him.

It was the time of the winter academic break at MGU, Moscow State University, and with most students away and at this hour on a bone-chilling night there was little activity around the school. Still, he wanted to be careful so he strolled for several minutes along the overlook. Below to his right shone the lights and glittering monuments of the city. He stopped and leaned on the balustrade. Across the river bend in the foreground was the Luzhniki Stadium and in the mid-distance the illuminated walls of the Kremlin and beyond lay Red Square and St. Basil's with its gilded onion domes. Many couples came to the hills on their wedding day if the weather was good to have photos taken with the city in the background. It all looked like a fairyland from up here, but Vladimir knew that fairy tales always included an ogre, or troll, or some wicked spirit. That was true of Moscow as well.

A young couple, the boy with his arm around the girl's waist, approached on his right and stood next to the rail and embraced. Vladimir stood upright, turned away, waited for cars to pass, then crossed the street and walked toward the university entrance. The building loomed ahead. Spotlights were aimed at the facade and the center spire with its blood red star on top. The whole construction was designed in the Stalinist wedding cake style. In fact, Stalin himself had approved the architecture. The large thermometer on the side tower registered a temperature of minus nine degrees Celsius and the clock showed it was already eight thirty-five.

Vladimir pulled down the ear flaps of his fur hat and stopped to tie them under his chin. As he got closer to the front of the building he could see the ground layout described in the Americans' broadcast and he reasoned that rather than walk all the way to the entrance then turn around and re-trace his steps, he could find the spot they had indicated by approaching from this direction. Now he looked back. The young couple had disappeared. A taxi stopped about forty meters behind him and someone, a man, was getting out. Vladimir skirted the octagon and started counting the junipers. He moved out farther from the tree line to create a better angle to those ahead. Now he could see the farthest tree and he counted back from there. Suddenly, a man appeared from beyond the last tree. He was walking in Vladimir's direction. Vladimir pulled up the collar of his coat, turned down the front flap of his hat and lowered his head as if leaning into the wind, even though the night was calm. The man passed, but by then Vladimir, himself, was beyond the point the Americans had described. He had to turn around. The man was moving away, but there was the young couple again. They crossed to the far side of the street stopping occasionally to kiss. He began to shiver, but it was now or never.

Vladimir stepped onto the landscaped area and walked behind the trees. Between the third and fourth evergreens he squatted and searched the ground. "The devil take them," he thought. They should have told him to bring a flashlight. He continued to hunker down and now leaned first one way, then the other to create angles of light against the street. He still saw nothing. How could he be sure it wasn't buried in the snow? They had already made that mistake. He was becoming angry then he spotted a lump very near the base of the third tree. At first he thought it was part of the trunk. It looked to be the size of a grapefruit. He had to get down on his knees and stretch and hold one hand up to protect his face in order to get under the lowest limbs. The branches were stiff with hoar frost and when he disturbed them, powdered snow fell down over his hat and under his coat collar. When he cupped his hand under the object the needles pricked his palm and even after he managed to withdraw this irregular ball he wasn't sure it was what he had come for. Still, there was nothing else. Of that he was certain. So he took the plastic sack from his coat pocket, stood and put the ball in the bag.

On the way back, no one got on the trolleybus with him and in the seats there were only three people, none of whom paid him any heed. He sat looking out the window. Occasionally, he opened the bag to look at his find. All the while he seesawed between fear and anticipation. Had anyone had seen him pick it up? He kept thinking back. There was only the couple, and the man who came at him, and the man getting out of the taxi. But none of them had been there when he went into the trees. Perhaps it had even been that approaching man who had put the package there to begin with. It didn't appear that the thing had been there for very long. Vladimir had never gotten a close look at the fellow. He could have been an American. Still, if this was the package, he was desperate to know what it contained.

In the flat, he took off his coat and hat and sat again as he had that morning at the kitchen table. He hastily plucked away the juniper sticks and used a large knife to cut into the shell. It was some kind of molded Styrofoam or soft plastic. When he had created a split in the material, he pried it apart with both hands. Inside, there were perhaps half a dozen clear plastic bags. The first one he pulled out contained watches. He spread them on the table and laughed. There were five and they were the knock-off Seikos he had intended to buy in Rio but had to forego when he ran out of time. "Bless Boland," he thought.

In a second packet was a tightly rolled sum of rubles with a rubber band around them. He counted them: six hundred. That concerned him. What did they represent? Was this supposed to be his compensation for what he was doing? What were they up to? Then he saw the note: "Spending money for incidentals." What the hell did that mean? The next item was wrapped in clear plastic bubble paper. It was a Minox camera. Taped to the back was a note: "Film already loaded." Also, there were printed instructions from the camera's manufacturer and ten extra rolls of film with thirty-six exposures each. He held it up to his eye and looked through the viewfinder at the ceiling light. In another mini-bag was a Cartier pen exactly like his old one and the one he had brought back to Moscow with the Mylar code sheet. There was also a small tin with four pills and another paper. This one said "Lethal Pills," and below was written, "One pill will kill instantly. Two additional pills are contained inside the pen."

Vladimir unscrewed the pen cartridge. At the tip of the ink container was a fourth pill. He screwed the pen together and put it in his shirt pocket. Finally, there were four sheets of paper folded in four. They were sandwiched between hard cardboard squares. On the first was a message. It was encoded, again in five digit groups. Vladimir was forced to set up the ladder and climb to the attic to retrieve his code list and use his magnifying glass. When he deciphered the message it read:

"Here is the chemically treated sheet for secret writing. The second sheet here is a back-up sheet." They went on to tell him again how to layer the papers to write his messages. He read on. "Also, inside the pen we have put an additional one-time pad for future messages. Please continue to use your present pad until it is finished then use the new one. In your first message, please tell us your address, floor and apartment, the office in which you work, the route you take each day. Does your building have a mailbox on the ground floor? Do you have a car? What is your work schedule? Who is your boss? On what floor do you work? Do you ever travel out of town?

"As of today, you have a balance of $70,000 US in the Banque de Suisse in Geneva. The last sheet is a message from your friend."

Once he read that, Vladimir pushed aside everything else on the table. The letter from Justinha was written in Portuguese. It brought tears to his eyes.

"*Amor*,

"I received the postcard. My friend has told me she will get this letter to you and you can write to me through the same channel. I am

143

desperate to hear from you. It has now been eight months and since you left, all the light has gone from my life. Please, *amor*, give me some word. Let me know you will come and rescue me and that we will have a future filled with our love. Conceição and Maria send kisses. I send every feeling I have and will ever have. Come back to me.

    J."

He looked at his watch. It was already ten thirty-five. He re-packed all of the material in the plastic baggies, climbed the ladder and hid everything under the floor of the attic. He put his coat and hat back on and stuck one half of the Styrofoam shell in each pocket. In the basement of his building, he took a piece of coal from the bin and put that in his pocket as well. Three blocks from his flat he caught the metro to Komsomolskaya Station on the north side of town.

He wondered why the Americans had chosen this place. It was a haven for pick-pockets and drunkards. Still, with seventy thousand dollars he was already wealthy by Soviet standards. And he could take care of himself if he had to deal with low-lifes.

He came up out of the metro to the columned pavilion. It wasn't immediately clear to him on which column of the next building he was to make his mark. He walked outside and to the middle of Komsomolskaya Square. From there he saw where he was supposed to go. He approached the main station entrance all the way to the hooded arch with its incongruous combination of Soviet crests and reliefs of Arctic fisherman, then turned left and continued along the station façade to the next building. At the third column on the far side of the building, he took the piece of charcoal and made his mark waist high without stopping. In the metro, he threw away the Americans' empty package in trash receptacles at two different stops.

It was almost midnight by the time he got to Natasha's room. From the back stair entrance he let himself in as quietly as he could. He hoped she was asleep. If she wanted sex tonight, he was not sure he could oblige. Spying, he had discovered, took a lot out of a man.

Chapter 21

Steve Cooper was waiting in his apartment on River Road for Boguslav Rzepnicki. His hip had stiffened up on him as it usually did in winter and February had been a cold month. When the knock came, Steve's limp was more pronounced than usual as he went to the door.

"Hello, Bugs."

The little man was clearly surprised. Steve knew Rzepnicki had expected Betty to greet him.

"Your wife is not here?"

"Not right now. Come in. She had to go to New York."

Boguslav did step inside the door, but stood there apparently undecided about what to do next.

"Maybe I shouldn't stay." He half turned back toward the hall, but Steve was already closing the door behind him.

"Nonsense, Betty is due back in about an hour. In the meantime, there's a lot we have to talk about. Let me take your coat." Steve loomed over the little fellow and lifted his jacket from his sagging shoulders almost before Bugs had a chance to react.

"Talk about what?"

"Relax, just a chat. Go ahead and sit down. Then there's something I want to show you."

"What? What are you talking?"

"Bugs, I'm not going to rob you, or hit you over the head. I'm a colleague. We both do the same thing. I just want to talk a bit about my writing." Steve had hung the coat in the closet by the entrance and now he stood between Bugs and the door and gestured toward the living room. "Please, come in and sit down." The little man shuffled across the room, still wary and unconvinced. "Can I offer you a drink? Vodka? Betty said you take it without ice."

"No, nothing." Boguslav continued to stand, but now he was next to the yellow sofa. He had his head down and seemed to be staring at the floor trying to decide what he should do. Then Steve saw that his guest noticed the tape recorder and the Polavision unit on the coffee table and that clearly made him even more nervous. "No. I think I go."

"Okay, but just one drink. That will only take a couple of minutes." Steve kept one eye on him and watched with the other to pour two glasses from the bottle of Smirnoff, which he had already put out on the counter. "You see, I'm writing this spy thriller. And it's hard because I can't find out how things really work. A guy like you is worth his weight in gold to me. You have the inside story. I'll bet in all the years you've worked you must have covered hundreds of cases."

Bugs turned and looked up at him listening perhaps for the first time.

"Sure, but I can't talk about that."

Steve came with one drink and extended his arm.

"There, that's for you." He set the glass on the coffee table on the same kind of coaster as before then went back to the counter to get his own drink. "Come on, sit down for a bit." Steve went to the other end of the sofa carrying his glass and with his outstretched leg leaned back into the cushions. Bugs finally took his seat at the other end. "Chin-chin." Steve didn't reach all the way across the middle cushion, but gestured toward Bugs's glass as he raised his own. Rzepnicki took a swallow. "So, you've been spending a lot of time in Athens this past year, right?"

"Yeah."

"I guess that's tough, all that time away from home." Bugs said nothing. "Is it for one operation, or do they expect you to do many things at the same time?"

"Just one."

"So how does that work? I mean, what is it you transcribe?"

"What I hear."

"But Betty tells me you said it's hard work."

"Goddamn right." Steve almost chuckled at the little man's belligerent tone. He knew it was really aimed at him. Bugs wanted to show him how tough he was.

"So what happens? You have to listen to phone conversations?"

"Sure." Now Bugs took several swallows of the vodka. "You are not recording this?" He pointed to the tape recorder on the table.

"No, not at all, there is a tape already in there that I wanted you to hear, though. Do you want to listen to it now?"

"I have no time. I got to get back."

"Oh, it will take only a few seconds for you to recognize it. But first, you should probably see my new system. Have you ever heard of Polavision?"

"No." Bugs set his glass on the table and moved to the edge of his seat. Steve figured he was about to try to leave.

"It's this film system from Polaroid. It's self-contained. As soon as you do the filming, you can watch it in this little viewer. Here, I'll turn it on. You're on the film."

"What?" Bugs had mostly avoided looking at Steve, but now he turned suddenly and was obviously surprised.

"You're a movie star. Go ahead. It's started." Steve sat back and took a sip of the vodka.

Rzepnicki leaned over the boxy viewer. It took him no time at all to realize what had happened. Steve knew the fellow was watching Betty, bare-breasted and smiling, moving across the room to join him on the bed.

"Oh, Christ, you took pictures?"

"Yes. Aren't they great? And listen." Steve pressed the play button on the tape recorder. "Sorry, the audio and video aren't synchronized."

Betty's voice came on.

"There, is that better?" she said again, and then Bugs's command, "Come here." Bugs had stopped watching the film. Now he was staring at the recorder. It gave off his sounds of satisfaction as Betty moved over him. Steve reached over and turned off both machines.

"I was going to skip to the part where you talk about your wife, how terrible she is, but you get the idea. I suppose it's ironic that I was able to catch an audio specialist on tape, hoisted by your own petard, as they say." Steve chuckled. "Relax, I'm not about to play these for anybody but you. When Betty's here, you can watch them together."

"No. You can watch it if you want. I won't come back." Bugs suddenly got up and started toward the door.

"I think you mention on the tape that your wife is a real German bitch, if I remember. I don't think she will be happy when she hears that."

Bugs had gotten almost as far as the closet when he stopped dead in his tracks and turned.

"What the hell do you mean?"

"Listen. I'm trying to be your friend. You're taking all this too seriously. Come on. Please sit down again, just for ten minutes or so."

"What are you saying to send it to my wife?"

"No. Of course she won't hear that, or see the film. We're adults, not kids. Just relax. There's no need to be upset. Come finish your drink." Bugs walked slowly back and stood by the sofa. "Anyway, about Athens, it means a lot to me to be able to write my book and I want to do it right. So tell me, how they make these phone taps. Come on. Relax. Sit, for God's sake." Steve thumped the middle cushion twice with the flat of his hand. Bugs reluctantly sat on the edge of the cushion.

"I don't know. I am not goddamn technician."

"Yes, of course. But do they have our people go up on telephone poles, or do they go into the target's house? At least you know that."

"I do know that. And lot more. But already I told you I don't talk about it."

Instantly, Steve threw his glass across the room and rose up in one synchronized movement despite his hip. The glass shattered against the far wall and the vodka had left a streak across the carpet. He extended his arms as far as they would go and loomed over Rzepnicki and screamed.

"Listen, you arrogant little shit. Who the fuck do you think you are? You won't talk to me? You come here and fuck my wife. You drink my drinks and you say you won't talk to me? You're going to talk to me and right now. And you're going to answer every fucking question I put

147

to you and if you don't, your wife is going to see that film and hear that tape. You're marriage will go down the shitter and then I'm going to make sure you lose your job and if that doesn't impress you, I'll cut your fucking balls off." Now Steve's face was inches from Bugs's startled eyes. Steve had planned it just this way. He knew that he resembled a mad whooping crane and he could see that Bugs was out of his wits. The little man must have felt like a plump paralyzed bullfrog stuck in some reedy Masurian swamp with this huge menacing bird about to pluck out his innards.

"You're crazy," was all Rzepnicki could think to reply, but he said it with awe rather than defiance. Now Steve modulated his tone. He was still loud, but no longer at the top of his voice.

"You're fucking right I'm crazy, crazy enough to do just what I said. You're just like all those operations officers who think they're too superior to share anything. But I'm going to write my book and you're going to help me. You got that straight?"

"Okay. Okay." Bugs had his palm up between them. "If this means so much that you would do such things just to write book."

"That's better." Steve reverted immediately to his pleasant self. He smiled. "Since I'm up, I'll get myself another drink. Can I refresh yours?"

"No." Bugs sat for a moment, then picked up his vodka and took a swallow. Steve crossed the room, talking over his shoulder. "I really need your help and I'm not out to hurt you. Once I understand how things work, if you don't want to come here any more, you don't have to." At the island in the kitchen he poured another glass of vodka. He came back to the sofa holding the glass in front of him and taking satisfaction from the fact that his hand was steady as a rock. "Now, where were we? Oh, yes. I was asking about the teltaps. So you know how they put them in?" He set his glass on the table and took up a notepad and pen. Bugs had to take another moment. He was still shaky.

"Different ways." He seemed to have trouble switching to the topic, but when he got started, he was coherent. "Sometimes they get help." Now he seemed to be concentrating. "Local security service uses their man in central exchange. If that don't work, they can do like you said, climb up and attach something to wire. I'm not sure."

"But then they have audio bugs, too, microphones in the home? I suppose that's how you got your nickname."

"Yeah."

"How do they set them up?"

"Again, local service may help. If they do, we give them my work when I finish so they know what Soviet is up to. That helps them."

"Suppose the service won't help. What then?" Steve was busily taking notes.

"Case officer tries to recruit neighbor of target and drill through wall, or ceiling. Other times they go in when the guy is out. They put in piece of furniture, like lamp, chair."

"They put the microphones in the furniture?"

"Yes, transmitters, but lots of times these don't work right and they expect me to be magician and tell them what guy is saying when nobody can hear goddamn word."

"Is that what happened in Athens?"

"It was station that put in audio device. They don't want Greeks to know we are interested in this guy. First time it was in wall, but no good. We could hear only when he shouted at wife. So they waited until he went away and they went into his flat and put bug in his sofa."

"I see." Steve reached over and took another sip of his vodka. Bugs finished his. "Listen. You're at home here. Go get yourself a refill. It's not always easy for me to get up." Bugs did as he was told. Steve talked to him as he crossed to the kitchen. "So why are we interested in this fellow? I mean how did they decide he was worth pursuing?"

Bugs talked as he filled his glass.

"They think they can recruit him. Also, they want to know cases he is running. He's KGB guy. I already heard him talk about one agent in Italy. This summer in August when he goes again to Moscow, he will go first to Roma to meet this agent. Station in Roma is now setting up to catch both of them." He came back to the sofa apparently no longer frightened. All along, Steve had intended after the blow-up to ease him into this conversation and he saw he had succeeded.

"Wow. That's great, all because of your good work?"

"Yes." Bugs took his seat again.

"But what I'm asking is how does a station decide just who should be a target?"

"They got all these profiles. They make psychological model. If someone is willing to break rules, if someone is different, don't get along with comrades; don't get along with wife, such stuff. It's all bullshit."

"Why do you say that?"

"Because after all that, Soviets don't cooperate."

"You've never worked on a case where one was recruited?"

"No, because then they don't need me. What would they need me for to listen when the guy would be talking right to them?"

"Sure. I see." Steve was satisfied. He had gotten the little fellow to take the first step. Now he changed the conversation. For the next fifteen minutes, he asked about Bugs's life, just as Betty had, and he got the answers he had already heard. Now it was time to send the little man on his way. "Well, look. I said that Betty would be back in an hour, but I'm really not sure of that and I don't want to keep you from other things. Besides, I guess you would still feel uncomfortable about having sex with her while I'm around." Bugs said nothing. "Next time you come, I want to talk about how they do recruitments, how they follow people, what they say, that kind of thing." Steve now rocked forward and pushed off the armrest to stand. Bugs got to his feet. Now he was silent. Steve started across the living room. "Listen. I'm sorry I lost my composure there. But you see how easy it is just to talk. I'm not asking anything classified and even if I did, I'm cleared for it." He draped his arm over the little fellow's shoulder. "And you don't know what a help it is to me to be able to write things that sound real. Only a guy like you knows the inside story. I just sit on the outside looking in. You're the one who does all the exciting stuff, the dangerous stuff. It must take nerves of steel."

"Yes," was all Bugs said in reply. Steve took his coat from the closet and held it while Bugs fit his arms into the sleeves.

"I want you to come back again. Let's say in two weeks. I looked at the travel schedule in the office. I have to process your accountings and so on and I saw that you won't be going anywhere for a while."

"No. That's right."

"Well, come over again. You call me, or I'll call you. If you're not there, I'll just talk to your wife." Bugs looked up. Steve saw there was fear in those furtive eyes, which was just what he had intended to put and keep there. The little man left without saying a word.

That evening Steve went out for his constitutional. The air was cold, but not bitterly so. Ever since the dog incident, he had been even more careful than usual on his walk. This time, when he got to the farthest point from the complex, he stepped off the path to the corner fence post. The smiley face was still there, but it had been dulled by the elements. Steve took a penknife and scraped it away. He reached in his pocket and took out a small sticker. It was Barney Rubble, the Flintstone character. He peeled off the back and stuck it where the happy face had been. Then he snapped the knife shut, put it back in his pocket and moved on for the last part of his walk.

Later that evening Betty called to tell him to pack his slippers. He was grateful for her reminder. On his last trip to New York he had forgotten them. He'd had to walk barefoot on the hotel room carpet. He hated that. You never knew what others might have done on that carpet. People were capable of just about anything.

Chapter 22

Vladimir Shurin got off the metro at Smolenskaya Station at eight forty on the morning of the second Thursday in March. He walked up Arbat Street to a neighborhood coffee shop. In contrast to the sharp sunrise frost outside, the air in the small room was steamy, almost syrupy from the cooking and brewing. There was the pungent smell of onions mixed with the unmistakable aroma of fresh bread and coffee. All this combined with the smoke from thirty or forty cigarettes. Men were standing two deep at the bar puffing and drinking. Natasha was one of a handful of women in the place. She had just come off her night shift and was waiting for him at a back table. Vladimir could see that her eyes were heavy as she watched him snake his way through the crowded space.

"Today is the day," she said as he leaned over to kiss her cheek.

"At nine o'clock." He sat down.

"Finally he seems to be ready to transfer you."

"I'll find out why it has taken so long, I suppose." Suddenly, behind them a waitress dropped a clear glass teacup on the wood-planked floor. It shattered. The patrons clapped and hooted. These were mostly laborers many of whom were taking their morning vodka, but Vladimir even in his suit and tie felt comfortable among them.

"Another one is leaving," Natasha said, "Morozov, so it's the perfect moment. Vorontsov has no other candidates."

"Then I have no worries, do I? But you told me the same thing five months ago. Any last word of advice?"

"He is not a bad chap." She sipped her coffee. Vladimir knew it was sugary. Natasha liked her coffee sweetened. "He is part of the *treugolnik*." At first Vladimir considered that unusual. The *treugolnik* was the political triumvirate in every Soviet agency. Normally it was made up of the head of that agency, the chief of the local union, and the communist party secretary. But he quickly realized that Andrei Gromyko, the foreign minister, could hardly be expected to head up a local political committee. Mstislav Vorontsov, at his level, would be the more logical candidate. "If you don't antagonize him at the start, he will accept you," Natasha said.

"Do I antagonize people? Have I antagonized you?"

"I'm just suggesting that you be, let's say respectful in the beginning. Aren't you having anything?" Natasha saw the waitress who had just had the mishap coming to their table. Vladimir held up his hand to stop her before she reached them.

"If I get there late, that would not be respectful. I'm sure Comrade Vorontsov expects me to be punctual."

He got up and kissed her again.

"I hope you're going in with the right attitude." She looked concerned, but he thought perhaps it was just her fatigue. "Let me know as soon as he makes the decision." She reached out and for a second took his hand. "This is important for our future."

Vladimir trotted across Smolenskiy Boulevard and took the shoveled steps of the foreign ministry two at a time as he had done almost every working morning since his return to Moscow. In all those months, he had been assigned as an administrative officer in the Latin American section. Today he hoped that was about to change. On his way up in the crowded elevator, he acknowledged to himself that he was using Natasha for his own ends. But so what? He had no qualms about it. In the Union, everyone used everyone else. It was a fact of life. Now he would use this bureaucrat, Vorontsov, to get what the Americans wanted even though Vladimir realized that the Americans were using him, Vladimir Shurin, as well.

He went in to the anteroom outside the office of Mstislav Antonovich Vorontsov, the deputy-director of management of the foreign ministry. He gave the secretary his name. She had him sit until ten minutes after nine, then opened Vorontsov's door and announced him.

The inner office was hardly imposing, but it did have a maroon carpet over the parquet floor. Vladimir thought it had probably been larger once, but partitioned to create space for lesser members of the ministry's hierarchy. A large framed photo of Leonid Brezhnev hung on the wall behind the deputy-director along with the always watchful photo of Vladimir Ilyich Lenin. Vladimir Shurin carried his coat over his arm. Vorontsov actually stood to greet him, which Vladimir took as a good sign.

"You are Vladimir Sergeyevich." Vorontsov shook his hand across the paper-strewn desk. "Natasha Osipovna has spoken of you. She recommends you highly. Sit down, please."

Vladimir saw that the fellow was in his early fifties, chunky and somewhat lethargic in his movements. But he had two more noticeable features, one real and one artificial. The first was a cleft lip that may have extended into his palate. It was prominent and seemed to divide his face into two halves. And there was the other unusual thing. The black plastic frame of his glasses had obviously cracked over the bridge of Vorontsov's rubbery nose and he had used a heavy white tape to secure the two sides. It only accentuated the dichotomy and it was very distracting. A real two-faced fellow, Vladimir thought.

"I appreciate her recommendation," Vladimir said. "She told me about this opening six months ago and I had hoped to meet you before this, but I know things should not move too quickly and I appreciate that you can see me today." Vladimir had to concentrate to engage the fellow's look. He half expected Vorontsov's eyes to roll in opposite directions like those of some Brazilian lizard.

"If I understand correctly, Brazil was your first foreign posting?" Vorontsov asked.

"Yes."

"Well, there you have it. I did need someone six months ago, but my hands were tied. Since you never had the experience before I suppose you didn't realize that for the first six months you are back home, the security lads do their work to be sure there are no complications. Now they tell me we can proceed, provided, of course, that our chat today goes well."

"So that's it."

"You understand don't you that your work in the center will be every night from midnight until eight in the morning?"

"Yes."

"In the beginning, that will include weekends. You will have off one day and one half day during the week to compensate."

"Good."

"Tell me about Brazil. Things there cost a lot?"

"They have luxury goods that are expensive. But the every day staples are cheap."

"I suppose you brought back souvenirs?"

Vladimir expected this. Despite the fact that the swine needed him, he still required some kind of sweetener, as Natasha did with her coffee. From his coat pocket Vladimir took a small package wrapped in pale pink paper and tied with a little gold ribbon. It was the fourth of his phony Seiko watches. He had already presented three to other supervisors and he intended to keep the last one for himself.

"I got a few things."

"There are a number of candidates for this position. Can you tell my why you think I should choose you?"

Vladimir knew this was a blatant lie and Vorontsov must have understood full well that Natasha would have been aware that there were no other volunteers. But this was the way the game was played.

"The shipment of my household effects was delayed a bit and when it came, my wife stored some boxes where I couldn't find them. But just a few weeks ago, I found this. Please do not consider it extravagant. It's not much, a trifle, but as I hope we are to work together, comrade, I would ask you to accept it as a token of my enthusiasm for the things we can accomplish. That enthusiasm is why I believe you should pick me for the position." Vladimir handed the box to Vorontsov, who smiled an almost reptilian smile.

"Aren't you the considerate fellow." He slipped off the ribbon and tore away the flimsy paper. When he opened the box, he was obviously surprised and pleased. "'A trifle,' you say, my God." Then he quickly caught himself. Vladimir was amused. He saw that the maggot understood he had to maintain his superior position so Vorontsov immediately tempered his gratitude. He put the watch back in its box and stuck it in the side drawer of the desk. "It will come in handy. In the meantime, I will tell the duty supervisor that you will start tomorrow night. Natasha Osipovna is also working then and she has volunteered to show you how things are done. I am glad you came in. We can use good workers."

"I will do my best, comrade." Vladimir said.

That was the end of the interview. Vladimir stood. Vorontsov did not. Vladimir reached across the desk and they shook hands, then he turned and left the office. Outside at the foot of the ministry steps, woolen-swathed, beet-cheeked babushkas the size of sumo wrestlers with arms like staves and legs like birch trunks were lifting and dropping iron pikes to break up the ice on the sidewalk. Vladimir timed his walk to move around them without having his feet smashed and headed back to the metro.

The following night, just before midnight Vladimir greeted the night guard in his militia uniform at the ministry reception desk, showed his pass, and walked to the elevator bank. He was carrying a black haversack and up on the seventh floor he turned right down the hall and noticed that beside every office door was a trash can. A stocky granny was dipping her mop in a bucket and swabbing the floor at the far end of the corridor. Vladimir turned right into the message distribution center. Natasha was there, leaning over a wooden table that was covered with papers, apparently communications from various diplomatic posts. She was alone.

"The others have already left?" he asked as he kissed her on both cheeks.

"You're on time. That's a good start. Yes. I told them to go." He took off his coat and hung it on a hook behind the door. "I'm glad to see you're wearing a sweater. It gets chilly in here at night. They turn down the heat in the building."

The room was perhaps four meters square. Covering three of its walls were slotted rows of wooden containers, their edges rubbed bare of varnish and finish. Each had a metal tag holder on the front just below the opening. In the middle of the room was the large wooden table with the messages. It was obviously used for sorting and collating.

"I'm ready to begin. Just tell me what to do."

"There's nothing to it. I'll take you down the hall to the communications center in a bit. We go down and pick up incoming telegrams every fifteen minutes or so and bring them back here, separate them, and route them to the various offices." Natasha walked to the back wall and held up her finger. "The white cards on each of these slotted holders have the office designations." She went to a large box by the door and took a message that she brought to show him. "Each telegram already has a time stamp. The communicators put that on. And each has an action recipient line and an information recipient line." She held out the paper and looked up at him. He saw she was holding a message from the Soviet Embassy in Ottawa. "You know that already. So you put the top copy in the action office box and the second in the information office box. The third copy goes to the minister's office, there." She pointed to a large container next to the door. "Then a copy for the archive box there." She gestured toward a second big box next to the minister's box.

"As simple as that?"

"Because of the time difference, we keep getting messages in all night. Those from Western Europe have already been processed by our comrades. By the time we start our shift, the ones from Western Hemisphere countries are arriving. We process those. By morning about the time we leave, the Asian messages are beginning to get here."

"That's it?"

"Yes. In the morning the secretaries come from each of the sections to pick up their messages. Let's go down the hall and I'll introduce you to Marisa Vasiliyevna. She works with the communicators and we pick up everything from her." Natasha moved to the door and put back the Ottawa telegram. As they walked down the hall, Vladimir saw the same cleaning woman still sliding her mop back and forth across the tile floor. She didn't appear to have made much progress.

Behind a kind of Dutch door open at the top sat Marisa Vasiliyevna. She was a slight listless creature with short straight mousy hair that might or might not have benefited from a washing. In fact, Vladimir thought, that was one of the most striking differences between western women and those in the Union. The Soviet women had no real shampoo available to them and the result was lackluster hair. He wasn't about to offer that observation to Natasha, who introduced him to the girl and took from her a stack of messages.

"Is there any time for a break in this routine?" he asked on their way back up the hall.

"Yes, often. We can spell each other and take catnaps. Since Morozov left, I haven't been able to do that. That's why I've been so tired lately."

"Are we able to lock the door once in a while?" He smiled. She looked at him and it took her a second to get his meaning.

"I'm not sure we should think about that."

"But we are able to lock the door."

"I suppose."

"Perfect." They turned into the distributions center. "As I was coming here tonight I thought winter is ending and we should go skating before the ice melts."

"I would like that, when?"

"Let us say Sunday afternoon. We'll meet at the main entrance to Gorkiy Park on Krimskiy Val. At three o'clock. What do you think?"

"What about tomorrow?"

"My wife will be home and I should be. But Sunday I can make it. I'll tell her I'm going to a martial arts workout. That way I can take along some extra clothing."

It was about two in the morning when Natasha went to the ladies room. Vladimir stuck his head out the door and watched her go. He saw that by now the cleaning lady was moving down the hall emptying each wastebasket into a large gray canvas sack that she dragged behind her. He picked up the wastebasket from the corner of the room and put it out in the hall beside the door. He called to the woman.

"Auntie, I'm leaving this here for you."

Then he closed the door and turned the dead bolt. He took the Minox camera from his sack. He had it stuck tightly in his glove and had to struggle to get it out. Immediately he went to the slot marked USA. Several times during the night he had stuck those telegrams written by Anatoliy Dobrynin, the Soviet ambassador in Washington, in the back of the stack. Now he took out just those and quickly cleared a space on the sorting table. He glanced at his Seiko. He had already focused the camera at home to eighteen inches, so he had to make only slight adjustments as he snapped away. He had decided ahead of time to limit himself to three minutes, but was surprised that he finished the ambassador's messages in less than one. He then went to the French desk's slot. Since he had not anticipated being able to get more than the USA photos, most of his time was spent sorting. He was able to take only a few shots before his three minutes were up. He put the camera away, reinserted the messages in their slot and unlocked the door. Natasha took another three minutes to come back. He figured that he would time her each night, take an average, and work well within that limit. Then another possibility struck him. Something he should have thought of before. For the next hour as they worked together, he continued to stick messages from the Soviet ambassadors to the United States, France, Great Britain and Germany in the rear of their containers. When Natasha went down the hall to get a new batch of messages, he carefully put the ones he had selected in his haversack trying not to bend them.

"I have to go where even the Czar went on foot," he told her when she got back.

"Of course, the wonderful thing about this job is we work at our own pace."

In the men's room, Vladimir locked the door to his stall, closed the lid of the toilet and set his sack on the floor beside it. He took out the first message, centered it on the flat lid, leaned over and snapped. Each subsequent message he put on top of those he had already done. The Americans had told him in their instructions that the film was high-speed, able to create images in low light without a flash. He had to replace the film canisters twice and he finished three rolls. He repeated the process at four-thirty. All in all, by the end of the night he figured he had taken well over one hundred photos. He considered that a good night's work.

The following day, Saturday, with Irina out shopping, Vladimir sat in the attic. This time he took up a cushion to avoid the splinters. He followed the Americans' instructions and wrote out his first message on the special paper.

"My Dear One,

I tell you first that I will come back. It is all working as I planned and by the time I get there we will have no worries of any kind. My time here has been dreary. You cannot imagine what winter is like. The sun is shut away in some heavenly vault and we go about like tattered, stiff-limbed blind men feeling our way. Next to you, the light of Rio is what I miss most. But I intend to see and bathe in it again soon. It and you will wash away all my sorrow. Be patient, my darling. Kiss the girls for me.

Eugenio."

Next, he wrote a short note to the Americans.

"Friends,

As you see, I have used up the film you gave me. Next time send more. Also, the rubles you gave me are gone and I need more of those, too. For the time being, I cannot answer your questions about where I live except to say that I have access to a room in a building in the Arbat section. I pass on Kalinin Prospekt often if you have to spot me. I also received the pills. Let us hope I never have to use them.

Eugenio."

Vladimir put both messages in one of the clear plastic baggies. He put all the rolls of film in a second baggie and stuck both of them in an old sock. He used the rubber bands from his first package to secure the sock.

The next day, he got off the metro at Oktyabrskaya and crossed the street to the grand arch at the entrance to Gorkiy Park. The street was crowded, but Natasha was nowhere to be seen. He looked at his watch. It was five minutes after three. Now he looked around. He had gotten into the habit of looking these days even though he had been reassured by Vorontsov's comment about the KGB investigators and by his acceptance into the new job. It seemed to him that they would not have put him in that position if they had any doubts about him. Once again in the crowd he saw no one who looked out of place. Still he was nervous.

He waited another five minutes that seemed like thirty and was just about to go into the park alone when he saw Natasha crossing over Krimsky Val.

"Sorry. I overslept. I usually don't get up until four," she said. Her breath looked like smoke signals from American Indians.

"After we finish here, we'll go back to your place, and get in bed again then go on to work," he said.

They went to the rental shop and fitted themselves for skates. They laced them up then started out immediately for Pushkinskaya Naberezhnaya, the broad path next to the Moscow River. All the paths were artificially flooded and frozen over for most of the cold season and at night they were lighted. Now the afternoon sun was low and the air cut to the bone. But Vladimir's adrenaline was surging. He guided them directly to the spot the Americans had chosen. It was far enough from their starting point that he could reasonably suggest that they sit. Both he and Natasha were breathing heavily. Vladimir unzipped his leather jacket, took a cigarette from his shirt pocket and lit it.

"I'm fit for martial arts, but not for this."

"Still, it's great fun."

"Look at that fool. Someone should arrest him. He's a menace." Vladimir pointed to a boy in his late teens who had built up great speed and was twisting by the skaters ahead of him, most of whom were startled by his passing. As Natasha watched the speeder, Vladimir switched his cigarette to his left hand, reached in his jacket pocket and took out the sock. He draped his right arm over the back of the bench and with a flip of his wrist, tossed his little package toward the base of the light pole. "Ready?" he asked.

"Yes, but let's go a bit slower this time."

They got up from the bench with Vladimir holding Natasha's arm to support her. He puffed on his cigarette as they started off. Once again he looked around, but no one seemed to be taking any notice of them. But would KGB men allow themselves to be spotted so easily? For the rest of the afternoon, he felt uneasy just as he had in the Lenin Hills. He figured it would always be this way, but that's why the Americans were paying him all that money.

The next evening, Vladimir left home early. Irina complained that this new working arrangement was intolerable, but he ignored her. Let her suspect he was up to something romantic. At least that way she would not guess the real game he was playing. At seven-thirty it was already dark and he stood at the stop for the number twenty bus in front of the Moscow Workers' Publishing House. Several people were forming a queue by the signpost that indicated bus numbers, but Vladimir remained off to the side. When the bus arrived, he stood scanning the windows. He removed his rabbit fur hat and scratched his head. As the bus pulled away, he wasn't confident that anyone had seen him. He had studied every male face near the windows. It was only several minutes after the bus had departed that he recalled seeing a woman. What struck him in the image of her that he retained was that the hair that fell below her own fur hat was clean and lustrous.

Chapter 23

With three days left before his departure for Budapest Frank sat in the room two doors down from Tony's office reading files, going over the details of each case he would handle in Hungary. Harriet Upshaw, Tony's secretary, poked her head in the door.

"Tony would like to see you."

Reluctantly, Frank marked the page he was reading, closed the file and left it on the desk.

"What's up?"

"Francis, Bagatelle has sent us another batch of films. We've struck the mother lode. You, lad, are the man of the hour." Tony clapped once then reached out to grasp his hand. "Congratulations."

"Bill Marshall deserves the credit. He stuck with the case."

Tony motioned for him to sit.

"Bill is euphoric. The messages from their ambassador back to Moscow are on the President's desk as we speak. They give Soviet positions on just about every policy they have formulated for dealing with us. I've put you in for the Intelligence Medal of Merit, pretty heady stuff for a new GS-11."

"Thank you, Tony. What about Julie? She worked on this as well. In fact, she saved the operation."

"I put her in for a commendation."

"Maybe that will get her career back on track."

"You are also to be congratulated on your language scores. The best of any student we've sent to FSI for Hungarian. Is there anything you don't do in outstanding fashion?"

"It was a good course."

"Splendid. Now one cautionary note: Bill wanted me to remind you of your conversation with him in the fall. You are single. He had to convince the DCI that it would be all right to give you this assignment. The Hungarians will see a young, good looking hormone happy fellow and start lining up all the Zsa Zsa Gabors in Budapest to run by you."

"Did you ever drive a cab?"

Tony tilted his head to one side clearly not knowing why the question had been put.

"I must say I never did."

"I drove one in Philadelphia after I got out of the army. You get a lot of female passengers who try to convince you it's a barter economy and they have something worth more than the fare. But I kept my eye on the road. What I'm saying is that I've had experience with women and

Bill is better off sending me than he would be sending an unhappy husband, or some guy who just came out of Holy Orders. Besides, at this point there's only one woman I'm interested in."

"Yoiks, zounds and odds bodkins, the truth will out. Should I venture to say who it might be?"

"It doesn't matter. She shot me down."

"Ah, she can be that way. Which reminds me," Tony twisted sideways and bent over to the file drawer, "there is one case I haven't shared with you until now." He held up a single thick manila folder in his pudgy right hand. "This is a case that has gone dormant, but if we can resurrect it, I believe it will be extremely productive."

Frank reached across the desk and took the file from his soon-to-be boss. He looked at the label.

"Spats?" He opened the cover and started skimming the cables from back to front.

"That was his code name. He was deputy chief of the AVH office in Paris and he was recruited by someone we both know and of whom we are very fond." Tony gave just the hint of a smile.

As he looked through the early reporting on the case Frank noticed the date on the recruitment cable, November 21, 1978, and the pseudonym of the reporting officer, Pushteau. He looked at Tony.

"Julie?"

"I once told you that she had a Hungarian connection. She accomplished the recruitment and worked the case skillfully. Unfortunately, as you will see, the fellow never made his first contact after he returned to Hungary."

"Do we have any idea why he didn't show up?"

"None, so please look through it. Since you will get out there before I do, I would like you to make it your first priority to find Mr. Spats. I had hoped that you could discuss the case with the recruiting officer before you left, but she had to attend to family business." Tony tried to conceal his sly smile by pursing his lips and looking down at the stack of papers in front of him.

"Julie's here?"

"She's in New York." Tony raised his head and now his look was serious. "Her father suffered a stroke. She arrived from Brazil on Monday. Since she was to return here anyway in June, the station chief allowed her to pack out early. I'm anxious to have you look for her lost agent, not only to redeem our fair Julie, but because he was such an excellent source of information."

"I'll do my best."

"Given what you've accomplished already, I'm more than happy to settle for that. You are a rare combination, Francis. You possess the things that cannot be taught, but you have worked hard to learn the things that can." Tony twisted his chair, stood and tugged his trousers up over

160

his paunch, but by the time he got around the desk they had slipped down again beneath his belly. "I have to attend an off-site meeting. How does one say *bon voyage* in Hungarian?"

Frank stood.

"*Szerencés utat kívánok.*"

"By the time I could master that, you would be in Budapest. Instead I'll say that you go with all my best wishes. I consider it a stroke of the greatest fortune that I will have you there with me." Tony reached up and Frank stooped a bit. The smaller man held him for several seconds and patted him on the back. "Next time we're together, we'll drink some bull's blood."

Back at his temporary desk Frank pushed aside the file he was working on and opened the one on the Spats case. He was half way through it when he picked up the secure phone and punched in the number of a friend in LA Division. Five minutes later he had Julie's New York address. On the open line he called McLean Florists and ordered a bouquet of yellow roses sent to her home.

It took him another thirty minutes to finish his reading. He put the files in the room safe and walked across the hall to the administrative section. He told the secretary that he had come to check out. She looked at her desk calendar.

"Steve Cooper will take care of you. He's in the third cubicle on the right."

Frank passed several clerks then stuck his head around the third partition. Cooper was on the phone. Frank fidgeted a bit. He looked around the office. There were the usual posters, scenes of exotic places, the Taj Mahal, Ankor Wat, a night photo of the castle at Chenonceaux surrounded by its glittering moat. All of these people would certainly prefer to be there rather than on the bureaucratic treadmill. And he was headed for one such place, provided he could light a fire under this fellow Cooper, who had held up his processing until the last minute. The admin clerk put down the phone.

"Steve, I'm ready to check out."

"Sit down. All your personal affairs wrapped up?"

"Pretty much."

"Ever been to Budapest?"

"No."

"Okay. Since Don Kearns left early and Tony Valletta won't be out there to replace him until August, you'll be living temporarily in Kearns's apartment in the *Népstadion* building. It's back by the soccer stadium. The embassy has promised to find another place for you by the beginning of July. It will be for a single man. You're single, right? No dependents?"

"None."

"Just want to be sure what I have on paper corresponds to the facts. Okay. You sign these papers, here and here." Cooper reached over to hand Frank a pen. It slipped in the exchange and fell off the side of the desk. Frank bent over to pick it up. Down low he noticed Cooper was wearing Allen-Edmonds shoes and had them laced in the European way. Sharp dresser. Frank picked up the pen and signed the insurance forms. "Here is your diplomatic passport. Sign here to show you received it." Frank did as he was told. "Your flight is out of Dulles on Sunday at four. And these are your tickets and your advance. You connect in New York, then New York to Frankfurt on Pan Am. You change planes in Frankfurt on Monday morning still on Pan Am. Here's the receipt. You sign at the bottom." Cooper pointed again to an X on the bottom line. Frank signed again. "That's it. I'll send out the cable letting the station know your arrival time. Somebody from the embassy will meet you at the airport. Good luck."

"Thanks for your help." Frank got up. Cooper did not, but he did extend his hand. It was long and bony. Only then did Frank notice the cane by the coat rack.

Downstairs, Frank headed toward the cafeteria. In the south hall he saw Boguslav Rzepnicki coming toward him. The little man wore his typical scowl. Frank was not enthusiastic about chatting with the fellow, but saw no way to avoid him.

"Bugs, I haven't seen you since Rio."

"I come in only few times. This week I am courier from our building over to here."

"And I just finished nine months of Hungarian."

"I thought you went back to Brazil."

"That fell through. They got somebody else."

"I been out in Athens. But that's over. I don't go again there."

"I leave for Budapest on Sunday."

"So, good to get away from this place."

Frank found it curious. Here was a man who claimed he hated to travel, but couldn't wait to get away from wherever he was. Rzepnicki behaved like a victim and therefore he had become a victim. Now for a moment they both stood there silent. Finally, Frank had to move on.

"Good to see you, Boguslav. I have to hurry, first to lunch, then a lot of errands to run."

Down the hall, Frank turned to his right to go into the cafeteria. He looked back the way he had come. Between the bobbing heads of people coming for lunch he saw Boguslav Rzepnicki again and he was walking in the direction of the admin fellow who had just processed Frank's paperwork, Steve Cooper. Frank had the distinct impression that Cooper was watching both of them.

At four o'clock on Sunday afternoon, Frank flew out of Dulles. When his plane landed at JFK, he walked in a stream of people down the corridor of the Pan Am terminal toward his next gate. Slung over his shoulder was a black garment bag with the suits he would wear when he started at the embassy. He was also toting a carry-on bag with his toilet articles and a copy of a biography of Benjamin Franklin, another Philadelphia boy, to read on the plane.

As he approached the lounge he saw Julie. She was standing under the globe of the blue and white Pan Am logo. She resembled the logo itself, with a sky blue skirt and white blouse that showed her smooth complexion and dark hair to best advantage. When she spotted him, she smiled broadly. Frank couldn't believe it and as he got closer, he was shaking his head.

"What are you doing here?" He set down the carry-on piece and took her hand and kissed her on the cheek. His look showed his puzzlement.

"I just thought it would be nice if you had someone to see you off." She seemed happy at having pulled off the surprise.

"That's it?"

"Yes. Aren't you pleased?"

"I'm delighted, especially since you're the one person I haven't stopped thinking about for the last two weeks."

"Come on. Let's sit down." She walked with him to the crowded gate area and they sat in the row of blue cushioned seats by the broad, high window that overlooked the runways. One 747 was lifting off and moving away from them to the southeast. "I called Tony. He told me that you wouldn't have family up here."

"How did he know that?"

"He said he read it in your file, something he hadn't noticed before. So you really need someone here to wave."

"That's so kind of you."

"You were kind to me. I have never forgotten how you held me that night on the beach just to comfort me. You didn't try to kiss me or paw me." Frank thought "Thank you, Jesus." "And yellow roses are my favorite flower even if they were for my father."

"How is he?"

"A bit better, even two weeks have made a difference." She looked out the window then smoothed her skirt. "Also, Tony said that if I did come out, he wanted me to talk to you about Spats." Frank must have looked crestfallen. "Believe me, Frank, that is not why I came."

"Okay. I certainly don't want to question your motives again. I did that at Christmas and this time around I hope we can get off to a better start."

"We already have." She smiled. He recalled the first time he saw her, stunning and brimming with confidence. Now she seemed less self-assured. She brushed her dark hair back behind her ear. He had the urge to do it for her. What kept going through his mind was that even when she was angry at Christmas, Julie had admitted that she had thought

163

about them seeing each other if he had been single. Now he was, but he intended not to push things."

"Spats looked like a great case," Frank said.

"That's what I thought," she answered.

"And he was the one you had all the trouble over?"

"The rumor was that he was my 'fancy man.' That's what they were calling him in headquarters. But that didn't start until later. His name was Szebrenyi and his first name, if you can believe it, was Attila. I guess you saw that in the file."

"How did he get the code name Spats?"

"He was a snappy dresser. Another case officer met him before I did at a diplomatic lunch. He reported that Attila was really interested in classic cars. Right after I met him, I ordered a number of books on cars from the States, so when I saw him the second time, I talked about Bugattis and Zephyrs. He loved it. I recruited him, or thought I did, in 1978." Obviously she was speaking from memory and seemed to be gazing into a past she found disturbing. She looked back down the concourse for a moment and then turned back to him with her forehead wrinkled in concentration. "I ran him for almost a year. We went through the same drill as you did with Bagatelle, trained him in internal commo."

"If he wasn't after you," Frank realized instantly that he didn't want to start down that road, "and I believe you totally when you say he wasn't, what was his reason for cooperating?"

"Money and his dream car. Just before he left for Budapest, he bought an antique Jaguar, forest green with an inlaid wooden dash, leather seats. He was supposed to make his first meeting on the Danube near the parliament building. Kearns waited, but Attila never showed."

"The file said he didn't show up for the alternate meeting either."

"True. That was the last we heard of him. That's when the rumors started. People at home said that the only reason he saw me was to have sex and the fact that he never showed up once he got back to Budapest was because he got what he wanted. Headquarters said I made up a lot of it."

"So that's the reason you warned me on the beach that I should expect the same thing?"

"Yes. Peter Halley was our deputy in Paris and when he was named chief of station in Brazil and wanted me to go with him, the gossip-mongers had a field day. By now you've probably heard that he was going to leave his wife for me, right?"

"I never believed it. I know how you are about married men." Had that sounded sarcastic? He almost kicked himself. "Nothing provocative" was the thought that went through his mind, but Julie didn't seem to react.

"When a friend of mine told me the rumor, I was sick."

"Helen Hassan?"

164

She looked surprised.

"How did you know?"

"I met her at Christmas just before I saw you."

"Anyway, I didn't deserve it, but more important, Peter and his family didn't deserve it. Tony told me his main goal when he gets to Hungary is to find Spats and I know he wants you to look for him as well."

"And all we really know is that he drives an antique green Jaguar?" he asked.

"Yes, forest green."

"We have no idea where he lives?"

"No."

"And he may not drive the car around every day, or he may have bought it to sell once he got back to Budapest."

"That's certainly possible. He never told me what he intended to do with the car, though I doubt he would part with it."

"Was there anything he liked to do, tennis, soccer, collect stamps?"

"He did like to sail."

"He might go out to Lake Balaton. I'll keep my eyes open. Maybe we can find some way to smoke him out."

Julie nodded and smiled, but it did not appear to be a hopeful smile.

"That's really all there is. Everything else was in the file."

They chatted for forty-five minutes about everything, work, families, people they knew at the agency. He told her about Patrick Kerrane.

"He's going to Prague as the deputy. He's an unusual guy."

"Helen would agree with you."

"Patrick was never one to smooth talk the ladies. He's Irish, born in Belfast, but Catholic. He came here when he was seven or eight." Frank leaned back against the seat, but the hanger of his garment bag dug into his back so he sat forward again. "His father came first and he used to send the family a little money. By the time Patrick's mother brought him over, his father had taken up with another woman. So we had that in common."

"Your father left your mother?"

"No. I mean that he had no father. But at least I ate every day. Patrick once told me they were so poor that for weeks the only thing he took to school for lunch was grapes. Some kid said to him, 'Man, you sure must like grapes.' His mother had to heat hot dogs over a light bulb in their apartment. He told me all this once when he was drunk. He's a pretty angry drunk, and a compulsive gambler. Last time I saw him he was headed for the race track in Laurel. He said he had to score big."

"But what about you? Did you ever know your parents?"

"Yes."

"And how did you lose them?"

Frank hesitated. He looked out the plate glass window at the line of planes taxiing down to the takeoff point. This wasn't something he talked about casually, and he just wasn't sure how to respond. Finally he thought he had found a solution.

"Why don't you come out to Hungary? We'll have dinner up on the Fisherman's Bastion with a gypsy orchestra. I'll tell you the whole story while they play sad songs."

"I'm sorry. I didn't mean to pry. I would like to see Budapest. I've never been there."

The departure announcement came. They both stood.

"Write and let me know when you'd like to do it. Any time is fine with me." Frank swung the garment bag over his shoulder.

"You'll be pretty busy for the first couple of months, but maybe in the fall." She smiled. Frank moved toward the attendant who was checking tickets at the entrance to the corridor leading to the plane. A line had formed ahead of him, but suddenly he stepped aside.

"I want you to know how much I appreciate your coming out here." He stood close to her.

"I hope everything goes well for you. If you should ever see Attila, give him my best. And take care of yourself."

He leaned over and kissed her on the cheek. She stayed close and he could feel and smell her sweet breath.

"That's the same perfume you wore in Santa Teresa."

"Amazing sensory perception, but I've known from the start that you were an extraordinary guy. I'm sorry that I never let you know that." Frank was taken aback. She had tears in her eyes.

He didn't think he was misreading the signals.

Until now their relationship had been like driving over rolling hills with a lot of ups and downs. He had seen himself outside the moat of a castle that he had circled several times without finding a way in. Now the princess was lowering the drawbridge. He kissed her on her full lips and she responded willingly. He kissed her again. She reached up and put her hand on his cheek.

"I guess it's that time," he said. He stepped away and presented his ticket watching Julie all the while.

"*Bon voyage.*"

"Come out in September," The thought that came to him was that love was like jazz. If you had to have someone explain it to you, you didn't get it. He didn't try to figure it out, but as he looked back up the enclosed walkway to see Julie smiling and waving, he knew she was hitting all the right notes.

Chapter 24

In 1982, Janos Kadar was first secretary of the Hungarian Communist Party and president of the country. He had come to office after the 1956 uprising and the fact that he had navigated the shoals and storms of treacherous waters for all those years was one measure of his political seaworthiness. That he had managed to hang on and still keep the relative good will of his fellow Hungarians was further testament to his cunning.

Still, Kadar was a communist and the Hungary that Frank entered was tightly controlled and hostile to the United States. Relations had improved somewhat when the American government returned the Crown of St. Stephen in 1977, but the security services were not about to relent in their effort to neutralize American evildoers. In the eyes of the AVH, Frank Manion was one such devil. He got his first look at their tactics at Budapest's Férihegy airport.

He went through the arrival formalities on his own, which he had expected to do, but in the reception area no one from the embassy was waitng for him. He stood outside the main building for another twenty minutes. Several taxi drivers took a few steps to approach him, but then they backed off. At first Frank didn't understand why, but when he followed their look he knew what was happening. A knockout blonde female driver with a navy blue Mercedes taxi, the only one in sight, was parked parallel to the queue and they were obviously deferring to her.

Finally, Frank got tired of waiting. He shouldered one bag and picked up the other and started down the steps. The blonde woman's taxi pulled up beside him. She got out and came around to open the trunk. Frank saw she was about twenty-something, probably a year or two younger than he was and she was wearing tight navy blue slacks that matched the color of her car and accentuated her well-proportioned curves. She spoke in Hungarian.

"You are going to the city?" She stood by the open trunk.

"Yes."

"Where?"

Frank had to decide. He wasn't sure whether anyone in his apartment building would have a key to the Kearns place, so he figured he should head for the office.

"To the American Embassy on Szabadság Tér."

She nodded and he stuck his bags in the trunk. She didn't hold the door for him as he got in the back. Still, he figured he would tip her well.

No sense in getting the AVH angry right off the bat. She pulled out of the parking area onto the highway.

"You are American?"

"Yes."

"From what part of America?"

"From the Philadelphia part."

"Are all Americans as good looking as you?"

"No. I had a special diet."

"Of course you are joking."

"Yes."

"Are you from a Hungarian family?"

"No."

"But you speak Hungarian so well. How did you learn it?"

"In our diplomatic school."

"For how long did you study?"

"Nine months."

"Again, you are joking."

"This time I'm serious."

She continued to ask questions. Frank knew she would have to fill out a biographic report on him after the ride. He didn't mind answering her, but at the same time he took every opportunity to watch the passing scene. Even allowing for the fact that many airport roads ran through the seamier parts of a town, Frank was not favorably impressed by what he saw. The city had been called the "Paris of the East". He figured it might have deserved that reputation once, but not any more. Things were run down. The trees were in full bloom and there were a lot of them. But the building facades, the shops, the statues all could have used a sand blast. The cars were small and clean, but tinny looking and he could tell they were not well engineered. Traffic moved smoothly enough and it was heavy, but normally that would have indicated prosperity. Not here. This was not Paris. It might be a poor relative.

On Szabadság Square, he got out of the cab, took out his bags and paid the young woman.

"If ever you need a driver, here is my number." She handed him a business card, but there was no company name. Frank was sure she was not in business for herself.

"Thank you. I enjoyed speaking your beautiful language and seeing your beautiful city." This time she didn't ask if he was joking and he didn't say. Let her wonder.

Frank walked toward the door of the sandstone building. It was a thick, beveled glass art-deco style portal covered with heavy black metal grillwork. A gray uniformed militiaman stepped from the booth to the right of the entrance. Frank produced his passport and the fellow saluted and stepped back. Frank rang the bell and someone buzzed him in. At the

168

top of the interior steps a Hungarian receptionist greeted him from behind an elevated desk.

"I'm here to see Mr. Gardener, the commercial attaché." Frank showed his black diplomatic passport.

"Mr. Manion? I am Zhuzha Fekete. Welcome to Budapest. I'll call him." She dialed an extension and apparently talked to Gardener. Thirty seconds later a well-dressed black man with a neatly trimmed beard came out the interior door into the lobby shaking his head. He smiled as he introduced himself.

"I'm Ty Gardener. I really apologize. We only got the telegram fifteen minutes ago saying you were arriving today. I don't know how that happened. Did you have any trouble getting through immigration?"

"None, it wasn't a problem."

"That's a terrible beginning for your posting. We meet everybody at the airport. Anyway, welcome to Budapest. It's just as well that you didn't go to Népstadion. They're repainting the Kearns place. It won't be ready for another week or so. We've got you in the Royal Hotel on Lenin Körút. Do you want to hang around here a bit and get to meet people, or do you want to go there first?"

"I think I'll go to the hotel, at least to unpack. Can I get a cab?"

"Not at all, I'll drive you. It's the least I can do. I'll get my keys."

Frank was pleased. His cover was as a second commercial attaché and he would be working with Gardener, who was a legitimate State Department officer. Frank's immediate impression of the man was that he would be easy to get along with.

Gardener reappeared and they started out the door.

"Let me help you," Gardener offered. He shouldered the garment bag while Frank continued to carry the larger suitcase. "My car is up the street."

As they walked Frank read the inscription over the door of the building next to the embassy. It was the National Bank. He looked out across the square. There was a monument in the center, an obelisk.

"Where are you from Tyrone?"

"Call me Ty. I'm from Detroit. But we've been in Bethesda since 1970, except for three years in Cameroon. We got here two years ago."

"Do you like it?"

"It's been good. We have a new ambassador. You'll meet him, Walter Crittenden. He's a Republican, a political appointee."

"Easy to work for?"

"I've had no problem."

Gardener's car was a little red Toyota. They put the larger of Frank's bags in the trunk and the other on the back seat and started off across the square. Frank lowered the vanity mirror and watched as they drove, but in the five minutes it took them to get to the Royal he saw no one behind them. A red streetcar passed them on the left as Gardener got out on the driver's side. He walked ahead of Frank into the hotel and across the lobby to the front desk.

"This is Mister Manion. He has a reservation made by the American Embassy. It was for tomorrow, but he arrived a day early."

Once again, it struck Frank that the hotel, like the city in general, had seen better days. The elevator creaked and shuddered a bit as they went up to the third floor and the red and gold patterned hallway carpet was faded and even threadbare in some spots.

"I'll leave you to get settled," Gardener told him. "This is the welcome kit. It gives you all sorts of information. Here." He handed Frank a calling card. "This is my number. If you need anything, just give me a call." He took a map from the plastic envelope and spread it on the bed. "Here's where we are on Lenin Körút." Gardener pointed to a spot on the map. "This is the embassy. We won't expect you in today. Tomorrow, you can either get a cab, or if the weather's good, you might want to walk. Nancy, my wife, also reminded me that we'd like to have you come to dinner. How about tomorrow evening, say six o'clock?"

"That's kind of you. How do I get to your place?"

"We live up on the Vár. My address is on my card. Any cab driver can find it."

"Fine, and what are the embassy hours?"

"We start at eight-thirty. Most people get in around eight-fifteen."

Frank unpacked only what he figured he would need that day. He put nothing in drawers. As he looked around the room, he couldn't understand the logic of the layout. There was a stand-alone chiffonier in one corner with a mirror on top, but it slanted out from the wall. Double doors opened to an adjoining sitting room and again in the far corner there was a mirror that was oddly placed. It was only when he put his toilet articles on the shelf over the sink in the bathroom that he realized why things were positioned that way. He turned from the sink and it immediately struck him that with his back to the bathroom mirror and with the other mirrors angled as they were, he could see every nook and cranny in both rooms. That meant that the mirror over the sink, which was fixed firmly on the common wall with the next room down the hall, was a see-through mirror and behind it was the observation post. Someone was sitting there watching him.

The next morning before he left the room, he partially unzipped one of the compartments in his carry-on bag and counted the notches on the zipper, then with map in hand he set off for the embassy. The morning air was pleasantly cool with the promise of a warming sun to come. He entered Liszt Ferenc Square and stopped on the other side of the statue of the composer and looked back briefly, but saw no one. That troubled him. The AVH knew he was there, but where were they?

At the embassy he passed the same receptionist then rode the tiny elevator to the third floor where he rang the bell outside a vaulted room. Charlie Noble, the communicator, swung open the steel door.

"Hey, I been waitin' for ya. Now I don't have to go to any more staff meetings." Noble stood about five feet eight and had a stocky barrel-chested build. He was dressed in a plaid short-sleeved cotton shirt, no tie, khaki pants and gray athletic shoes. His hair was black, his skin was pale and his teeth were bad with a very prominent gap between the two top teeth in front. He wore glasses that made his eyes look abnormally large. He looked to be in his late thirties.

"Is it okay to talk?" Frank asked.

"Yeah. I got the audio shield on." Charlie raised his arm toward the ceiling. Frank thought that was a good thing since Charlie had a booming voice that sounded even louder in the cramped space. "Headquarters screwed up as per usual. We only got your travel cable just about the time your plane was gettin' here." Frank looked around. The room was tiny, probably six by eight. It was divided by a table with open shelves in the center that could serve anyone sitting on either side.

"That's what Ty Gardener said. But the admin guy promised to send out my itinerary a couple of days ago."

"He didn't." Now Noble just stood there with a matter-of-fact expression on his face. He looked as if he could become testy pretty easily. He may have thought Frank was questioning his veracity or his competence, or he could have been trying to size up the new kid on the block. Frank didn't know which. "With Jack Dorsey on home leave, I been jumpin' more than a shit house mouse, but I guaran-damn-tee you there was no message."

"Not a problem. I made it."

"Now that you're here, I got to send out your arrival message. You want to write it, or should I?"

"I'll be happy to do it since you're so busy. But if you do it, just say I got here fine."

"Good. I'll do it. This is the real commo shack."

Just off the tiny room was one that was half that size and it was crammed with transmitters and receivers.

"Where are you from, Charlie?"

"West Virginia. Clarksburg, coal country. My old man's still back there. He's got emphysema from all the coal dust and the cigarettes. I smoke only cigars."

"Anything I should know before I go to the staff meeting?"

"Nah, it's all the same old bullshit. They'll do some butt sniffin', but don't let it bother you. After it's over I'll meet you in your office. Just go up the stairs behind the marine house. You'll see the vault door at the top."

Frank went out into the hall and walked to the far end. Several people were ahead of him and he followed them through another ciphered door. Inside he saw what looked like a room under construction. The walls were stripped and in the center of the space sitting on wooden beams was a plastic cube, a room within a room. It was known in all embassies as "the bubble." The door was open and staffers were taking their places on uncushioned chairs around a long table. At the head sat a man who was obviously Ambassador Walter Crittenden.

Frank's first impression was that Crittenden had just stepped out of central casting. Even seated he appeared tall and thin. He was dressed in a charcoal gray pin-striped suit and a black tie with tiny white dots. His silver-gray hair was combed back from his high forehead. He had sharp blue eyes, a bit darker than Frank's. He held forth for about ten minutes then went around the table and each person spoke. Crittenden spoke when it was Frank's turn.

"And this is Frank Manion, a Philadelphia boy. Frank's going to be working with Ty and doing that funny business on the side."

"Great," Frank thought. Crittenden's sense of security left a lot to be desired. The ambassador extended his hand in Frank's direction and Frank waved to everyone. But Tony had assured Frank that he would handle all dealings with the ambassador. Frank figured his new boss would have his hands full. Afterward, he climbed the back stairs as Charlie Noble had told him to.

"Welcome to your home away from home. This is where you'll sit for the next two or three years if you don't get PNG'd." Frank was surprised at the size of the room. It was probably thirty-five by twenty-five with two desks positioned at the far end. Charlie walked to one of them. Frank watched over his shoulder as Charlie opened a cabinet behind the desk and switched on the audio defenses.

"Okay now?" Frank asked.

"Yeah, but you should always try to keep the talk to a minimum even with this thing on. The Hungarians are smart monkeys. With these common walls we got with the buildings they control, they're always tryin' somethin'."

"Like what?"

"Last year they got into the embassy. They came through the third floor window. They rappelled down from the roof, sawed through the bars and put some wooden pieces in their place. Overnight they machined the bars so they could screw them in and out. Then they came in at least once a week."

"I never saw that in the files at home. How did you find out?"

"We caught 'em. Me and the gunney figured somethin' was odd, so we stayed for three or four nights. Sure enough, we got 'em in the hall."

"What happened?"

"The gunney had his pistol out. We marched 'em down to the front door. We knew we were in trouble when we got 'em outside and the militiaman saluted them. You got your hands full. This is their ballpark. You don't play by their rules they're gonna slap you upside the head."

"I'll keep that in mind. Let me ask you something."

"Shoot."

"How would the AVH have known I was going to arrive yesterday when nobody in the embassy did?"

"Beats me. What makes you think they knew?"

"How many blonde bombshells have you seen here driving Mercedes taxis?"

"Like I said, they're smart monkeys."

That evening, Frank checked the zipper on his bag and saw that someone had been through his luggage. Outside it was still light when he caught a taxi and rode across the Danube and up the hill to the fortress. This was where the Germans had taken a stand when the Russians were chasing them back to Berlin in World War Two. But despite the shelling the houses had retained their medieval look, with pastel shades and tiled roofs. The Gardeners' home sat at the far end of the thick wall that formed the enclave. Nancy Gardener greeted him at the door.

"My, my, aren't you easy on the eyes." Frank had to laugh. "The word is already out there's a handsome sport in town. The lady bees are going to be buzzing around you, honey."

Nancy was as ebullient and bouncy as Ty was taciturn. She had short hair, dark brown eyes and a well turned figure.

"There's only one queen bee I'm interested in right now."

"Well she'd better get out here fast. I hear that the ladies in Népstadion intend to get you in the laundry room and not let you out until they've washed your socks."

Frank laughed again.

In the enormous living room on a sofa against the wall sat Charlie Noble and his wife Joanie. For the first time Frank understood that there was a class division in the embassy. There were the officers with college degrees and accompanying privileges, then there were the service people, who constituted a kind of sub-culture. It struck Frank as ironic that the black man was the former and the white man the latter. Gardener was Harvard-educated, polished and urbane. Charlie was earthy and sometimes crude. That didn't appear to pose any problem for either one.

For Frank it was his first meal with black people. In his school years at Stephen Girard he had lived in an enclave with a ten foot brick wall separating him and the other students from the surrounding black community. "Injun country" many of the boys called it. On several of his outings Frank had gotten into confrontations with the local blacks. He had come back to the school infirmary twice with knife wounds. He wasn't going to bring that up at dinner.

Afterward the Nobles dropped him off at his hotel just before eleven and he arrived in the office by seven-thirty the next morning. Charlie was still working on the cable traffic for the day so there was nothing to read. Frank started a letter to Julie.

"That was quite a send-off," he wrote. "All night on the plane I could think only about your kisses. Right after takeoff, we flew over Shea Stadium. The sun was low in the west, but it hadn't set. The lights were already on and I could see the Mets or the other team out on the field. I've left the country several times before, but this time it was harder to say goodbye to America. The song says, 'It's a long, long while from May to December.' For me September can't come soon enough. I hope you'll decide to visit me."

For the rest of the week every evening he wandered the streets. On Friday night he stood outside a movie theater near Rákóczi Street studying the glass-covered displays. They were showing what looked like a Hungarian swashbuckler from the fifties. There was an additional advertisement around the side just past the entrance and he walked to it. Suddenly, someone came around the corner behind him. Frank turned and saw the fellow as he was walking away. He was wearing blue jeans and on his left back pocket he had an elaborate embroidered design. For Frank, it was like Moses' burning bush. He had seen that same pattern at least as long ago as Monday night, the day he arrived. There couldn't have been another like it. He realized that he had been under surveillance the whole time and had never spotted it.

With that sighting everything changed. Frank recognized that there was a difference between suspecting he was being followed and knowing that he was. On Saturday, he saw two more of his watchers. But it was on Sunday, a day he would later call "Bloody Sunday," that the floodgates opened and he finally understood what he was up against.

Strolling with the weekend crowds he noticed young people, men and women in their mid-twenties or so wearing T-shirts with the logos of U.S. universities. On his way back to his hotel, he entered a sweets shop. The place was crowded. Frank studied the assortment of cakes, éclairs, Napoleons and meringues in the glass cases then stood in the queue to order some bread for sandwiches. As he was waiting for his turn, he looked out the plate glass window. On the other side of the broad avenue he saw a tall fellow he had noticed earlier that morning. He was wearing one of the school shirts. Surrounding him were twenty to twenty-five more young people, many of them with shirts from different universities, but probably half were wearing other outfits. The taller fellow at the center of the gathering was talking to this team and obviously instructing them, positioning them to pick Frank up when he came out of the shop. When he did walk outside, Frank knew he was stepping into a new

174

world, one inhabited by lions and tigers and bears, "Injun territory." He had promised Tony and Julie that he would do his best to find Spats. He had dealt with more than his share of adversity in his life and come through it intact and confident. But now for the first time in a long time he wondered whether his best would be good enough.

Chapter 25

Vladimir could see that Natasha had settled into her room and routine. After their lovemaking, she had neatly spread a light green coverlet over the bed and placed a small leaf-green pillow embroidered with daffodils at the head. The widow who owned the flat had been away fifty percent of the time in winter and was absent all the time now that it was summer. Apparently she had taken to Natasha and allowed her the run of the small place with kitchen and bathroom privileges and she had enough influence with the building super that he didn't report her. Either that or the old lady was paying him off.

On this late June Saturday morning an oppressive heat had settled on Moscow. The air in the flat was stuffy. Vladimir sprawled on a sofa with synthetic covered cushions and one broken spring and read an old issue of *Ogonyëk* as Natasha fixed breakfast for him in the kitchen. She wore a yellow and white daisy apron over an asparagus-green dress. She was singing to herself, *Kalinushka*, one of her country songs. He could smell and hear the sizzle of the onions she was frying.

"Volodya, come join me. It's almost ready."

"I'll come when it is ready."

"Well it is, yes. It's ready now." He got up reluctantly. The odor and heat were stronger still as he moved into the kitchen. Natasha was standing at the stove. "Would you like water?"

"No. We should open the window. It's stuffy in here. Air out the place while we can."

"The windows are stuck. You should do it after we eat."

"By then I may have suffocated."

"You are always exaggerating. And why are you so angry? I feel that just below your skin you are simmering and ready to explode."

"You've been standing near that stove too long in this heat. You have combustion on the brain. I may explode. You will simply melt."

"I got some milk. Would you like some in your tea?"

"I already told you. No."

"On the farm we used to take whole milk, add a little vinegar, let it sit, pour off the whey and the rest was firm. The top layer still had wonderful cream. At this time of year we used to eat dilled new potatoes with sour milk."

"Listen to yourself. You're always talking about food. If you go on this way, you'll be one hundred fifty kilos by the time you're forty-five."

"And you're always talking about Rio. But you can get the same thing here."

"No. You are wrong. I miss the sun."

"And what is that in the sky that is roasting us?"

"It's not the same. You have to see the difference to understand. I never used to care about it. But you see, when all of your world is gray, you can't know that there is a blue and a green and a yellow. Once you see the colors, you cannot go back. You can never understand your own condition until you know some alternative. It's like Adam and Eve."

"What are you going on about?" She carried the frying pan in one hand and held a wooden spoon in the other. She had buttered bread for him and brewed tea and now she covered the bread with the fried onions. On the other side of the table, she spooned another portion onto her own slice of bread.

"What I'm saying is that the devil did not lie to Adam and Eve. He told them that if they ate the forbidden apple, they would have a knowledge that only God had. Until then they had known only good and happiness, but they never understood what happiness was because they never knew misery and evil. When they ate the apple they knew misery and evil. They knew what God knew. That's when they understood what they had lost. For us here in the Union everything is gray and misery and evil are all we've ever known."

"You can get yourself in a lot of trouble talking that way Vladimir Sergeyevich." She used his name and patronymic for emphasis, he thought. "Here where it's cold you stay stiff. Out there in the heat it is you who would melt."

Vladimir, too, had his routine. Rather than sleep immediately after their night shift, he preferred to get out in the air and even attend his martial arts classes out at the Dynamo Sports Complex. But today, Saturday, he had promised that before he went for his lesson, he would accompany Natasha to GUM, the state department store on the eastern side of Red Square. She had pestered him to use his wife's pass to gain admission into Section One Hundred, a special clothing store for the party elite. After breakfast they took the metro and got off at Revolution Square. As they walked across the great expanse and with a blue sky above them, Vladimir should have felt uplifted. Instead, he missed Brazil even more.

"Have you told your wife yet?" Natasha asked.

"No. Do you think she would have given me this pass if I had?"

"When do you plan to tell her?"

"Soon."

"You said that six months ago." Natasha now expected him to marry her. He had not really promised that he would, but he had to admit to himself that neither had he entirely disabused her of this notion. "Sometimes I get the feeling that you are just using me."

177

"For what, what are you good for little farm girl?" He laughed and squeezed her, his fingers pressing the muscles of her upper arm, soft and cool in her short-sleeved blouse. She pulled away angrily.

"I don't like such talk. I helped you get your position."

"And you would still be living with your cousin if I hadn't told you about the flat. We don't use each other. We help each other as good comrades should."

"Do you plan to marry me or not?"

"First I have to rid myself of that harridan. She's a millstone around my neck."

"And when do you expect to do that?"

"Soon."

Inside the store, they walked through the main arcade. The steel frame and glass construction called to mind the great train stations of Paris and London designed by Eiffel. They rode the polished brass-trimmed elevator to the top floor and Vladimir presented the pass to the guard, who waved them along.

"My God, Italian clothes, French designers," Natasha covered her open mouth with her hand.

"I can't spend too much time here. I have to get out to Dynamo. And my wife will be home this afternoon. I should be there."

The room was crowded and Vladimir noted that most of the clients were older men, a few with young women on their arms. These girls tried to appear more sophisticated than Natasha, but Vladimir could see the glow of avarice in their eyes.

"Cashmere," Natasha held a bright red sweater up to her chest and looked down. Now she brought the garment to her face and rubbed it gently around her cheeks. "But it costs five hundred rubles."

"We'll take it. Here." Vladimir counted out the money. "Now you can't say I'm not a good comrade. Take it and let's go. I find this place depressing."

At eleven-thirty, Vladimir was perspiring profusely and the heat was only partly responsible. He had gone through his drills and had a good workout with his instructor and was now delivering one-legged side kicks and punches to the body bag. Suddenly, someone called from the door of the gymnasium.

"Kick the bastard again. Yes. Harder." Vladimir dropped his arms and turned. There in the doorway stood Anatoliy Barchuk.

"Tolya? What the hell are you doing here? Are you back for good?"

"I might ask you the same thing? How did you manage to get in here?" Barchuk came closer and they shook hands. He was wearing soccer shorts, a sopping wet Dynamo T-shirt and cleats. In a conspiratorial voice he asked, "Have you joined the organs?" Vladimir understood that Barchuk was referring to the fact that the Dynamo sports complex was mostly limited to KGB personnel. It was known throughout the Union that KGB people referred to themselves as the organs. Vladimir didn't know the origin of the term, whether it was musical or sexual, but in Moscow parlance it was an unwelcome word.

"My wife got me the pass through her father. You remember Irina?"

"Yes, of course. How is she?"

"Well." Vladimir knew that Irina would certainly have told this swine that her husband had found out about their affair in Rio. But there was a certain protocol involved. Neither man would mention it to the other.

"So, have you finished your workout?" Barchuk asked.

"Yes, just now."

"Come, we can change and have lunch."

"I'd like to, Tolya, but Irina is waiting. I haven't been home since yesterday afternoon. I'm working the night shift at the ministry and I came here from there." Vladimir had thought quickly. He figured that if he told Barchuk about his night work, the son-of-a-bitch might realize that Irina was free every evening and probably for much of the day as well while Vladimir slept. If Vladimir got the two of them back together, Irina would be away from the flat even more often than she was and she would be less able to impede his own activities.

"Well at least walk with me to the locker room," Barchuk draped his arm over Vladimir's shoulder.

"Yes. I've done enough damage for one day. So, I ask again. Are you finished in Rio?"

"Yes. We got back only two weeks ago. It was getting chilly there when we left."

"Chilly? Have you forgotten so quickly what winter is like here?"

"No. I remember. And I'm looking forward to it. Rio was too goddamn hot."

"Maybe you're referring to the women, not the weather."

Barchuk laughed.

"Them, too."

In the shower they were alone. Vladimir soaped himself and glanced occasionally at Barchuk. The fellow may have begun to work out on the soccer pitch, but he had a long way to go to get in shape. His legs were spindly and his arms were like toothpicks. He did have an ample belly, but it sagged. If Irina had found this guy attractive she must have been looking only at his face, which was handsome in a rugged way. She could not have been seduced by his cock, which was so short it was almost covered by the surrounding hair. Somehow it did not disturb Vladimir to think that the man's member had penetrated his wife.

"Volodya, you enjoy coming here, right?" Barchuk asked as he soaped his armpits.

"I get a good workout."

"We have the best facilities in Moscow."

Vladimir understood that once again, Barchuk's "We" meant the KGB.

"Yes, top notch."

"Have you ever considered joining the organs?"

Vladimir was taken aback by the question. While he had been briefed by the KGB before he went to Rio, he had never been approached to join them, though he knew other lads in the ministry who had been.

"I never thought about it, no."

"You should. I could put in a good word for you." Barchuk dropped his soap. As he bent over, Vladimir saw how scrawny his ass was. "Think about it." Vladimir realized that he resented this fellow not because of the affair with Irina, but because he was of the class Vladimir hated. For an instant he thought about kicking this sorry sod to death and leaving him on the shower floor with his blood running down the drain.

Ten hours later at the ministry, Natasha took her first break.

"I'm going to the ladies room."

"Of course, take your time."

Vladimir watched her start down the hall. He closed the door and immediately went to his satchel and removed the camera, then grabbed the Washington cables from the rear of the slots where he had stuck them. He cleared a space on the table and stacked the messages in the middle and began to photograph them. He had gotten this down to a routine by now, but it still took him about thirty seconds. When he finished with the Washington stack, he put the camera on the table and was replacing the messages in their slot when he heard the door open. He felt a chill come over him. He had forgotten to lock it.

"What is that for?" Natasha looked from the camera on the table up at Vladimir.

"That was quick."

"I forgot my purse. You didn't answer me. I asked about the camera."

"Go powder your nose. When you come back, I'll show you."

She just shook her head on her way back out the door. If he had needed time to come up with some explanation, Natasha's absence would have given him five minutes. But, in fact, Vladimir had decided instantly what he was going to do even though he had not given any thought ahead of time to what he would say if he were caught. Natasha came in the door once again. He still had the camera on the table.

"Close the door and lock it." She looked surprised.

"Why?"

"You'll see. Just do it." She shut the door and flipped the small dead bolt.

"What are you doing?" She looked up at him as he began to unbutton her blouse. At first she put her hand on his to stop him, but he took his other hand and put it between her legs and began to caress her. Now she didn't resist. He undid her skirt and she stood there wearing only her bra and panties.

"Take them off." Vladimir picked up the camera and changed the focus.

"My God, what are you going to do?" Natasha asked the question as she was unsnapping her brassiere. But this time a smile played on her lips.

"Take off your panties." Again, she did as she was told and now she giggled.

"You're crazy. Is this the kind of thing you did in Brazil?"

"Sure." He put the camera on one of the piles of paper and lifted Natasha onto the table.

"This won't make a flash, will it?"

"No. It's low light film. Now show me what you have." She laughed, but began to take different poses. "Hold it." Vladimir snapped the shutter. "Another." Natasha twisted to her side. "Good."

"No one can see these, Volodya."

"Just you and me. Now the other way, yes, that's it." He snapped again. After several more shots he put the camera down again. "Now stay there." He undressed and climbed onto the table and on top of her.

After their adventure, they both got dressed.

"I have to go back to the ladies room to wash up."

"Sure."

When Natasha had gone, Vladimir put the camera in his haversack and stuck the remaining messages he intended to photograph in his shirt and buttoned it. This time he had been careless, but he would finish his work in the men's room and from now on that is where he would take his photos. He laughed out loud. He was thinking that he would love to see the Americans' faces when they developed this batch. Spying was truly an unpredictable business.

Chapter 26

The chauffeur-driven black Moskvich arrived at the main entrance to the Lubyanka headquarters of the KGB at eight fifty-five precisely. For Russians living under the Soviet regime, the ancient prison had always been a place of horrors. In everyday parlance, it was known as the "Government Terror." Many went in, but few came out. The driver stepped from the car, walked around and opened the rear door for his Hungarian passenger. Imre Galos straightened, stood beside the limousine for a moment and looked back across the square past the statue of Felix Dzerzhinsky to the Children's World Toy Store and made a mental note to buy some souvenirs for his grandchildren before he returned to Budapest.

Just as General Peter Acs had predicted, Galos had been appointed director of the AVH, the Hungarian Security Service. With the promotion in 1976, Galos, too, had become a general. In the following six years as director he had dealt often with the head of his Soviet counterpart service, the KGB. For this visit, however, he had requested a meeting with the heads of the First and Second Chief Directorates. He had met both men before, but usually with their boss. Today Vitaliy Nekrasin, the chief of the KGB, was traveling, so Galos would talk directly to the two subordinates.

Although the offices of Peter Borisovich Kuzminsky's First Chief Directorate had been moved out to Yasenovo beyond the Moscow ring road, he had consented to join Galos and Alexander Pavlovich Voroshilov, boss of the Second Chief Directorate, at the Lubyanka. The young aide assigned to escort General Galos greeted him on the steps and walked with him past the guards at the entrance. They took a private elevator to the second floor. From a small anteroom, Galos was shown into a spacious, blue-carpeted conference room. At the far end of a long polished mahogany table sat the two men he had come to see. They stood and welcomed him.

"Comrade Galos, Imre, good to see you." Voroshilov shook hands and kissed him on both cheeks, as did Kuzminsky. A white-jacketed young attendant stood off to one side. Voroshilov motioned to him. "Will you take some coffee?"

"No, thank you, Alexander Pavlovich."

"Cognac, perhaps?"

"Thank you, no. I just had breakfast at the guest house."

Voroshilov waved again at the waiter, who walked back into the shadows and left the room by a side door.

"So, to what do we owe the honor?" Voroshilov asked. "It's unusual that you requested to talk with both of us." Kuzminsky nodded. He was leaning forward with his elbows on the table, his fingers intertwined under his chin.

"I realize that. And I'll get to the point quickly in order not to take up too much of your time." Galos reached in his shirt pocket and took out a pack of *Munkás* cigarettes and pulled one of the copper ashtrays toward him. "Do you mind if I smoke?"

"Not at all," Voroshilov answered. "Would you prefer a cigar?" He stood and stretched for one of the four humidors spaced down the length of the table. "They're Cuban."

"No. Thank you." Galos lit his cigarette and leaned back to exhale the smoke toward the ceiling then looked at the two men. He coughed a raw hacking cough. His constant smoking was finally taking its toll. His complexion had turned gray and his legendary work habits left little time for exercise or distractions. He was not a well man, but as always he put aside any thought of his own well being and got to the matter at hand. "Some years ago, we acquired a source who has been giving us the names and biographic data of personnel of the American CIA. We have passed that information on to you as we received it."

Galos, as a security man, was practiced in the art of dissembling. What he had just said was not correct to the letter, but the product handed over to the Russians was accurate and genuine and Imre's tone and facial expression did not waver or reveal uncertainty.

"Yes, and we have appreciated your consideration in doing so," Kuzminsky said. "Our lads who work abroad have a great advantage in knowing who it is they're dealing with. And I can't think of one instance when you have given us erroneous information."

"And with what you have given us," Voroshilov added, "the boys in my directorate have been able to concentrate our efforts to neutralize the activities of those CIA people here in Moscow and up in Leningrad rather than having to waste time looking at all of their diplomats and trying to figure out which of them are the spies. This saves us a lot of manpower. I second what my comrade said. You have never been wrong." He gave Galos a military salute.

"That is because the person passing that information is someone who works inside the CIA itself," Galos said.

"We guessed as much." Voroshilov looked at Kuzminsky, who nodded again. "We didn't want to pry, of course. And we are certainly grateful for what you have told us." This was a bold faced lie. The KGB had exerted constant pressure on the AVH to run this case jointly, which meant they wanted to control the whole thing. Imre Galos had resisted their overtures. Voroshilov took a sip from the demitasse in front of him. "Is there a problem now?"

"Not at all," Galos hastened to reassure them. "On the contrary, our source now seems to be expanding his contacts. Up to this point, those identities were all he seemed able to acquire. But recently he sent us new information that concerns the KGB directly and, in fact, must be of interest to each of you in your respective positions."

Both Russians looked at each other then back at Galos. Kuzminskiy took his arms from the table and straightened in his chair. Galos puffed on his cigarette then positioned it on the edge of the ashtray.

"You have our attention." Voroshilov smiled.

"Apparently one of your officers in Athens has been the target of an audio operation mounted by the CIA. Our chap has not provided his name. Presumably he is not in a position to know it. But it has come out that your officer will be returning to Moscow in August, but going by way of Rome. And while he is in Rome he intends to meet an Italian agent he recruited some years ago. The CIA is in touch with the Italians and they plan to set a trap to catch both of them. From that information, even though it is incomplete, I presume it will not be difficult to figure out who the target is."

Voroshilov looked directly at Kuzminsky. It was the job of the First Chief Directorate to conduct intelligence-gathering operations outside the Soviet Union, so this clearly fell into Kuzminsky's basket. He reached for one of the many pads of notepaper and took a pen from the box on the table and scribbled a few sentences. Then he looked up.

"Is that it?" he asked.

"Not quite," Galos answered. "I have another bit of information and it may concern both of you." Galos picked up his cigarette and took another puff. He felt he could take his time now and that no matter how quickly or slowly he delivered his report, they would bear with him. He coughed four or five times, took out a handkerchief and wiped his lips. He reached for a silver water pitcher, poured himself a glass and took several swallows. "This same source reported that the CIA attempted to recruit one of your diplomats last year in Rio de Janeiro. This chap became sexually involved with a Brazilian woman. No doubt the CIA tried to blackmail him to gain his cooperation. We are not certain that he was from the KGB. He may have been from the Foreign Ministry. It was in March and April."

Kuzminsky's mouth opened and he stopped taking notes. Clearly, he was surprised, but he appeared to recover quickly.

"That happens from time to time, of course," he said. "Most of the time our boys report the approach. Occasionally they do not, but if you give details, I can look into it." He looked at Voroshilov. Galos understood the intra-service rivalry. If a KGB man serving abroad had been recruited, it would certainly be a black mark against the First Chief

Directorate and Kuzminsky himself. But Galos had to let the chips fall where they might, but at the same time he wanted to be precise.

"I would repeat that we do not know for certain that the diplomat in this case was a member of your service. However, in this instance," Galos went on, "our source believes the CIA succeeded. The reason I asked you both here is because this fellow is now back here in Moscow."

"So this is where it concerns me?" Voroshilov asked. But it was a rhetorical question. Once a KGB man or any Soviet returned home and was under suspicion, the Second Chief Directorate would take over the case.

"Yes," Galos said. "But I must stress that the information I have given you is known by only a handful of people. Within my service we have kept knowledge of our source strictly limited, so I must ask that whatever investigation you undertake not be connected to the AVH in any way."

"I understand. Do you have a name this time?" Kuzminsky asked.

"Yes," Imre Galos replied. "The CIA has given him a code name: Bagatelle." Now he took one long drag on his cigarette and exhaled very slowly. He had that tickling scratchy sensation that usually required a cough, but this time he suppressed it. "His real name is Vladimir Sergeyevich Shurin."

Chapter 27

Early on the morning of July fourteenth, Frank Manion swung open the vault door, punched the cipher buttons and walked into the ever-cramped communications office. The day before, he had met the second communicator, Paul Dorsey, who had returned from six weeks of home leave. Dorsey was twisting dials on one of the receivers. He only looked back at Frank and waved. He was as quiet and reserved as Charlie Noble was voluble and garrulous. Today, Frank was there to talk to Charlie, who was sitting on the far side of the small desk collating the sheets of multi-page incoming messages and chewing on an unlit cigar.

"It's all set?" Frank asked.

"Yeah, here are the keys. Joanie's gonna leave it parked out on Pushkin behind the National Museum. It's a dark blue VW. There's a pair of baby shoes hangin' on the rear view mirror. They were my son Richard's."

"I appreciate it, Charlie."

"Don't mention it. I hope it works."

At precisely noon, Frank took the elevator to the embassy basement. He was carrying a brown shopping bag. The night before, he had sent his navy suit, a white shirt, navy and silver striped tie and black cap-toe dress shoes home with Charlie in another shopping bag. Charlie's wife Joanie was supposed to take them with her today in their car. The whole idea was that Joanie was never under surveillance when she went out, whereas the surveillance on Frank had increased in intensity, so Frank would use her car. All he had to do now was to get out of the embassy unnoticed and make it to the National Museum where the car was parked.

In the basement men's room Frank entered a stall and slipped the bolt on the door. He had left his suit jacket in his office and now he took off his shirt and tie, pants and shoes. From the brown sack he pulled out a Hungarian workman's outfit, blue bib coveralls with shoulder straps, a blue denim shirt and a cotton cap. In the bottom of the bag was a pair of worn workman's boots. He had to balance first on one foot, then the other and lean against the walls of the stall as he put the old clothes on and stuffed his own in the bag. Finally, he took a small plastic kit and his bottle of actor's glue from the pocket of the coveralls. He dabbed the glue above his lip, let it grow tacky then attached a moustache from the kit that matched his dark hair. He flipped open the case and looked in the small mirror inside the cover to be sure his new addition was on straight.

Finally, he put on a pair of clear lens glasses and stuck the cap on his head.

Down the hall from the bathroom he walked into the commissary. The side door stood open and as he did each day at this time, a deliveryman was carrying in crates of produce. Frank walked straight through the store and out the side door. He lowered his head slightly, turned right and headed down Perczel Street and through the open double doors into the closed market on Rosenburg Házaspár. At midday the market was crowded. Frank went to the pepper stalls on the left side of the cavernous room. He stood where he could watch the entrance. Customers, mostly women, were milling about examining the produce. Only a few people came through the main doors and none of them looked suspicious. After several minutes Frank knew he had eluded the massive surveillance that blanketed the embassy and he walked back through the market and out the opposite doors on Vadász utca.

It took him almost twenty minutes by bus to get to the National Museum and to find Charlie's car, but it was just where the communicator had said it would be. The suit, shirt and tie he had sent home with Charlie the night before were hanging on the hook above the rear window. His dress shoes were on the floor. So far, so good, but this would all be wasted without a bit more luck.

He drove for almost a mile along Rákóczi Street then pulled to the right and slowed down as if he were looking for a parking place. He turned right on Berzsenyi utca. Still there was no sign of surveillance. There were almost no parking places and he went down two blocks, turned again and passed the French Embassy. Several guests were arriving for what Frank knew was the Bastille Day reception. He himself had received an invitation and had considered going, but had decided to take this approach instead. He turned slowly into Kenyermezö utca. He could see that the roots of the thick-leafed plane trees had lifted some of the cement blocks on the sidewalk. This was an old neighborhood. The brownstone buildings along the street were handsome and he wondered what it would be like to spend one's life in one of them. His daydream ended when he looked ahead again and saw the forest green Jaguar.

The first thing that came to Frank's mind was that this was just like finding Shurin's car in Rio. The Jaguar was parked half a dozen cars ahead of him on the right side of Kenyermezö. He passed the car slowly. It was squeezed in too close to the car behind it for him to be able to see the license plate, but he knew he had found what he was looking for.

He drove around the block. As he pulled back into the street, a man and a little girl stopped beside a yellow Lada two cars in from the corner. Frank pulled to his right and waited. The man unlocked the passenger door and the little girl got in. He went around to the driver's side, got in and pulled out. Frank backed the VW into the spot. Now he needed only one final blessing from heaven. As he sat waiting, he thought that luck played a major role in this work. You could do all the planning you wanted, but without luck you would never succeed.

Frank sat for over thirty minutes. He had lowered his window. The sun was almost directly overhead and created a narrow strip of light between the trees down the middle of the street. The day was as pleasant as could be, but Frank was perspiring. Once again, he checked the moustache. He was tempted just to pull it off, but thought it might keep some roving surveillance team from identifying him by sight.

At the far end of the block from the direction of the French Embassy, a man and woman turned into the street. The man was walking behind the woman and Frank had caught only a glimpse of him from this distance. He saw that the fellow was wearing a dark suit and tie. He might be coming from the reception.

As the couple passed each car in the row and got closer, Frank's heart began beating faster. The woman stopped at the passenger door of the Jaguar and the man came from behind her to open the door. Frank had all he could do to keep from shouting for joy. The fellow was about five eight and a hundred fifty pounds. His navy pin-striped suit was snappy. Frank guessed it was an Armani or Pierre Cardin. He was wearing a red tie, probably Hermès. He had a black goatee, which didn't appear in his file photo, but it was definitely Spats. The only problem was that he was with a woman who was probably his wife. Frank couldn't approach him now.

Frank started his motor and when the Jaguar pulled out, he followed, but stayed several car lengths behind. But as Spats approached the major intersection at Jozsef Kőrút, Frank closed the gap. He didn't want to risk getting stuck at the light. They turned left and Frank followed. He kept one eye on Spats and the other on the rear view mirror to be certain no one was tailing him. At the next major avenue, Üllöi Út, Spats turned left again. Two streets in he turned right. Frank saw the street name on the blue and white sign attached to the corner apartment building: Páva Utca. Two blocks farther on the Jaguar pulled to the right and stopped, but didn't park. The woman got out. She pushed open the heavy door to an apartment building as Spats drove off.

Frank had to make up his mind. If he continued to follow Spats, it was true that some roving surveillance team might just spot him, or he could be pulled over in a routine traffic check, or Spats himself could realize he was being tailed. Besides, it was a working day for Hungarians and Spats might well be returning to the office where Frank would have no opportunity to approach him anyway. Frank took a chance and pulled into a parking spot in the next block and walked back toward the building the woman had entered.

From across the street Frank looked carefully at the front entrance. He couldn't see the upper floors because of the trees. He crossed over and just walked in. The entryway was dark and for a few moments he had trouble seeing the names on the apartment mailboxes. But when he leaned closer, sure enough, there it was: Szebrenyi, third floor. Frank left the building. He drove around the neighborhood then stopped beside the park two blocks down. He did some contortions and changed clothes in the car, pulled off his moustache and glasses and drove back to the National Museum. From there he caught a bus to the embassy and walked right in the front door.

Frank had decided to say nothing to headquarters about what had happened. His hunch that Spats would be invited to the Bastille Day reception was a good one and now he knew where the long lost agent lived. But he still wanted to wait until he had actually talked to Spats before sending a cable home.

For the next week, Frank kept to his routine. He had taken possession of his BMW and drove it to the embassy around eight fifteen each morning. He normally stayed late at the office, then came back to cook a meal in the apartment on those evenings when he wasn't invited out by one of the embassy families. He wanted the surveillance teams to be lulled into thinking that what they saw was what they would get.

By Monday of the following week, He was ready to make his move. He had waited until then because there was a soccer match scheduled for that evening. When he got back to Népstadion around six-thirty, on his way in he unscrewed the light bulb in the entryway just inside the back door. Upstairs, he had a tuna fish sandwich and a glass of milk then changed into a pair of light blue pants and a dark blue shirt he had bought in the department store on Rákóczi Út. For the next two hours he sat on the sofa. At least a dozen times he went over his plan and checked the note he had written in the office in Hungarian. Finally, around ten o'clock he figured the soccer match should be almost over. He moved to the bedroom and watched through the window as the first fans began to move down the street. Gradually, the number of people increased. Within five minutes, the street was literally jammed with people. They filled the sidewalk across the street, the street itself, and the sidewalk in front of Frank's building. Now was his chance.

He left the apartment and stood for a moment inside the back entrance. He knew that the Hungarians had an observation post in the building to the rear to watch people coming and going through this door. He figured with the light out, if he moved quickly, he could slip by. He opened the door, walked quickly down the side of the building and stood by the black metal gate. He turned the knob, pulled it open, closed it and slipped into the crowd.

The night air was cool, but Frank was perspiring. He went along with the throng, slowly making his way out into the street to the middle of the flow. During the day, the thigh muscle he had pulled in his tennis match the day before had given him little trouble, but as he moved along slowly in the lemming-like crowd, it began to tighten up. At the end of the street, he walked with everyone else through the City Park and caught a bus on Dózsa György. He was forced to stand in the aisle, but this served his purpose since he was able to look through the rear window to watch what was happening behind. He saw nothing; so far, so good.

He got off the bus at the old Industrial Trade Museum on Üllöi Út and walked for several blocks to be sure he was still clean of surveillance. He was limping noticeably. By now it was ten twenty-five and it took him another five minutes to get to the building on Páva utca. Once again because of the trees he couldn't see the upper floors. He walked in the front door. Now he did what he should have done the week before when he looked at the mailboxes. Szebrenyi was on the third floor and he saw that one of the two apartments on the fourth floor was occupied by a man named Lajos Nagy. Frank fingered the note in his pocket and struggled up the stairs.

On the third floor landing, Frank rang the bell of the apartment on the left. The door opened and there stood Spats. Even though the light from the apartment was behind him and his face was in shadow, Frank knew this was his man. He had sharp features, dark hair, the goatee and a small vertical scar that intersected his left eyebrow. He was wearing a maroon silk robe with navy blue piping. Beside him on a small table in the tiny drab foyer were the incongruous pale purple blossoms of an orchid. Frank couldn't tell if it was real or artificial. It made him think of Spats's Jaguar, something fine that didn't quite fit in. Over Spats's shoulder Frank spotted the woman he had seen earlier. She was wearing a pink, terry-cloth robe and she walked out of the front room toward the back of the apartment. Frank spoke in Hungarian.

"Excuse me. I am looking for the apartment of Mr. Nagy, Lajos."

"You made a mistake. Mr. Nagy lives on the fourth floor." Spats didn't seem pleased at the late intrusion.

Frank took the note from his pocket. It was in a small envelope. He put his left index finger to his lips and extended his other hand to Spats.

"I'm very sorry to have bothered you."

At first, Spats looked at the envelope without understanding Frank's purpose. But Frank watched carefully and saw the instant change in Spats's expression when he realized what was happening. He accepted the note then looked over his shoulder. By now his wife was out of sight. Frank turned and instead of going upstairs, went back down the way he had come.

Outside, he turned right and walked two streets over to the two square blocks of park on Ferenc Tér and sat on a wooden bench. In his message to Spats Frank had said that this was where he would wait for him. It had also mentioned that he brought greetings from Julie d'Andrade.

Frank looked around. A young couple locked in an embrace sat several benches away. In this park and the one across the square, a few people were walking their dogs. One middle-aged man passed Frank. He was holding one of those expandable leashes and at the end of it was a black Puli. A light breeze, cooler than Frank had felt since he arrived eddied through the trees. Perhaps it was a first hint of fall. He felt his leg stiffening even more as the air passed over him.

It was ten very long minutes before Szebrenyi appeared. Finally, Frank saw him enter the park on the diagonal path from the corner. Frank pushed himself up with both hands as the Hungarian approached the bench.

"Who are you? Are you Hungarian? What do you want?" Frank could tell that the note had scared Attila out of his wits.

"Frank Manion. I'm an American diplomat." Frank had weighed the possible benefit that might come from giving a false name. But this man was an officer in the AVH and he could have identified Frank pretty quickly at the embassy, so Frank gave his true name. Julie had done it in her diplomatic status, and he had decided to do the same.

"I am not authorized to have anything to do with Americans." Attila turned on his heels and started to walk back the way he had come. Frank knew the Hungarian was afraid this was a provocation by his own service, a test of his loyalty. Before he could get very far, Frank called out to him.

"Julie said you like escargots. It used to make her squirm when she watched you eat them. You found that amusing." Spats stopped. He stood for several seconds then walked back to the bench. "And in the game season you loved the pheasant at Le Coq d'Or behind the Pantheon."

"How did you find me? I am not listed in any phone directory. I never told Julie where I would live."

"We knew about your Jaguar. I saw you at the French Embassy."

"You followed me when you were being followed yourself?"

"No, not at all. I planned this very carefully. I took every precaution and I was free of surveillance."

"Who in Washington knows that you have come to my flat?"

"Absolutely no one and I mean no one."

"I trust Julie. Since you found me, I have to trust you. You must promise me you will not come here again."

"I won't come here. But can you meet me someplace else in town?"

"No."

"If you're not able to meet in Budapest, is it possible for you to get out of the country?" Spats kept looking around. He seemed especially attentive to the young couple. "Please," said Frank, "just sit for a few minutes. You're less conspicuous sitting than you are standing up." Attila hesitated then sat down, but only on the outer slats of the bench.

"Do you swear to me that no one knows you are meeting me? Remember, I am in the same profession as you and I know that such a situation is almost impossible. Someone else always knows." Spats put his hand to his forehead. At first Frank thought he might be trying to conceal his face, but no one appeared to have noticed them. Attila rubbed both temples. Frank wondered if the fellow had a headache, or if Frank himself was causing him pain.

"I do swear it. My headquarters wanted me to find you, but they don't know that I've succeeded."

"I have permission to go to Vienna in the third week of September. The windshield of my car has a crack and if I have to buy the replacement here, it will cost me a thousand dollars in forints for the window and the labor to install it. If I go to Vienna and bring back the new glass, it will cost me a hundred."

"Do you know the exact date yet?"

"No, but it will be between the fifteenth and twentieth of the month."

"I'll meet you there. Look for me in St. Stephen's Cathedral. I'll sit in one of the back pews near the rack of candles by the main entrance. I'll be there every day between nine and nine-thirty, twelve and twelve-thirty, three and three-thirty. Every three hours, got it?"

"I won't come if Julie is not there."

"I'll ask her to come."

Again, Spats looked around. The young couple was getting up from the bench. They still had their arms around each other's waist, but they began to walk out of the park.

"I have to go back. My wife will wonder. I told her I was going for a short walk, to digest my dinner."

"I'll be waiting for you in Vienna."

Suddenly, Spats grabbed Frank's right hand and gripped it firmly.

"You haven't asked me why I did not come to the first meeting after my return from Paris."

"We thought you might have had second thoughts about cooperating."

"I am not a coward, but neither am I a fool. To have come would have been to sign my death warrant. You must take every step to limit the number of people who know about me. My life is in your hands."

"Does someone here suspect you?"

"The problem is not here. This information is very tightly held within the AVH, but I have heard that they have a source who reports to them from inside your service."

"Are you certain?"

"Almost."

"Who is it? Do you have his name?"

"No. Normally, we recruit American military men in Germany if they have Hungarian relatives here. Usually they are enlisted men, sergeants, corporals, privates. You should look for anyone with such background who entered the service of the CIA. I was fortunate. When I first returned from Paris, a friend was leaving for Canada, Montreal. He should not have told me, but he did. He said his only task was to travel once or twice a month into the United States to meet this source. My colleague is now in Budapest on summer holiday. I am to see him next week when he returns from Lake Balaton. I will try to find out more before I come to Vienna, but it won't be easy." Spats squeezed Frank's hand harder. "Just remember, my life is in your hands."

Frank got up as Attila did. Now Frank's leg was rigid. They shook hands and Spats walked down the path toward his apartment building. Frank hobbled off in the other direction.

As he left the park, Frank was glad he had waited before sending a cable to Washington. Now he had something to write home about. Spats's claim that the agency was penetrated would give the Raven a lot to chew on. Frank's message would have to go in a privacy channel directly to Bill Marshall to limit the distribution, but he would ask the division chief to share the information with Tony. Tony would be delighted, and as icing on the cake Julie would come to Vienna.

Chapter 28

Vladimir Shurin stood in the doorway to the kitchen. His wife Irina was brewing her morning coffee.

"So, Tolya is back from Brazil?" he asked.

"Yes...I mean...is that right?" At first she looked at him then turned quickly back to the coffee pot. "Where did you see him?" Vladimir laughed out loud. She wasn't quick enough. He was certain that she and Barchuk had resumed their liaison and her lame attempt at deception confirmed it.

"Your reaction time has slowed down. In Brazil you were able to lie even without thinking."

"Fuck your mother, you bastard." Irina shouted, but she was yelling at Vladimir's back as he turned and walked across the small living room and out the door.

Out on the street, it was a typical mid-August Sunday in Moscow, with the sun already hot at nine in the morning. He swung his black rucksack onto his shoulder and was still smiling at the thought of Irina squirming, but his mood changed instantly when he spotted the man across the street. Actually, Vladimir did not see the whole man, just his body from the chest down under an awning. Vladimir's involuntary reaction was to reach to the chest pocket of his shirt and finger the pen with the pills. When he got to the corner and looked back, the man was gone. All the while on the metro he watched people, but no one seemed to show the slightest interest in him and by the time he arrived at the stop near Natasha's room, everyone appeared to be preoccupied and normal.

When he came up the metro steps, to the left there was a makeshift flower stand. Vladimir stopped and looked around again, but spotted no one. Perhaps it had been a case of nerves.

"What kind of flowers are these, comrade?" He pointed to bright pink blooms with long stems.

"They're daisies."

To Vladimir, the vendor looked Georgian. He was a swarthy fellow with black hair and a thick moustache. The man reached a hairy arm into the tin bucket beside him and pulled out the pink bouquet.

"I thought daisies were yellow and white."

"These are a hybrid, Gerber daisies. I grow them in a hot house."

"I'll take two bouquets. Wrap them separately," Vladimir said.

"Don't cut the stems," the man told him. "I put match sticks in them. That keeps the blossom from getting too much water." He took another bunch from the bucket and several sheets of newspaper and wrapped the stems.

"Well, at least Pravda is good for something, eh?" Vladimir pointed at the newspaper.

"You can wipe your ass with it as well." The fellow smiled and Vladimir paid him and headed for Natasha's place. As a last minute precaution, he turned into an alley and cut through to a side street, then walked quickly through another alley. He went to the apartment by the back stairs as usual.

"You brought me flowers, Volodya?"

"One bouquet is for you, the other for later." He kissed her on each cheek.

"What do you mean later? You bought these for someone else? Who is she? I thought we were going to the pet market."

"No one else. We are going. You'll see. It's a surprise."

She turned from him and carried the flowers into the kitchen.

"I'll put them in water." At the sink, Natasha removed the newspaper.

"I'll take that," Vladimir said. "It will keep the others fresh." Natasha took a knife from the counter. "You can't cut the stems," Vladimir told her. "Besides, you shouldn't use the good knives I bought you to cut flowers." He was annoyed. At Natasha's insistence he had paid almost a hundred rubles for that set of Wüsthof German cutlery.

"The old lady doesn't have a vase. I'll just put them in this." She began to arrange the bouquet in a clear glass jar along with the ferns the vendor had included.

Vladimir walked into the tiny bathroom and closed the door. He set his rucksack next to the small tub, lowered the lid of the toilet and sat down. From his bag he took the most recent rolls of film he had put in the plastic baggies. He removed the newspapers from the second bouquet and fit two rows of film canisters around the lower part of the stems. He secured them with rubber bands. He folded another of the plastic baggies with his latest message to the Americans and a letter to Justinha around the canisters and used another rubber band to keep them in place then he re-wrapped the bouquet in the newspaper. He added the Pravda sheets from the first bouquet and put rubber bands around the outside.

In his last message to the Americans, Vladimir had told them that their choice of sites posed serious risks for him. He insisted that he would now choose the sites himself. He knew western diplomats were limited to a forty-kilometer radius from the Kremlin, and he intended to stay within that range. Today's site was in a cemetery.

Vladimir carried the flowers as Natasha took his arm and they walked to the metro. They took the train to the Taganskaya super market. From there they got on the number sixteen trolleybus along Taganskaya Ulitsa.

They got off at the fifth stop and cut through to Kalitnikovskaya Ulitsa. Even before they reached the pet market, Vladimir could hear the barking of dogs, chirping of birds, even the high pitched squealing of monkeys. He had promised to buy Natasha a canary.

The main alley of the market was formed by stalls, but on Sunday the street was packed with unofficial vendors as well. People were selling German shepherd guard dogs, several breeds of herding dogs, and simple mutts. As Vladimir and Natasha passed, women hawkers held up wire cages with colorful songbirds and even parrots and myna birds.

"These fly wild in the trees of Brazil." He pointed to a brace of parrots.

"There you go again. I don't believe you anymore. And I'm sure there are snakes and monkeys as well." Natasha gestured with her thumb to the stalls on her left where the monkeys were sitting on the counter with strings around their necks. On the right were glass tanks with colorfully-patterned snakes.

"In fact, there are. Don't you know anything about the rest of the world?"

Vladimir's reverie of Brazil was destroyed when one of the parrots greeted them in Russian. "*Privyet, privyet*," ("Greetings, greetings.") it squawked. Natasha laughed.

They stopped at the next stall to watch the slow random movement of colorfully striped and patterned exotic fish, then Natasha let go of his arm.

"Look, Volodya, the canaries." Natasha skipped ahead. When he caught up with her, she was standing by a man who had four cages filled with the yellow songbirds. "Maybe I should get two, one to keep the other company."

Vladimir stood looking at the birds. Through the wires of the cage he saw a young man, probably in his late twenties, standing back by one of the monkey vendors. Vladimir was certain the fellow had been watching him and when Vladimir took notice, the guy turned away. This was no coincidence and not his imagination. He was being watched.

He thought fast. For him to put down the film now would be folly. Still, the Americans would be expecting it. In their last message, they told him he had accumulated one hundred seventy thousand dollars in his account. That was a fortune in the Union, but in the West it wouldn't be enough. He had been putting packages down each month now for the past six months and he was determined to continue.

"As you like, but first we have to do something."

"What?"

"Let's keep walking."

They left the market street and meandered back toward the Church of St. Nicholas. The walls were decorated with red, white and blue kokoshniki and sage-green pendentives. Above them were turquoise shingled onion domes. As they passed through the church's tent-roofed archway, Vladimir handed Natasha the bouquet.

"Did you know this used to be the entrance to the Old Believers Commune?"

"No," she answered.

"Many of them are buried here." They walked through the gates of the Rogozhskoe Cemetery. "One of them is an ancestor of mine."

"Are you serious, who?"

"Timofei Morozov. Did you ever hear of him?"

"No."

"He was the son of the founder of a textile empire. All of the factories were confiscated after the Bolsheviks took over. We never got any of the money." While the essence of the story was true, the part about his being related to the Morozovs was not, but the lie served his purpose. Vladimir nodded to his left. "Take the bouquet and put it on the grave. It's the third one from the left in the second row. You will see the name on the headstone. Remember, Timofei Morozov. Don't unwrap it. Just lay it by the headstone. I'll go back and wait for you by the canaries. Maybe I will have a surprise for you." Vladimir turned on his heels. Back by the archway, the same young man stopped and turned also to go back the way he had come.

All the while Vladimir had been thinking that the organs of state security were grinding and he could be crushed. He felt himself on the verge of nausea, but kept walking. Back at the canary vendor, the bird-keeper tried to show him the difference between the male and the female he bought, but Vladimir couldn't see the distinction and wasn't really interested. He was going over in his mind the times he had picked up or placed packages, messages, and what he had seen in each spot. He had always looked carefully and was pretty sure that what he saw today had started today. Now the fellow had not seen him go into the cemetery at all. And this surveillant apparently had paid no attention to Natasha. For all this watcher knew, she was simply laying flowers at the grave of someone close to her. After several minutes, Natasha rejoined him.

"I got you the cage as well," Vladimir said. "Otherwise, he was going to put each of them in a tiny cardboard box. By the time you got them back to your place, they would have been dead."

"I love you, you know? You are very thoughtful." She held the cage up and whistled to her new friends.

Three days later, Vladimir was working out in the gym at the Dynamo complex. Anatoliy Barchuk approached him. The KGB man was wearing cotton slacks, a shirt and tie.

"Tolya, have you finished your workout?" Vladimir asked.

"I didn't come today to exercise. Actually, I was looking for you."

Vladimir stopped punching the heavy bag. He wondered if this was to be a moment of confession, contrition or confrontation.

"Well, here I am."

"Volodya, are you going abroad again?"

"Not soon."

"Have you changed jobs?"

"That was some time ago. Why?"

"I shouldn't be telling you this, but a lad from the Second Chief Directorate came to see me in my office on Monday. He was asking me about you."

Vladimir reached up with the rough leather glove and tried to wipe sweat from his forehead. A drop ran from his eyebrow into his right eye and he had to blink several times.

"What were they asking?"

"How you conducted yourself in Brazil, whether you had close contacts with foreigners."

"What did you tell them?"

"I said we all had close contacts. That was why we were there."

"Then you spoke honestly."

Barchuk nodded.

"Of course, but what I wanted to tell you is that if they should interview you, don't mention anything about helping me get that stamp in Duffy's passport."

"Who?"

"Remember I asked you to get a stamp in a passport from your chap at the airport?"

"Oh, yes."

"Did you know that the man I asked you to get it for disappeared?"

"Defected?"

"Maybe." Barchuk looked around the room and back at the gym door. "Still, say nothing."

"Of course, you can count on me."

Vladimir now understood the reason Barchuk had approached him. The scoundrel wasn't doing this out of the goodness of his heart. He was just trying to cover his own ass. Vladimir went back to punching the bag. He was sure that he had gotten away with his little ploy on Sunday and that the Chekist would never even have thought to go into the cemetery since he never saw Vladimir enter. He believed he could continue to outwit them. The question was for how long. It all depended on how lucky he was.

Chapter 29

Tony Valletta arrived in Budapest on Friday, September 10, 1982. Frank was delighted to see him not only because Tony relieved him of the obligation to attend daily staff meetings, but also because Frank needed another operations officer in the station. That was especially true now that he was in contact with Spats. Increasingly, Frank felt the burden of being responsible for someone else's life and well-being. Even with Tony there they would be hard pressed to do the work they had to do. It had occurred to Frank several times that Americans didn't realize how few the CIA officers were in number and how much bounce the taxpayers were getting for their buck.

After the Wednesday morning staff meeting, Frank stood outside the bubble while the principals filed out. Several said hello or nodded to him. Crittenden was engaged in conversation with Roger Hallek, the deputy chief of mission. He looked at Frank, but never acknowledged him. Tony was waiting in the secure room.

"Francis, it is absolutely wonderful to see you." Tony hugged Frank. His head came to Frank's chest. Looking down Frank saw that the comb-over was a bit frizzy and the pouches under the eyes were more ample, otherwise, Tony looked the same as he had in Washington.

"A year ago I didn't know if we'd both get here," Frank said. "Thanks to you we did. How was your trip?"

"Long, but uneventful. Sit down, dear boy." Tony had to inhale to fit between his chair and the long table in the cramped space.

"I want to offer you my condolences on your father's death."

"Thank you, Francis. He was ninety-two so he had a full life." Tony smiled, but Frank could tell it was a forced expression. "You know, we came from San Gimignano, a little village in Tuscany. I went back to see it when I was stationed in Italy. It's lovely, with vineyards and olive groves covering the hills. It was one of those unusual instances when childhood recall didn't deceive or disappoint. But when we arrived in America, strange that I don't recollect this, my mother told me that we lived in North Jersey. That was in the Depression. Hard times. He walked ten miles every day and crossed the bridge into New York to look for work. He went from door to door all day long and trudged another ten miles to get home. Can you imagine that? He did it for his family." Tony turned away to face the transparent plastic wall. When he turned back, Frank saw tears welling up in his eyes.

"Sounds like a singular man."

"He was that, tough as an old boot." Tony took a white handkerchief from his pants pocket and blew his nose. "Anyway, I do apologize for the added burden my tardiness imposed on you. I fully anticipated being here in August."

"I understand. I was able to keep it together."

"I would say you achieved somewhat more than that. Bill Marshall is convinced that you can walk on the Danube and turn cobblestones into Hungarian dumplings. What you have done is truly remarkable. I say that after many years in this business, Master Francis. Kearns and his deputy spent three years looking for Spats and you managed to spot him in less than two months. Those few who are familiar with both Bagatelle and Spats, including a certain fair damsel, are in awe of what you've accomplished. What ever gave you the idea that you might spot him at the French Embassy?"

Frank smiled. He knew that only a handful of his colleagues would be aware of what he had been able to do, but he considered it a stroke of great luck that Julie was one of those few.

"I thought about it and I suspected that the AVH was probably like us in some ways. They spent money to train this guy in French. They sent him to Paris. He got all that experience and made a lot of contacts. Would they throw all that away? I didn't think so, not unless he was in trouble. Instead, I thought they would probably keep him as a French specialist to get their money's worth and they would want him to maintain those contacts. Anyway, I figured it was worth a shot."

"Extraordinary. No wonder everyone sees you as a Messiah."

"All except Harry O'Meara, right?"

"For a time when it was clear that Bagatelle was exceeding all expectations, Harry had ceased his fulminations. Now he has another carcass to peck on. He has seized on the Spats case. He is convinced that Spats is under hostile control, that the Hungarians are simply trying to lure us into some unforeseeable trap."

"I guess he has to have something to be suspicious of or he doesn't get paid."

"What about Spats?" Tony turned aside and coughed. To Frank it sounded like the cough of a reformed smoker. When he turned back, Frank noticed that his eyes were bloodshot. "You can be absolutely candid," Tony said. "Now that we're abroad no one is looking over our shoulder. What do you think of him?"

"I think he was scared that night. He came out to the park about ten minutes after I knocked on his door so he had enough time to call someone. But while he was sitting with me he was constantly fidgeting. That could have been an act. But the thing that persuaded me that he was straight was that he could have set up another meeting here and had the AVH nab me, but he decided on Vienna instead."

"That sounds entirely plausible."

"What was Harry's reaction to Spats's claim that there's a mole in the agency?" Frank asked.

"At first he didn't know what to make of it." Tony pushed his chair farther back from the table to give himself room, took a deep breath and exhaled slowly. "Then he decided it was self-serving, a contrived excuse for why Spats never made his first meeting with us."

"We'll find out more next week in Vienna if he shows up."

"That reminds me. I bring you greetings from the glamorous Miss d'Andrade."

"She plans to be there, right?" Once again, Frank concealed his emotions. He didn't want to appear overly anxious, but seeing Julie was important to him, possibly just as important as seeing the agent.

"Yes. Marshall approved her trip." Tony smiled knowingly.

"Spats may be telling the truth about a mole. I didn't put this in a cable, but the AVH was expecting me when I got here. The embassy didn't know I was coming, but the service had a woman taxi driver waiting for me when I walked out of the terminal at Férihegy."

"Tell me what we are up against here." Tony said. "What have you seen so far?"

"This is the A-team. The denied area ops course trained us, but it was like training future astronauts to handle weightlessness in a swimming pool. Now we're on the moon and there are little green men everywhere." Frank went on to recount some of his experiences. "I was looking at shoes in a department store. They were stuffed with paper to keep their shape. I picked up a pair and put them back down. Suddenly this guy grabbed them. He was sure I had put a note in those shoes. When he walked away, he thought he had his next promotion in his hand." They both laughed.

"You've learned a great deal in a very short time, Francis. Well done."

"I may need to be able to get out of the embassy again without them knowing it's me."

"And how would you accomplish that, by posing as a delivery man again?"

"I took some photos at the Fourth of July reception at the ambassador's residence. They're of a fellow named Csaba Fenyvesi, a translator in the USIS office. He's my height and weight, carries himself about the way I do. I saw he wears a navy raincoat and I bought a duplicate. That's why I went to that department store. Now all I need is his face."

"What do you have in mind?"

"I'd like your permission to go up to Frankfurt and have a mask made, one of those rubber things in his likeness. I could do it on Monday then go down to Vienna to see Spats."

"Francis, I can refuse you nothing. Go with my blessing. I'll muddle through while you're gone."

The following Sunday, the twelfth, Frank took a Lufthansa flight from Férihegy to Frankfurt-am-Main. He wanted the Hungarians to be aware of his destination and the timing of that segment of his trip so they wouldn't connect him with Spats's travel to Vienna.

His correspondence with Julie had increased in frequency and candor. On the plane he read her latest letter for the tenth time.

"Dear Frank,

"Did you know that I can tell people's fortunes? My grandmother taught me to read cards. She read mine before I left New York and told me I would have good luck with a very special younger man. I'm anxious to know who that younger man might be and what his future holds. I'll bring the cards with me.

"Did I also tell you that I was an English major at Cornell? I believe I did. I always fancied myself a good writer, but you put me to shame. I've come to know you so well in just two months and all because of your letters. I know this sounds crazy, but I feel as if I'm falling in love by mail. I can't wait to see you."

Every time Frank read the part about falling in love he had to smile. He told himself that the money he spent on that bouquet of roses was the best investment he had made in his life.

On the afternoon of his arrival in Frankfurt-am-Main he walked into the CIA's technical office on Kaiserstrasse. It was located on the seventh floor in one of the many high rises that gave the city its nickname: Mainhattan. The two technicians who met him, one a short, peppy, red-haired woman and the other a tall, thin, quiet fellow in his mid-forties, weren't overjoyed about having to work on the weekend, but they were used to it. That afternoon and twice the following day Frank sat for a fitting of the mask he had requested by cable. It was fortunate he wasn't claustrophobic or suffering from a cold because for several hours he had only two nostril holes to breathe through while the cast was being taken. After the mold solidified, the two techs worked from the photos he provided of Fenyvesi, the Hungarian translator, to color it. They promised to send the finished product to Budapest in the classified pouch.

By eight o'clock on Tuesday morning, Frank was driving a rented Audi south on the A-5 Autobahn. At Munich, he headed east across Austria. When he passed Salzburg, he felt like a horse that smelled the stable. He knew Julie would be waiting.

In Vienna, he found the building of flats, the Cordial apartments at 5, Kustlergasse, parked in the small courtyard and took the steps two at a time to the third floor. He knocked on the door and Julie opened it immediately. Although he had looked forward to this moment for three

202

months, he had never decided what he would do when they met again. She was barefoot and looked up at him. He stepped inside and Julie closed the door. Frank was breathing heavily from his climb. He started to speak, but she reached up and put her finger on his lips. She took the lead.

She moved to him and he kissed her, just a light brushing of skin. Then they kissed again, a deep, luxuriating kiss.

"You said you know how to keep a secret. I hope you can keep this one." She took a step back. She was wearing an ash-gray sweatshirt and burgundy sweat pants with "Cornell" down the right leg in white letters. She simply lifted and removed the shirt and dropped the pants and suddenly she was nude.

She had obviously planned it this way and she was just as he remembered her from Copacabana, but now even more exciting with the promise of what was to come. He was still breathing hard as he kissed her voraciously, moving from her mouth down to her neck then her breasts. He held her under her arms and she bounced up and wrapped her legs around his hips. She straddled him as he carried her down a hallway that he assumed led to the bedroom. He turned into the last door and laid her on the sheets. As he stripped off his shirt and unbuttoned his trousers, she smiled.

"I've known from the start you wanted to fuck me. I had to be sure you were a free man and that I could trust you."

Now fully aroused he moved to the bed.

"You're wrong. I never wanted to fuck you. What I wanted from the first moment was to make love to you because that's what I felt and that's what I'm going to do."

Whatever he may have said, or done, or written up to this moment had gotten Julie to surrender herself. But for Frank, the seduction had just begun. He wanted to give her more pleasure than she had ever known to ensure that she would want more still, so he moved slowly.

The second time they coupled he was in control. He worked her in different positions creating new angles and frictions and using every way he had learned from the other women he had known to delight her. He could feel and move every muscle at will. She climaxed right away. Shortly after that she came again.

"What are you doing to me?" Now she started into a continuous orgasm. With each thrust she came more. Tears began to run back across her temples into her already matted hair. But any concern for appearance was gone. This was sheer abandon. Then he exploded and it was over. They lay panting, spent and content.

"Why were you crying?"

At first she didn't answer. She seemed to have trouble finding words.

"I...I'm just so happy. That was incredible. You're like a sailor home from the sea." She laughed and ran her index finger through his short dark hair and twisted it in little ringlets. "God, if I had only known you would do that, I wouldn't have wasted all this time."

"I'm glad. I read once about free diving. Men go as deep as they can without oxygen. Some succumb to what's known as rapture of the deep where they don't know which way is up. I guess this is what it's like." They lay side by side for a time, saying nothing. Finally he broke the silence. "I was afraid they wouldn't let you come."

"They almost didn't. If it hadn't been for Bill Marshall, I wouldn't have gotten the approval. When I saw him he spent most of his time talking about you. I think he may consider you the son he never had. He has three daughters." Julie turned toward him, bent her elbow and rested her head on her hand. "Tell me, did Spats really say he wanted me here, or was that your idea?"

"No. He insisted."

"Well, arranging this was a bit complicated. There's something I have to tell you. I didn't say it in my letters because I didn't want to write about work. I transferred to the Directorate of Intelligence."

"What? Why?" The September sun was well to the west and the breeze coming through the window had turned cool. Frank noticed Julie's perspiration and reached down to pull the sheet up over her.

"I decided I'd had enough of being a case officer."

"But you were great at it. And DI officers don't get to work overseas."

"That's not a bad thing if you're a woman." Frank tried to look sympathetic, but apparently didn't succeed. "I know you've heard this before, but for female case officers the problem isn't just with our male colleagues. We're sent to cultures where men think a woman is good for one thing, two if you count cooking." She turned on her back with her head on the pillow and it was Frank's turn to roll toward her and prop himself up.

"But you're tough, remember?"

"When I have to be. I put in my five years overseas, so I can retire early if I stick around that long. But with my father's illness I want to be close to home. I have an obligation to be there for him."

"I don't have that..." Frank was about to say "problem," but chose another word, "...responsibility."

"That reminds me. Did you ever know your parents?"

"Yes."

"How did you lose them?" He hesitated, but she persisted. "You said you would tell me when I came out here, remember?"

He turned on his back and looked at the ceiling. Maybe he wanted to keep some distance from her for this, or maybe he had to steel himself to pick at an old wound.

"When I was five years old my mother took me to the hospital, Frankford Hospital, to have my tonsils taken out. I was in the room with another boy who was a bit older. I remember we had all these comic books spread across our beds and the beds were separated by a glass partition. It was before the operation and we were tossing the books over the glass to each other after we read them. A lot of them ended up on the floor." He looked at the window where the sheer curtains were billowing.

"A nurse came in. She looked very serious. I thought it was because we were making a mess. But she didn't say anything. She just got me out of bed and took me down the hall to an office where the doctor, Doctor Gibbs, sat behind a desk. She closed the door and I stood there in front of the desk then sat on a chair. I remember that I had no slippers and the linoleum felt cold on my feet so I was happy to sit." He actually lifted each foot slightly from the bed as he recalled that moment.

"He told me that my mother and father had been killed. The house in Tacony where we lived burned to the ground. Firemen thought it was my father. He was probably sleeping on the sofa. When my mother came home from the hospital they went upstairs, but apparently my father left a cigarette between the cushions. The place turned into an inferno before they ever realized what was happening. After that they still took my tonsils out." Frank half chuckled.

"The hospital arranged for me to move to St. Vincent's, an orphanage in my old neighborhood. Then a year later, Doctor Gibbs had me moved to Stephen Girard College. It's a school for fatherless boys. That's all there is."

At first Julie stayed quiet. They both remained on their backs.

"Did no one ever try to adopt you?"

"I stayed in touch with Doctor Gibbs, or he stayed in touch with me. He told me just before he died a couple of years ago that my chances of being adopted were better in the orphanage, but he said it would have been a crap shoot. I could have ended up with an abusive couple, or drunks. He said he saw something in me that made him believe I could make it on my own and that Stephen Girard was a great school so I would benefit."

"I guess he was right. You turned out great." She leaned over and kissed him on the cheek.

"So if you can't travel, when will we see each other?"

"I will get to take short trips. If this goes well, maybe I can go wherever our friend goes."

"I hope so. I'll keep trying to push for that from my end. That reminds me. I don't think I finished pushing."

He looked down and Julie followed his gaze.

"Again?" she asked. "I think you've done enough pushing and diving for one day. Besides, we've got work to do. We'd better go out and decide how we're going to set this up for tomorrow."

Frank smiled. She was taking charge again.

"Assuming he comes. You have the room at the Park?" he asked.

"Three-twelve."

"Maybe we can get a sandwich or something," Frank said. "I haven't eaten since seven this morning."

They washed up and dressed. Out on the street, they walked along Wienzeile for three blocks and entered the Naschmarkt from the southern end. Stall after stall was stacked with fresh polished fruits and vegetables. They passed through spaces defined by their aromas. There were spices, peppers, herbs, garlic, bay laurel, and smoked meats, sauerkraut, pickles. Colorful Pheasants and ducks hung in braces above the butchered body parts of pigs.

"How about a Doner sandwich?" Julie asked, pointing to a porcelain-topped counter manned by a big-busted woman in a white apron with blonde hair pulled back in a bun. "It's lamb and onions in a yogurt sauce on a fresh roll."

"Perfect." They waited while the woman stuffed the ingredients into the bread and wrapped it in a waxy paper. Frank ate as they walked.

"I think we should look at the streets around the cathedral," Julie said.

"I thought you were an analyst. You still sound like a case officer." She was wearing a cricket green sweater over a white blouse and had a matching green silk scarf on her head. Frank couldn't resist the urge to lean over and kiss her cheek. She wiped away the smudge of yogurt he left behind.

"Are you going in or should I?"

"I told him I would wait for him inside the main entrance."

"Well, I can do the counter-surveillance," Julie said. "I looked at it this morning. He could get to the church from several side streets, but the best view of the main door is probably from the Stock-im-Eisen Platz. There's an American Express office where I could hang out and watch him go by if he comes that way. There's also an optical store that has a postcard stand outside. I could browse there and spot him before he gets in the door. You'll see it when we get there."

"How is your father?"

"He's able to walk with a cane. A little wobbly, but he gets around. Thank you for asking."

Frank finished his sandwich quickly, balled up the paper wrapper and put it in a cylindrical trash can. At the far end of the market street on the Rechte Wienzeile they passed a hair salon. In the window was a naked male mannequin sitting astride a Harley-Davidson motorcycle. On his head was a blonde toupee all in curlers. Frank laughed.

"This is an interesting city. See what you're going to miss if you don't travel. Would you ever see that at home?"

"I'll travel a bit, probably to the Middle East."

"You mean Latin America."

"No. LA Division didn't want me. A fellow named Bill James gave me a job in the Near East Division. He's a La Salle man."

"He's married, right?"

"Yes. And you know how I am about married men and he has a loving wife, so there's no reason to be jealous." She squeezed his arm at his biceps.

"Who said I was?" He tried to be nonchalant, but knew he couldn't pull it off. He was hooked.

It took them almost ten minutes to get to the area around St. Stephens. There was a steady wind blowing from the west. It was one of those days when the sun was shining brightly one minute only to be obscured by heavy clouds the next. Frank saw the spot Julie had described. There was a small Toto-Lotto umbrella covering a postcard stand. It would serve as an observation point, but only for a short time and provided it was not raining. There weren't many people about. It was the coffee and pastry hour for most Viennese.

"I think if you hang around there for long, you'll look conspicuous. I would wander back and forth between the postcards and the American Express office. And you can window shop there." Frank pointed to a women's clothing store, Deckenbacher and Blümner.

They crossed the square. Only the top third of the cathedral's main spire was visible. The other two thirds were surrounded by scaffolding and there were metal construction platforms draped with green canvas over the main door. As they walked underneath, Frank looked up to be sure nothing was about to fall on them. Inside, they crossed the black and white tiled floor to the racks of votive candles. Tourists and worshipers mingled, the former with cameras that flashed occasionally, and the latter adding to the rows of lighted candles that flickered each time the breeze passed through the door as it opened behind them. Up front there was a raised pulpit to the left of the main altar.

"I'm going to be sitting there." Frank nodded to his right toward the rows of wooden seats separated from the rear by a grilled gate. "I'll be able to watch the door. When he comes in, I'll come back here to the candles."

"What happens if I see he's brought people with him?" Julie asked. "What will be our danger signal?" Both had moved to the right side of the church and spoke just above a whisper.

"Just come into the church and walk up the aisle. Don't look back. I'll spot your scarf. Sit in one of the seats close to the altar. When I see you, I'll break off the meeting. Otherwise, I'm just going to pass him a note to go to the Park, room three twelve."

Outside, the sun was sinking fast and a hint of autumn was in the air.

"I haven't told you how extraordinary you are," she said. "I was amazed that you were able to find Attila so quickly." Julie took his arm again as they headed back to the apartment. He realized that she had hardly let go of him since he got to Vienna.

"It won't count for much if he doesn't show, or if he brings some bad guys with him. Have they started to look for the mole at home? I understand the Raven doesn't take this very seriously."

"I talked to a friend of mine who works in his office. You met her, Helen Hassan."

"Yes."

"Helen told me that the CI office is waiting to see what happens here."

"So am I."

Around eight they had dinner in a place called Zum Kuckuck. It was a bit of old Vienna, with vaulted ceilings and old prints of Viennese scenes from the time of Emperor Franz Joseph. The tables were covered in pink linen cloths with lighted candles in pewter candelabra and fresh flowers.

When the waiter came, Julie ordered a beef rouladen marinated in red wine. Frank chose duck in a honey and green peppercorn sauce.

"How about a bottle of Chateau-Neuf du Pape?" Frank asked. "Red for meat and game, besides, someone once told me that drinking white wine was like kissing your sister."

Julie just nodded. Instead of answering his question, she asked one of her own.

"Where are we going you and I?"

"Tomorrow? The Park Hotel."

"No. I mean us. You asked how we can be together, but that will be hard to do if you're three thousand miles away."

"Are you saying that's my fault?"

"Not at all. I'm just wondering where you'll go from here."

Before he answered, the waiter came and Frank asked for the wine. He handed the wine list back to the white-jacketed Austrian.

"I guess we just try to see each other as much as possible. I'll try to get home whenever I can get leave. And you can come to Hungary and stay at my place. I'd love to show you around Budapest."

"I already asked. Headquarters won't approve that."

Frank was silent. He looked around the dining room. It was two thirds full. The two men they had passed on the way in were paying their check and were about to leave. He noticed two couples seated together at a table for four. They wore traditional dress, the men in lederhosen and the women in dirndls. The waiter came with the wine.

"I don't know. What do you think?" He broke off a piece of dark bread.

"I'm not raising this because my biological clock is ticking, and I don't expect that after one roll in the hay I can rope and brand you. I just think that we've started something and I'd like it to continue. I don't know how we can do that." Julie took a swallow of her wine, put down the glass and looked at him with those bright green eyes.

"I'm the one who wanted things to move fast, remember? I still do. I'm crazy about you. I think of you night and day, every day. Don't worry. We're two smart, able people. Even if I weren't, I love you and that makes up for a lot. We'll figure out a way to be together more." It was the first time he had used the word love other than in his letters and he could see that it had both a calming and then an exhilarating effect on Julie, so he said it again and meant it unstintingly. "I love you."

That night, they both slept fitfully. It was because of the lumpy bed, and the bolsters rather than pillows, and, undoubtedly, the strange surroundings and the anticipation of what the next day might bring. They made love in the middle of the night. Both were still tired in the morning.

In a café on Gempendorferstrasse they ate a continental breakfast. Frank took two cups of the dark Viennese coffee. He figured he would need the extra buzz.

"We got a break," Frank said. "The weather is good. You'll be able to stand outside." He looked at his watch. It was eight forty-five. "We'll have to walk fast."

They got to the square and split up. Frank went inside the cathedral and Julie moved from spot to spot as they had agreed. At nine forty, Frank came back out.

"Did you see anything?" He asked Julie.

"No. He was a no show."

"There's no reason I have to be the one to meet him. Why don't you go in at noon? That way you can sit rather than walk around."

"Great. My feet hurt from these cobblestones."

"Hey. We're only starting. This could last for days."

"That's another reason I like being an analyst. No hurry up and wait."

They came back for the noon shift, but reversed positions. Still nothing. At three, it was Frank who sat in the pew. He thought of praying for Spats to show up. Instead he asked God to protect the fellow whether he came to Vienna or not. Then he added a line.

"And thank you, God, for bringing this wonderful woman into my life."

Chapter 30

It took three more days for Spats to appear. When he came in the main door Frank saw him look intently at each of the people standing in the back of the church then at those in the pews beyond the candle racks. He was wearing a gray plaid suit over a navy shirt that was open at the collar. Frank started to get up, but Spats saw him. The Hungarian looked around again before he moved forward. He took a seat that was one removed from Frank's. He stared straight ahead and spoke in a low voice in Hungarian.

"Where is Julie?" were his first words. Frank was reassured. His partner had done her job. Spats had not spotted her.

"She's here in Vienna. When can you meet us?"

"My car is in the shop. It will be ready today by five. I have to leave first thing tomorrow. I can meet tonight."

"Seven o'clock?" Frank, too, kept facing the altar.

"Yes."

"Take the subway, the U-4 line to the Hietzing stop. Come to this hotel, room three twelve." Frank put a church flyer on the seat between them. On it he had written the subway line and stop, the name Park Hotel, and the address in the thirteenth District, Hietzing. "Please sit here for another five minutes. It's all on the paper." With that, Frank got up, walked to his right out of the row of seats and left the church.

Julie approached him when he got to the dress shop.

"I saw him go by. He had nobody with him. Did he spot me?"

"No, you were perfect."

At six o'clock they took a taxi from a cab stand on Kartnerstrasse. As they approached the hotel, Frank caught a glimpse to his left of the Schönbrunn Palace, the summer residence of Austrian emperors. The driver let them off across the street from the Mietzing Gate that opened to the palace grounds. The hotel had a windowed hallway that faced the wall surrounding the royal gardens. Julie went to the desk and got the key, and they went up in the elevator.

Julie had taken a suite. The furnishings were dark and heavy, the walls were covered with an ornate flower-patterned paper. The impression Frank had was that the room would have looked this way fifty years earlier before Hitler marched into town. On the round linen-covered table, Julie had put a basket of fruit wrapped in yellow cellophane, two bottles of Austrian wine, one white and one red, an assortment of cheeses on a plate and an enormous bouquet of yellow roses. Julie saw he was looking at the flowers.

"They're his favorite," she said. "We had that in common."

Precisely at seven, there was a knock at the door. Frank and Julie looked at each other. They had worked out their meeting plan but had neglected to anticipate who would answer.

"You do it," Frank said. "It will put him at ease."

When she opened the door, Spats was obscured. Frank had not gotten a good look at the man either on the street on Bastille Day, at the apartment door, in the park in Budapest or in the church. Now he realized that the Hungarian was shorter than Julie. She stepped aside and allowed him to pass and Frank saw that Spats's hair was black with a touch of gray at the temples and combed straight back, but not flat on his head. If it had been, he would have been shorter still, perhaps five feet seven. The goatee exaggerated his pinched, pointed features and he resembled a caricature of a Serbian terrorist looking to assassinate Franz Ferdinand.

Julie turned from the door and Spats kissed her on each cheek and they hugged each other. Frank had been curious to see this moment. He had developed a talent for walking into a cocktail party and spotting which people were having some kind of affair with other people there. It happened mostly because Beth used to drag him along to social functions given by her law office and it was she who would gossip about her colleagues. He had noticed that people who she said were intimate were more animated, almost manic when they dealt with each other socially. Their eyes seemed to light up. Frank saw none of that now and he was sure that whatever had happened between Julie and Spats, they had not been lovers.

At first Frank spoke in Hungarian.

"Mr. Szebrenyi. I'm so glad you were able to come." They shook hands. Frank looked at Julie and realized that language was another detail they hadn't thought of.

"Attila and I always spoke in French." She said that in French and Szebrenyi nodded. Now she spoke to the Hungarian. "It is marvelous to see you and to know that you are well. How long has it been since we saw each other the last time?"

"More than three years, no?" Both of them were smiling.

"And how is your wife? Well, I hope."

"She is very well, thank you, and happy to be back in Budapest." For the first time, Szebrenyi looked at Frank. "Do you speak French?" he asked.

"Yes, happily, I do," Frank answered.

Julie led Spats to a chair. Up close and in the light of the room Frank saw that Spats's grey suit was of good quality worsted wool and his cordovan shoes were probably British.

"Would you like some refreshment, Attila? You prefer red wine, if I remember. Someone recently told me that drinking white wine was like kissing your sister." Spats laughed. Julie looked at Frank and he took the corkscrew from the table, opened the bottle and poured, but it was Julie who handed over the glass. Frank reminded himself to be patient. This was to be his case from this point on, but so far it appeared that for Spats and Julie he was an afterthought. He filled Julie's glass and his own.

"Can you tell us how much time you have this evening?" Frank asked. Once again, Spats's answer was to Julie rather than Frank.

"I can stay for perhaps one hour. I have to say that I must put an end to the relations we have. I cannot take the risk of seeing you in Hungary as I had promised when we were in Paris."

"To your health, Attila. We are both grateful that you came today." Julie touched his glass with her own. Frank couldn't resist toasting him in Hungarian.

"*Egészségére.*"

"Some cheese?" Julie asked as she extended the plate. Spats simply held up his hand to refuse. She put the plate down. "You said that our service is penetrated. Is that the reason you can't see us any more?"

"Yes." Now he turned to Frank. "I told you to look for an American with Hungarian background, possibly a military person. As Julie knows, the AVH has had some luck with sergeants from the American army in Germany." Now he looked to Julie, who was sitting across the table. "I think I am right about the German connection."

"Why do you say that?" Frank asked.

"They have given him a code name. It is German: Fassbinder."

"But you think he's American?" Frank asked.

"He is CIA. Don't you have to be American to be in the CIA?"

"Yes," Julie said.

"If he was an American stationed in Germany, do you know where his base was?" Frank asked.

"I am not certain he was there, but if he was, I don't know where." Attila sipped from his glass.

"How did you get the name?" Julie asked.

"I talked with my colleague, the one who is handling the case. I did not learn much, but he told me that he goes down from Montreal and he meets his man most of the time in New York. Our embassy in Washington tells him when the source is able to travel."

"And he gave you only the name?" Frank asked.

"Yes."

"And that's all he said?" Frank crossed his arms.

"Yes. I could not ask a lot of questions."

"Of course you couldn't. We understand," Julie said. Frank looked at her. For now he would have to follow her lead. His inclination was to push a bit harder for information, but she knew how to handle this fellow. She went on. "I came from Washington and I can assure you that Frank alerted us to the problem and the need to restrict this information until we can find this person. Can you spell the name for me?" Julie got up and went to one of the night tables and returned with a yellow legal pad.

"F-a-s-s-b-i-n-d-e-r." Spats used the French pronunciation of each letter.

"And that is all you know about him?" Frank asked.

"Yes." Frank noticed that Attila occasionally parted his lips and made a strange sucking sound as he separated his teeth. Frank wondered if he was wearing dentures.

"How long he has been in the United States? When did he leave Germany?" Frank leaned forward, his forearms on his knees.

"I told you. I am not certain about Germany. It is just my suspicion and that was strengthened by the name."

"How did the AVH recruit him?" Frank was trying to get any minor detail that might help the investigation that was underway at home.

"I asked my friend if he had recruited the fellow and he said 'No.' I said, 'Whoever did must have gotten a handsome bonus and a promotion,' and I asked him who had done it. He said, 'No one.' I said, 'So he was a walk-in?' He said, 'Something like that.'"

"Do you have any idea what he meant by that?" Julie asked.

"No. Perhaps this Fassbinder volunteered in some other way, maybe by mail."

"Is there anything else you can tell us about him?" Frank asked.

"Nothing, I assure you, nothing at all." Frank could see Spats was losing patience. Julie stepped in and Frank understood they would go at this as good cop, bad cop and he would clearly be the latter.

"Attila, you're in the same profession as we are, so you know that any small piece of information can be helpful." Julie spoke softly and evenly and the Hungarian answered her in the same tone.

"I know nothing more. But surely with the name and the possibility that this person came from Germany you will find him."

"We'll certainly do our best," Julie assured him. "And until we do, we promise you that we will protect your identity. Is there anything else you can tell us about the AVH now?"

"Yes. For one thing, they are entering the British Embassy once each week to read classified messages."

Frank recalled Charlie Noble's story about the operation mounted against the U.S. Embassy. To him it made sense, but Julie appeared surprised.

"How do they get in?" she asked.

"Just as with the American Embassy, they come from the roof. Once inside, they enter the secure area. It was the British air attaché who was responsible."

Frank had met the man at a cocktail party, Wing Commander Peter Gross. Frank recalled that he was puffed up like a poisoned puppy. His face had the multiple folds of a hound. A French diplomat had told Frank that Gross's fellow Brits called him Gross Peter, putting his last name first as Hungarians did.

"You mean he let them in?" Julie asked.

"No, he brought his sons to the embassy and allowed them to open the vault. He told them out loud the combination and our microphones picked it up. For this reason, I hope you have never shared my name with the British." Spats seemed to address every severe comment to Frank.

"Never," Frank assured him. "What about the U.S. Embassy? Have they tried again to get inside?"

"No, but they have another means. They have drilled a tiny hole in the common wall where you have your plastic room. They photograph documents. The angle is sometimes difficult, but they have had some minor success because your people do not close the curtains." Frank looked at Julie. He knew it was true. In the time that Frank was attending staff meetings he had actually gotten up from his chair once to draw the green curtains, but Crittenden had let it be known that he was a bit claustrophobic and insisted that they remain open. "Now they are trying something new. It has just begun. There is a man who, I don't know how to say this in French. He watches the movements of the mouth and can tell what words are being spoken."

"He reads lips," Julie said to Frank in English. Then she spoke to Attila. "Yes, we understand."

"He does not speak English," Spats said, "but he sits on a high platform by the ceiling and looks through the lens. He speaks into a tape recorder and says what he hears phonetically. He can tell what all those who are sitting against the far wall who face him are saying."

Frank thought immediately of his conversation with Tony. He remembered that he had sat sideways in relation to that common wall Spats was referring to, but Tony had faced the hole. As best he could recall, it was he who had given the possibly compromising information in answer to Tony's questions.

"We are really grateful to you, Attila for what you've told us," Julie said.

"We have resumed the payments to the account we are holding for you," Frank said. "I realize you're not doing this for money, but if you need anything, please tell us."

"I could use perhaps five hundred dollars."

Now was the moment Frank had hoped would come. He wanted to have some quid pro quo beyond what Spats had already given them. Frank took a plain envelope from Julie's large purse and counted out five one hundred dollar bills while Spats watched.

"I know that you don't want to meet in Budapest, but what if I could tell you a way we could do it that would be secure? Would you be willing to meet me?" Frank held the money, but did not hand it over yet.

"No. The risk is too great." Attila eyed the bills.

"And if we could cut the risk to almost nothing? You told me you were not a coward and I believe you. You also said that the reason you did not come to the first meeting three years ago was that you had discovered there was a penetration of our organization and you thought that he would learn of your contact with us. We have always restricted all knowledge of you to just a few people and you haven't been compromised. Thanks to you, we'll catch this fellow you've told us about so that reason will cease to exist. Can I explain to you what I have in mind?"

Spats sat for a moment. He no longer appeared interested in the money. Instead, he looked around the room. His eyes fixed on the yellow roses and he smiled. That look transformed his face. So far, he had worn a stern expression. Suddenly, Frank saw another side of the fellow and he understood that the first time an agent was recruited was not the only time he would have to be talked into doing something he might not want to do. This was a different kind of courtship. Attila looked at Julie.

"Thank you," he said. "You remembered." Then he turned to Frank. "I am certainly disposed to listen."

Frank thought it was such a waste that Julie had become an analyst. She had those people skills that couldn't be taught.

"On the thirtieth of October I will have a party at my apartment. I live in the Buda hills. I intend to invite about fifty people. Everyone will be wearing costumes. It will be at night. If you stand in a deserted place, maybe across the street from the park where I saw you, I can have a car, one without diplomatic plates pick you up. The driver and his wife will have a costume for you with a mask. You can put it on immediately. You come in with them. We'll be able to talk in one of the bedrooms. Afterward, you go out the same way."

"The AVH is watching your apartment."

"Yes. The observation post is across the street. They have my phone tapped. They didn't know I would be the one to take the apartment, so they didn't have time do to a proper audio installation. They have hot-wired the phone and they use it to monitor my calls, but also to listen to what I'm doing in the apartment. I've tested it. I know when they turn it on and off. They will see you come in, but they won't know it's you and there will be plenty of background noise, music and the crowd, so they won't be able to hear us."

Spats sat for another moment. He looked again at the flowers, but this time he didn't smile. Then he looked at Julie. Frank was counting on the fellow's sense of adventure. Most denied area agents had it. He thought, too, that Spats might want to impress Julie with his courage.

"Yes. Okay. Tell me precisely what I have to do."

Frank went on to explain the particulars of his plan, which he had kept simple. He was aware that Julie was watching him and he did his best not to preen or posture.

"If for some reason you cannot make that meeting, is there a chance you will get out of Hungary again?" Julie asked.

"It is possible that I will go to Paris at the end of the year on AVH business."

"If you do, here is a telephone number to call." Julie was drawing on her Paris experience. She jotted the number down on a three by five card. "Say you are Monsieur Boyer and that you are inquiring about the Ford that was listed for sale. The person will say that they regret that the car has already been sold. Frank or I or both of us will meet you at the Hotel Lutétia near Le Bon Marché department store."

The rest of the meeting was uneventful. When Spats left fifteen minutes later he kissed Julie's and shook Frank's hand. Frank had the impression that the fellow did so with more warmth than he had when he arrived. Perhaps that was wishful thinking. Frank knew that the real measure of Spats's confidence in him would come on the thirtieth of October.

With the Hungarian gone, Frank stood beside Julie and motioned to the bed.

"It would be a shame to waste it," he said.

"Let's just go over the room to be sure we don't leave anything behind. You'll get yours later." She poked her elbow in his ribs.

A taxi brought them back to the Kartnerstrasse about half a mile from their apartment. They began to walk in that direction. Julie pointed to her left.

"If you're still hungry, we can get a Sachertorte, or a bloody Mary." Frank saw the lettering of the Sacher Hotel and the café. "It would be appropriate. They filmed part of 'The Third Man' here."

"Orson Welles. Joseph Cotton."

"Yes. But you don't look anything like either of them."

"Funny, we've never gone to the movies together. I don't know what kind of music you like. What books you read."

"But we've spied together. How many couples can say that?" Julie was wearing a yellow rain slicker and she turned up the collar around her neck. "So what did you think of him?"

"So far so good, what he said about the Brit rings true. I don't know how headquarters will pass the information to MI-6 without blowing Spats, but that's their problem."

"And how will you deal with your own ambassador?"

"Tony handles that end of things. Crittenden doesn't understand what it's all about, but Tony will find some way to persuade him."

They made love again that night then they both dozed off. At about three in the morning, Frank got out of bed and sat in the yellow-cushioned armchair by the window. It had a musty smell, but he didn't mind. He just sat looking at Julie. She was curled and sleeping like a crescent moon. He knew this image was all he would have to sustain him for the next few months. Then she stirred and reached her arm across the bed. When she sensed he wasn't there, she began to move her legs. He stood and tiptoed across the hardwood to join her again under the sheet.

The following morning they moved out of the apartment by eleven. Frank put his suitcase in the car trunk and they drove the Audi to Salzburg, where he checked his bag at the train station then turned the car in at the Hertz office. Julie planned to take a bus back to Vienna, but first she wanted to visit Mozart's home.

"You asked me what kind of music I like," she said. "I like classical music."

"I would have fit in better in the forties. I like big band stuff, classical, too, but best of all, Nina Simone. There was a station in Philadelphia that used to play her songs late at night. I drove a cab and I used to listen. It was dark, quiet, cold, nobody around. I'd be cruising, or parked at a stand on some corner. I've always identified her with that, being alone."

She looked at him.

"You have incredible eyes."

That gave him pause. Beth, in one of her few uncharacteristically complimentary moments, had said the same thing. She told him he looked as if he could see something no one else could and that made him appear knowing and spiritual.

Frank took Julie's picture sitting at the young Mozart's harpsichord. They walked for ten minutes. A couple approached them. The woman was leading a rottweiler. He was broad-shouldered and solid. His body was almost black, but his face was mahogany, with a white crescent mark between his eyebrows.

"He reminds me of my Fritz," Julie said as they passed the couple.

"When you were a kid?"

"No. I had him when I taught school in Massachusetts. I had a garden apartment. I used to cook on the grill in the summer. Some of the kids would try to steal steaks, but Fritz would just walk up and look at them and they skedaddled. He wasn't much for chasing balls and he never ran after the kids, but he was a great watch dog."

At the train station on the platform, neither knew how to say goodbye.

"You haven't told me about the movies you like," she said, "old ones?" He carried his bag in one hand and she held tight to his free arm and put her head on his shoulder. He could tell she was struggling to keep things normal.

"Yes, and when I go to the theater, I get there early and sit in the middle seat of the middle row. From there you see the film the way the director intended to show it."

"You take everything so seriously." She smiled.

"I take you seriously. I love you." Frank kissed her, then held her, then kissed her again.

"I'm counting on that. Keep resisting those Hungarian temptresses." For a moment she held her hand on his cheek. "Tomorrow in Vienna, I'll go in to the embassy and write up what we did. I'll send an info copy to Budapest."

He hoisted his bag onto the step of the first class car and looked back.

"I won't stay in Budapest more than two years. I'll come home in eighty-four. Then we'll see how we can work something out together. But first I'll try to get some leave. Maybe we can meet in London."

"Spats said he would come to Paris."

"There, too," Frank said. An announcement came over the loud speaker in German. Frank figured it was the call to board. He kissed Julie's hand.

"I have to ask you something." She continued to hold her hand close to his mouth. "You're sure that you don't mind that I'm older than you?"

"I've always loved older women." Frank climbed the metal steps, walked down the corridor and stood by the window. He reached up and lowered the wide pane. Julie stood on the platform. Neither said anything until the train began to move. Julie walked along beside the car, but as it built up speed, she began to lag behind.

"And I love you, Francis Manion. We'll go the movies. Did I tell you I can read cards? When we get to Paris I'll tell your fortune." she called after him.

Frank remembered the first time he saw her in Rio, the café, the ceiling fans. Now it was "Casablanca" again, but this time it wasn't sultry.

"Right, remember, we'll always have Paris." He waved and blew her a kiss.

Chapter 31

At eleven thirty on the morning after her return to Washington, Julie sat in Bill Marshall's office. She didn't realize it, but she was on the same sofa and in the same spot Frank had occupied over a year ago. Harry O'Meara was sitting to her right. He looked at her only when he had to.

"If the AVH is really trying to take pictures of papers, that's penny-ante stuff compared with the old days, right Bill, the tunnel in Berlin?" Julie figured this was intended to put her in her place, a newcomer who couldn't have hacked it in "the old days."

Marshall smiled, but didn't comment. Instead, he turned to Julie.

"We've gone over your report on the meeting. It looks as if Spats may be back in business. Good job, young lady."

"Thank you. But if Frank hadn't found him, we would still be wondering what happened." She didn't bother to acknowledge O'Meara. She figured him for another male chauvinist. But Marshall was pleasant. Maybe he was that way because he had gotten used to dealing with women. He had four of them at home. "I'm just sorry that he didn't know any more about the mole," she said. "Do we have enough to identify him?"

Marshall looked at the Raven.

"I'm not sure you have the need to know that." O'Meara glared at her.

"For Christ sake, Harry, she's the one who got us the information in the first place, she and young Manion."

"I'll tell you what we don't know," O'Meara groused. "We don't know anybody named Fassbinder. We are looking at several people. There is a guy who was from Vienna, but it's not likely that he could be telling them very much. He's not in a position that gives him real access."

"I talked to Clive Calhern, MI-6's Washington man." Marshall was addressing Julie. She realized that he had probably already coordinated with O'Meara what the agency would pass to the Brits. "I told him we've been doing a general check of our denied area stations because we had a tip the Soviets have a new method for trying to get into our secure areas and they're doing it not only in Moscow, but in the Bloc embassies as well. I said we were changing all of our combinations as a first step. I advised him to do the same. We're going to have somebody in the Pentagon ask them to get that air attaché out of Hungary before he shoots off his mouth again." Marshall leaned back in his chair and half turned to

219

the plate glass window. "They'll say Gross isn't working well with our own DEFATT. Something like that. That will protect Spats."

"What about the security at our own embassy in Budapest?" Julie asked.

"We'll leave that to Tony Valletta and Frank." Marshall smiled. Julie wondered if he had any idea what was going on between her and Frank, but she was pretty sure he didn't. Even Tony wasn't fully aware unless Frank had told him and she knew Frank could keep secrets.

The Raven stood. He seemed to do so in segments and when he straightened as far as he could, he still looked stooped and gaunt. Julie felt sorry for him. It must be terrible to lose a child, she thought.

"I suppose that's it, eh?" O'Meara asked.

"Yes," Marshall said. Julie got to her feet. "No. Please stay on a bit, Julie. I want to talk more about Frank Manion." Julie sat down again. The Raven looked at both of them, shrugged his bony shoulders and walked out. After he had gone, Marshall winked at her. "That business about Berlin was a bit of puffery. Harry glossed over a lot. What we did wasn't all that great. The Sovs knew about the tunnel all along. And some of the things we did in the old days were stupid. We dropped a lot of émigrés into Russia and the Ukraine, got them all killed."

"I guess we've learned this business the hard way." Julie shook her head.

"You know, I followed the Spats case from the start. I was chief of operations then and I believed all along that you had recruited this guy."

"Thanks for your confidence. A lot of people doubted that I had."

"I was sorry to see you had switched over to the DI. You had the makings of a fine case officer."

"Thank you again."

"I want you to stay involved with Spats at least for the time being, but I also want you to continue with the Bagatelle case. That's going gang-busters. In his last package he sent us an advanced copy of the speech Brezhnev plans to give in Baku about improving relations with the Chinese. He gave us the analysis they're sending out about the likelihood that Helmut Schmidt will lose the election in Germany and how that will affect their approach to the SALT talks in Geneva. And he passed us a copy of a telegram to Dobrynin, their ambassador here, instructing him to go to the State Department after the twenty-sixth of October to inform them that the Soviets are testing a new ICBM. It's going to be launched that day from their test center in Plesetsk, a solid-fuel job. That's the kind of information we're paid to get and Bagatelle is helping us earn our money."

"Frank said all along he was an unusual fellow."

"You seemed to work well with Frank." This time he didn't smile in a knowing way, or any way at all. "I also want you to go down to Rio every month or so to hold Bagatelle's girl friend's hand. Will you do that for us?"

"I don't know if my office will..." Marshall didn't let her finish.

"Don't concern yourself about that. I'll work it out with Bill James. He's a good fellow. He'll let you go. You wouldn't mind a few days in Rio every month or so, would you?" Marshall smiled. Julie noticed age spots on his forehead. She thought Marshall must like the sun. Frank had told her the division chief had a twenty-five foot day cruiser he sailed out of Annapolis on weekends. And there on his credenza were his nautical knots. She returned the smile.

"I'm ready to answer the call of duty," she said.

"That's what I like to hear." Marshall got up and came around his desk to escort her to the door.

Julie went back to her office, but only to pick up her purse. Just after she had arrived that morning she had called Helen Hassan to set up a lunch. She hurried to the elevator. The meeting with Marshall had lasted a bit longer than she had anticipated. It was five minutes after noon when she walked quickly down the corridor to the cafeteria. Helen was waiting outside the double doors. She waved as Julie approached.

"Sorry. I got tied up with Bill Marshall and your boss."

"I know. He came back from the meeting grumbling about having to wipe CT's noses. He thinks nobody ever gets beyond the career trainee stage."

They snaked their way through the lunch line, paid separately and met at a table on the upper level of the cafeteria. Julie preferred it since it was usually less crowded up there.

"So, how was your trip?" Helen asked.

"Very successful, I guess you've seen the cable I sent back."

"Yes."

"I sent an info copy to Frank Manion in Budapest." Julie had ordered a bowl of soup and a salad and sprinkled a bit of salt on both.

"I don't know if I told you, but I met him at Christmas time." Helen ripped open a small plastic envelope of mustard and spread it on her ham. She was not Muslim and had no dietary restrictions. Though she was Lebanese, she was Christian.

"You didn't mention it, but he did," Julie said.

"What a hunk. He told me you two had worked together in Rio."

"Yes."

"It was obvious he was smitten," Helen smiled as she said this.

"That could work both ways."

Helen had started eating her ham and peas and the potatoes with a cheese sauce and now put down her fork.

"Oh, my God." She looked at Julie and smiled again. "Don't tell me he's now your significant other?"

"Could be." Julie smiled herself between spoonfuls of tomato soup.

221

"It's about time," Helen said, "a beautiful girl like you. All I can say is you two could make lovely babies together. What a gene pool!"

"Please don't say anything to anyone about this, okay?"

"My lips are sealed." Helen took her paper napkin from her lap and wiped her mouth then pressed her lips together and pointed to them.

"In the meeting Harry wouldn't say much about the mole. Have you been able to come up with anything yet?"

"There's a guy we're looking at. I can't tell you his name. If it goes anywhere, there will be a criminal indictment. But he's in admin and we don't think he's a likely candidate as an AVH penetration. I did go over to the German desk this morning to talk to a friend of mine there, Gertrude Buckholz. I haven't even told this to Harry yet. I wanted to find out if that name Fassbinder was unusual in any way or if it was a common name. She said in German it means a barrel-maker. I don't know if that has any significance." Helen cut off a piece of ham and was about to eat it when Julie spoke.

"You mean a cooper?"

Helen's ham never made it to her mouth.

Chapter 32

On Saturday late in the afternoon, Vladimir Shurin and Natasha Chernenko wandered through the Arbat. The area had become famous both in Russian literature and in reality as Moscow's Bohemian quarter. There were crowded cafés everywhere and many of the pastel painted buildings had housed artists and writers through the previous century.

The couple passed the Empire style sky blue Pushkin house on Arbat Street, where the poet had lived. Vladimir recalled the poem he had written out for Boland. If that day in Rio had been a new beginning, any day now could prove his end. More and more he felt the noose tightening. Almost every night as he left for work at the foreign ministry or when he returned to his flat in the morning he noticed men lurking around the entrance to his building. But on his way to this rendezvous, he had intentionally lost his tail by going down into the metro, melting into the crowd, and exiting without getting on the train. He didn't want the organs to know what he was up to today.

They walked back to the square surrounding the Church of the Savior in Peski. Behind the church stood rows of parked cars, most of which were for sale. Natasha was like a child in a toy shop. Vladimir had promised to lend her the money to buy a used automobile with the understanding that she would repay the loan over two years time and allow him to use the car whenever he needed it. He had gotten the money from the Americans in their last drop to him.

"What about that one?" Natasha pointed to a shiny BMW.

"I said I would lend you money to buy a car, not a golden carriage. You had better lower your expectations. I'll show you the one." They walked up and down the rows, passing Pobedas, Chaikas, Moskvichs, Zhigulis and Ladas. In one of the side streets, Vladimir spotted the pea-green Opel Olympia he had seen the previous week. "This is what you need."

The owner, who had been sitting at the wheel reading a copy of *Krokodil*, tossed the magazine on the passenger seat, got out and met them at the front fender. The hood to the engine was already up.

"So, comrades," The man took off his cap to reveal that he was bald as a bottle. "Newlyweds? You need wheels, I suppose."

Natasha was about to answer, but Vladimir squeezed her hand.

"Yes, comrade, the car is for my wife. She just got her license last week from the GIBDD. This is how old? Seventy-two I would say."

"Correct."

"How many kilometers?"

"Eighty three thousand, and it runs perfectly."

Vladimir studied the body. Several spots had rusted through and been replaced with lead plugs and painted over. If the odometer had eighty three thousand kilometers, it was certainly because it had been turned back. But everyone had to play the game.

"It looks as if you have steam cleaned the engine." Vladimir ran his finger around the distributor cap. "But I see the body has corroded."

"What can you do in Moscow?" The fellow slapped his cap against his thigh. "I keep a canvas cover over it and I park it in the courtyard of the building, but on these streets you're bound to get a little rust. Still, the paint job is not bad, would you say?"

"So, why are you selling this chariot of the gods?"

"I'm able to buy a BMW, but I need money to do it."

Vladimir hesitated. Anyone who could afford a BMW must have some connections. He wondered for a moment if this fellow might not be KGB. If so, his efforts to get away from his tails could be for naught. He knew it would be imprudent to ask personal questions.

"And how much are you asking, comrade?"

"Well, for a couple starting out, I would say eight thousand."

This time it was Natasha who squeezed Vladimir's hand. He didn't know what that meant, but he knew eight thousand was only a starting point. For the next five minutes, he and the car's owner went back and forth. Between bids and counter-offers, they discussed sports clubs, the world situation, crime in Moscow. Finally, at six thousand five hundred, Vladimir thought he had taken the price as low as he could.

"My wife will come next Saturday to close the deal."

"By next Saturday, it may be gone." The man half turned away.

"If it isn't, she'll take it. I will not be here, but she'll give you six thousand five hundred. No more."

Even if baldy tried to jack up the price, Vladimir knew Natasha wouldn't pay it. She would haggle. He had discovered that she was good at haggling over just about anything.

They walked back the way they had come.

"Why didn't you buy it on the spot?" Natasha asked, obviously disappointed and a bit angry. "He won't go lower and you said it was worth it. He's right. By the time I come back, it may be gone."

Vladimir lowered his head, closed his eyes and pinched the bridge of his nose. He thought this was all understood.

"I told you. I don't want to be connected to this deal. When I separate from my wife, she could claim ownership if my name is on the registration." This seemed to mollify Natasha. In fact, the real reason was that Vladimir simply wanted use of the car without the KGB knowing he had it. Now they continued for three more blocks to the foreign ministry. They were working a middle shift, from four to midnight on this Saturday night and they arrived with five minutes to spare.

At eleven-thirty, Natasha made her run to the communications room. Vladimir tucked the messages he had selected into his shirt and when she got back, he headed down the hall to the toilet. Opening the door to the darkened lavatory he reached to his left to flip the light switch then froze. Over the two toilet stalls he saw pencil thin shafts of light from the ceiling to the floor. Somebody had drilled holes in the ceiling. He had to swallow hard and force himself to move normally. He entered the stall and did his business quickly. He never removed the cables and at his first opportunity, when Natasha stepped into the hall he put them into the distribution bin with the others.

At midnight, he headed home. He had told Natasha that Irina was expecting him. It wasn't true. His wife had gone, as usual, to her parents' dacha. Although he spotted no one on his way to the flat, he continued to feel queasy, and when he walked through the door, his stomach took another turn. He had gotten into the habit of putting individual pieces of hair over doors and checking each time he came home to see if they had been disturbed. Irina had left at midday but his inspection now showed that someone had been in the flat. He took everything off the shelves that he used as a ladder and climbed into the attic. Up there he had put two tiny strips of paste across the edge of the board that concealed the radio and cipher pads. He was relieved to see that they were unbroken.

He slid the ceiling cover back into place, climbed back down and sat at the kitchen table. What to make of it? As nearly as he could figure, they had come in to search the rooms, but evidently they never realized the storage space existed. He was certain that if they had, they would have taken up every loose board. Had he left anything in the flat that might compromise him? No. It was all up in that attic. He forced himself to calm down and go over day by day what had happened since he had seen that first watcher across the street. He was sure he had never led them to Natasha's place. He had taken great pains to give anybody the slip in the metro. He thought of the times he had put down or picked up packages. He thought of the days when he had encrypted messages at this very table. He concentrated on the nights when he had photographed documents at the ministry. But each night, he had turned the light on and turned it off in the men's room and this was the first time he had seen any sign that someone might be watching. At the end of this exercise, he took a bottle of icy Stolichnaya vodka from the tiny refrigerator and poured himself a full glass. He reached in his shirt pocket, took out the Cartier pen and unscrewed the top. He fingered one of the suicide pills then screwed the top back in place. He sat and tilted his head slightly, rubbing his index finger beside his ear.

"Not yet," he decided. "If they have anything on me, they won't let me go to Prague in one month. I'll know soon enough." He lifted the glass to his lips. "To a new beginning."

Chapter 33

Frank rolled over in a half-sleep. Dreams crowded together like furtive migrants trying to slip across the border into waking time. There was Julie. She had been in the dark wearing an Arab chador. Now that garment had become white, diaphanous. He could see her breasts, but was not allowed to touch them. When he woke fully, he was facing the window and she was gone.

Frank's place was in the Buda hills on the top floor of a three story building. Its best feature was a deep balcony, a veranda without a roof that ran the width of the apartment and overlooked the Danube and almost the entire city. The bedroom windows faced east across that veranda and often he woke with the sun. On this morning, he was awake even before dawn. After his sexy dream, the cityscape was a disappointment, a monochrome gray, like a great sheet of photographic paper waiting for its catalyst. Frank had taken to watching the leaves on an acacia tree that in summer had formed the first luminescent green before all the other colors of the city showed themselves. Now those leaves were a dirty yellow. Still, it was perfect weather for a Halloween party. And Frank had invited over fifty people for Saturday night.

On Friday in the office, he and Tony went over the drill for Spats's pick-up with Charlie Noble. They stood around Tony's desk studying a map of Budapest.

"Charles," Tony said, "he should be waiting just here." Tony used the tip of his pen to point to the spot. "Francis, how does one pronounce this name?"

"*Városligeti Körút.*"

"Devil of a language, but I've seen it and Francis has recommended it. It's very dark under the trees in this corner of the park."

"Yeah, I know the place." Charlie stood, legs slightly spread, his feet pointing outward and his hands on his hips. He appeared dismissive, but Tony persisted.

"It's very important to get there at the appointed hour. If Mr. Spats is forced to stand for any length of time, he will certainly be inclined to return to the security of hearth and home."

Charlie tilted his head back and slightly to the side, his ever-present unlit cigar butt in his mouth. Here, Frank thought, was a clash of cultures if there ever was one. He could tell that Charlie just didn't like Tony. Had he picked that up from body language, or through some gift of insight? Whatever the explanation, Frank knew that Charlie had been Kearns's man and that he hadn't been able to adjust to the change of bosses. But he also knew that however Tony conveyed the instructions, they could count on Charlie and his wife to carry them out.

"I put Spats's get-up in this grocery box with your costume and Joanie's." Frank pointed to the box on the floor next to the wall. "You'll have to come in tomorrow to get them. I think it's better not to leave them lying around in your apartment overnight."

"Fine, I have weekend duty anyway," Charlie replied.

"Try to get to my place between seven-fifteen and seven-thirty," Frank said. "That's when the crowd should be arriving. You'll probably have to park down the hill, but that will be good because your car won't be spotted from the observation post across the street. Afterward, you drop him off here, Mátyás Square." Frank indicated the site on the map.

"Yeah, I know."

"Right, then," Tony said, "we're as prepared as we can be. Thank you, Charles for your assistance." Tony reached out to pat the communicator on the shoulder, but couldn't quite reach that far and wound up sliding his hand on the front of Charlie's flannel shirt.

All the following day, Saturday, Frank was uneasy as he was before any operational act. He wondered whether this stress might lessen his effectiveness. And he knew he was under stress. On his flight to Frankfurt, he had noticed how relaxed he became when he left Budapest and how tense he grew on his way back in.

In the morning he went to the diplomatic club just uphill from his apartment and jogged around the extended lawn of the large dilapidated manor house that sat on the property. The grounds were owned by the embassy and had been converted into a tiny four-hole golf course. Half of his run was uphill on the near side and the other half back down on the far side. The surveillance cars behind him always stopped downhill from the club. He was sure that must be because the AVH observation post at this site was in a modern apartment building, the only one on the hill that sat directly opposite the club and looked down onto the tennis courts.

That afternoon, he went to the Jordanian Embassy to pick up his costume from a third secretary with whom he played tennis. Then two ladies arrived at his place. Normally they worked in the Széchenyi building, an American-owned apartment house that sat next to Parliament Square on the Danube. But tonight they would earn some extra money by preparing the food for the buffet dinner. A dark-haired young man who would serve the drinks showed up. He was the custodian at the Népstadion building, also owned by the embassy. Frank knew these people would report to the security service after it was all over, but he was counting on the costumes to carry the whole thing off right under the noses of the AVH.

The guests began to show up at seven and Frank greeted each one at the door. Most of the foreigners had never heard of Halloween, but they had accepted the invitation to a costume party with delight.

The first to arrive was a group of Finns dressed as a gypsy band. They were followed by a Frenchman and his wife. He was a Roman legionnaire and his attractive dark-haired wife was dressed as Cleopatra. She even carried a rubber snake, which she dangled in Frank's face.

"I thought you might like to see my asp," she said in English.

Several people were clowns. An Austrian and his Canadian girl friend were Andy and Raggedy Ann respectively. A Mexican came as Pancho Villa, but his wife was Pippi Longstocking. Tony came as a prizefighter replete with sixteen-ounce gloves and a long red satin robe with the word Rocky in big white letters on the back. He wore white satin shorts and a narrow black mask, high-topped white sneakers and black silk knee-high socks. His spindly legs showed he hadn't done his roadwork for his next fight. There were pirates and a Hungarian count. An American secretary was Hester Prynne with a scarlet letter A on her chest. Ty Gardener showed up as Abraham Lincoln. Frank wondered where he had gotten the stovepipe hat.

"Nancy made it for me out of cardboard. She painted it black."

Nancy Gardener was a Playboy bunny. Vitorio Cabrini from the Italian Embassy waddled in dressed as an enormous lion.

"I rented the costume from the National Theater," he told Frank proudly.

Frank wore slip-on sandals, long white pants, a dish-dash, which was a one piece long-sleeved white shirt with buttons at the neck. Thick leather belts with cartridge holders criss-crossed his chest and connected to the wide black belt around his waist. On his head he had a white kaffiya and a gold iqal, three braided strands that circled his head. In his waist belt he had a dagger just in case. Over it all he wore a half-sleeved white abbaya that reached to his heels. He was Lawrence of Arabia.

He had started the music, Chicago, Rolling Stones, Jefferson Airplane. And the table was covered with cold cuts, broccoli and dips, potato salad and Hungarian specialties. Most important, there were open bottles of wine, whiskies, liqueurs, beer and Hungarian palinka, a potent apricot brandy. In no time the place was rocking. The gypsies danced with royals. Clowns seemed to prefer pirates. The Roman soldier appeared to be getting on well with Hester Prynne on one of the sofas that had been pushed to the side of the room. This was of obvious concern to Cleopatra.

At seven-twenty, Tony sidled up to Frank.

"Our chap has not made his appearance."

"There are still a lot of people to come. If he's at the right place, Charlie will get him."

Suddenly, Tony tried to grab Frank's arm, but couldn't quite succeed with the boxing glove.

"There he is." A tall fellow preceded by a woman in a black veil made of Spanish lace and carrying castanets came in the door. The man was dressed as Zorro, all in black, with a tasseled hat, a black sash at his waist, polished black boots and a sword. They were from the Portuguese Embassy.

"No. It's not him," Frank said. "That's all we need, two Zorros."

In the next group of five were a Bonnie and Clyde couple, Charlie and Joanie Noble, who both wore oversized fedoras and carried Tommy guns. Behind them was the missing Zorro. Frank greeted them.

"It went all right?" he asked Charlie.

"No problemo. He was waitin' for us."

Frank spoke to Spats in French just loud enough to be heard over the music.

"You see, my friend? You're perfectly safe. Just come with me."

The young Hungarian waiter was on the other side of the living room serving drinks to the few people who were seated. He never looked beyond the dancers as Frank led Spats to the back bedroom and locked the door from the inside. Frank had also locked the living room doors to the balcony and drawn the bedroom curtains to cut off the view from the outside. The noise of the music was almost overwhelming even in this adjoining room, but to be absolutely certain their own conversation was private, Frank turned on a portable radio on the bedside table. He motioned to Spats to sit in an upholstered chair. Frank sat on the bed and leaned close.

"Where is your telephone?" Spats asked in a whisper that was difficult to hear over the music.

"Out in the hall."

"The people who watch you are in the building across the street.

"Yes, I know."

"They listen to everything through the phone."

"I know that, too. If you remember, I told you that in Vienna."

"How do you know?"

"I don't think they realized that I would be the one living here. I went outside when I first got here and I noticed that the phone line stretches from my building to the building next door. It runs up the street, then across the street, back down and into the building facing this one. More than that, they don't know it, but when they turn on the listening device, a surge of electricity comes through the line and it rings the phone bell, just one quick ring, 'ping.' When they turn it off, the same thing happens."

"I have brought you something." From inside his black shirt, Attila took a packet of papers. "These are the schematics for the AVH's audio installations into your other buildings." He got up from the chair awkwardly as he had to hold the sword straight in front of his leg, and he spread the papers out on the bed cover. "You see. Here is your building back by the soccer stadium." He made that little "tsk" sound with saliva and his teeth. Frank stood and leaned over to look at the drawings and immediately recognized the area. "And here is the observation post." Attila pointed to each in turn.

"I thought it would be there," Frank said as he looked at the outline of the building behind his former apartment.

"The audio lines run underground and enter through the laundry room in the basement of the building. You see?"

"Yes."

"Then all the lines run up this wall into the apartments."

"Right," Frank said.

"For the building on the river, all of the microphone lines run down to the mezzanine floor and out through this room." Again, Attila indicated the location on the map and the schematic.

"Where we have the American school?"

"Yes. They go into the building next door. The listening post is right there, on the other side of the wall. And here are the names of the employees of your embassy who are reporting to my service."

Frank scanned the list. While not all of the local employees were on it, most of them were.

"Thank you, Attila. These will be extremely helpful." In fact, Frank saw little value in the drawings or the names. The Americans posted to Budapest had been briefed many times on the effort made by the Hungarians to bug their apartments and phones and monitor their activities, but Frank was certain most people either didn't believe what they had been told, or forgot periodically that everything they said was overheard. But he was not about to say that to the agent. "What about the mole, any news?" Frank gathered the papers and stuck them under the mattress.

"Yes." Attila tilted his sword again and sat back in the chair. "My colleague told me before he left for Montreal that he crosses into the United States only on weekends of the first and third week of each month. Our embassy in Washington tells him which weekend it will be. All the meetings are in New York, but not always in New York City."

"Do you know his real name?"

"No, only the name Fassbinder."

"So you know nothing more about him?"

"No, nothing."

"Is there anything else you're able to tell me?"

"We know that you have a security team here. Our men have shut down all of our technical operations at your embassy and in the residences of all of your diplomats until these men leave."

"Anything else?"

"Not for now."

"Do you have access to President Kadar's office?" Frank asked.

"None."

"Ministry of Foreign Affairs?"

"No."

"Ministry of Defense?"

"No."

Frank learned a couple of lessons. First, a recruited agent in the security service of a country was worth his weight in gold because he could provide counter-intelligence information, but unless he was high up or posted to another office where policy was made, he had little other useful access. Second, Frank realized that he liked the recruitment part of operations a lot better than the debriefing part. He was a head hunter.

"So, will you be able to meet in Paris?"

"For now, it's scheduled for the end of December."

"And you still have the number Julie gave you?"

"Right here," Attila took off his hat and tapped on his temple, which was covered by a black bandanna and the string of his mask.

"Before you come to Paris, I would like you to get the names of as many AVH people as you can and tell us what they do, those serving abroad and the ones here in your headquarters. Don't write them down. Just try to remember who is where."

"I can do that. Do you want the names of people on the surveillance teams?"

"Yes. You won't be able to remember everyone, of course. But try to think of the names of officers, those high up and those who look as if they will move up, anyone in a position of importance."

"I understand."

"Great," Frank said, "and our first priority will continue to be whatever you can find out about Fassbinder. What reason did you give your wife for being out tonight?"

"I told her I was on official business."

"Good. Now let's just enjoy ourselves. The food is in the dining room. Dance, have a good time. When people start to leave, you can go out the door with my friends. They will drop you off on the other side of the park. You can leave the costume in their car. I want to thank you for your courage in coming tonight. Maybe we can have a fine dinner together in Paris when Julie comes, the three of us."

"I look forward to that."

They shook hands and Frank unlocked the door. Spats went out first. Just outside in the hall, a British man dressed as Horatio Hornblower, or maybe Lord Nelson stood in front of Spats.

"And what have you two been up to then? So, Zorro, the old sword still has a point, eh? Buggering Lawrence were you?"

Spats said nothing. He probably didn't understand. Frank saw that he headed straight for the buffet table and poured himself a stiff glass of Johnny Walker Black Label. Frank ignored the Brit and walked to the living room to join the dancers.

"Everything went well?" Tony asked.

"Fine, he didn't have much to say. I'm not sure it was worth the risk. But Paris is still on."

They stood on the living room floor and Frank could actually feel it bounce to the rhythm of the music. He figured he had to displace some of the weight and went to unlock the balcony doors. Dancers spilled outside onto the veranda. A Swedish gypsy he knew from the diplomatic club approached him. She was married and had been quarreling with her husband. She was obviously well into her cups. Maybe she had been drinking before she arrived.

"I love you," she said to Frank.

"Yes, but will you respect me in the morning?" he asked. She appeared stymied and Frank figured her English was probably not good enough to appreciate the humor.

Over the next few hours, Frank kept his eye on Spats. He noticed that the Portuguese Zorro was watching his competitor. Finally, with a wobbly step he approached the Hungarian out on the balcony.

"*Voce não pode ser o verdadeiro. Ha um solo Zorro. Eu sou o unico Zorro.*" (You can't be the real thing. There is only one Zorro. I am the only Zorro.) Frank realized it was a challenge and moved quickly when he saw the Portuguese actually start to draw his sword. Frank grabbed the swordsman's arm and spoke in Portuguese.

"*Voce e sem duvida o verdadeiro. Ele e so o seu substituto. Voces dois juntos vão eliminar o mal.*" (Without a doubt, you are the real one. He's only your deputy. Together, the two of you are going to eliminate evil.)

"*E justo. Exato.*" (That's right. Exactly.) With that, Alfonso, the Portuguese, appeared to consider Attila his long lost little brother and draped his arm over Spats's shoulder. For the first time, Frank figured Marshall was right. His Portuguese did come in handy.

The party didn't even start to break up until almost two in the morning. Charlie and Joanie Noble took Spats out in a crowd of revelers. Many of them had to hang onto the railing of the outside steps to steady themselves.

The next day, Frank slept in. When he finally got up, he surveyed the damage. The place looked like a war zone. Glasses, dishes, bottles, aluminum cans, balled up orange paper napkins were everywhere. He figured he would have to spend the rest of the day cleaning up. He went to the bathroom, lifted the toilet seat and started to pee. Suddenly, he broke out laughing. Urine splashed out of the bowl and he cursed, but went on laughing. Scratched into the wall above the toilet tank was a capital Z.

"The real Zorro," Frank said out loud. He had to remember to tell Julie.

Chapter 34

On the one hand Frank felt confident. Bagatelle was following his instructions to the letter. It was twenty-five minutes before nine o'clock on a drizzly marrow-chilling night, Thursday, November twenty-fifth, and few people were about. The Russian exited the Prague metro at the I. P. Pavlova station and walked around the square of the same name.

Frank's training had not prepared him fully for the kind of surveillance he had encountered in Budapest. But one thing it did teach him was that when he was not the target of surveillance and could watch teams at work from a distance, they were as obvious as stripes on a zebra. Frank was wearing his navy blue Hungarian raincoat and stood beyond the ellipse formed by the streetlight and close to the buildings at the edge of the square. He was carrying a net bag with two bottles of vodka and a worn leather loose-leaf binder with a zipper. In the darkness he listened as the high/low bleat of an ambulance or police car rose in intensity somewhere in the distance then faded slowly away and he watched Bagatelle, who appeared to be walking quickly to the tempo of the siren. Frank was certain that Shurin was free of surveillance.

On the other hand, Frank was uneasy. He spoke no Czech and he was not used to being in a place where he didn't know the local language. He had to buy the vodka without understanding a word the clerk said. And he was in his Boland disguise and that always made him uncomfortable.

Still, he knew he couldn't operate on emotion. What counted was that he had no doubt that he was working black and so was Shurin. In fact, from the time Frank crossed the Austrian border into Czechoslovakia, he had not seen one sign of surveillance. He was carrying Irish identity documents in the Boland name and the border checkers and train officials had not shown the slightest interest in him. Now he walked to Wenceslas Square and got the metro to Republic Square. He crossed to the intersection of Prikope and Hybernska and entered an apartment building at the tip of a wedge that from a thirty-degree angle overlooked Republic Square.

Frank rode up in a clanking, shuddering cage elevator to the fourth floor, got out and with a long brass key opened the door to the meeting place. He flipped the switch to turn on a dim entry light then walked across the main room to draw the heavy, dusty brocaded curtains. That left the room murky. He switched on the few wall sconces and table lamps, but they didn't cast much additional light. The ceilings must have been twelve feet high and remained in shadows. About eight feet up on one side of the main room was a loft. Frank could see the edge of a mattress. Below on a small table between two armchairs was a radio sitting on a lace doily. The furniture appeared to be catch-as-catch-can and was mostly thick-cushioned and old. Still, he would not be there long and comfort was not a consideration. He took off the raincoat and hung it on a wooden hook by the door. There was a small rickety wooden table near the window and two spare wooden chairs. He set the vodka bottles and his binder on the table and sat down to wait.

Precisely at nine o'clock, there was a gentle knock. Frank got up and turned on the radio. A symphony orchestra was playing a work by Mahler. When he got to the door, it struck him as appropriate that the first shadowy glance he had of Bagatelle was through the spy hole. Neither man said anything until Frank closed the door.

"Boland, *skol'ko lyet, skol'ko zim*?" ("How many summers, how many winters?"). The two men hugged each other and Bagatelle kissed Frank on both cheeks. Frank knew it was a traditional greeting, but was still touched. When he stepped back, Vladimir put his hand over his heart. "It is good to see you, my friend." He was wearing a black leather hip-length coat with the collar turned up. The leather was wet from the drizzle. He looked older than Frank remembered, certainly older than thirty-six.

"Wonderful to see you, Volodya. You had no trouble getting away?"

"My colleagues went out carousing. I told them I was not feeling well. It was not hard to persuade them." He pointed to a lump under his left eye that appeared still to be swelling. Frank figured it was from the Tae-Kwan-Do tournament and Vladimir confirmed it. "I lost my match today and truth is I have headache." The Russian put his fingers on top of his head, then tipped it back, arched the thumb of his other hand and jerked it several times toward his open mouth. "What do you have to drink?"

"Vodka, I just have to find the glasses. How much time do you have before you might be missed?" Frank crossed to the area that served as a tiny kitchen. He opened three cabinets before he found what he was looking for. He held two mismatched glasses up to the light. They looked clean enough and the alcohol would probably kill off any remaining germs.

"Perhaps one hour. No more. Do you have ice?" The Russian took off his coat and hung it over the back of the chair.

"I didn't remember that you took ice," Frank said.

Vladimir laughed.

"Not for my drink," he pointed again to his face, "for my cheek."

Frank looked in the small refrigerator. He took out a plastic tray of tiny cubes. In one of the counter drawers he found a dishtowel. He twisted the ice holder and dumped the cubes into the towel. When he went back to the table, he handed them to Shurin.

"So," Frank said. "You've done amazing things. The few people who know about you at home instructed me to tell you that they are honored and delighted that you are helping us."

"Richard, I understand that you have to say such thing, but for you and me we don't talk bullshit. I am doing this for money and to see Justinha." The Russian pressed the ice against his cheekbone.

"That reminds me. Here." Frank took an envelope from the inside pocket of his sport coat and handed it to Vladimir. "I got it in the diplomatic pouch. We knew you were coming to Prague, so I decided to bring it with me rather than put it in a package for you." The letter was from Justinha Marques and Frank had decided to get it out of the way first.

Vladimir studied it intently. He dropped the ice on the tabletop. He even ignored the glass of vodka Frank had set in front of him. Frank had read the letter. And Julie had told him in Vienna that Justinha had taken up with a former Brazilian boyfriend. The text didn't mention that, of course, but it did implore Vladimir not to believe anything he might hear about her, presumably through the Americans. That should have been a giveaway that something wasn't right. Frank gauged the time it would take for Shurin to get to that point. He could see the concern come over Vladimir's face and Frank thought, who better than a traitor to catch the slight scent of treachery? But then he realized that he did not think of Bagatelle as a traitor. Instead, Frank saw him as one of the millions of poor souls caught up in a lousy system. The difference was that Shurin had decided to do something about it. But with women there was only so much a man could do.

"She asks for money." Vladimir put the letter on the table, reached one arm across his body and fiddled with his wristwatch, then held his ear lobe between his forefinger and thumb. He appeared to be thinking fast. "Can you get money to her?"

"Sure. I just have to have your approval since it will come out of your escrow account. How much do you want to give her?"

"What about five thousand dollars?"

"Consider it done."

"Since it is all about money, how much do I have now?"

"At the end of this month you'll have two hundred thousand dollars."

"What about bonus?"

"It was approved. If you stay for a full three years and come out again, Washington will add one hundred forty thousand to make an even five hundred thousand."

Shurin smiled then held out his right hand palm up. Frank reached over and slapped it.

"Excellent. Now let's drink," Vladimir said. If he was upset by the letter he didn't show it.

Frank raised his glass. "Here's to swimmin' with bow-legged women."

Vladimir laughed loud.

"This I never heard. Again."

Frank repeated his toast. That was one of the benefits of dealing with foreigners. Old jokes became new. Shurin laughed again. They both drank.

"Okay," Frank said. "Let's get to some business." He unzipped his binder to take notes. "What the hell were those porno photos you sent a few months back? Nobody could figure it out."

"There is girl." Bagatelle picked up his ice towel again and applied it to his cheek.

"That much we understood."

"She helped me get position in distribution center. I fuck her. She found my camera one night and I had to think quick. So...." Shurin took several more swallows of his drink. "She thinks I am going to marry her. She wants me to go meet her parents. She has wicked temper. Last week she tried to cut me. She used knife I bought for her. Bloody hell."

"But she doesn't suspect that you're helping us?"

"Not at all, but things are becoming difficult."

"What do you mean, with the woman?" Frank leaned forward, his elbows on the table, which rocked a bit to one side.

"Suppose I cannot stay three years? I still get money, right?"

"What's going on, Volodya?"

The Russian lowered his head a bit, closed his eyes for a moment and pinched the bridge of his long nose.

"It is possible the organs suspect me." Shurin finished off his glass and reached for the bottle.

"What makes you think that?"

"People are following me." Vladimir tipped his glass and drank deeply. "They searched my flat, but they did not find radio or camera or papers."

"Is that why you stopped sending the film?"

"Yes. I believe they tried to catch me taking pictures at ministry, so now I just memorize messages and write them in code."

"But they let you come here. Would they have done that if you were under suspicion? You weren't followed here. I'm certain of it."

"You watched me come?"

"Part of the way."

"Possibly they have not found out nothing. I believe I can continue, but what happens if I am convinced that they will arrest me? What I mean to say is suppose I find out they are coming for me. Is there no way you can get me out of Soviet Union? Otherwise, I have to take poison."

Frank stood up. He hadn't eaten dinner and even the few swallows of vodka he had drunk caused him to be a little light-headed. But he had to think and he walked across the room. He put one hand in his pocket and the palm of the other on the back of his neck. The boards creaked under his feet.

"I don't think I can work this out on the spot. Washington will have to help. You don't have a car, right?"

"I can use one when I want, the girl's car...the Opel, Natasha's."

"What about a place where you could go, say for a day or two to hide out and wait?"

"I think her room. I have been very careful not to lead them to her place."

"Okay, write down the address. Maybe we can set something up now." Frank tore off a piece of yellow legal-sized paper and handed over his pen. "The address, the floor, right or left on the landing, the car, its description, license plate. The one thing we can agree on is a new danger signal." Frank knew the people in Moscow Station would have to get involved, but he figured if he could have Shurin place the signal in a spot they would have reason to pass regularly, it would work. Frank remembered that the embassy was on the Garden Ring and they had a travel limit of twenty-five miles in a radius from that point outward just as he had in Budapest. He waited while the Russian listed the information and all the while he thought. He enjoyed the independence that came with the case officer position, but there was a concomitant demand to be able to think on one's feet and solve problems on the spot.

"There." Vladimir handed him the sheet of paper.

"Volodya, this will have to be approved by Washington. But if they change the plan, they will let you know in the next package they put down for you. Otherwise, I want you to park the car..." Frank looked at the paper, "the Opel, on a street and get one of those matushka dolls, the largest one, and put it on the dash board of the car. The question is, where can you leave the car so that someone going to or from the American Embassy would see it? You know where the embassy is, right?"

"On the Garden Ring Road."

Frank had to be careful. He was not about to commit Moscow Station officers to anything without their agreement. In fact, he would not even tell Bagatelle that the CIA had people in Moscow.

"Is there a department store nearby? What about that big one, the GUM?" Frank recalled the name from his Russian language lessons in California.

"Yes. Not too far."

"Better still, what about a library?"

"There is Lenin Library near Kremlin."

"Is there a street close to the library where you could park the car?"

"Ulitsa Snamenka."

Frank wrote down the name and jotted notes about the plan.

"If you know you're in danger, park the car there with the doll on the dash between eight and nine in the morning, or six and seven in the evening. Let's add something. If the KGB is forcing you to give this emergency signal, put the doll on the dash in front of the passenger seat. That will mean they have you in their power and you're just along for the ride. If they do not have you in custody, put the doll on the driver's side. That will mean that you're still in control."

"Then what will happen?"

"Good question." Frank wanted to ask, "How the hell should I know?" But he realized he had to show and inspire some confidence. He sat back down. "What I think will happen is that someone will meet you at the girl's apartment. Does it have a window that faces the street?"

"She has only one room in flat. There are two windows. Yes, on street side."

"Okay. If you're in trouble and you park the car on Snamenka, go back to the room. If it's safe for somebody to meet you there, raise one window shade and pull the other one all the way down." Frank knew denied area stations had ways of exfiltrating agents. In Budapest he and Tony had worked out their own method. The question was whether headquarters and Moscow would go along with this plan.

"Will you be man who comes?" Shurin asked.

"I don't know. I'll try."

"How shall I know who it is if you cannot?"

Frank reached in his pocket and took a Hungarian ten forint note from his wallet.

"I could give you some parole, a recognition signal, but you might forget it." He tore the bill in half. "This might not seem professional, but it will work." He handed Vladimir half of the bill and put the other half back in his wallet.

Shurin looked at the torn piece of currency.

"Does it have special mark?"

"No. But whoever comes will have this half of the bill and he will say 'I bring greetings from Richard'." Frank held the torn piece at eye level over the middle of the table. "Now listen, Volodya. Use this only in an emergency. Don't run if they're not chasing you. Brezhnev is dead. I just heard today that Andropov was voted into the presidium. More than ever we're going to need you to tell us what he's going to do so there won't be any miscalculations that could start a war."

"Of course, I am not going to run away without reason. I want to stay. I said I would. Do you know why they have chosen this moment to elect Andropov?"

"No."

"It is because delegation is about to arrive from Middle East. I saw message from Soviet ambassador in Damascus. King Hussein from Jordan and Prince Saud, Foreign Minister of Saudi Arabia, will head this group. There will be major Soviet initiative to re-establish relations with moderate Arab states. In 1972, when Sadat expelled all Soviet diplomats from Egypt, we lost such relations. Without being member of presidium, Andropov would not be authorized to represent government with foreign delegations."

Frank wrote down what he knew would be an intelligence report if he could get it to Washington in time.

"When is the visit to take place?"

"Very soon. In next days. Also, from same ambassador we lost eleven of our lads in Lebanon."

"How?"

"Israel Air Force bombed Israeli plane."

At first, Frank thought there was a linguistic problem.

"I don't understand. You mean a Syrian plane?"

"No, Israel had plane go down in Lebanon. They came back to destroy plane because they had to prevent Syrians, who could get electronic counter-measures devices that Jews put in plane. Ambassador said Syrians told him these devices were developed by Israelis themselves. By then, our boys were sent to remove these devices. Israelis bombed this plane and killed eleven Soviet men."

"Do you know the date of the incident?" Frank continued to write. It was another intel report.

"No. Was only one or two weeks ago."

Frank was able to picture the situation easily. Whenever an enemy had a chance to get technical gear from a weapons system, they would swarm over it like ants on a dead beetle.

"What did the ambassador recommend in response?"

"Nothing. But he also said that our program to replace all military equipment lost by Syrians in last summer battle with Israelis in Lebanon was almost complete. There are T-62 and T-72 tanks, three hundred of them with armed personnel carriers were shipped, also eighty jet fighters, MIG-21s and MIG-23s. Syrians did not lose any MIG-25s because they never took part in battle. Also, there is new anti-jamming radar and new missile tracking devices. When Hafez al-Assad came back from funeral of Brezhnev, he said that Israeli superiority of arms would not continue. This is because of Soviet re-supply."

All the while, Frank took notes and Vladimir continued to drink. Unlike Spats, this guy was a treasure trove of intelligence.

"This is new," Frank said, "before you seemed to be concentrating on reports from your European embassies."

"Yes. But now that I take no photos, I read everything and try to remember most important things. I saw report from our ambassador to

239

Kabul. This confirmed that our boys are using toxins to kill Afghans. Ambassador wanted confirmation since this is violation of weapons convention of 1972."

"What kind of toxins?"

"I don't know."

"What evidence did he have that this was happening?"

"Only what he heard."

Frank understood that would not be a reliable report, but he would submit it anyway. And he knew he wouldn't be able to flesh things out at this meeting. When Vladimir was photographing cables, they were turned into ready-made reports. Now that he could no longer take pictures of documents, his efforts to recall and write about issues were sketchy.

"Volodya, we don't have time to teach you how to write reports in our format, so all I can tell you is that when you're writing up what you remember of the messages you've seen, keep two things in mind. First, don't write anything you're not certain of. Second, when you do write about sure things, answer these questions: Who? What? When? Where? Why? We call them the five Ws. Can you repeat that?"

"Yes. Be sure of what I write. Who? Why?"

Frank went over it again and again and had Vladimir repeat the little cant in sing-song fashion. "Who said it? What did he say? When? Where? Why?" Then he reviewed the emergency signal and what would happen once it was spotted.

"I understand, even when you say it once." Vladimir was showing the effects of the alcohol.

"What about coming out again? Is there any chance of an assignment for you?"

"Not yet."

"How about another trip, where is the competition next year?"

"In Warsaw."

"Tell me more about this girl, Natasha."

"She is spoiled kid, daughter of lesser privileged people. Her uncles are party hacks. Now with room and Opel, she believes she has world by balls. But really, she is simple country girl."

Frank looked at his watch.

"Our time is just about up, my friend." Frank wanted to end the meeting on an encouraging note. "Look. You made it through twenty months. You have just sixteen to go. We're letting you pick the drop sites and that's something we don't normally do. But we want you to be safe. That's the most important thing."

"I, too. What I said before is not true. It is not just for money or for Justinha I do this."

"I didn't think so." Frank smiled.

"I had uncle, my father's brother. Like my father, he was soldier in Great Patriotic War." Frank understood this was the Russian term for the

Second World War. "He was hero. He fought at Stalingrad. You cannot imagine those conditions. But after fighting he came home. Then one day in 1951, he said something bad about Stalin, some joke. One of his neighbors denounced him. He was sent to Gulag. He was called 'Enemy of People.'"

Frank knew many of the Soviet terms from his Russian textbooks. But that one he remembered not from a book, but because one of his teachers in Monterey had told his students he had been known in the Soviet Union as a "Son of an Enemy of the People." The man walked with a severe limp from the beatings he suffered after his arrest, and in Monterey he became the butt of jokes. The accepted way of announcing his arrival in class was ""Here comes the 'Son of an Enemy of the People.'" But Frank never found it humorous. He could see that the man's body and spirit had been broken. Frank had almost come to fist city with a classmate over the cruelty and that finally put a stop to the ridicule.

"Did that cause problems for you?" Frank asked.

"No. But his wife was forced to divorce him and my cousin, who was older than me was not able to enter university. I know the system well, Boland. It has not changed. I want to stab it in the heart."

"You're coming close, Volodya. But I'm afraid you'll have to go now. Otherwise, you'll be missed." Frank got up from his chair.

Shurin stood slowly. He looked exhausted. For a moment he even had to steady himself by holding onto the back of the chair as he pulled on his coat. He left the ice bag on the table.

"You know, Richard, I never thought of this until now. What do I do if Justinha doesn't wait for me?" The Russian stared at Frank with rheumy, almost pleading eyes and Frank was at a loss. He stepped forward and the two men hugged each other.

"You keep going, my friend. That's what men do when they are alone in the world."

Chapter 35

On Friday, the day after his meeting with Bagatelle, Frank caught the morning train from Prague to Vienna. He arrived just after noon, stored his baggage in a locker at the station then knocked around town all day checking for surveillance. He did some shopping and visited the Schönbrunn Palace. That evening as he walked along dimly-lit Buchfeldgasse, he stripped off his moustache, removed his glasses and put both in a paper bag. Three blocks from Auerspergstrasse he entered a café and spotted Derrick Carmichael, a Vienna station officer who was waiting for him at a back table. Frank handed over his Boland documents and the disguise and picked up his true name diplomatic passport and papers that had been pouched to Vienna. The two men had a beer, chatted for a bit then parted company. Frank walked back to Auerspergstrasse and checked into the Hotel Auersperg, where he spent the night. The following day, he got on the train back to Prague.

The whole point of the maneuver was to persuade the Hungarians, the Czechs, and ultimately the Soviets that for the few days he was absent from Budapest he must have been in Vienna and that he had gone to Prague only after Bagatelle departed. That way the two would not be connected.

The evening of his arrival back in Prague, Frank followed Patrick Kerrane as the tall raw-boned redhead maneuvered between tables to the vestibule of the U Kalicha restaurant. They were being serenaded on their way out by two musicians, one dressed in a black uniform with red trim and the other in a gray uniform with gold braid on his hat. The black-suited fellow sang as he played an accordion while the other man puffed on a polished brass tuba. Frank didn't understand a word of the song, but Patrick, who was just over the crest into drunkenness, had given them a twenty dollar tip in U.S. currency and they were only showing their overwhelming gratitude, especially the tuba player, whose reddened cheeks looked as if they were about to burst.

"We have to leave a note." Patrick said. He stopped and teetered for a moment in the entranceway. Frank saw messages scribbled on the walls in many languages. "It's the custom." Patrick took a black crayon that hung from a string and began writing on the wall.

They had partaken of a fine meal. The room behind them was crowded and smoky and the customers seemed unusually animated for Czechs. Their table had been under cartoon drawings of the "Good Soldier Schweik". The place had become famous because of the book of the same name written by Jaroslav Hasek and the sketches had been done by Jaroslav Lada before the First World War. Frank and Patrick had avoided discussing work at the table. They were both well aware that all the Bloc security services bugged restaurants as well as apartments. But Frank was no longer in disguise and felt relieved that his mission was complete. He was looking forward to seeing this ancient city as a real tourist, with no operational strings attached.

Patrick stepped away from the wall and Frank looked at the uneven scrawl.

"There once was a man named Miholic.

A peasant and confirmed alcoholic.

He stirred with his dick

like a swizzle stick,

so his martinis tasted slightly bucolic."

Frank was hardly surprised. Patrick had spent most of the meal denouncing Stan Miholic, his boss.

"Does he ever come here?" Frank asked.

"Sometimes."

"And you don't think he'll know you wrote that?"

"As if I bloody well care." Patrick pushed open the door and Frank felt the rush of autumn wind and dampness as they walked out onto Na Bojisti Street. "So, no more microphones, now you can tell me what you're doing here, X."

"I came to visit you. And to get my passport stamped. Miholic didn't tell you?"

"We don't talk much. His head's a box of rocks."

Stan Miholic was the chief of station in Prague. The cable traffic that flew from Moscow and Washington and Prague to set up Frank's meeting with Bagatelle had gone in a restricted channel to him. Patrick had not been informed of the case.

"It's the techs," Frank said. "Haven't you heard about their border crossing program?"

"No."

"They'll probably have you do this sooner or later."

"Do what?"

"All the Bloc services change the stamps they put in passports each day. They use inks that show up under ultra-violet light. Sometimes they use different stamps for diplomatic passports than they do for tourist or business passports. Our techs monitor them so that if they ever have to produce false passports, they can include the right stamps. One of the techs came across today with a tourist passport and I came across on the same train with my dip passport. It's right here." Frank patted the chest of his sport jacket.

He had made up the story and he wasn't sure Patrick would buy it, but he thought the cross-border explanation would have been pretty convincing for most people.

"So you weren't in town yesterday?" Kerrane looked straight ahead. Frank figured the redhead wasn't interested in seeing a facial reaction. Instead, he would listen for any hesitation or unusual tone in Frank's response.

"My train got in this afternoon."

"Funny. We had a NOC come in from Germany as a businessman to get a safe apartment. All hush-hush. Miholic never said what it was for. I thought it might have been connected with your visit."

"Hey, take a look." Frank pulled his diplomatic passport from the inside chest pocket of his sport coat. "There's the entry stamp." He marveled at Patrick's instincts.

"Sure." Patrick never even glanced at the document.

They walked past the arched windows of the restaurant in silence toward I. P. Pavlova Square. Patrick scuffled along, his shoulders hunched, his head slightly bowed. Frank recognized the signs. Patrick usually became maudlin or angry when he drank. Tonight he was a bit of both.

"I got only one agent here, a Czech colonel. But the son-of-a-bitch is under control. The Czechs are just running him at us. Miholic thinks this guy's ass is the rising sun. I keep telling him the Czechs are diddling us. He threatened to send me home."

This sounded like a repeat of Patrick's London disaster.

"That wouldn't help your career any. You've got a year and a half to go. Why not stick it out?"

"I can't go home." Patrick's tone was one of resignation combined with dejection. "People are still lookin' for me there."

"What people?"

The alcohol may have loosened Patrick's tongue. Or else he just wanted to get this off his chest.

"Some wise guys, I owe them a lot, gambling debts."

Frank had maneuvered to the window of a crystal shop. He wanted to buy something for Julie. At first he studied the Herend figurines and tried to read the prices in the unlit display to compare them with Budapest prices. But hearing what Patrick said, he switched his focus. He studied the surreal rain-dappled reflection of his friend. Even in the darkness of the glass, Patrick seemed overly pale and drawn. His beard was fuller now, no longer a goatee, but it was matted against his cheeks and chin. He resembled the face of Jesus Christ on the Shroud of Turin.

"How much?"

"It was about thirty-eight thousand when I left. It's a lot more now with the vig."

Frank wasn't completely surprised, but he was disappointed.

"Shit, Patrick. You don't have anything to give them? No savings from London?"

"You can't save anything there, boyo. Besides, I gave most of it to the cause."

"The IRA?"

"Yeah. Now me ma is sick. She has cancer. No insurance. I've been sending her what I have."

In their army days, Frank was often amused by Patrick's grousing and his predicaments, of which there had been many. Later he became more interested in what made this man what he was. Now he was simply worried about his friend.

"I'm sorry. What kind of cancer?"

"Breast, but it's spread already. I tried to include her on my insurance, but it can't be done. Fuckin' Americans."

Once again, the tone of the criticism sounded venomous. And this time Frank was taken aback.

"What the hell does that mean? You don't consider yourself American?"

"It's just like you. You say you're not Irish."

"Not the same."

"Well, that's one thing I always liked about you, X. At least you're not one of those bloody yanks that play at revolution. Sing all the old songs in the pubs when they come over and drop a hundred dollar bill in the box. Stop a minute. Mr. Twinkle has to tinkle." Patrick turned, unzipped his trousers and urinated against a wall. Frank stood to the side.

"Actually, since I met you I realize how much of what I grew up with was Irish."

"Such as?"

"My mother. I don't remember a lot about her, but she had a real problem showing emotion, or giving praise. She never hugged me and I never heard her say once that what I did was admirable. It's the Irish way. 'Playing it down.' Even today I don't accept compliments well."

"Sounds familiar."

"And the humor. We always fall back on it to keep from showing true feelings. Patrick, if you need help, I have money. Not a lot, but some."

"Nah. I'll get through it. Always have. But I've got to stay. I can't let Miholic send me home now even though he just gave me shitty grades on my fitness report."

They turned away from the building and resumed walking. Frank saw a car pull across the square ahead of them and drop off two passengers.

"Your escorts?" Frank said.

"They're interested in why you're here," Patrick said. "You can't throw a dead cat here without hittin' a surveillant. Since you're spending the night at my place they'll be outside all night. How will you go back tomorrow?" Patrick asked.

245

"Train to Vienna." They reached the corner and stepped back from the curb as a Skoda turned and splashed water from a puddle. "So what are you going to do?" Frank asked.

"I don't know yet. But I've got to stay this time even if it means kissing somebody's arse."

"What makes you so sure this colonel is bad?" They started across Katerinska walking downhill toward the Vltava River.

"He gives us nothing. Sure, he hands over a few manning tables, some order of battle stuff. He was their military attaché in Damascus and down there he never gave us anything, but everybody figured when he got home he would get to see the real good stuff. They pay him a piss pot full of money in an escrow account."

"That's it?"

"Not all. I fucked up once, X. I thought I had lost my surveillance. I picked him up for a car meeting south of town. When I dropped him off, surveillance was waiting for me a couple of blocks from his car. They knew I would be there. They bloody well knew it. But he showed up for the next meeting and he continues without any problem. He's their man all right."

"Did you report that to headquarters?"

"Miholic refused to let me. He said I must have been seeing ghosts since the asshole was never arrested. It's all one great sham. Headquarters in its wisdom promoted the fella who recruited him in Damascus and they never take back a promotion."

Frank wondered if the AVH mole had somehow reported on Patrick's activities too, but he wasn't about to raise the matter of the investigation underway in Washington.

"All I can say is hang in there. Do the right thing. It will work out."

"Always the philosopher, X. This time you're right. Things are going to work out. I'm going to make sure of it."

"What does that mean?"

"Keep in touch. You'll find out."

Chapter 36

Betty Cooper had done most of the driving. Steve had napped off and on as they traveled north on Route Ninety-Five to New York City. It was one in the afternoon when she maneuvered the Saab into a parking spot in front of a high-rise apartment building across from Central Park. She went to the trunk and got her suitcase out, then stood on the sidewalk by the open door on the passenger side. Steve had walked around the front of the car and taken the driver's seat.

The party this month was to take place at the capacious, glitzy apartment of a Jewish couple, the Rosens, Sam and Barbara.

"Make my excuses," Steve instructed her. "Tell them I have a meeting, but I'll show up this evening. If I should be late, save a sweet little thing for me, maybe Barbara Rosen herself."

"Be careful. The road is slippery."

"I'll be fine if I can get this goddamned heater to work right. Why the hell did you ever want a Swedish car in the first place?"

Betty did not respond. She just closed the door and Steve started off. He made his way through weekend traffic and continued north in the drizzly December chill on the New York Thruway. The heater in the little car blew either too much or too little air and he kept turning it on high and being roasted, or off and shivering. His leg had stiffened, but he ignored the discomfort and concentrated on keeping within the speed limit. He didn't want to attract any attention.

Two hours later, he approached the U.S. Military Academy at West Point. He spent the next hour taking the visitors tour. When the guide canvassed the group, he discovered that of the twelve people there, nine were from the Midwest.

"And you sir, where are you from?" The tall, spare, regular army sergeant with close-cropped hair looked up at Steve.

"Washington, D.C.," Steve answered.

"And what is it you do there, sir?"

Steve thought it funny that the fellow addressed all the males as sirs.

"I work for the Bureau of Labor Statistics." That was the answer he gave whenever he wanted people to cease their stupid questions.

From three to four o'clock, they wandered around the grounds with the sergeant reciting his prepared delivery on Custer, Lee, Grant, MacArthur, Marshall, Eisenhower, the renowned graduates and the attempt by Benedict Arnold to turn the fort over to the British in the Revolutionary War. From the overlook, the Hudson below was barely visible, but Steve wasn't interested in the sights or the information. He simply wanted to assure himself that no one had followed him this far.

When the tour broke up, he headed west on winding, one-lane mostly mountain roads. There was no sun and the diffused gray light almost disappeared against the stark, dark confines of the hollows. These were ancient hills, not peaked and craggy like the Rockies, but worn, rounded and smoothed over by the scouring and sanding of time and the elements. It took him forty-five minutes to find the place he was looking for. The wooden sign on his left had faded yellow letters against a peeling green background: "Rip's Retreat". On this day it would require a lot of imagination to conjure up the notion of a pre-Revolutionary country bumpkin falling asleep in a warm, sunny mountain meadow and day-dreaming away the next thirty years.

Cooper's tires crunched the gravel as he rolled slowly downhill on a drive that led to a parking area below. There were clapboard cabins and a shuttered office long since closed for the winter. Just outside the office sat a Volkswagen Vanagon mounted on gray cinder blocks. It was missing its wheels. That van had not been there the last time he had come here. It looked like a cast-off remnant of the sixties, with white doves and rockets and flowers painted in profusion. The colors may once have been psychedelic, but were now faded and forlorn, like the sixties themselves.

He saw no one in or around the van. It struck him that if it was an FBI stakeout, J. Edgar Hoover must be turning over in his grave. Steve turned right and moved slowly across to the far side of the lot. A light blue Chevy caprice with Montreal tags was parked at the edge of the tree line. Steve stopped, shut off his engine and reached to the floor behind his seat to get his walking stick. He got out and steadied himself against the car. As he stretched to get the kinks out of his back muscles, he looked back at that van. It appeared completely abandoned. He walked around the back of the Saab, past the rear of the Chevy to the passenger side. The driver had leaned over and pushed open the door. Steve slid in to join him.

"Good to see you, my friend. Did you have any problem getting here?" The driver was in his early forties. Steve knew from their earlier meetings that the man was shorter than he was. Most people were. He was wearing a coffee-colored car coat made of some synthetic material with a faux shearling collar. He had even, undistinguished features. He looked like a typical Canadian and he spoke in that clipped northern way. Perhaps that was why he had been chosen for this assignment.

"Have you been here long?" Steve asked.

"Not a problem. I don't mind waiting."

"That's not what I asked." Betty had always told him that he was quick to lose patience. She had even said that people found him haughty. He didn't give a shit. In this situation he wanted an answer to the question he had asked. It was he who was taking the risks.

"About thirty minutes," the driver answered.

"What about the van? Any sign of life?"

"None, calm down. I know how to do my job. I was careful when I chose this site. I wouldn't put you in danger."

"Can't you turn on the heater? I'm freezing my ass off."

"Sorry. Sure." The driver turned the key and started the engine. The heater came on instantly. It had not been turned off when the motor was. Now the fellow took a pack of Marlboros from the pocket of his coat and pressed the car lighter below the radio. "I have been instructed to tell you that everyone at home continues to be delighted with what you have done."

"Why shouldn't they be? They never thought this would go anywhere."

"Right, so what have you heard from your source?"

Steve knew the question was coming. It was always, "What have you done for me lately?" He had passed information on several of the cases Rzepnicki had talked about. The problem was that the little bastard was always traveling. Steve had not seen him since September.

"Nothing for now, he's still in Cairo. It's what they call a tdy, temporary duty."

"When will he be back?"

"Can you open the window?" It was more a command than a question.

"I thought you were cold."

"I'd rather be cold than suffocate." Steve waved his long slender hand back and forth in front of his nose and mouth. The fellow had been puffing away for less than a minute, but already the smoke had begun to irritate Steve's nostrils.

"Sorry, old boy. I can wait." The driver lowered the window and tossed out his cigarette. "So for the time being we're back where we were. The only thing you see is names and assignments."

"Right, but that's a lot more than you had before I got this job."

"We're not complaining, not at all." The fellow's tone was almost jocular. Steve found it cloying. He reached up and adjusted the center mirror to look out the back window. It was steamed over and he could barely make out the van at the other side of the lot. The driver re-set the mirror in its original position. "But I have been instructed to ask you. Are you certain that the Soviet diplomat you spoke of, the one in Rio de Janeiro, was really recruited?"

Steve turned to look at the man.

"My source said he was sure he was."

"And how reliable do you think that judgment was?"

Steve was annoyed. After years of passing only biographic information and assignments of agency personnel, the Shurin recruitment had been his first report of real substance and he wanted it to stand.

249

"Good. He was there when it happened. Is there some doubt?"

"The KGB has been tailing him now for several months. They have spotted nothing unusual. They searched his flat. No sign of anything. We want you to check again with your man."

"I will when he comes back to the country."

"From now on, try to meet him on a Sunday. The FBI doesn't work then."

"I think I know what I'm doing. By the way, I'm taking flying lessons."

"Lessons? What do you need lessons for? Where? Why?"

"At Dulles Airport. You have to take lessons to get a license. If I get a license, I can fly wherever you want to meet, even to Canada. That will certainly increase our security, don't you think?"

"I don't know if that's such a good idea. They might do another background check." Steve looked at his man in disgust, but the fellow persisted. "Let's keep things simple. Don't take offense, my friend. This is the country of 'The Headless Horseman'. We just want you to keep yours."

Chapter 37

Nineteen eighty-two was ending. The halls and offices at the CIA were as sparsely occupied as they were in the vacation months of July and August. The only difference was that there were Christmas decorations on most of the doors. For Bill Marshall, though, it was business as usual. Intelligence operations, with their attendant ups and downs, went on year round. Overall, he thought, it had been a good twelve months, but it was ending on a sour note, this business about a mole.

On the last Wednesday of the year, Marshall sat at his desk listening to Harry O'Meara. The two went back a long way, to their training days together. While Harry talked, Bill reflected on that fact and their present relationship, that of supervisor and subordinate. It hadn't started out that way. Harry's father-in-law, now deceased, was Lieutenant General Marty Collins, one of Douglas MacArthur's aides-de-camp, and when Harry started out in the agency he had benefited from that cachet. But he just didn't seem to have the rounded, diverse abilities necessary for success as an operations officer. Mostly, he lacked people skills. And despite his family connection, he was no good at Washington politics. But there was no question that he had found his calling in this counter-intelligence work. Basically, Marshall thought, that was because Harry always liked to find fault.

Outside the broad windows, snowflakes were falling and the trees pointed their branches in defense like bared claws against an attacking sky.

"He's our guy," The Raven said. "The FBI alerted the Canadians. They followed this Hungarian, Fárago, from Montreal to the border and the bureau took over there and stayed with him to some place in the Adirondacks. Cooper met him there. It's the second time they've met in the same place. The bureau boys had left an old van there just in case. They photographed the meeting, but the results weren't very good. It was at night."

"What's his motivation, money? I mean the guy seems normal. He substitutes sometimes for Tom McAfee at the morning staff meetings when McAfee is on leave or sick or something. What's his financial situation?"

"He has a swank apartment over off River Road, but he's had it since he came down here from New York. That was five years ago. But here's the interesting part. He's naturalized."

"What?" Marshall leaned forward with both elbows on his desk. "We're just finding that out? Why the hell didn't you tell me that?"

"When we started looking at him, personnel sent us the wrong file. There's another Steve Cooper. He's an analyst in the DI. When we finally got the right file, we saw that he came here from Austria. At least we think he did."

"Really? You know I actually talked to him at the Christmas party. He doesn't have any accent." Marshall opened the side drawer of his wide mahogany desk and took out a thick white cord. He began to twist it as he listened. Then Harry's comment struck home. "What do you mean you think?"

"We sent a message out to Vienna asking the station to get in touch with the Austrians and check this guy out. They have a record of him under the name Fassbinder. Spats told us that was his code name, but it was his real name. The file goes back to the end of 1968, but somebody expunged whatever was in it before that."

"So where does that leave us?"

"They're going to continue to check. They think it may be that he was originally Czech and might have come out with that big wave of refugees when the Soviets moved in back in sixty-eight."

"That doesn't make sense. Why would the Hungarian AVH be running a Czech?"

"Beats me," Harry reached up and scratched the top of his head. From his shirt pocket he took his ever-present pack of Camels and lit one. "Over the Christmas break Security had the techs put a camera in the drop ceiling over his desk. He's under surveillance twenty-four hours a day, every day. So far, he hasn't taken one paper out. He doesn't take any notes. The only thing he sees is admin stuff. He doesn't even carry a briefcase."

"He's got that bad leg. Should we move him to another job?" Marshall asked as he tilted back in his chair and continued to twist the cord.

"I think we should wait for another two months. For one thing he doesn't see much where he is, just admin stuff, like I said. He has no access to the restricted channel traffic or sensitive cases. We'll do a damage assessment, of course, but my guess is that the only thing he could have given away is names, the identities of our people."

"That's pretty damaging. It's hard enough for our guys and gals to do their work overseas without every goddamn hostile service knowing who they are before they even get where they're going." Normally, Bill Marshall didn't curse, but he wanted Harry to know that he didn't like the way this was going.

"I agree, Bill. But we don't want to tip him off that we're watching him. The bureau has to build their case against him. He's due for a normal rotation in two months anyway. In the meantime, maybe we can give him one final project. We might even concoct some phony case and let him see the file somehow, see if he takes out any documents."

"How the hell did he get this far?" Though he wasn't about to admit it to Harry O'Meara, Bill Marshall knew that if this thing weren't handled right, it could end up as a black mark on his record. Nobody got to be a division chief in the CIA without paying attention to the politics of the agency. Black marks were ammunition for snipers who lurked behind all the other polished mahogany desks in all the other big offices.

"We've got it under control now."

"Thanks to young Manion whom you bad-mouthed. If he hadn't found Spats and Spats hadn't told us about this son-of-a-bitch, he could have gone on for five more years, or forever till he goddamned retired and we gave him a medal for thirty years of service." Marshall yanked on both ends of the cord that snapped and tightened in his hands. The rope was knotted, but when Bill Marshall looked at it, he saw that it wasn't at all the knot he had intended to tie.

Chapter 38

Travel by automobile in early January on the Minskoye Shosse was always uncertain. With winter's heavy snows and blowing winds, drifts could build surprisingly quickly and in the event of a breakdown for a driver there was little recourse but to fix the problem himself. Service stations, motels, restaurants were non-existent in the ramshackle hinterland beyond Moscow's outer Ring Road. Vladimir Shurin and Natasha were bundled against the cold as he drove the Opel Southwest out of town. At six in the evening, it was already dark and the road was virtually unlit. Snow seemed to cascade against the windshield to the point where Vladimir had the impression that he was moving steadily into some swirling black hole in space. One advantage, possibly the only advantage of these conditions, was that the car that was tailing them would have great difficulty spotting what Vladimir intended to do. He had planned it this way.

"Keep your eyes peeled. I can barely make out the markers." Vladimir rubbed his hand across the inside of the windshield. His wipers were on as well as the defroster, but the glass kept fogging up.

"We're not close," Natasha said. "We have to go to the twenty-one kilometer marker. The last one I saw was only seven."

They were headed for the dacha of the elderly woman who had rented the room to Natasha. The old lady had returned to town for the New Year celebration and because her clapboard cottage even with its two wood-burning fireplaces and cast iron stove was too cold for her at this time of year. She had given the dacha key to Natasha, for whom she had developed a liking. She had no children. Perhaps she hoped Natasha would take care of her if she fell ill. Natasha and Vladimir planned to spend the weekend in the house.

"There's something wrong," Vladimir said.

"What do you mean?" Natasha twisted her cheek against the pulled-up fur collar of her great coat to look at him. His chiseled features were barely illuminated by the dimly lighted dash.

"I'm going to have to stop. It's not just the snow. There's some kind of drag in the back. We may be getting a flat tire."

"Oh, God save us."

Vladimir smiled to himself. He recalled what he had told Boland in Rio about communists who called on God when they were in trouble. He steered to the side of the road, or at least the spot where he thought that would be.

"I'll have to look." He pulled up the collar of his coat and opened the door. Snow swirled in his face and onto the seat when he stepped out. As he walked to the rear of the little car on the driver's side, he took his Swiss army knife from the pocket of his coat and pried out the sharp metal punch. Just as he was about to kneel beside the tire, he could make out the faint headlight beams of the Moskvich he had seen following them out of town. He reached down quickly and drove the punch into the sidewall of the tire. In the snowy silence he heard the unmistakable hiss of escaping air. He continued to kneel. The knee of his woolen pants compressed and melted the soft snow beneath his leg. The black tail car moved slowly by and the passenger looked straight at Vladimir, but when Vladimir returned his gaze, the fellow turned away. "It's not flat, but it's low on air." Vladimir twisted back into the driver's seat, turned the key in the ignition and started off again. "It may have a slow leak. We'll have to see if we can get as far as Peredelkino. If not, I'll have to change it. Bloody hell!"

Less than a kilometer farther on, Vladimir spotted their surveillants. The car had pulled over and as Vladimir had anticipated the driver and his passenger had remained inside. At the ten-kilometer marker, Vladimir pulled over again.

"That's it. It's gone flat."

"Do you need any help?" Natasha made the offer, but Vladimir knew it was half-hearted.

"No. You stay, no sense in both of us freezing. I'll have to change it. It's hard enough trying to steer when all four tires have air."

Once again he stepped into the cold and swirling snow. He had taken the keys from the ignition and unlocked the boot. Inside he had two tires one on top of the other. He pulled out the lug wrench and the car jack. Kneeling again beside the rear tire, he used the crowbar end of the wrench to pry off the hubcap. He was loosening the lug nuts when the Moskvich went by again. They never stopped to offer any assistance and Vladimir certainly didn't want any. With the nuts turning freely, he fitted the wrench into position as the jack-handle and pumped away to raise the rear of the car. When the rear tire had cleared the ground, he stood at the open trunk.

The top tire was not mounted on any wheelbase. Nor would it have served well as a spare. It was bald and the sidewall was cracked in several places. In the inner wall, Vladimir had secured eight film canisters with black tire tape. They were the result of his most recent efforts. He knew Boland and the Americans would be pleased to see he was back into photography. He had simply reverted to his initial way of taking the photos in the sorting room when Natasha took her breaks. Now he lifted the tire and carried it to the ten-kilometer marker. It would have been easier to roll it, but he didn't want to leave any track in case the Moskvich came back to check. He stepped off the road into the woods. His leg sank knee deep into the snow even over the top of his boots. He waddled five meters downhill and set the tire beside a conifer, scooped out a snow pocket, laid the tire flat and pushed snow back over it just enough to cover the rubber. Once again he took out his Swiss army knife and pulled open the main blade. On the side of the pine away from the road, he carved out a strip of bark and threw it into the snow then he made his way back to the car and finished changing the wheel. The ten-kilometer marker and the cut in the tree would serve as the reference points for the Americans to find his latest drop. He went into the woods again and urinated against the tree. If the tails checked, they would think he had stopped to change the tire and had to pee.

"You're covered," Natasha said.

Vladimir took his seat behind the wheel.

"Yes. But we shouldn't have any trouble now." He started the motor and rolled on.

"When we get there, I'll make you a good hot cup of tea," Natasha took his free arm and squeezed it.

"Fine."

"Maybe after we're married we can get a dacha for ourselves. The old lady might even help us. She likes me."

"Maybe."

Once again they passed the Moskvich.

"That car must have trouble just like us," Natasha said. "They go on for a bit then stop."

"Maybe we should stop to see if they need help," Vladimir said.

"No. They did nothing for us." Natasha shook her head.

"You're right. They did nothing for us." Vladimir smiled. "People can be mean-spirited, can't they?"

Chapter 39

Tony had turned on the audio shield and was seated at one of the two desks in the station office when Frank arrived on Tuesday morning. But what the station chief had to say was hardly secret.

"Francis, apparently the ambassador thinks you don't have enough to keep you fully engaged. He has asked me if you would be so kind as to chaperone and act as translator for a group of ladies from the embassy who in the January chill have come to realize they are in dire need of fur coats."

"Tony, most of the time I'm able to discern the essence of your praiseworthy discretion and circumlocutions, but this time you got me. You want me to take them shopping?"

Tony gave a baritone chortle.

"The ladies need someone to take them to the fur factory."

"Where is the fur factory?"

"I have the address right here. They will assemble just outside the library tomorrow morning at nine-thirty. The embassy van and a driver will be at your disposal."

"Aren't you concerned about exposing me to eight women? I thought I was supposed to steer clear of women."

"I apologize most sincerely, Francis. But as far as any romantic overtures are concerned, I doubt you have anything to fear. All of these ladies are married."

"They may be married, but a few of them have already let me know they need more than a new fur coat to keep them warm."

The next day, Frank greeted the eight women. He knew most of them. Maisy Crittenden, the ambassador's wife, came out of the library. She appeared to be the group leader.

"Our escort is here, ladies. Shall we go?" Maisy led the way past the commercial office, through the reception area and out the front door to the waiting van. Frank followed. He sat in the front seat with the driver and the women squeezed into the remaining places in the back.

The factory, when Frank saw it, looked like most other Hungarian industrial plants, red brick with a tinny ramshackle roof. But the driver pulled around the building to the front of what appeared to be a more elaborate theater and stopped at the foot of the steps leading to a set of double-doors. He just pointed up the steps.

"You go in there," he said in Hungarian.

That was the extent of the interpreting Frank was called on to do. As he opened the door on the right to allow the women to pass, a tall, slim, attractive, middle-aged woman with slightly graying hair pulled back in a bun, greeted them all in English.

"Welcome to our exhibition, *Mesdames*. Please take your seats closest to the stage. Our girls will show you everything that we have available."

The women tittered a bit as they walked down the aisle. Most of them were unaccustomed to being treated like royalty. Mrs. Crittenden seemed to take it as her due. Frank waited by the partition that divided the foyer from the viewing area.

When everyone had settled into their seats, the hostess climbed the center steps to the stage.

"Welcome again, ladies. Normally, I give some history of our manufactures, but I know that you may not be interested in such a thing so we shall move to our first offering..." With her right arm, she signaled to the model offstage. "a sable coat of knee-length, with wrap-around collar. The pelts were imported from Siberia. In fact, most of our furs come from Russia, Poland, Czechoslovakia, as untreated pelts and we process them here on site."

A tall, slim, dark-haired girl in her early twenties did the customary walk-on and spin-arounds. The embassy ladies ooohed and aaahed. The ritual continued for several minutes, with the exhibitors disappearing behind the curtains after each display. Frank wandered back outside. From the steps he caught sight of the driver, who had taken the van close to one of the doors almost at the side of the building. A man was leaning on the passenger window of the vehicle talking to him. The man turned to look up the steps. By now, Frank had come to recognize the characteristics of surveillance cars and people. This fellow was a surveillant. The man walked in the side door. Frank went back in the way he had come out.

Five minutes later a model showed a long shiny blackglama mink, but instead of retreating stage right as the others had done, she walked down the center steps and up the aisle to where Frank was standing. She spoke in Hungarian.

"Would you like to see what we have for gentlemen in the back?" She motioned to her left. Frank immediately smelled a rat rather than a mink, but he went along.

"Certainly." He had his raincoat draped over his left arm, but he gestured with a sweep of his right hand. "After you."

It was hard to determine just what the girl looked like under the coat. From what he had glimpsed, her face was striking, full-lips, dark eyes, long dark hair. Her calves and ankles were shapely above the shiny black stiletto heels she was wearing. She walked with only the slightest sway, the way models were trained to walk. She opened a door on the far side of the foyer and reached to her right to turn on a light then extended her arm.

"These are our men's coats."

Sure enough, hanging on rack after rack were coats of every description and size and length in furs and leathers and wools. Frank started down one narrow aisle and the girl followed behind. In fact, she was very close behind. Frank could smell her perfume. He thought someone should tell her to use it sparingly. He stopped when he spotted a long rough beige leather overcoat with a fur collar.

"This looks nice." He ran his hand down the smooth lapel.

"You can choose anything you like. Do you see something that could meet your needs?" With that the girl let the fur she was wearing slip open. Underneath she wore nothing more than a black garter belt and sheer black stockings. The dark triangle above her vagina was in sharp contrast to the whiteness and smoothness of her skin. Her nipples, too, were dark and her breasts were perfectly proportioned. She moved to within inches of his side.

Frank's first impulse was to see the humor of the situation, but he suppressed a smile. As he had told Bill Marshall, this was not the first time this had happened to him.

"It's hard to choose. Everything here is beautiful." He looked directly at the girl. Up close he could see that although her features were even and attractive, her facial skin was probably blotched or marked by acne. Her makeup was heavy to the point where it looked almost scaly.

"First we have to find your size," the girl said. She unbuttoned Frank's suit coat and helped him take it off. He draped it over the metal rack. She reached between his legs, but he took her hand, gently but firmly.

"I really do need a coat, but that will be all for today."

That evening, Frank was invited to dinner at the Nobles. As he and Charlie walked from the embassy toward the Széchenyi building on the river, Frank was wearing his new coat and he told Charlie about the episode.

"No shit? I guess that's why they call it the fur factory. So she wanted to check your size?" Charlie laughed his West Virginia holler laugh, which echoed off the walls of the Parliament building.

They had just started across Parliament Square. Suddenly, Frank heard the squeal of tires and out of the corner of his eye he saw a car careening toward them. He pulled Charlie with him as he dove to his left. The BMW had cut the corner of the cobblestone square rather than stay on the street. As it sped away, Frank saw the man in the back seat. He had his face to the window and he was laughing. Frank recognized him as the fellow he had seen that morning at the factory talking to the van driver.

"Sons-of-bitches," Charlie stood up and shook his fist at the disappearing car.

"Surveillance," Frank said calmly.

"They must not like you. You better hope they don't get you in a dark alley some night."

"They were just trying to scare me. Maybe this morning they gave me the carrot. Tonight it's the stick."

The following morning, Thursday, Frank flew out of Férihegy to Vienna. There was a newly-inaugurated non-stop Air France service to Paris, but once again he didn't want to establish any link between his travel and that of Spats, so he connected with a Lufthansa flight to Frankfurt and waited for another Air France plane from there. The departure was delayed because of some baggage-handlers strike in Paris. He didn't get into Charles de Gaulle until four-thirty in the afternoon. Before clearing customs, he went to the phone bank by the baggage carousels.

"*Hotel Lutétia, Bon jour*," the voice said.

"Room 507 please."

After two rings Julie picked up.

"Hello."

"It's me. I just got in. I'll come straight there, but traffic will probably be heavy and you may have to start without me."

"I'll wait until you get here to talk about the most important topic."

Frank took a Citroën taxi outside the terminal that dropped him off on the rue de Sèvres. As he got out of the cab, he saw that Le Bon Marché department store still had large green Christmas wreaths over the corner entrances. He carried his bag up the steps of the Lutétia and passed through the black-and-white-tiled lobby. In the elevator, Frank had to remind himself to concentrate on keeping the Spats case from becoming an afterthought. But when Julie opened the door to the suite, his professionalism almost slipped away. He could see Spats over her shoulder sitting on a green damask giltwood fauteuil. Julie smiled, but the only other sign of affection they shared was a squeeze of the hand before Frank followed her in and set his bag on the floor next to the wall.

"Attila, it's good to see you. At least this time you don't have to wear a mask and carry a sword." Frank shook his hand, which was thin and not very muscular. But once again, Spats was well turned out. He wore a charcoal gray pinstriped suit of fine worsted wool. He seemed partial to pinstripes. Maybe, Frank thought, his tailor had told him they made him look taller. His shirt was pale blue with a gold stickpin through the collar and he had a navy and white polka dot tie. His shoes were of polished black leather, probably from Weston's. He must have visited his Paris barber as his black goatee had been trimmed and his hair styled.

"Frank, welcome to Paris," Spats smiled. "I told Julie about Zorro."

Frank knew he was making progress. The fellow had called him by his first name. There was nothing like shared risk to bring people together.

"We've discussed a lot," Julie said. "I'll go over my notes with you after Attila leaves. But we left the two most important things. We wanted to wait for you."

"I'm sorry for the delay." Frank sat at one end of a small sofa with Julie at the other end. He looked at Spats. "I could have gotten here yesterday, but I didn't want to arrive on the same day that you did and I took a roundabout way of getting here just as a precaution. Then there was an air strike."

"That is the French for you," Attila said. "In Hungary we don't have to worry about labor strikes. That is one of the few advantages of communism."

"Would you like a glass of wine or some cheese?" Julie leaned toward the coffee table and the tray of assorted cheeses and an open box of Godiva chocolates.

"No, thanks." The TV was turned on. Frank noticed that it was tuned to one of the literary discussions the French obsessed over. The volume was high to mask their conversation.

"Then maybe the first thing we should discuss is the mole," Julie said. "Washington has some idea that he may be Czech." She looked at Frank. This was the first time he had heard this.

"That's not possible," Spats said. "If he were a Czech, he would be run by the Czech service."

"I'm not up to date on what Washington thinks." Frank looked down the sofa. What caught his eye for a moment was a vase filled with yellow roses on a round Louis XV console table by the window. They reminded him to ask Julie about her father. "Julie and I have not had a chance to discuss it. I didn't realize that we suspected he might be anything other than American."

"What if he's one of yours?" Julie asked.

"You mean Hungarian?" Spats replied.

"Yes, an AVH officer."

"That, too, is unlikely," Spats said. "We would not take the risk of sending one of our men to try to penetrate the CIA."

"If you can, I want you to look back in the files to 1968. Look for a man named Kadar," Julie said.

"Like the president?" Spats asked.

"Yes."

"And how did you find out that name?" Spats asked. Actually, it was the same question that Frank had in mind.

"We think he may have changed his name from Czech or Hungarian to the German translation, Fassbinder." Julie replied.

"I don't speak German." Spats shook his head.

"One of our people on the Hungarian desk said that Fassbinder in Hungarian is Kadar." Again she looked at Frank. She must have known that all this was news to him.

"Interesting," was Frank's only comment. "Have you been able to learn anything more about this man?" he asked Spats.

"No. But perhaps this name will help me. I will look for a file on Kadar."

"I apologize. I'm sure Julie has asked this question already, but what is your itinerary, Attila?"

"I will be here for one more day then I travel to Brussels. I am to be assigned there in July to be head of our office."

"Congratulations," Frank said. "That should persuade you that your service doesn't suspect you at all."

"Yes. I was concerned when my trip here was delayed. I was to have come three weeks ago. But it was only because the head of our office here had to be out of town then and couldn't meet me until now."

"Are you looking forward to the job in Brussels?" Frank asked.

"The weather is not the best, but there are more excellent restaurants per capita than there are here in Paris. And the work is important since it is the home of NATO."

"That brings us to the most important case here in Paris. Attila told me about it briefly, Frank, but I wanted him to tell you what he told me. Can you talk again about the Montrachet case, Attila?"

"Of course," Spats shifted in his seat and put his right elbow on the gilded top of his chair. His body was angled toward Frank. "I was tasked to do a survey of the cases being handled by the Paris office."

"And you've told Julie about them?" Frank asked.

"Yes. But the most important is a French military officer, a major. He is assigned as liaison to NATO. Although he works in Brussels, it is one of our Paris chaps who directs his intelligence collection."

"Can you repeat his name for Frank?" Julie asked. She had her pen in one hand and flipped over a new sheet of the yellow legal pad she had in her lap.

"Henri-Paul Montrachet. I read the file in Budapest before I came. Yesterday I talked with our man, Ferenc Molnar. He is the one who recruited Montrachet and continues to run the case." Spats made that sucking sound with his teeth. It seemed to happen when he pronounced the letter "s".

"When did the recruitment take place?" Frank asked.

"Two years ago, almost, February of 1981. Molnar meets him every two weeks in Belgium, Mons and Bruges, sometimes in Antwerpen. Once in the early stage of the operation they met at the exhibition park on the edge of Brussels at the space needle."

"Wouldn't the Soviets normally run that kind of case here?" Frank asked.

"Not at all. It is not so unusual. We are active against NATO. The Stasi also work against NATO. Besides, we have a long association with France. In the Dreyfuss affair it was actually a Hungarian who was responsible for providing information to the Germans." Spats smiled and that softened his features.

"What office does he work in and what are your requirements for him?" Frank asked.

"He is in the Logistics Division in a sub-element called the Office of Weapons Standardization."

"You don't have him working against the Operations Division or the Intelligence Division?" Frank looked at Julie, who shook her head.

"No. This is the area of greatest interest to us and to our Soviet friends because this is the area in which the United States and its allies share information on new developments in weapons research. He brings us reports of new weapons systems, manuals, schematics and such."

"If we alert the French to Montrachet's espionage, will it affect your position in Brussels?" Julie wanted to know.

"Not so much, but perhaps rather than arrest him, you could have the French move him first into some other position, some place where he will not see things of such importance."

"A good suggestion, we'll pass that on to Washington." Julie looked at Frank, who nodded in agreement. "Is it possible that you'll come abroad again before next summer?" Julie asked.

"I am to return here in April and once again I will go from here to Brussels."

"We should use the same communications plan, your call to the embassy with the same parole as this time." She looked to Frank, who held up his thumb to show he concurred.

On the mantel over the fireplace, an Ormolu clock with a bold shepherd stealing a kiss from a porcelain maiden chimed the hour.

"Yes, I agree. But for now I must go." Spats rose from his chair.

"You won't take any wine?" Julie gestured toward the bottles on the console and the trays on the coffee table.

"I am afraid not, but perhaps next time. Frank, I left with Julie the list of names of AVH men you asked for."

"Thank you, Attila. If there should be any problem in coming abroad again, we would like to know about it," Frank said. "I hope you will reconsider our request that you communicate with us while you are in Budapest." Frank could see this drew an immediate reaction and he held his hand up to stop the Hungarian from interrupting his pitch. "I don't mean personal meetings. We could work out a system of drops and signals that would be safe for you. If I come up with a plan, will you look at it next time?"

"I am willing to look, but no guarantees." He made that sucking sound again.

Frank didn't object to his departure. In fact, since Julie had gotten whatever intelligence the fellow had to offer, Frank was anxious to have him leave. He followed Julie, who escorted the agent to the door.

"Have a safe return, Attila. And don't worry," Julie said. "With the information you gave us, we now have a good idea of who the mole is and we are in the process of neutralizing him." Spats leaned forward and kissed her on both cheeks. He shook Frank's hand. "Just let me check the hall to be sure no one is out there." Julie leaned out the door then stepped aside to allow Spats to exit. Frank took several steps back into the room and turned to the door. As Julie closed it, she stood for a second then turned. She had a mischievous smile on her face. She walked to him.

"Now where were we?" she asked.

"Fun time," he held out his arms.

"All work and no play make Francis a horny case officer."

He picked her up and carried her to the bedroom. For the next hour they made love. It wasn't frenzied or acrobatic, just sweet and joyful. Afterward, Julie went into the tiled bathroom. From the bed, Frank watched her as she sat on the bidet.

"One of the little refinements of French culture," she called out. By the time she came out, he was aroused again. She looked at him. "Oh, no, we've got to get out of here." Frank got up reluctantly and began to straighten the bed. "Leave it," she said. "We're paying enough. Let them take care of it."

"Where are we staying?" Frank asked.

"It's not so grand as this, I'm afraid. It's a little place over by the old opera, Hôtel de la Paix."

Paris was normally mild even in winter, but there was usually a cold spell a week or two in late January or early February when the night temperature dropped below freezing. This year it had come early. As they walked down the steps of the Lutétia, the cold air hit them. Frank saw that the white Christmas lights along the roof of the Bon Marché were now lit. The streets were crowded and people seemed invigorated by the cold.

They rode in a Peugeot cab that dropped them off in front of the Opéra Garnier. Their conversation up to that point had not touched on operations, but Frank was anxious to find out about the mole. They started up the Boulevard des Italiens.

"So they found the guy? What was all that about the name?" he asked. "Who is he?"

"His name is Cooper. He's an administrative officer in SE Division."

Frank stopped in his tracks. Julie turned and looked at him. The people behind had to walk around them.

"That was the guy who checked me out of headquarters. No wonder the Hungarians were waiting for me at the airport." They resumed walking. Frank shifted his suitcase to his other hand.

"We talked about it. We figured that since he Americanized his name from German, he might have Germanized it from Czech or Hungarian. Attila said he wouldn't be Czech and people on the Hungarian desk told me that the translation of Cooper in Hungarian would be Kadar."

"Cooper to Fassbinder to Kadar?" Frank said.

"Like Tinker to Evers to Chance."

"That's another thing I love about you. You know your baseball."

"There's something else. They're taking me off the case," Julie said.

Again Frank stopped. This time, a man bumped into him from behind and excused himself.

"What the hell for? It's going well. Whose brilliant idea was that?"

"Now you're talking like a field officer. What does headquarters know, right? They want to turn it over to you. You're the one working in Hungary."

"But you're the one who recruited him," Frank said. "He likes working with you."

"I don't mind, really, except for not seeing you." She stopped at the corner of the Rue du Helder. "We turn here." The side street was far less congested. Frank saw the small neon light ahead on the right for the Hôtel de la Paix. "Marshall wants me to come out once more then disappear. But at least we'll have April in Paris, although generally May is a lot better."

The following day Julie went in to the embassy and wrote up the report of the meeting. For the two days after that, they walked the city. They avoided the tourist attractions, the Eiffel Tower, Arc de Triomphe, Notre Dame and even though the Bateaux Mouches were heated, the closest they got to them was a walk down the Quai Anatole France. Instead, they prowled the art galleries along the rue Bonaparte, bought cheese, cold cuts, wine and bread in the closed market behind St. Sulpice and had café crème at the Café de Flore. Julie lectured him on the reasons the Flore was superior to the Deux Magots just down the Boulevard St. Germain. Over on the rue Champollion, they saw a Jacques Tati film and on their last evening had one sumptuous memorable meal at Beauvilliers overlooking the city on the Butte de Montmartre. Frank told the sommelier that he wanted an extraordinary wine for a modest price and the fellow earned his tip. It was so good, that they decided to have another bottle. By the time they came out, they were both tipsy. They walked across the Place du Tertre to the steps leading down from the Sacré Coeur. Paris lay below them and below a layer of fog.

265

"What about Justinha? Did she take the money?" Frank asked.

"She sure did. I think she was surprised to get it. She used it for breast implants."

"What?" Frank supported himself on the railing that ran down the center of the steps and tightened his hold on Julie's waist to keep her steady.

"There's a famous cosmetic surgeon in Rio. Her Brazilian boyfriend wanted her to have bigger boobs. Now she's asking for more money."

"I wonder if we should tell Bagatelle."

"Better not to, I think. Let him find out for himself when he comes out. His life must be hard enough as it is." They crossed rue Montgolfier and continued down the steps. "I found it curious that you never talked about your marriage."

"I think it's a bad idea to talk about one woman when I'm with another one."

"So you compartment women the way you compartment your operations?" She was tweaking him.

"Kind of, but I'll say this: With every woman I've dated, there was something missing. Somewhere in the back of my mind I would hear this voice, like the whisper of a timid angel. He knew I'd argue with him, but he wanted me to know this wasn't the one. When I met my wife I ignored him, to my everlasting regret. With you there's no voice. You're the real deal."

As they went slowly and carefully down the steps he had another thought, one he wasn't about to verbalize. He knew he had to be careful this time around, but with Julie he figured that the agency had done a lot of his screening for him. She wouldn't have gotten in if she had been a criminal, or a deviant, or a druggie, or unbalanced. So he knew what she wasn't and he felt he had come a long way toward finding out what she was.

Back in the hotel they made love. This time they went at it with abandon. Julie moaned then screamed with pleasure. The bed bounced and Frank knew that whoever was on the other side of the thin walls wasn't getting much sleep either. When they finished, they were both still buzzing and not ready for sleep.

"At the train in Vienna I said I would tell your fortune," Julie said as she came back from the bathroom. She had on a dark green velour robe, but her breasts were visible as she bent over her suitcase. She took out a regular deck of playing cards. They both sat cross-legged on the bed. "Are you sure you want to know?" She smiled.

"If it isn't going to change your mind about me."

"Let's just see what we see." Julie riffled through the cards separating out the aces, face cards, nines and tens. She laid the piles on the sheet.

"How did you learn to do this?"

"My grandmother moved in with us when I was a little girl. She taught me. She's eighty-six now and she still lives with my mom and dad. I never asked her, but she may have been part gypsy."

"Your mother's mother, she's Portuguese?"

"Yes, my maternal grandmother. No, she's Italian."

"I love Italian women."

"I'll bet you do. How many have you known?"

"You can't grow up catholic and not know Italians. They run the company."

"Cut the cards three times." Frank did as she instructed. She turned over the four piles he had made and looked at the top card on each pile. Now she put them together in reverse order to form one pile. "Cut again, just once." He did. Again she reversed the piles and laid out the separated cards in three rows of eight. The first two cards were the Ace of Spades and the Ace of Diamonds in the top row. "Interesting," was all she said.

"I thought you did this with big cards that have pictures on them," Frank said. "You know, knights, fair damsels, knaves, jesters."

"In the old country they didn't have fancy cards. They did it with regular cards." Now she looked concerned.

"So what do you see? Does Justinha get a tummy tuck?"

"You have to be patient. I'm not sure that's one of your qualities."

"How fast you forget. I know how to take my time."

"That's true," she smiled. "Sorry." Now she was silent and intent. She put her finger on the Jack of Clubs in the bottom row. "Here you are. And here I am." Julie's card was the Queen of Spades. It was the last card in the bottom row. Their two cards were separated by the Queen of Hearts. "Here is your ex-wife." Beth was the Queen of Clubs, the card in the second row just above Frank's. Now Julie began to count, eight cards back from Frank, seven cards back from his wife, ten cards back from her own card. "This king," she had her finger on the King of Hearts, the third card in the top row, "is a man of some importance, a man of possible wealth and status. He and your wife are romantically involved. He's older than you. He may be a senior person in the same company with her." Frank smiled. He had never told Julie about Beth's affair, possibly because of his male ego. But it might well be something she could have guessed. "This man," she pointed to the King of Clubs, "will take some legal action. It looks as if your wife will marry, but then get a second divorce."

"That has nothing to do with me." Frank waved his hand back and forth in front of his face. He was still feeling the effects of the wine. "I see you and I are on either side of the Queen of Hearts. What does that mean?"

She smiled.

"I hesitate to say it. You might get more ideas." She looked at him for a moment smiling only with her eyes. "That means we'll be joined by love."

"I knew it." Frank held both arms straight up in his soccer player imitation. "It's what I've been trying to tell you all along."

"Down boy, things aren't all wine and roses."

"What do you mean? I know what I need to know."

"Not quite." She counted again. "That relationship is solid, positive, but professionally you're going to face some hurdles. A very tall man, you see this King of Spades? is going to cause a lot of problems for you. There will be some kind of inquiry. In the end, things will be settled in your favor, but not without a lot of turmoil."

"Harry O'Meara? If you had those picture cards, he would be a raven. Doesn't matter. Love conquers all. Continue Madame Lola." Frank tapped on the sheet next to the cards. Julie began to count again. This time she stopped, then recounted then stopped again. She just sat staring at the cards. "So, what happens next?" Frank gave a chuckle.

"I think that's enough." Suddenly Julie reassembled the deck. She looked at him and he was surprised by the sadness he saw in her eyes.

"Come on. You don't take all this seriously, do you? I don't, except the love part." He laughed again, but she didn't join him. "What? I go to jail for assaulting a man in a black suit?"

Julie reinserted the cards in their box and put it on the table. She sat now with her knees up and her arms crossed looking into the vacant fireplace.

"It was not about you." She pulled up the collar of her robe. "I just got a terrible chill. Come and hold me for a while."

Chapter 40

Vladimir Shurin huddled in the attic with a blanket over his shoulders and copied the latest encrypted message he heard over the radio. Irina had gone out. She said she was headed for her parents' apartment, but Vladimir suspected she had a rendezvous with Anatoliy Barchuk. Either way, he didn't care. He sat with earphones on and with his back to the opening down to the kitchen.

In his concentration he never saw his wife when she returned unexpectedly because she had forgotten her lipstick. She couldn't avoid seeing the ladder in the kitchen and almost silently she climbed up several steps and poked her head over the beams to see what was happening. By the time Vladimir finished copying the numbers and climbed down the ladder into the kitchen, she was gone once again. He went to the table and worked with his one-time pad to decipher the instructions that would lead him to his next package of high-speed film and a promised letter from Justinha. But he decided to wait until the following night to make the pick-up. That evening he went to Natasha's place.

"I am going to Perm next week. I want you to come with me." She stood by the stove slicing a long sausage with one of the Wüsthof kitchen knives he had bought her.

"That would be a long drive. How long will you stay?" he asked.

"I won't drive. I'll go by train. Five days. I want you to come with me," she repeated.

Vladimir girded himself for their usual argument. He didn't know how much longer this relationship could last. Over the previous weekend she had thrown dishes at him twice.

"I can't do that. How would I explain my disappearance for five days?"

"You'll think of some lie. You're good at that."

"And who will substitute for us at work?"

"Vorontsov will find someone. But those aren't the real reasons." This was when the dishes normally took flight. "You have no intention of leaving your wife. You never did."

"I have every intention of leaving her, believe me. And I will do so in the next year." His voice had the ring of conviction because he was telling the truth. What he didn't add was that he would leave his wife, but not for Natasha.

"Liar, my parents are expecting me to bring you this time. I won't be embarrassed." She turned and jabbed the knife in his direction as she made her point.

They went back and forth, but nothing was resolved. At eleven o'clock, they left the flat for the ministry. The eight-hour shift passed almost in silence.

When Vladimir walked in the door of his own apartment the next morning he saw in an instant that he had a major problem. Irina was in the kitchen. She stood by the Braun coffee-maker they had brought back from Brazil. The ladder stood in the middle of the room with the ceiling lid into the attic open. On the kitchen table was the Grundig Ocean Boy radio, the earphones, the one-time pads, secret writing materials, everything he had cached in the attic.

"You're back," he said because he couldn't think of anything else to say and because he needed time to figure out how to handle this. She didn't reply, didn't even look his way. The coffee machine made that gurgling sound it gave off when it was creating its mixture. "Your parents weren't there?"

"Papa is traveling. It was a shame, since there was something I wanted to talk to him about." She looked at the paraphernalia on the table. "He won't be back until Wednesday so I suppose I will have to call Anatoliy. He'll know how to handle this." Still she didn't look at him.

"Handle what?" He realized he was still standing at the kitchen entrance. Better to move in, he thought and determine how serious his problem was. Irina finally looked at him and showed her smile of disdain.

"A filthy traitor, that's what I married, a clerk who betrayed his country."

"What are you talking about?" He had decided his first approach should be to brazen it out. "Treason, that's a pretty serious word."

"You can forget it. I saw you yesterday up there." She jerked her thumb up toward the attic. "I came back last night and found all of this." She pointed at the gear arrayed on the table.

"The radio, so what? I listen to the BBC. There is a chance I'll be posted to London next. I practice my English."

"I won't waste my breath discussing this with you. You can save your explanations for Anatoliy and the organs. I don't think they'll be convinced. If you can't fool even me, you're not a good enough liar to deceive them." She walked out of the kitchen into the next room. He thought she might be going to the phone, instead he heard her running water in the bathroom. His mind raced. He could attack her. He was capable of snapping her neck, but she might scream in the process. Instead, he reached for the pen in his chest pocket, opened the top and took out the two L pills. He stepped to the counter and dropped both of them in the coffee pot. Irina came back to the kitchen.

270

"So your father was away? He would have told you this is all a delusion. You're always making things up. Did Tolya take you seriously?"

"I haven't spoken to him yet." She reached in the wall cupboard and took down a cup. From the tiny fridge she took out the milk. She took no sugar. He watched her pour the coffee.

"You're wrong. There is an explanation, but I'm not authorized to give it to you. I can only tell you that I have joined the organs. Tolya will verify that. It was he who persuaded me to make the switch." Vladimir walked into the bedroom. He sat on the edge of the mattress and listened to her movements. She went to the table. He heard the scraping of the chair, the placement of the cup. Now he was curious about just how long this would take. The Americans had promised it would be quick. Irina proved them right. In ten seconds he heard the slump and tumble of his wife's body on the floor. When he got to the kitchen, she was lying with her back to him. He walked around to look at her face. It was frozen, her eyes wide, her mouth slightly open, her lips twisted one hand close to her throat.

He left her lying there while he took the radio and the remaining gear to the attic and hid them. When he came down, he replaced the ceiling lid, put the ladder back against the kitchen wall and arranged the bowls and dishes, that part was easily accomplished, but what to do with the body? He knew he couldn't move it until after dark. He found he was perspiring even though he remembered that when he first came in the flat had seemed chilly. He needed to think things through and for the rest of the day that's what he did.

That evening he took a bus in the direction of Kudrinskaya Ploshchad, the ritzy section of town where Irina's parents lived. His surveillance, two chaps in a black Moskvich, followed along. Vladimir had calculated that he had to act quickly. He had been careful never to go directly to Natasha's place when he was being followed and he certainly did not want to do so tonight. It was important that he keep to his routine as much as possible until he actually had to make his move, but first he had to break free of his tail. He got off the bus at the Belorusskaya metro station. That forced his pursuers to split up. The driver stayed with the Moskvich, while his passenger, a younger fellow who looked to be in his early thirties, came down into the tube. Vladimir rode the train back toward the city center. He got off at Pushkinskaya and began walking in the direction of the Chekhov Theater. He had counted on the fact that a performance was scheduled for that evening and that the theatergoers would be arriving just about now, some of them in taxis. He spotted a cab coming toward him on Tverskaya ulitsa and waved it down. As he got in, he could see that his tail was left flat-footed.

The taxi dropped Vladimir off two streets from Natasha's room. He found the Opel parked one block away from her building and used his own key to unlock it. He headed back toward his place. He figured that it would take some time before his two surveillants could link up and by then they would figure that the next sure place to pick him up would be at the ministry. That gave him a little more than four hours to do what he had to do.

He found a parking spot on the street behind his building. When he got upstairs, he realized he was perspiring again and was short of breath from the climb and the stress of all this. Just inside the door of the flat, on the floor rolled in the imitation oriental carpet was Irina's body. He had tied the rug with cord. Now he hoisted and positioned it so his shoulder fit into her stomach. It was awkward trying to close the door and he didn't bother to lock it. No one was in the stairwell. Only one person passed him on the street and even though he had to struggle to fit the carpet into the small boot of the Opel, he managed it without being observed. He had to make a second trip to get the shovel.

The road out of town was not so treacherous as the last time he had taken it. The lanes had been cleared and the snow was piled in dirty mounds against the shoulders. Rather than go all the way to the Peredelkino turnoff, he pulled into a small clearing just beyond the twelve kilometer marker.

Even though he was fit for martial arts, he found himself puffing away as he dug the hole. But once he got through the frozen crust, he found the layers of snow and dirt soft and moist. Spring was coming. He figured that by the time anyone found the body, he would be long gone, so he went down only about a meter. He carried the carpet from the car and tugged on one end as the body rolled into the hole.

Back in town he pulled into a spot on Ulitsa Snamenka near the Lenin Library. Before he left the car, he reached in the glove box and took out a brightly painted matushka doll. He placed it on the dash in front of the steering wheel.

At work, Natasha barely acknowledged his arrival.

"I have decided to go with you to Perm to meet your parents."

She looked at him, first with some doubt, then with elation.

"Really, Volodya?" She came at him and jumped up with her arms around his neck and her legs around his waist.

"I told Irina I will be going to a martial arts tournament there. But I said I was leaving tomorrow morning, so between now and Wednesday, I will have to stay at your place. You'll have to talk to Vorontsov about my replacement."

She loosened her stranglehold and stood in front of him.

"Why don't you tell him?"

"Technically, you're my superior. I wouldn't want him to think there is anything unusual in my request, which should go through you."

"Yes. Of course I will arrange it. I'm so happy."

"Now that I have made my decision," Vladimir said, "so am I."

Chapter 41

Patrick Kerrane was more than fluent in Czech. He had done well in the intensive program at the Defense Language Institute in Monterey. A few years later, he had the opportunity to go through the whole experience again at the Foreign Service Institute, where he added to and refined his knowledge of the language. His vocabulary broadened. He gained cultural knowledge. And he learned to write flawlessly in Czech cursive.

On the tenth of February of 1983, Patrick informed his boss, Stan Miholic, that Pavel Francek, the Czech colonel who was Patrick's agent, had demanded payment of all the money he was owed for his espionage work on behalf of the United States. Miholic was surprised by the request, alarmed even, but Patrick produced a letter written in Czech in what appeared to be Francek's handwriting to support his claim. The letter assured its readers that Francek had no intention of severing his ties to the Americans, but that he had to have the money for a personal medical reason. Miholic, although still concerned, accepted Patrick's explanation of the situation. He sent a message to Washington reporting what had happened and after a bit of cable traffic back and forth, the money was pouched to the station.

On the twentieth of February at four o'clock in the morning Patrick drove south on E-14 toward Volice. He had lost his surveillance and was alone when he turned off the road to the edge of a now barren beet field. He was wearing his old army combat boots and he walked across the field to the tree line on the far side. A hunting platform had been built on four supports about ten feet off the ground. Patrick imagined a line between the two northern supports and continued east for three meters beyond the supports along that line. There he dug a shallow hole and buried a package that contained ten thousand U.S. dollars along with a note that read: "Final payment against the total of $250,000 we owed you for your service to us."

On the twenty-first of February, Patrick composed and wrote an anonymous letter ostensibly from a man whose wife had engaged in a sexual affair with Francek. The letter denounced Francek as a spy for the Americans. It said that Francek had boasted that he had gotten two hundred forty thousand dollars for his work and was about to receive another ten thousand dollars in payment. He would have to dig up the money in a field south of Prague. It gave the precise location of the site where the money would be buried. Patrick addressed the letter to the Czech Ministry of the Interior. He wore rubber gloves as he wrote it and went across the Vltava River to Francek's neighborhood to mail it. He figured the Czechs would suspect that the informant lived close by.

Two weeks later, in spite of the letter, Francek appeared on an isolated street corner for his scheduled meeting with Patrick. He made no mention of any difficulty, any letter of denunciation or any money. Patrick had known all along that the fellow was working under the control of the Czechs and Francek's appearance confirmed it. Patrick conducted the rolling car meeting as he normally did. Although the two men clearly did not like each other, both of them kept things civil. Patrick, too, did not raise any doubts or mention the money.

Once he dropped Francek off two miles from the point where he picked him up, Patrick drove the station car to the quai one block from the Charles Bridge. He left the keys in the ignition, popped the trunk lid with the lever beside the driver's seat, got out and took a heavy suitcase out of the trunk. He closed the lid and walked to the Staromestka metro stop, where he went down the steps. As far as Washington knew, the tall, thin red-haired Irishman might as well have descended into Hell. And that is what broke loose in CIA headquarters when Miholic cabled the message that his deputy had vanished.

Chapter 42

"What do we know, Harry?" Bill Marshall asked.

"Not much at this point. Security found out that Kerrane was up to his gonads in debt. He probably went over to the Czechs. They'll let the Russians interrogate him if they haven't already."

"Is there any connection to Bagatelle?"

"We believe there is." The Raven in his rumpled black suit and skinny dark tie squeezed a cigarette in his tar-stained fingers as he sat cross-legged to the right of Bill Marshall's desk. "Manion and Kerrane were friends. Manion was in Prague to meet Bagatelle. He goes out to Vienna then back in again and stays at Kerrane's place. Kerrane disappears. Bagatelle puts up his danger signal. I'd say that at the very least, Manion shot his mouth off."

"I'm not sure. For now I'll give him the benefit of the doubt. But I certainly intend to find out what the hell happened when I see him."

"When does your flight leave?"

"This evening. Manion's already in Vienna. This is something the director's going to have to approve. If he gives the okay, fine. But first Manion's going to have to convince me that Kerrane didn't know anything about Bagatelle and that the timing of the danger signal and Kerrane's disappearance are coincidental. I want him to look at me when he tells me that. Then I may let him go in."

"I'm against it." O'Meara leaned forward in his chair. He figured his best chance to derail this crazy scheme would be to couch his argument in personal and political terms. "If this blows up, it will go all the way to the White House. God damn it, Bill, you'll be down in the basement doing name traces. Your career will be over."

Marshall looked remarkably composed. He hadn't even reached for one of his nautical knots. His gaze was apparently untroubled.

"I've considered that."

The following day, Frank sat at a small, tile-topped table in a sparsely furnished Vienna safe house. Scenes on the blue and white squares were of Austrian hunters in Tyrolean caps firing at broad-chested stags. Frank was waiting for Bill Marshall to arrive from the United States and he used the time to write to Julie. His pen kept pressing into the grout between the tiles and poking little holes in the paper, but he wanted to explain the decision he had taken and knew he had to do it fast.

"Hi,

"By now I suppose you've heard where I'm headed. I don't know whether you would try to talk me out of it if you were here, but I think you would not. You once asked me why I decided to do this work. My answer was truthful, but maybe not complete.

"When I got out of the army I went to study in Paris. I met a Canadian at a party. He told me about his days in the international student movement. He said that in the fifties the Soviets had students come from all over the world to Moscow for annual meetings. Any students who didn't agree with the Soviet line were shouted down or excluded from meetings and committees. Then they had a meeting in Finland and the dissenters were beaten up in the street.

"The Canadian said he went to the next meeting. It was in Vienna. The Soviets thought they could still control things there. But the CIA went out and recruited a bunch of bully boys who were tougher than the Soviet bully boys and the Soviets never came out to play again. Nobody was willing to go to Moscow after that."

"No, I didn't want to be a bully boy. I wanted to be the one who defended decent people. I know this sounds chauvinistic and self-promoting, but I believe it. I grew up having more choices than people who live in other countries. A lot of people died so I could have those choices. I hope to have kids and I want them to have the same freedom to choose as I did. You don't deserve that freedom if you're not willing to risk something to preserve it..."

He heard a soft knock at the door.

"Got to go.

Love,

Frank."

He folded the letter and put it in the pocket of his suit coat.

"I came right from the airport." Marshall looked haggard and harried as if he hadn't slept well on the overnight flight. but knew he had to keep the adrenaline pumping. It had been two days since a Moscow case officer had spotted Bagatelle's danger signal. Time was running out for the Russian. Marshall slipped his black vinyl bag from his shoulder and let it fall on the threadbare sofa. He dropped his cracked leather briefcase beside it. They sat opposite each other at the small table by the window. "So, you want to go to Moscow?"

"I think I should, yes."

"I talked to the director. He approved it in principle, but before I give the go ahead, this is crucial," Marshall said. "I have to know what happened in Prague. Remember Watergate. The cover-up is often worse than the deed, so tell the truth now and we'll deal with it. Maybe you had too much to drink. If you slipped up and said something you shouldn't have, nobody will hold it against you."

Frank didn't believe that last part for a moment, but as far as he was concerned, that had no bearing on what they were discussing.

"I didn't have too much to drink. I recall perfectly what I did and didn't tell Patrick. If he knew anything about the Bagatelle case, it didn't come from me." His tone was firm, but not argumentative. "Personally, I don't believe he knew about Bagatelle. I know Patrick."

Marshall countered that statement.

"If that's true, why didn't you tell us he would defect?"

"I don't believe he did. At this point we don't really know where he is. He never trusted that colonel he was running. Maybe the Czechs figured he was going to expose the guy as a double agent. Patrick might be at the bottom of the Vltava for all we know. It's pretty deep."

"Maybe, but it doesn't look that way."

"No matter where he is I believe that if he suspected I was involved in a Soviet case, he couldn't have resisted teasing me about it. But he never did." Frank thought briefly of his conversation in the headquarters cafeteria when Kerrane had pressed him about his trip to Brazil. But he dismissed it. Patrick hadn't been sure of anything at that point and had never spoken of the trip again.

"And you would swear to that?" Marshall watched him as he answered.

"Yes."

"You'll almost certainly have to when you take the polygraph." The older man twisted in his seat to reach behind him and unsnap the briefcase. "Okay," he took out two manila envelopes, laid them on the table then put his hands palms down beside them, "then let's get to the business at hand. Moscow station doesn't want any part of this. Just between us, I think they still have their nose out of joint over the fact that we approved having Bagatelle choose his own sites. That had never been done before. Now they claim that since Shurin gave his danger signal, surveillance has intensified, doubled, and they can't count on getting anyone black to carry out the exfiltration. If we insist on getting him out, they want someone from the outside to do it. That's you.

"I know."

Now the division chief leaned against the back of the vinyl-covered chair. Small pockets had formed under his eyes and silver stubble was visible on his cheeks in the angled light from the window.

"Be that as it may, the question is whether you can pull it off. And it may not be worth the risk."

"Maybe not to us, but it sure as hell is worth it to Shurin." Frank realized too late that his voice had risen. He brought it down an octave. "Look, Bill, I'm not trying to be some kind of hero. But I made him a promise. If Moscow Station won't get him out, I have to do it."

"Most men don't plan to be heroes, Frank, but from where I sit it looks as if what you're doing qualifies."

Frank understood that this discussion had to take place even if Marshall chose to wax philosophical. But he couldn't help being impatient. Time was passing.

"What about Cooper?" Frank asked.

"What about him?"

"Did he ever have access to the files on Bagatelle?"

"No. He was in admin. He was never on the bigot list. He never set up the accounts. He had nothing to do with the case."

"Then I still want to do it." Now Frank leaned back in his chair just as Marshall had. For several moments they stared at each other in silence. It was Marshall who spoke first.

"There's one more thing. I talked about risk. Before I approve this, I want to be sure you understand how great that risk is. Even if nobody ratted Shurin out, the Soviets are like junk yard dogs. They may let you through the gate, but getting back across that border is another matter."

"I understand."

"You'll have to go in and out with the Irish documents. Can you do that?"

"I couldn't pass for an Irishman in Ireland and I couldn't pass for a Russian in Russia, but I think I can pass for an Irishman in Moscow."

"All right, you'll have to take Shurin's documents in with you. He'll have to pretend to be a Brazilian. What about him? Can he do it?"

"His Portuguese is fluent. I think it's the best chance he's got."

Marshall reached into the inside chest pocket of his suit coat.

"Here."

Frank opened the buff colored envelope. He leafed through the Brazilian passport and studied Shurin's photo.

"I think he's already shown us he's a pretty resourceful guy."

"Fine, but if it goes bad and your Boland identity is compromised, you are not to go near the embassy. And you cannot approach any of our people on the street." Marshall pointed his index finger at Frank for emphasis. "The KGB will nab you on the spot."

"So I'm on my own?"

"Not quite. The station has a young secretary who almost never comes under surveillance. She can't get near Shurin, but she will put down a set of American docs for you."

"Do I have to put up a distress signal?" Frank was growing concerned. This was beginning to sound complicated. If at all possible, he didn't want Moscow Station to be involved. Who was the girl? How could the station be sure she had never had surveillance? Did they believe that just because she had said so? What if it had been there and she simply hadn't spotted it?

"No signal will be necessary. If you're not on the flight to Vienna, we'll know right away and we'll cable the station to go ahead with the drop. The new documents will have all the right stamps to get you out the day after your scheduled flight to Vienna." Marshall pulled a black and white eight by ten inch photo from the top envelope on the table. "This is where you'll pick up the package." He took two sheets of paper from the second manila envelope. "Memorize the directions and instructions. They could save your life." He waited as Frank studied both the photo and the instructions. "If those don't work, you really are on your own. The stamps are good for only one day. You still want to go?"

"Yes." Now Frank reached into his own coat pocket and took out his letter. He put it in an envelope, sealed it and wrote "Julie" on the front. "I wonder if you would do me a favor and give this to Julie d'Andrade." He held out the envelope. Marshall didn't smile. He just looked surprised.

"I'll be happy to." He stuck out his hand. "Go with God, Frank. Bring him out alive."

Chapter 43

Frank spent the night in the safe house, but was too wired to sleep. The next morning, wearing his Boland disguise, he took the Austrian Air flight from Schwechat to Moscow's Sheremetyevo 2 Airport. The plan was simple. He was to spend the night, pass the false documents to Shurin and have them both fly out separately the following morning. Shurin's papers had all the necessary entry and exit stamps. Frank carried them in a concealed space in the side of his briefcase along with two thousand British pounds for incidentals.

On his arrival, he passed the usual guards toting Kalashnikovs. The airport had been built only three years before for the 1980 Olympics and the Soviets hadn't put in enough passport kiosks or luggage carousels. There were bottlenecks. He had to fill out a currency declaration. Then the customs agent took his time rooting through the two suitcases and the briefcase. But Frank knew the most critical moment would come when they scrutinized his passport. The official held it below the counter while he studied it. Frank knew he was using an ultraviolet light. The fellow appeared satisfied. He closed it and handed it back without a word.

In the concourse Frank exchanged three hundred British pounds. But as he walked out of the building Marshall's admonition stuck in his mind. The Soviets might let you in, but just try to get back out.

In front of the terminal five blue and white AEROFLOT buses were lined up. Most of them were destined for the bigger hotels in town. Frank waited only five minutes for a minibus that took him to the air terminal on Leningradskiy Prospekt. He left one suitcase in a storage locker and caught a taxi to the Rossiya Hotel, where he checked in. He left his other suitcase and the briefcase in his room, went downstairs and got another cab to Kudrinskaya Ploshchad out by the Garden Ring. He kept looking out the back window, but saw no sign of surveillance. He had dressed well for the trip in a gray British-tailored glen plaid suit with a pinpoint oxford shirt and blue tie with a silver pattern. He wore a Burberry raincoat and Church's shoes. The point was not simply to be able to show the British labels, but to be so well dressed that at first glance everyone would take him for who and what he was supposed to be: Richard Boland, Irish businessman. The taxi driver apparently did. Other than explaining to Frank that the square was commonly called Ploshchad Vosstaniya rather than Kudrinskaya Ploshchad, he never said a word the whole trip. It wasn't always safe to talk to foreigners.

It was one in the afternoon when Frank crossed the square and passed a pink, two-story house sandwiched between two taller buildings.

Several people stood outside. They looked like tourists. As he walked by the door, Frank noticed the nameplate: Doctor A. P. Chekhov. From his days in the language course in Monterey, Frank recollected that Chekhov, the writer, had been a doctor. He saw a small wooden stand with a sign identifying the place as the Chekhov House Museum. The hours were from eleven in the morning until four in the afternoon. He wished he could go inside, but knew any visit would have to wait until better days.

He kept walking. He was surprised at the width of the boulevards and the fact that the back streets were lined with trees. He pulled up the collar of his coat. The sidewalk was wet with dirt-encrusted snow piled along the edges. It struck him that it was a good thing the trees were leafless, otherwise he might have difficulty spotting the windows of the room where Shurin said he would be hiding. He turned into Granatnyi Pereulok. The street had about the same small number of cars as pedestrians. From across the street, Frank looked up at the fifth floor windows of a gray concrete slab building. They did have curtains. One was drawn and the other was open. He went into the building and stood for several moments in the vestibule before climbing the dank stairwell. The air was acrid with an underlying cabbage odor. He felt a chill and by the time he got to the top of the steps, his heart was racing. He waited for about thirty seconds to regain his composure then knocked.

"Boland, I knew you would come, but what delayed you?" Shurin looked like hell. He hugged Frank and kissed him on both cheeks. It was obvious from his stubble that he hadn't shaved in several days. He was wearing a wrinkled white shirt that looked as if he had slept in it. His hair was uncombed. But the most noticeable feature was his eyes, which were glassy and wild looking.

"Volodya, are you all right?"

"Now that you are here, I am better. But I have been like crazy man, trapped animal waiting for hunter."

Frank looked around and listened. He heard no sound. Apparently they were alone. The apartment may have been comfortable by Soviet standards, but Frank found it musty and cramped. From the door he stepped directly into the small living area. The tiny kitchen was off to the right. He figured the door on the left opened into a bathroom. Ahead was a short hallway with two other doors, probably bedrooms. Shurin waved his arm to have Frank sit on a stuffed, lumpy burgundy sofa. Frank took off his raincoat and put it on the cushion beside him.

"What happened? Why did you give the danger signal?"

"My wife saw what I was doing. She threatened to report me."

"Has she done it?"

"No. I stopped her, but only for now. The organs will know shortly that I am spy. I had to leave my flat and come here."

"What's the situation? Where is the girl who lives here?"

"This place is owned by old woman. She lives in outskirts. Natasha, this girl, is in Perm at parents' house. But she returns in two days. When I heard knock, I thought she might be back, but forgot her key. I cannot tell you how relieved I was to see your face at door."

"Will it be safe for you to spend one more night here?"

"Probably, I was always very careful never to lead my tails to this place. Still, authorities know that Natasha and I worked together. Sooner or later they will come here."

"I'm staying in a hotel." Frank thought it better not to give the name. "Tomorrow I'll come again and give you a Brazilian passport. It has your photo. There's a driver's license and other cards and a currency declaration along with your plane ticket. You remember the photo I took of you in Brazil?"

"Yes."

"My people added a moustache and glasses. I'll bring those tomorrow as well. If the KGB is looking for you, the moustache and glasses will change your appearance just enough so that with the false passport you'll be able to get by. It has all the necessary stamps in it. Your name will be Gilberto Morais. Your story will be that you're an administrator for PetroBras, the oil company. You were here to talk to NEFTORG, the foreign trading organization that handles energy contracts. Tonight I want you to fill in the details of the story. Keep to things you know and keep it simple. Memorize it. Can you do that?"

"Of course."

"But we have to leave tomorrow. That's when the visa in your passport expires. Mine, too. I want you to get cleaned up. I have a suitcase for you. It's packed with clothes from Brazil. They're in your size. I'll bring it tomorrow."

"Will we go together?"

"No. It will be safer if we travel separately. Now I'm going back to the hotel. Just to be sure, if everything is all right tomorrow, reverse the curtains, that one open, the other one closed." Frank stood and put on his coat. "Get some rest, Volodya. And shave. Clean yourself up. Tomorrow you start a new life."

"Richard, you are my brother. You have saved my life."

"So far all I've done is show up here. We're not home free yet."

Frank went back to the main intersection at the Garden Ring and caught a taxi to his hotel. At the desk he reserved a ticket for that evening's performance of Prokofiev's "Stone Flower" at the Bolshoi Theater.

As he sat in the audience with the lights down, he felt almost cocky. He was more accustomed to his disguise. He had gotten into the Soviet Union, made his contact with Shurin and tomorrow they would leave the country. It would work.

Chapter 44

While Frank was watching pirouettes and leaps that defied gravity at the Bolshoi, Natasha Chernenko was shivering in an isolated holding cell at the Lubyanka Prison. She had returned from Perm a day early, but at the end of the Pavelets Station platform two men stopped her. They knew her name, although she was certain she had never seen them before.

"Nothing to be concerned about, comrade, just routine business, really," said the first one, the taller of the two, who took her suitcase in one hand and flipped open a small blue and red folder with the other. His photograph was inside with the name, Belyagin, Viktor Yuryevich, major, Operative Detachment, Committee for State Security.

"What is this about?" Natasha asked. "Am I in some kind of trouble?"

"Not a bit of it." The shorter man laughed as if that were the most outrageous interpretation of what was happening. "It won't take very long, just a few questions. We believe you can help us straighten things out," he said as he hooked his arm under hers.

They hurried her outside, where a black Pobeda with darkened windows was waiting with the rear doors open. The squat fellow lifted off her backpack and pressured her into the seat. They drove her across Moscow and along Pushechnaya to Dzerzhinsky Square. The gray building in front of her was the Lubyanka Prison. The great steel doors were apparently on rails and slid open sideways into the walls, then shut again. The car was in a large central courtyard, deserted except for the new arrivals. They went through a normal-sized door, down a hall lined with other regular doors that were oddly close together. The short fellow opened one door on the right and gestured for her to precede him.

"This way, please."

They had been walking fast and in turning into that doorway Natasha had kept her pace. Suddenly she stopped. If she hadn't, she would have run straight into a wall. She was in a box, perhaps a meter and a half by three meters. The ceiling was high, another three meters. There was a plain permanent bench on one wall. She turned in confusion, but the door behind her was already closing. Above that door was a naked, intense bulb in a heavy link wire cage. And that is where she sat, cold, frightened and bewildered for what seemed like a very long time. She had no way of knowing how long. She had left her watch in her backpack. It was actually midnight when the door opened. A prison matron waved her out of her cell. Natasha tried to protest, but the woman simply put her finger to her lips and they walked on in silence. Natasha followed her through a series of corridors. They turned left. The doors were now wider spaced and the matron stopped and knocked lightly at one. Without waiting for an answer, she opened it.

"Go in."

Natasha entered a large room with wide floorboards and a huge barred window on the far side. She could see that it was night outside. To her right was a desk. A tall man with a pockmarked face was seated there. He was in a khaki uniform with two stars on his shoulder boards and a diamond shaped dark blue insignia on his lapels. About two meters from the desk was a wooden table with a hard wooden chair.

"Sit down." He pointed to the chair. "I am Colonel Mstislav Stepanovich Fersin. I will be your interrogator." His tone was business-like.

"Can you tell me why I have been brought here?" she asked.

Without looking up, the colonel held up one index finger as he turned the pages of a thick file on the desk. Natasha fidgeted on the chair. She really had to pee. After a few moments, he spoke.

"I think that is for you to tell me."

"But I don't know. I haven't done anything."

"Think about it." He raised his voice, although he didn't appear or sound angry. "I'm sure if you do, you'll understand your dilemma."

Natasha felt a chill run through her.

"I assure you, I have no idea."

"Let us not waste time. You work with a man, Vladimir Sergeyevich Shurin, correct?"

It was as if the first two pieces of a puzzle had been connected, but Natasha still couldn't guess at what the whole picture would be. Had Volodya done something while she was away?

"Yes, at the Ministry of Foreign Affairs."

"Just so. Have you ever been in his flat?"

"No."

"And you live on..." he turned back two pages in the file, "Polkovaya ulitsa, correct?"

"Yes, with my cousin." Natasha wondered if they knew about her move to the old lady's flat. It was illegal and if they weren't aware of it, she wasn't about to tell this fellow. But if they had found out, maybe that was what this was all about.

"Did you know Comrade Shurin's wife?"

"No." Now Natasha was uncertain again.

"But you did know that he was married." He affirmed this rather than posed it as a question.

"Yes." Maybe, she thought, they had found out about her love affair.

"She's gone missing, you know?" Again, Fersin said this almost as if it were not a question, but a statement of fact.

"Mrs. Shurin? No, I didn't."

"Did Comrade Shurin ever bring you an oriental carpet say within the past ten days?"

"No, not at all."

"We've been watching him for some time. We saw him leave his flat one evening with a carpet over his shoulder. He put it in the boot of your car."

"Oh." So it must be about the car. Maybe the papers were not in order. "Well, you see, Volodya, that is Comrade Shurin, loaned me the money to buy that car with the understanding that he could use it at any time."

"Do you know where your car is right now?"

"It's parked on the street near..." Natasha was about to say "near my room," but caught herself. "I can't be sure, I suppose. It's possible that Comrade Shurin moved it, of course. He was supposed to join me in Perm to meet my parents. We're going to be married, you know. But he didn't come. Has something happened to him?"

"How can you marry him if he is already a married man? His wife would be something of an impediment wouldn't you say?" Fersin had gotten up from his desk and was walking behind her from one side to the other. She kept turning her head to follow his movement, but felt her neck getting stiff. She had noticed it on the train when she had tried to sleep with her head against the seat back.

"He planned to divorce her." It surprised her that she was speaking in the past tense, as if that were somehow out of the question now.

"I suppose he would have to, unless he got rid of her in another way."

"What other way?"

"Has Comrade Shurin ever discussed his activities on behalf of a foreign government?"

"What?" Natasha had been somewhat surprised by the line of interrogation about Irina, Vladimir's wife. But this last question stunned her. The officer had come around her now and was looking at her face. She thought he must have recognized her shock.

"Has he been photographing documents? And have you been helping him?"

"Oh, my God," she crossed herself involuntarily, the camera, that bloody camera.

"You see, this fellow never intended to marry you. He planned to go abroad again for the ministry and marry a Brazilian woman. Did you know that?" He waited, but Natasha sat in helpless silence. "Perhaps you were not really helping him. Maybe he was just using you."

"I never knew..."

"We'll see." Fersin returned to his desk. He said nothing. A few minutes later, without any further explanation the interview ended. Fersin pressed a button next to the phone. The same matron came back and led Natasha to the same cell. She cried most of the night.

At eight o'clock the following morning, Mstislav Stepanovich Fersin walked down the fourth floor hall of the Lubyanka to the director's office. He had been at this work, the task of interrogating prisoners, since the mid-seventies. His family was actually of Scottish ancestry. Their name in the late nineteenth century when they came to Russia had been Ferguson, but over the years it was mongrelized. Their Scottish paterfamilias had emigrated from Scotland to run a textile mill set up by Nicholas II. He married a Russian girl and after three generations, Mstislav, in the family tradition was weaving threads, but now they were human threads.

Fersin stood in front of Alexander Pavlovich Voroshilov's desk. The head of the KGB's Second Chief Directorate had been following the case closely and had just received a full report of the night's activities.

"We planted the seed, Comrade General," Fersin said. "Shurin's on the run. We'll release her in about an hour and she'll lead us to him."

"I want you to give strict instructions that our lads are not to crowd her or interfere. If we continue to give them both some rope, they'll take us to the body and they'll hang themselves in the process."

"I understand, Comrade General."

"Now what about the espionage?"

"We had him under periodic surveillance and saw nothing. We believe he has just used the girl. She may not even know anything about the wife's disappearance or even his filthy spying. We intensified the surveillance these last weeks. We also have an observation post in a building across the street from his flat. It was from this point that we saw him carry out the carpet. Our audio device confirms that the wife found a short wave radio and spy equipment. She confronted him. After that her voice was never heard again. Our boys went into the apartment and found the spy gear in the attic. We are certain his wife's body was in that carpet. If we bring him in for the murder charge, we'll get him to confess to the other, sir."

"All right, let her go. But I give you fair warning. Keep a balance. Do not let her spot you, but also do not let her slip away from you. If she disappears, those stars on your shoulders might disappear as well."

Chapter 45

Frank stood waiting at the check out desk of the Rossiya. The place was enormous. It could accommodate six thousand guests and the lobby was crowded. Outside, he looked over at the Moscow River as he walked to the taxi line. He knew Muscovites swam in it and sun-bathed on its banks in summer. It was ice-free now, but still looked frigid and uninviting.

He instructed the cab driver to take him back to the air terminal. Inside, he switched bags at the locker, leaving his own suitcase and picking up the one he had brought for Bagatelle. He kept the crocodile briefcase with him. On the street once again he put the suitcase in the trunk of another taxi and held the briefcase in his lap as he went back to Shurin's neighborhood.

There were more people on the street today, a Saturday. Parents with children in tow were headed for the nearby zoo. Frank carried the bag back to Granatnyi Pereulok. Even on the side street there were more pedestrians and cars. When he reached the sidewalk across from the apartment, he saw that the curtains were in the right position and he went up the staircase, this time carrying the suitcase packed with clothes. Shurin opened the door even before Frank knocked. He still looked tired, but Frank could see he had shaved and combed his hair.

"You look better, Volodya." Frank set the suitcase on the floor in front of the sofa and opened it. Shurin had to step over it to get to his chair. "Pick out what you want to wear."

"This looks all right," Shurin said. He held up a grayish-blue suit. "But it is not well pressed."

"Shit," Frank said. Done in by details. Of course it was wrinkled. Why hadn't he planned for that?

"Don't worry. We are accustomed to such things. I can press it." Shurin carried the coat and pants into the tiny kitchen. Frank stood in the doorway. The Russian laid the suit on the table, opened a cabinet under the sink and took out a clothes iron. He filled it with some water from the tap, plugged it into the wall and stood while the iron heated up.

"Listen," Frank said. "I'll do this. It will save some time and we have to get moving. You pick out the shirt and tie, socks, shoes and put them on. Do you know your cover legend?"

"Yes. I can tell such bullshit that president of PetroBras would believe I am one of his employees." Vladimir stepped back into the living room, bent over the suitcase and took out what he needed. He walked to the bathroom and closed the door.

Frank looked around the kitchen. It was pretty sparsely equipped. He saw pots hanging on the walls, two dish towels, a vase of dried flowers, a knife rack. The iron began to hiss and he ran it back and forth over the pants first. When he finished, he carried them through the tiny living room and knocked on the bathroom door. Shurin opened it. He stood there in red jockey shorts.

"I'll work on the jacket now," Frank said.

Two minutes later, Shurin came out. He bent over the suitcase and took out a brown leather belt. Frank finished the sleeves of the suit coat and handed it to the Russian, who put it on.

"How does it look?" Vladimir asked. For the first time Frank realized there were no mirrors in the room.

"Okay. There's not much we can do about the raincoat, but you're supposed to be a traveler after all and things get wrinkled when they're packed." He closed the suitcase and went to his briefcase on the sofa. He opened it and pried the Velcro corners of the side panel loose. "Here are your passport and papers and the ticket." Vladimir took the envelope. "I..." Frank didn't continue.

Both men looked at the door. A key was turning in the lock. The door opened, but grated against the chain.

"Volodya, open up." It was a woman's voice and a woman's face looking through the crack. Frank quickly pressed the concealment panel back in place and closed the briefcase. His first inclination was to hide, but she had already seen him. Frank nodded to Vladimir. The Russian pushed the door closed and unhooked the chain.

"It's good to see you. How was your trip?" He tried to kiss the girl on both cheeks, but she turned her face away and pushed on his chest.

"You son-of-a-bitch." She swung her suitcase forward and pushed past him into the room. She had a backpack and she slipped the strap from her shoulder and dropped it outside the bathroom door.

"I know. I couldn't come, a last-minute business. I had to see a friend."

"Friend?" She looked at Frank with an expression that showed contempt.

"Natasha, I want you to meet...Henry."

"Stop your silly fucking charade you liar. This man is a foreigner. And you are a spy and a murderer. You killed your wife." All this was in Russian, but Frank understood it perfectly. Up to this point he hadn't said a word and he hoped he wouldn't have to.

"What are you talking about?" Shurin spread his arms in front of him with his palms up. He chuckled. "What is this nonsense?"

Now Natasha stood with her hands on her hips.

"I arrived yesterday. You embarrassed me in front of my parents. But that was not the worst. Where do you think I spent last night?" She waited for only a moment, but there was no answer. "I was in the

Government Terror." Frank understood the words, but didn't recognize the reference.

"The Lubyanka?" Vladimir asked. Frank certainly understood that.

"Yes. And all the questions were about you. They know everything."

Frank realized he had to move. In an instant he evaluated things. Shurin had his papers. He had the clothes, the suitcase, the ticket and the cover story. He could make it on his own. Frank figured he would have to do the same thing. They had a better chance to escape if they split up.

"Vladimir, I think I should go. I wish you all the best."

"Go downstairs...Henry. Go to corner. I will catch you up there." He spoke in English.

Frank didn't say anything to the girl. Instead, he went out the door and down the steps. At the bottom, he heard the door to the flat open and Natasha's screams echoing down the staircase.

"So what they said was true. You have a Brazilian woman. You never intended to marry me."

Frank didn't go out on the street immediately. He stood and heard Shurin coming down the steps. He heard, too, the suitcase bumping against the metal railing. At first the girl didn't seem to be following. Then he heard the apartment door being flung open and Natasha was coming down the staircase. Frank went outside. The day had turned sunny and there were even more people on the street now. He crossed to the other side and started walking slowly toward the corner. He knew how Lot's wife must have felt and against his own better instincts, he looked back. Vladimir came out of the building. In an instant, the girl was behind him. She spoke to Shurin as he headed in Frank's direction, but her voice was lower now and Frank couldn't make out what she was saying. He saw Vladimir stop and turn to her. She walked up to him and they exchanged some words. Things appeared to have calmed down. Shurin looked across the street at Frank and actually smiled. The Russian shook his head, pointed to his temple and rotated his index finger. Then, the girl raised her left hand as if to strike Vladimir's chest. He grabbed her wrist, but suddenly, he got a strange look on his face and both he and Natasha looked down at the space between them. Natasha twisted her left hand free of Shurin's grip and Frank saw a flash, a reflection of metal. The girl had reached up and there was a burst of red from Shurin's neck. His right hand went to his collar. The girl took two steps back and began screaming again.

"You dragged me into your filthy business." People were passing Frank on the sidewalk. A father was holding his little boy's hand. They looked across the street. "Now I will lose my job, the car, everything because of you, you bastard."

"Boland," Vladimir called out. "Richard." Frank crossed the street running. Shurin was on his knees. Natasha was standing back, tears rolling down her cheeks, a knife in her lowered right hand. Blood continued to pulse from Vladimir's neck. It was a bright red accent to his white shirt and a dull spreading spot on the broad lapel of the navy raincoat. Frank laid the Russian on his back. He took off his own raincoat and wrapped one sleeve around Shurin's neck and pressed the carotid artery on the right side below his ear. "She cut me."

"Quiet, Volodya."

"What bitch," Shurin said. Frank wasn't sure if he was referring to the girl or to life itself, which, to Frank's confusion, seemed to be slipping away from the man. Shurin's face and hands had turned the color and almost the consistency of just-poured cement. Frank couldn't understand why since he saw he had stanched the flow with the coat sleeve, but the Russian was clearly dying.

Frank heard the two-note cadenced bleating of a police siren.

"Vladimir, can you hold this yourself?" Shurin didn't react.

"Thank God, tyrant is dead," the Russian murmured. He was trying to say something else. Frank leaned closer to try to make it out. Only when he straightened did he look down the length of Shurin's body. He spotted the pool of blood on the sidewalk between the dying man's legs. She had cut his femoral artery as well. Frank heard a kind of gurgle and leaned forward again and looked into Shurin's eyes.

A crowd had gathered. They formed a circle around the scene. An unmarked Chaika pulled up. Two men got out. KGB. Frank stood and stepped back into the group of spectators as the men approached the body. One man knelt while the other took the knife from Natasha's hand and held her by the arm. Frank kept moving back and when he was behind the last onlooker, he walked purposefully across and down the street. At the corner he looked back. No one was following him. Only when he got out to the boulevard did he realize what Shurin had said: "Brazil."

Chapter 46

Natasha Chernenko was unable to tell if the cell she was in was the same one she had occupied the night before. For all she knew, all of the cells may have been identical. But this time she was led away after only five or ten minutes by another stocky matron to the same interrogation room, where the same officer seated at the same desk confronted her.

"You killed him," Fersin shouted.

"Yes."

"Do you know what will happen to you now?"

"I can guess."

"Perhaps you can, but maybe you can't." He drew a stiff forefinger across his throat in a simulated cutting motion. Natasha shuddered. Fersin lowered his voice. "What I can tell you is that if you cooperate fully with us, we are in a position to recommend leniency. He was, after all, a traitor. Am I right?"

"You said so, comrade. He never admitted it, but there was that other man."

"What other man?"

"He was in the flat when I got there. Volodya said his name was Henry. He said they had business together, but it all looked shady to me." Fersin suddenly stood and approached the small table. He leaned on it with both palms. She could smell his breath. He had been drinking vodka.

"And where was this other man when you killed Shurin?"

"He had crossed the street, Granatnyi Pereulok. He was on the other side, but he came back."

"He came back?"

"Yes. He was the one who tried to stop the bleeding. When the officials took me away, he walked off."

"This is some kind of bloody fantasy." Fersin smacked his palm on the table. This whole thing had blown up in his face. General Voroshilov would cut his balls off because the girl had killed the chief suspect. The surveillance team had not reacted quickly enough to stop her. Their explanation was that they had orders to keep their distance. Now she was talking nonsense. They had never reported that there had been another man involved. "I think you were traumatized. Shurin bled to death on the sidewalk. No one helped him."

"No, comrade, he was there but..."

"But what, who was this man?"

"A foreigner."

"Foreigner?" Fersin's voice rose again and he leaned within centimeters of her face. "What nationality?"

"I don't know. When I came to the door of the flat, before I opened it I heard them speaking in English. And Volodya said other things to him in English. He could have been British, or American. And that was not his name."

"What do you mean? What name?"

"Volodya said in the flat that the man's name was Henry. But out on the street he called him another name, Boland. Yes, that was it, Boland, Richard."

Once again, this time at two in the afternoon, Colonel Fersin reported to his boss. General Voroshilov would normally continue to skim through papers while his underlings delivered their reports, but this time he had pushed the stack of papers to one side. Fersin had his full attention, and possibly would feel his focused wrath.

"The girl was telling the truth. We contacted all the hotels. There was a Richard Boland at the Rossiya. He checked out this morning. He had an Irish passport. The hotel kept it overnight and the police checked it, but they returned it to him this morning. He conducted no business here that we know of. That is difficult to determine since it is the weekend, but he had only a two-day visa. He was to depart today."

"Have you checked the airports?"

"Yes, Comrade General, he was booked on an Austrian Airlines flight to Vienna. That was how he came here. But the plane left thirty minutes ago and he was not on board."

"What about trains? Warsaw, Budapest, Helsinki?"

"We have alerted our operatives in all eight stations, even those with trains to the interior."

"And the border posts?"

"All are on alert for this man. We have given his description."

"What if he is traveling in disguise?" Voroshilov looked smug, as if he had caught his subordinate unprepared.

"We have cautioned all of our people that this is a possibility. On the other hand, he cannot change his height and weight and we have given that information to everyone involved."

"Cut off access to the American Embassy. I want that place harder to get into than a nun's pussy."

"That was the first thing I did, Comrade General. I doubled the militiamen outside the gate."

"Do we have any idea where he went when he left the Rossiya this morning?"

Now Voroshilov had caught him. Fersin had that information and had failed to give it.

"Yes, Comrade General. He took a taxi from the queue in front of the hotel. The doorman remembers that he told the taxi driver to take him to the air terminal on Leningradskiy Prospekt."

"I want you to send additional men there. Check the papers of everyone coming in or going out. He may be long gone from there, but you never know. Also, I want our men to go through every storage locker in the terminal. He may have left his baggage. He can hardly wander around Moscow with it. It would make him easier to spot and he may come back for it. And the girl never said he was carrying a suitcase, did she?"

"No, Comrade General." Fersin did not admit that he hadn't asked the Chernenko girl if she had seen a suitcase. He would have her brought from her cell to the interrogation room to get the answer.

"Check all the museums, the theaters, anywhere a tourist might go. Mstislav, in a situation like this I don't want us to be following this fellow from place to place. He is probably an American agent sent here to take Shurin out of the Union. Shurin had Brazilian papers, a plane ticket. He got them from this man. What we have to do now is anticipate what he will do next. Be one step ahead, not one step behind. He may have a plan to contact his people in the embassy. I want you to shut that down. No such contact will be possible, do you understand?"

"Yes, Comrade General."

"And anyone coming out of that embassy is to be surrounded by our people. If they take a piss, we grab their balls."

"At your order, Comrade General."

"Good. We may have lost our bird in the hand, but there is still the one in the bush. I want us to surround that fucking bush and set it on fire and catch whatever flies out."

Chapter 47

Frank had been a long distance runner in college. Those tests of endurance gave one a lot of time to think. Mostly he had thought about getting his second wind and when that kicked in, he concentrated on his pace and breathing, and toward the end the fatigue and the need to push beyond the pain. He had been good enough to know what it was like to have people behind him trying to catch up. The difference between his situation now and those long fall days in the woods was that if these people caught him, he would have to suffer more than just leg cramps.

At Kudrinskaya Square, he had been tempted to head straight for the airport. He calculated how long it would take to get there, how long he would have to wait for his flight. He tried to measure that against his estimate of how much time the KGB would need to pressure the girl to give them his name. It wouldn't take long at all. The airport was out. They would be waiting for him. Instead, he got a taxi back to the air terminal. He took the brass key, went to the storage locker and took out his suitcase. On the floor in front of the wall of lockers, he opened it, knelt down and picked out the clothes he wanted. He put the suitcase back in the locker, deposited another ruble and pocketed the key once again. He carried the briefcase with him.

Down the hall he saw the sign for the men's room. Just inside the door a babushka, probably a war widow who had been given this concession, sat at a small table. Prominently displayed on the table was a basket with a layer of coins. Frank passed by and entered one of the stalls. He took off his suit and put on a pair of jeans, a black woolen turtleneck sweater, cordovan Cumberland Oxfords and a tobacco brown leather jacket. Opening the briefcase, he pried loose the side panel and took out British pounds. He stuffed as much as he could in the pockets of his jeans and jacket. Just before he left the stall he realized that he wasn't sure when he would have his next opportunity, so he peed in the dirty bowl. On his way out, the old woman, gnarled as an oak, held out a soiled damp cloth. Frank made a gesture to dry his hands, but thought better of it. He dropped two rubles in the basket and in two perfectly coordinated movements, with his back to the woman but still not visible to anyone in the corridor, he stepped out the door, knelt and bent his head as if he were tying his shoes and stripped off the moustache.

On his way down the hall he removed the glasses. He stuffed the suit and his shoes and shirt into the locker and threw the glasses on top of the pile. For the last time he looked at his false passport and the identity documents that said he was Richard Boland. He put them, too, in the locker. They were worse than useless now. If he were stopped on the street and had to produce them, they would be like an alarm bell going off. He slammed the door of the locker shut, twisted the key and dropped it in a trash bin on his way out.

Strangely, his first sensation was one of freedom. Unless he was stopped, he would be okay. The trick was to act the way everyone else acted. He had some time, but he needed all of it to think. He had to last one more day. The American documents and his plane ticket would be waiting for him in the morning. What he hadn't considered was where he would spend the night.

He decided that for now he would hide in plain view. Where better to do that than the zoo? He considered going there on the metro, but was sure the Soviets were like the Hungarians, the Germans, the British, and the French who had cameras in every tunnel. Even though the girl's description of him might include his moustache and glasses, the Soviets were smart enough to put out an all points that would caution the cops and the KGB people to keep in mind that these could be removed. The upshot was that he took a cab.

In the taxi Marshall's admonition came to mind. The Soviets guarded their border like wolves and at least for twenty-four hours he was on his own. The sensation of freedom gave way to fear in the pit of his stomach. But he remembered the time he almost drowned in a rip tide off the beach at Carmel, California. His first thought then was "Don't panic." He had floated with the current and allowed the water to carry him out until the force diminished and he could swim to shore. That's what he had to do now.

For the next three hours, he wandered among the animal cages. He remembered an outing from the orphanage to the zoo and how he hated the smell of the elephant house when he was a kid. Some things never changed.

At three o'clock he sat on a bench and concentrated. Even if he went to the embassy in contravention of orders, there were militiamen outside the gate and without documents he could never get past them. Besides, they, too, would have a description that might help them spot him. Speak of the devil. At that very moment, two of the gray uniformed cops walked slowly by chatting to each other. Frank turned his head away to look back at the bear cage. They walked on.

He thought about waiting for the American staff to leave the embassy and approaching one of them on the street if they were on foot. But if Marshall was right and Moscow Station had been honest, they were under blanketing surveillance. And today was Saturday. No one would be going in or coming out until Monday. And then he remembered something: Saturday, Saturday hours, the Chekhov House. It was open until four on Saturday.

Frank waited until three-thirty before crossing Kudrinskaya. He approached the pink house at number six. He paid a ruble to enter, about the equivalent of thirty cents. A custodian, this time an old man wearing the dark khaki jacket of a Soviet infantryman decorated with a chest full of ribbons from World War II, took the money and handed Frank a pink flyer in Russian. Two women came down the steps from the second floor and went out as Frank went in to the living room. There were four more people in there all speaking quietly as if they were in church. For Russians, this was almost a spiritual experience. They loved their writers.

Frank read the flyer. It said that Anton Chekhov, his brother and his parents had lived in the house from 1866 to 1890. During those years he had practiced medicine and still found time to write over a hundred short stories, a novel and three one-act farces. Frank walked through Chekhov's study and consulting room. The doctor/writer's leather bag was on a table. Another three people. He was counting them as he progressed. He went back to the entrance. The door had a simple deadbolt. Now he watched the old soldier. The keeper had been attentive to the people who came in to be sure they paid the admission fee, but when the three people who had been in the study left the house, the old man didn't look up. That was what Frank had hoped for.

He continued to wander. Chekhov's bedroom and that of his brother were Spartan. There were few furnishings and no embellishment. Frank went upstairs. These rooms, the family salon, Chekhov's mother's workroom with her sewing machines and easel, and the bedrooms were much more elaborately furnished with gold-brocaded sofas and chairs. The dining room had been converted to a display area, with advertisements of Chekhov's works, first editions and playbills and a photograph of Chekhov with Tolstoy. Frank went to the parents' bedroom. A white spread covered the bed and hung down almost to the floor. A young couple was in the room. As soon as they went out, Frank went to the far side of the bed, knelt down and rolled under. He checked his watch: three forty-four. For the next sixteen minutes he watched shuffling feet. They were fewer as the time passed. At one minute to four he heard a man, almost certainly the custodian cry out.

"Four o'clock. As the sign says, we close at four precisely."

There was no one in the bedroom, but Frank heard some people going down the stairs. In two more minutes, he heard the slow footsteps of the old soldier. Now Frank could see his shoes, down at the heels, the black leather cracked. Frank held his breath. The veteran stood still for several seconds, then turned and went out. Frank heard him walking through the other rooms, then footfalls going back down the steps. The old timer opened the door downstairs and apparently was on his way out when Frank heard him speak.

"You can't come in. We are closed. Do you see the sign?"

There was another voice.

"Not yet, Daddy, we have to ask you some questions. Let's go back inside."

"What is going on?" the old man asked.

"Nothing to worry about, we are looking for someone, a foreigner. He would be almost two meters tall, eighty-five kilos, dark hair, blue eyes. Have you had such a visitor today?"

"A foreigner? A German?"

"You have Germans on the brain, Daddy. No, this man is possibly American. He could have claimed to be Irish. Have you seen anyone like that?"

"Maybe, but there are a lot of people who come in, and all visitors are gone now."

"We'll just have a look around."

Frank heard movement. A minute later he heard the voice of a third man.

"What's upstairs?"

"The salon, the family area, bedrooms."

"We'll just have a look."

Frank heard the footsteps on the stairs. The men passed through the salon then Frank saw a pair of black polished shoes and the drooping cuffs of gray woolen pants. The shoes stopped about two feet from the bed. Frank stopped breathing again. He could feel his heart thumping. It was so violent that he wondered if it could be heard outside his chest. The man walked out.

"So, no one left but you, eh Daddy?"

"No one." They went downstairs again.

Frank heard the front door open. The caretaker locked it on their way out. Frank was alone except possibly for Chekhov's ghost.

Chapter 48

"Our boy wasn't on the plane. We just got a message from Vienna." Harry O'Meara had called Bill Marshall at his home in Chevy Chase and was careful not to mention any names. Marshall's wife had gotten him out of the shower where the division chief had gone following their Sunday afternoon sex and now he stood in the bedroom, a towel wrapped around his middle. He was dripping on the carpet.

"What about the fellow he went to get?"

"He didn't show either. We heard from Frankfurt."

"So they're still in the dog pound?"

"As far as we know."

"Did you tell the station to put down the other docs and the plane ticket?"

"It's done, but there's a problem. The station says that they're blanketed. They say they've never seen anything like it. The secretary loaded the drop, but she thinks she may have been under surveillance, too. The kid may be walking into a trap."

"God damn it, can't they give him a danger signal?"

"It was never built into the plan. She didn't spot the tails until after it was all done. The tape was up, the package was down."

Marshall knew he would have to brief the director, but he decided he would wait until tomorrow. No point in disturbing him on Sunday. Besides, maybe Manion was bumped from his flight but would make it out by then, or maybe the girl was wrong about the surveillance. Still, if Manion was trapped, Marshall knew he would take it in the neck. Why the hell had he let the kid talk him into this?

"And the other guy, the redhead, anything?"

"No. But it's a hell of a coincidence that the two of them have gone missing together. They may have planned this. They may have gone over together."

"For Christ's sake Harry, give it a rest, will you?"

"You know as well as I do it's happened before. Burgess, McLean, Philby? What about those kids in Mexico City, Boyce and Lee?" Marshall said nothing for a moment. It was true. You could never tell what predicaments people could get themselves into, or what motivated them. Still, Frank Manion? He didn't think so. The kid was a solid citizen. The Raven must have read his mind. "Boyce was an altar boy."

"What about tonight," Marshall asked, "the other thing?"

"We're still on," Harry said. "Our pigeon has flown north." O'Meara was referring to Steve Cooper. "His wife went with him. He's taking annual leave tomorrow. They don't plan to be back until tomorrow night. We'll go in around ten."

"Remember, Harry. This is the bureau's case now. Don't get in their way. You're just along for the ride."

"I understand."

"Keep me posted. And tell those station guys in Moscow to earn their goddamn pay for once. Figure out how to get our boy out of there." He slammed the phone into its cradle.

That afternoon, Marshall received another call, this time from Julie d'Andrade.

"I'm sorry to bother you on a Sunday, but I was wondering if you had heard anything."

"Neither of them arrived where they were supposed to. Obviously, something unexpected happened. In our business we have to expect the unexpected."

"What are his options?"

"Our people in Moscow have put down fresh documents for him. He just has to get through tonight and I suspect that at this point he's pretty much flying by the seat of his pants."

"Can't he go to the embassy?"

"Negative." There was silence at the other end of the line. Marshall wanted to end the conversation on a positive note, like a comedian who always left them laughing. But this time there was nothing to laugh about. "As we both know, he's a pretty resourceful fellow. He'll find the new passport and be on the plane tomorrow. We certainly can't give up on him yet."

But Bill Marshall already had.

Chapter 49

For Frank, sleep was out of the question. The peanuts he bought at the zoo were intended for the elephants, but he was glad the animals' odor had kept him from feeding them. He ate the nuts now and was careful not to leave the shells anywhere. Even though he moved to the bed rather than the floor, he was not going to suffer Goldilocks' fate and he found himself jumping at every little noise. He thought often of Shurin. Had it been worth it? America had certainly benefited from the Russian's treason, but Shurin himself had rolled dice with the devil and lost. Frank knew he could end up the same way. He kept going over in his mind the instructions for retrieving his new documents. They were his lifeline, his only way out now. And lying awake he realized that he had another problem: money. He had plenty of it, just not the right kind. After paying his hotel bill, buying his meals, purchasing a ballet ticket and covering cab fares with rubles, he had given Bagatelle an envelope with the ruble equivalent of one hundred British pounds for incidentals. He needed more Russian currency. But in order to change pounds into rubles, he would have to produce a passport, unless he did it on the street. And where better to find black market money-changers than in a place where tourists gathered. But his first task, by far the most important, was to get his new passport and ticket.

At seven fifteen it was barely light. He peered through the sheer curtains at the street below. There were few people about and he decided he had to make his move. He stood and straightened the bed. Downstairs he twisted the deadbolt on the door and realized as he went down the steps onto the street that he had stiffened up in the night. It was the same muscle he'd pulled before he first saw Spats and he grew concerned. He figured that at some point in the course of the day he would have to be able to move quickly and that wouldn't be easy if his leg wouldn't cooperate. He spotted the metro sign at Barrikadnaya from a block away, limped down the broad stairs and used the change left over from his last taxi ride to buy a ticket. He exited at Leninskiy Prospekt.

His heart leaped. In Gagarin Square on the pole supporting the sign for the number seven trolleybus was a black piece of tape, the load signal. It meant that the secretary had been able to put down his new passport and ticket. Now all he had to do was find the drop site and pick it up.

From the square the number seven went uphill on Ulitsa Kosygina past the Pioneers Palace, with a mosaic of young pioneers blowing bugles under Lenin's avuncular gaze. Frank had no idea that he was following the same route Bagatelle had taken to pick up his first package and that the drop site would be the same: Moscow State University. The Soviet desk at headquarters had decided they didn't want to compromise another site and it wasn't something he needed to know. Now Moscow Station's instructions called for him to get off in front of the school, but he went one stop farther. Maybe it was instinct, maybe it was training, or maybe it was that he had always kept in mind advice he had gotten from Father Daniel, the priest at St. Vincent's, who told him when Frank went back for one of his periodic visits that most people weren't very bright and if he wanted to succeed in life, he would have to think for himself. Whatever the reason, he decided to come on the scene from a different perspective.

As he walked back uphill from the bus stop and out onto the esplanade, he reminded himself to do so with purpose and not to appear to be surveying the situation, though that, in fact, was what he intended to do. And it struck him immediately that something was wrong. Moscow State University had over thirty thousand residents. True, it was only eight o'clock on a Sunday morning, but where were they all? At the far end of the boulevard close to the central building with its swags and statues he saw that a wooden barrier had been placed across the walkway and people coming out of the building were being directed to walk along the side of one of the residence halls.

Out on the open prospect he saw something that he found even stranger. Near the trees where his package should be there was a man throwing a ball to a dog. It suddenly struck him that it was the first dog he had seen in Moscow. And this was not just any dog, but a German shepherd, a guard dog heavy and muscular. He remembered Julie's rottweiler. Some dogs didn't chase balls. Frank kept walking along the balustrade. What he saw next sent a chill through him. The man lobbed the ball. It was obvious that the fellow was not used to the throwing motion. But after he did so, he lowered his head into the front of his leather jacket and Frank saw his lips move. Then the fellow looked in the direction of the street on the southwest side of the residence halls. Frank saw a black panel van. He kept walking and didn't look back.

He started downhill. As nearly as he could calculate, he was about two and a half miles from Red Square and he wanted to walk. He thought he might have to throw up, but there was little in his stomach and he hoped that the walking would loosen him up and settle him down. Above all, he needed time to think. The KGB had the site staked out. Just as he had in Rio, he meandered, wandered into side streets, crossed at traffic signals, did the things that enabled him to look back naturally. After about a mile he was convinced no one had spotted him. But now what?

Leninskiy Prospekt was broad and clean, antiseptic. Stalin had built it for show. This was, after all, the country that had created the original Potemkin villages. The day was overcast, and although there were now more people on the street, a good number of them were drunks.

It took him almost thirty minutes before he spotted the wall of the Kremlin. All the while, Marshall's admonition stuck in his mind. Those documents had been his last chance. Now he was on his own. He had no idea how to proceed. He was cold and exhausted and continued to feel sick.

The south wall was imposing. He wondered how an enemy could approach it and he, after all, was an enemy. He walked north and as he got closer to the square, even at this hour of the morning he passed countless visitors buses. Passengers were stepping down from a blue one and Frank heard them speaking Hungarian. He looked at the lettering on the side of the bus. It was from the Ibusz Tourist Agency. On the glass panel over the driver's front window was the word Budapest. He waited nearby until the last person had gotten off. The driver stayed in his seat and closed the door. Frank followed the visitors at a distance.

They were colorfully dressed and the girls looked chic compared to the Russian women he had seen on the street. For that matter, the girls looked very attractive compared to girls from anywhere. They could have passed for models.

The group followed a woman who seemed to be a tour leader. From this distance Frank couldn't make out what she was saying. Half the time she spoke over her shoulder, but she led them across the enormous square toward the geometric ochre-layered monument that was Lenin's Tomb. The final resting place of the first Bolshevik leader was built into the wall of the Kremlin. Inside, Frank knew, Lenin's body was preserved like some kind of modern mummy. The lines that formed every day to see this curiosity were always long and mostly reverential. The Hungarians appeared less so. They chatted away as they stood waiting to enter.

Frank stood behind a fellow about his size and age. Most of the women were farther ahead in the line.

"So, comrade, is this your first visit to Moscow?" Frank asked in Russian. He knew that all Hungarians were forced to study Russian in school. After all that the Soviets had done to Hungary, most wouldn't speak it in Budapest, but these people had come to Moscow, so he thought the man wouldn't be offended. The fellow looked quickly at Frank trying to size him up. Frank realized that except for the fact that he was unshaven, he probably looked more like a KGB man than an average Russian. But the Hungarian didn't seem intimidated.

"No," the man said. "The group comes about once each year. It is my third trip." He had turned away to face forward as he said this.

"I am from Krasnoyarsk," Frank said. "For me it is only the second time I have come to Moscow. You have been to my capital more than I have." Frank chuckled. "Did you come by train? That is how I came."

"No, by coach." For the first time, the man turned to look steadily at Frank. Then he turned away again. He seemed to be hoping Frank would go away.

"And will you stay longer?"

"No. We leave right from here to go back to Budapest."

"By coach. It must be a long trip."

"We stay tonight in Kiev. We arrive in Budapest tomorrow evening."

Frank could see that the changing of the guard was about to take place. Two gray-uniformed young men with high polished boots were marching stiff-legged slowly past the blue spruces along the wall to take their place outside the tomb entrance. He noticed, too, that one of the girls in the Hungarian group kept glancing at him. She was wearing sunglasses with large lenses and a black frame. He thought that was somewhat affected since there was no sun. She nudged the girl beside her and she, too, turned to look at Frank. It reminded him of high school dances.

"I think I will watch this from another spot," Frank said. "All the best to you, comrade, I hope you have a safe journey."

Frank wandered back across the square. He was still looking for money changers, but he saw none. That was a bad sign. Usually they could spot trouble and they avoided it. If they came around, it meant that they had cased the site carefully and were sure there were no police or security people on the scene.

Ahead Frank spotted the plainclothes men. They had stopped a couple, obviously foreigners, and had demanded to see their papers. Frank went in the other direction and circled back to the place outside the wall where the buses stood side by side. He found the blue one again. This time he approached from the driver's side and saw that the fellow was dozing in his seat. The front door to the bus was still closed. Frank thought of knocking, waking the man and offering him a bribe to allow him to ride the bus, half now, and half when he got safely across the border. But he knew that Ibusz was a state-controlled agency. That woman who was leading the group was at the very least an AVH co-optee and this driver would never risk his steady job even for a large chunk of British pounds. At best, the fellow would take the money and turn Frank in somewhere along the way. And the woman who was the watchdog would check all the passengers before they started out. Then at the border the Soviets would probably check Hungarian papers almost as carefully as they checked anyone else's. Frank had to find another way.

He went around behind and to the other side of the coach. As he did so, he looked to be sure no one was approaching. There were two baggage compartments in the underbelly of the bus. As quietly as he could, he lifted the metal handle to the front bin and pulled up the side panel. The compartment was full. Suitcase was piled upon suitcase. There was absolutely no free space whatsoever. He lowered the lid carefully and cringed when he snapped the handle into place and there was the clink of metal on metal. Frank quickly walked to the back of the bus and watched. The driver didn't move. Now Frank waited as a group of people passed by headed for the square. When they had moved on, he went to the second luggage compartment and opened it. It, too, was heavily loaded. There were suitcases, along with a great many packages. But there was space at the top of the pile. He hesitated for a moment. If he decided to try this, his chances of succeeding were next to none, but if he stayed in Moscow he had absolutely no chance at all.

Frank crawled in and had to use all his arm strength to keep the side panel from slamming shut. There was an inside mechanism at the handle for opening and closing, but he couldn't reach down to secure it. He had to let the side lid remain slightly ajar. He shimmied across the top of the baggage pile to the side farthest from the opening. He re-positioned some bags to create a little burrow and moved down into it. He was surprised that many of the packages seemed so soft. They were wrapped in that waxy brown paper the Eastern Europeans used and tied with white cord. They gave off an odd odor like that of a dog that needed a bath, but he figured he could live with that. For now, he decided not to disturb them. All he did was wait.

After about thirty minutes he heard talking and movement outside the bus. Then he heard the door open and could feel the vibration as people climbed aboard and walked down the aisle over his head. Suddenly, the side panel lifted. The daylight made him blink. He remained down behind the bags. The driver must have been checking the space. He slammed the side panel shut and climbed back on the bus. The engine roared to life. Frank could feel the movement as the driver backed out of his space, then the slow shift as the coach turned and pulled forward. Frank checked his watch. There was a tiny edge of light down each side of the lid, but otherwise the compartment was dark enough so that the only way he could see the time was by the luminescence of the hands. It was twelve-fifteen. By twelve forty-five, they were out of the stop-and go movement that meant they were in traffic and the bus was rolling steadily. They must be outside of Moscow and on a highway. The road was bumpy and uneven and the bus suspension left something to be desired, but Frank settled in for the ride.

With the rock and rhythm of the road he thought back to his year driving a cab. He remembered the wave of robberies that had begun just after he started. The Philadelphia Police Department had assigned plain clothes officers as drivers and two of them were robbed, but as the robbers got out of the cabs the cops got out and shot them dead. From that point on, every driver figured any robber would shoot first and take the money afterward. All of them, Frank included, rode uneasily from then on. It was that way now.

Still, he was curious about the packages. When he had gotten into the compartment and had seen them in daylight, they all seemed to be about the same size and the same dimensions. With nothing but time and working just by feel he untied one and peeled back the wrapping. It took him several seconds to realize that what he was holding was fur, an uncured pelt. It was smooth and soft, but it was also the source of the odor. The passengers probably intended to sell them when they got home to pay for the trip and make a bit of profit as well. Frank nestled among them and as the adrenaline was depleted, with the sway and roll of the bus he fell asleep.

Several times he awoke to check his watch. It was almost midnight when the bus resumed that stop-and-start pattern. He could hear other cars moving beside them and past them. The Hungarian had said they would overnight in Kiev. They must be in the city. He worked quickly re-arranging the bags. He pushed and stacked the suitcases closer to the opening of the compartment and shifted the packages away from the opening. If people were going to retrieve their bags to take into a hotel, he would still have sufficient cover and concealment. It was almost twelve-thirty when the bus came to a final stop. Frank listened to the chatter and movement as people got off. The driver opened the front compartment and he ducked down as the side lid of his hiding place opened. The pile shifted a bit this way and that as people pulled out their bags. No one spotted him. The lid closed again. This time Frank thought he heard the sound of a key in the handle. Then the bus started up and moved for a short distance. He heard the driver get out and in another minute the door closed and everything was quiet.

Frank wouldn't have minded staying where he was. The furs had kept him warm so far and he knew he would wake up when he heard the passengers returning. But nature was calling and he didn't want to spoil the passengers' booty and have to ride with an additional unpleasant odor.

He waited another fifteen minutes. There was total silence outside. With most of the suitcases gone, he could maneuver more easily and he got to the handle. The lock was a cheap affair. From the inside, all Frank had to do was to turn the little cylinder and push the handle. He lifted the lid slowly.

He could see to the sides before he could see what was in front of him. The bus was parked in some kind of yard. He stepped out stiffly and lowered the lid quietly but didn't close it. One of his legs was still sore and both were weak. There was a cold drizzle. He stayed close to the side of the bus. The front was facing the wall that surrounded the yard. There were four other buses in a row. The hotel itself was large, not so enormous as the Rossiya in Moscow, but still pretty big. It must have been ten stories high. There were few lights on at this hour. At first, Frank saw no one in the yard then he looked at the large wooden gate that was closed. There was a small shed next to it. A tiny light flickered for an instant. Someone was puffing on a cigarette. Frank walked to the front of the bus, did his business against the wall and got back into his temporary refuge. He thought of Bagatelle. Only God knew what tomorrow would bring.

Chapter 50

On Sunday night at ten o'clock precisely, Harry O'Meara accompanied by three FBI agents made a surreptitious entry into Steve Cooper's Bethesda apartment. The bureau's surveillance team in New York had confirmed that the Coopers were still in the Big Apple, and in the parking lot outside the apartment, another bureau agent was sitting in a van monitoring the comings and goings of other residents and visitors.

The men all wore rubber gloves and black flannel coverings on their shoes and they moved silently from room to room to be absolutely certain that no one was in the apartment. Then they split up, with each man starting his work in his pre-assigned search area. The Raven wandered into the bedroom. The agent who was to search this part of the apartment had started in the master bathroom. Harry could see the focused beam of the man's penlight moving back and forth. Harry, himself, scanned the bedroom with his own tiny flashlight. He spotted the louvered double doors of a walk-in closet. He was grateful the bureau agent hadn't started his search there. Harry stepped into the closet. There were several sweaters each in its own clear plastic zippered bag on the shelf to the right. Harry took one down. He looked back over his shoulder and saw that his bureau colleague was still active in the bathroom. Harry opened the plastic bag. He unzipped his jacket and removed a small packet of papers. He fitted them into the fold of the sweater, re-zipped the bag and replaced it on the shelf. Then he walked out of the bedroom and waited.

It was another fifteen minutes before the bureau man came from the bedroom. He was holding the papers in his hand and waving them back and forth.

"Do these look like agency documents?" the fellow asked. He held them out to Harry, who scanned them with his flashlight.

"Yeah, they're cables from Moscow."

"We got him."

Bill Marshall got the call around midnight.

"The bureau found classified papers in his apartment," Harry said. "They're going to arrest him tomorrow as soon as he gets home before he has a chance to do anything with them. They have the warrant."

"How the hell did he ever get them out of the building? I thought we had the camera on him the whole time," Marshall asked.

"Beats me, but maybe we ought to start thinking about a trade. We give them this bozo and they give us back our fair-haired boy."

"He has dark hair, Harry. Besides, this morning you were sure he had defected."

"I never said I was sure, Bill. What I'm saying now is that we've got a bargaining chip no matter which way this thing goes."

"I'm glad I'm not one of the synapses in your brain. I'd get pretty worn out blinking on and off. Get some sleep. And Harry…"

"Yes?"

"You done good."

Chapter 51

Frank knew they were getting close. He didn't remember how far it was from Kiev to the Hungarian border, but it was almost two in the afternoon and the bus had been moving steadily at a good speed, so they couldn't be very far now. He figured they must be traveling along the same route Soviet tanks had taken during their suppression of the Hungarian revolution in 1956 and the Czech uprising in 1968. That must be why the road was kept in such good condition. They would probably cross at the Zahony Bridge.

He had started rummaging through suitcases and had found several jars of Beluga caviar, more contraband to sell in Budapest. He opened one and ate it. He found a wire hanger and took that out. If he made it into Hungary, he intended to wait for the bus to stop somewhere and use the wire to pop the lock on a car, hot-wire it and drive to Budapest. He rearranged the contents of the bags and closed them.

Realistically, he had little hope of getting across. In the night he recalled the horror stories, all true, of CIA case officers who languished for twenty years and more in Red Chinese jails. The agency had never admitted that these people were its own and the Chinese refused to let them go without that admission. Frank was confident that the Soviets would not handle his case the same way, but he knew he faced some period of incarceration and that it could last for several years depending on the political climate, which right now was not good. He thought of Julie and how she would handle it. But more often he thought of his stomach. He hadn't eaten in about thirty hours and he was feeling cramps. At least in prison, just like the army, he would get three hots and a cot.

The bus slowed. He could feel the shift in pressure as they came to a stop. For the next thirty minutes they rolled slowly, then stopped, then rolled again. They were in some kind of line. Then he heard the dogs barking. His stomach sank.

With another stop, Frank heard the pneumatic door of the bus open. There was a woman's voice speaking in Russian. Frank figured it was the group leader. The dogs were just outside the baggage bins and they were barking madly. They sounded like German shepherds, with that loud, deep-throated bark. Frank heard one stern voice.

"*Otkroitye.*" (Open up.) The side lid lifted. They had opened the rear bin, Frank's bin, first. The dogs were growling. Frank heard and felt one of them up on the pile of bags. "*Shto eto takoe? Borya, smotri.*" (What is that? Boris, look.)

Another man and another barking dog.

"*Krisi.*" (Rats.)

Both men laughed.

"They're going crazy over these skins," the first fellow said.

A woman's voice.

"*Nutrii.*" (Nutrias.)

The lid closed and Frank heard the inspectors working on the forward bin. He couldn't believe it. He might actually get across. He remembered that one of his Russian teachers, Mrs. Alexander, had called nutrias "the working-woman's fur." That was only fitting in the land of the proletariat.

The guards must have given the contents of the front bin a good going- over. It was forty minutes before the bus moved on. It took them five or six minutes to cross the bridge. On the Hungarian side, more dogs, but this time the inspectors concentrated on everything in Frank's compartment including him.

"Come out of there," the Hungarian said. He pointed a Kalashnikov automatic rifle at Frank, and suddenly all the fatigue and stress of the past two days overcame him. He could barely climb over the few remaining suitcases. "Who are you?" Then the guard said in Russian, "*Vy Russkii?*" (Are you Russian?)

The bags were scattered on the ground in a large parking area and the passengers had gathered just beyond the luggage. Two other guards approached and took Frank by the arms. They began pushing him toward a concrete building with a plate glass window. He could see other officials inside. One guard who was apparently the senior of the three said in Hungarian, "Latsy, go ahead. Call the Soviet side. We'll have to send him back." Suddenly, a woman's voice called out still in Hungarian.

"He's an American."

Everyone stopped. The guards and Frank looked to see who had spoken. The woman came to the front of the group of passengers. Frank saw it was the girl who had been looking at him in Moscow by Lenin's Tomb. Now she took off her sunglasses. It took him a moment to realize she was the model who had tried to seduce him. Now it all fit, the furs, the trip to Moscow. He remembered the woman at the fur factory saying that they got most of their pelts from Siberia.

"I'm an American diplomat," Frank said in Hungarian.

"What are you doing hidden in a bus? Where are your papers?" asked the senior man.

"I had too much to drink. Somebody robbed me. They took my passport and stuffed me into the baggage compartment."

At first the officer and his underlings just stood there looking at him trying to comprehend the situation. Finally, the officer took the usual military way out.

"We'll let the colonel deal with this," the officer said to the other two, who started pushing Frank again toward the building. He pointed to the girl. "You come, too," he said.

For two hours, the passengers sat on the bus. The model told the Hungarian colonel what she knew. He talked to Frank, who gave the same story about losing his papers in Moscow and finding himself in the bin on the bus. The colonel was having none of it. He called his superior in the Ministry of Security in Budapest who apparently told him to release the passengers, but hold on to Frank. The burning question in Frank's mind was whether they intended to send him back across that bloody border.

An hour after the bus pulled away Frank saw a Black Mercedes drive into the lot. Two men got out. Frank recognized one of them. It was the fellow who had laughed when his car almost ran Frank and Charlie down in Parliament Square. In the ten months he had been in Budapest, Frank must have identified sixty or seventy surveillants. Why did they have to pick this guy? Frank was sitting outside the colonel's office. The two passed him and the one Frank recognized gave him a knowing smile, but said nothing. Nor, despite Frank's effort to get them talking, did they or the leather-jacketed driver speak to him all the way back to Budapest. They had him in handcuffs between them in the back seat.

Frank was encouraged. Obviously someone high up had made the decision to deal with him in Hungary rather than send him back into the Soviet Union. But he was a lot less pleased when the car rode right through the capital and continued traveling out along the river road.

"Where are you taking me? My embassy is in Szabadság Tér."

Neither man replied. They entered a small town. Frank saw the sign: Vac.

There are strange connections in life. Frank had no way of knowing it, but for the next three days when he was not being interrogated he occupied the same cell in which Istvan Pinter, the young Hungarian air force officer, had been incarcerated before he escaped and was shot down over Lake Fertö. But unlike Pinter, the chances of Frank's escaping were zero.

The second day was the worst. There were two interrogators. They kept going over the same issues, what he had been doing in Moscow and his espionage activities on Hungarian soil. One of the two was tall and lanky. Frank sat on a chair in the middle of the room. Most of the time the two circled him like vultures, firing off questions. But late in the evening on that day, the lanky fellow must have had a burst of adrenaline. As Frank faced forward, the fellow asked him again what he was doing in Budapest.

"I'm a diplomat. I'm a commercial officer. I deal with your chamber of commerce, with your foreign trading organizations..." Suddenly, Frank felt a stunning blow on his left ear. It was totally unexpected and knocked him off his seat. His head was ringing.

"Stop it, Peter," the shorter interrogator said to his colleague. "Here, let me help you up." The second man started to lift Frank by one arm, but when Frank had risen to his knees and his middle was wide open, the first man, Peter, kicked him in the belly. Frank doubled over. He immediately became nauseous. It was the only time he was grateful for the fact that he'd had almost nothing to eat for two days. He heaved what little there was in his stomach. Choking on his own bile, he struggled to his knees. Suddenly another kick struck him in the ribs and he went down again, face first and cracked his nose. Two guards came in and dragged him back to his cell.

Imre Galos had, of course, been told of Frank's capture and his subordinates kept him fully informed of the results of the interrogation. He realized full well that the arrest could have political consequences. He briefed the Minister of Internal Affairs, who in turn reported the matter to the president. Still, Imre was surprised when, at eight o'clock on the third morning after the American's arrest, he got a call directly from Janos Kadar.

"Tell your men to let the American go."

"Yes, Comrade President."

"Bring him back to Budapest. Tell them to contact his embassy and have them pick him up on Roosevelt Ter."

"Yes, sir."

"No last minute rough stuff. He's not to be harmed. We will, of course, declare him persona non grata. The Foreign Ministry has already notified the American ambassador. The spy will have to leave the country within forty-eight hours."

It was Ty Gardener who came to get Frank. He accepted the letter the Hungarians had addressed to Walter Crittenden, who had already been chastised by the Hungarian Foreign Minister. There was no question of using the full forty-eight hours the Hungarians allowed them. Frank's left ear was still ringing, but worse, he had a terrible pain in his stomach. Crittenden called Tony into his office.

"I want him out of here today, if possible," Crittenden said.

"I agree, Mister Ambassador. They inflicted pretty severe damage. Francis needs medical care as soon as possible. We were hoping to send him to our military hospital in Frankfurt, but the timing won't permit it. Instead, our best choice would appear to be the non-stop flight to Paris. I have asked our station there to make arrangements for him to be met at the airport and taken by ambulance to the American Hospital."

"Ty should go with him. Terrible business. How the hell did all this happen, Tony? Why wasn't I briefed on it?"

"It was an extremely sensitive case, as you can imagine. We never anticipated that it would end this way, of course."

"You people never do."

Chapter 52

Two days after his appendectomy, Frank lay in bed with an intravenous solution dripping into his left hand. The French surgeon had caught the appendix as it was about to burst, but Frank was still badly dehydrated by the time Ty Gardener and Ronnie McKinsey, a Paris station admin officer, had gotten him to the American Hospital in Neuilly, just outside Paris. McKinsey had insisted on being in the operating room when Frank was anesthetized. That was agency policy, though it took a lot of persuasion and a personal plea from the American ambassador for the French doctor to accommodate an outsider in his workspace.

With the appendix removed, Frank was out of danger. Still, he had suffered two broken ribs when the Hungarian interrogator kicked him. He couldn't discover any movement that didn't cause him pain.

Ty stood beside Frank's bed. He was about to leave for Budapest.

"Don't worry about anything. Nancy and Joanie Noble will pack you out."

"I didn't have much there anyway."

"It's all set up for you to recuperate at the McKinseys' place. They have an extra bedroom and the doctor says you'll be up and moving in a couple of days, but you can't overdo it."

"That won't be a problem. With these ribs it hurts just to breathe. I don't think I'll be playing tennis for a while."

"Then I'll be going."

"Thanks for everything, Ty. It was great working with you, even if it didn't last long."

"You would have done the same for me." Ty Gardener grabbed Frank's hand. "By the way, you have a visitor. He's outside. He wants to talk to you alone. I'll send him in."

As Frank lay there, he went over in his mind everything that had happened. He had given Tony the bare bones of the story and he tried to talk to McKinsey about it, but the Paris officer had no news, so Frank was pleased to see Bill Marshall walk through the door.

"So, you just had to take a tour of Moscow, eh? I bet you'll think twice before you try that again."

"Sorry. It all blew up in my face." For the first time in a very long time, Frank broke down. Tears ran down his cheeks. He began to sob convulsively, but with the pain that caused he got control of himself quickly.

"It's okay, Frank. Don't hold it back. You've been through the mill."

"I'm all right. I never thought I'd get this far, I guess."

"I got Tony's cable," Marshall said, "but it was pretty sketchy. You feel up to talking about it?"

"I've wanted to do that for days."

For the next forty-five minutes, Frank told Bill Marshall everything that had happened.

"I still don't get the part about how you got across to the Hungarian side."

"The Russian guards figured the dogs were reacting to the skins, not to me, although I probably smelled just like the skins by that point. I was pretty ripe. Do you want me to try to write it up?"

"I think I've got it, at least for now. You can put it all on paper later. By the way, the bureau picked up the Hungarian from Montreal who was meeting Cooper. We were going to trade him for you if they had decided to keep you. Since the Hungarians let you go, we're going to turn him over to them, but not without some roughing up. The bureau boys love it when we tell them they can take the gloves off. We're keeping Cooper, though. He's a U.S. citizen."

"What about Tony? How's he going to handle everything?"

"We're sending out a replacement for you, another first tour officer. He's coming out of language school a couple of months early, but he'll be fine. I want you to stay here while you recover and since that will take some time you may as well stick around to meet Mr. Spats. I've got to get going. And you have another visitor who's waiting for me to leave."

"Thanks for coming, Bill."

"Not at all, don't worry about anything. We'll sort it all out when you get home."

Frank had a pretty good idea what that meant. But he didn't have much time to stew about it. Two minutes after Marshall left, Julie walked through the door. She was carrying a bouquet of yellow roses.

"Is this the room of the happy wanderer?" She leaned over to kiss him. Frank rose a bit, grunting with the pain. "Hey, stay where you are. I'm here to get you better, not make things worse." She put her hand on his cheek. Frank started to cry again. He didn't know why. "That's not much of a greeting," she said.

"Sorry. I didn't know if I would see you for a while."

"Well I'm here. I have six weeks of home leave I never took when I got back from Brazil. I'm taking it all now. The doctor said that's about how long it will take for you to recover. I'm going to nurse you back to health."

"Six weeks in Paris together? Americans say when they die they get to go to Paris. I didn't even have to die."

In two weeks, Frank was walking regularly even though Julie wouldn't allow him to overdo it. Rather than stay with the McKinseys, they had moved into a little hotel on the rue Dauphine by the Luxembourg Gardens. Frank made love to her day and night, but carefully.

After four weeks, they were able to stroll for hours around Paris. His ribs were still sore and he had ringing in his ear, a slight case of tinnitus, but his nose had healed and he had never been so happy. At the end of the second week of April, they started going back regularly to the Flore for lunch. They ate upstairs. Frank usually had a plate of crudités and a steak tartare.

"This summer I want you to come up to the Cape to meet my family. They've heard all about you."

"You don't think I'll be in jail by then?" Frank had taken to holding his fork in his left hand and his knife in his right. His fork was turned around in the European way and he speared a gherkin and brought it to his mouth.

"You'll be fine. O'Meara and the security people keep telling Marshall that you could never have gotten across that border without having agreed to spy for the Soviets. I guess after the bureau arrested Cooper, Harry had less to occupy himself. They'll put you on the box, but don't worry. It will all sort itself out."

"I'm not worried. I decided I'm going to stay out of those office fights. You wind up with a lot of paper cuts. Besides, after having the Hungarians work me over, an agency polygraph will be a piece of cake."

On Monday of their fifth week, after lunch they walked down to the river and along the *quais* past the bookstalls. Julie asked him about those last moments with Bagatelle.

"He would have been terribly disappointed with Justinha," she said.

"I'm not sure of that. I think he realized she wasn't going to wait and when he said 'Brazil,' I think it represented a lot more for him than just Justinha. I suspect it may have come to mean freedom."

At the National Assembly, they crossed over to the Place de la Concorde and headed up the Champs-Elysées. The air was a mixture of fine drizzle and mist. Julie was on his right side, the only place where she could hold his arm without giving him pain.

"April in Paris," she waved her right arm in the air. "You know, it was that movie 'American in Paris' that made me start ballet lessons."

"Why did you ever give it up?"

"I got tired of schlepping over to Julliard every day." They were almost at the Rond Point. The center circle was filled with red gladiolas surrounded by green leaves. "But I loved the dancing." Suddenly she walked to a bench next to the sidewalk. She rested her left hand on the top slat, extended her right hand, arched onto her toes and bent sharply at the knees. "*Pliez*." Without warning, she took two very respectable bounds across the broad sidewalk and leaped. "*Jetez*." When she landed, she did a pirouette. A white-haired, elegantly dressed boulevardier with a wide bow tie applauded.

"*Charmante. Bravo*."

Frank understood why she did it. They both felt like kids again.

"We'll always remember this time," she said.

"I know we will," Frank answered.

That night, Julie got a call from the station.

"They want me to come in tomorrow. They say there's a message for me."

On Tuesday, while Julie went to the embassy, Frank did some shopping at Cartier on the avenue Montaigne. Afterward, they met for lunch. This time they ate outside the Café de la Paix across from the Opéra Garnier. Julie told him what she had found out.

"The cable was from Bill James. He wants me to join him. We're going to be supporting Paul Namr's mission. We have to go to several stations in the Middle East."

"What about Spats, he gets here on Monday?"

"You'll have to start without me. I'll be here by the nineteenth, that's Tuesday. By the way, you know what I heard in the office?"

"What?"

"Bogey committed suicide."

"Rzepnicki?"

"Yes. He hanged himself in his basement."

"What the hell? Why do they think he did it?"

"Nobody knows. His wife just found him hanging there. He didn't even leave a note."

"He was always strange. I think he was pretty angry at life, and a little afraid."

"He must have been to take his own life." They sat quietly for a moment. Julie took the copy of the Herald Tribune and turned it over on the table. The waiter brought their tea. "I'll pack tonight."

"Okay, but clear your schedule. No plans tomorrow. I want to take you to my favorite place. It's going to be a special day." Frank smiled.

"What's up?" she asked.

"Wait and see."

Frank still had difficulty climbing, but he made it up the steps of the Jeu de Paume Museum with only moderate pain. They went through the turnstile of the former royal stable that now housed the collection of French impressionists. For about thirty minutes, they wandered through the first floor collections, Monet, Manet, Renoir. They stopped at "The Wild Poppies," "The Bridge at Argenteuil," "The Winter Garden at Giverny" and "The Lady with a Parasol."

"Pisarro is upstairs. He's a favorite of mine," Frank said.

On the second floor they walked by the snow-dappled winter scenes, the dusty summer landscapes of immortalized peasants walking down rutted roads.

"He really uses just a few basic colors," Frank said. They studied the greens and blues of the "Young Girl with a Stick," and "The Harvest at Montfoucault," with its yellow field and haystacks, blue sky with white clouds and the green trees in the middle distance.

Frank led Julie to a red velour covered bench in the middle of a long wide gallery.

"Are you tired?" she asked.

"No. Please sit."

Julie sat down and patted the seat next to her with her palm.

"You, too."

"Not yet." Frank reached in his pocket. He knelt down in front of her.

"Frank, what are you doing? You'll hurt yourself." She started to pull him up, but he resisted. She put her hand on his cheek.

"I want to do this right. I brought you to my favorite place to ask you something." He flipped open the top of a blue velvet Cartier box. Inside was an emerald-cut one carat diamond ring. "This shouldn't be a surprise to you." Now she took her hand from his face and held it in his. "I was going to try to say this eloquently. I decided instead to say it simply. I love you, Julie. I'm asking you to be my wife. You should know what that means. I don't want you to be mistaken. I'm not looking for a mother. I want a lover, a friend, someone who will share every day and every night and on every one of those days and nights I'll work to make you happy. I'll give you all that I have and all that I can become. It means I will always be faithful to you. I will defend you and take your side against anyone who tries to hurt you. I will care for you when you're in pain. If we quarrel, I'll be the first to ask forgiveness. We'll laugh together and when you're sad I'll console you. We'll come closer each day and by the time we're old, we'll be one heart and one spirit. Please say you'll marry me."

It took her several moments to say anything.

"My knight in armor."

Frank pulled the ring from the box and slipped it on her finger.

"Will you?"

In spite of what Frank had said, she was clearly surprised. She raised her hand to admire the ring then looked in his eyes.

"Frank, I do love you. When I thought you might not come back, I was sick with worry. But this is a pretty big decision. I...Well, I don't know what to say. Can I have some time to think about it?" He was disappointed and it showed.

"When I went through my little adventure, I realized that we never know how much time we have. I believe the work we're doing is important and it doesn't happen in Washington, it happens overseas. But if you want to stay close to your family, I will. You're the person I want to be with wherever you want to be."

"We can't work out the logistics of a lifetime. And it's not the details. It's just that it's so important to be sure. Please don't be upset. Just give me a few days. I promise I'll tell you when I come back next Tuesday."

On Wednesday afternoon, Frank saw her off at Charles de Gaulle. "Please think about it," he said.

"I doubt I'll be thinking of anything else." She waved as she rode up on the moving sidewalk toward her departure gate.

Frank had changed hotels. He was staying on the avenue de la Bourdonnais at a hotel of the same name. On Monday he walked past the front desk in the small lobby. Through the archway, people were scurrying about at the excellent restaurant on the ground floor preparing for the luncheon crowd. The desk clerk called to him just as he was about to leave for his meeting with Spats.

"Monsieur Manion, a telephone call. You can take it just there." The man in a white shirt and striped tie pointed around the corner of the lobby. Frank looked at the calendar. The date was the eighteenth. He looked at his watch. It was three minutes past eleven Paris time and he knew Julie was two hours ahead.

"How is everything going? Has our friend arrived?" she asked.

"I'm about to go meet him."

"I won't keep you. I just had lunch."

"Where are you? Can you say?"

"I can tell you that we're in an embassy that looks out on the Mediterranean. It's on a corniche. It's beautiful."

"Is the food good there?" he asked. "Did you have any mish-mish?"

"What's that?"

"Apricot."

"Yes, but we weren't at a restaurant. I'm calling from a pay phone just outside the embassy cafeteria."

"You had lunch with Bill?"

"Yes. Are you jealous?"

"Who, me? Why should I be when I can have my pick of any model in Budapest?"

"Don't worry, he's married and faithful and you know how I am about married men. And that's why I called. Time is going by and I didn't want you to wait any longer for an answer." Frank suddenly held his breath and strangely, the thing he noticed was that his ribs didn't hurt with the tension of his muscles. "You're going to be a married man again and this time I'm going to be your wife."

For a moment he said nothing. And he would always remember his silence and his elation.

"I'll do everything I can to make you happy."

"The first thing you can do is meet me at the airport tomorrow, okay? My flight gets in at ten in the morning."

"Fine, what airline? Julie?…Julie?…."

They were cut off. He looked again at his watch. It was 11:05. He stood by the phone for five more minutes thinking she might try to call him back then he decided he had to get to his meeting with Spats.

He caught a taxi from the stand on the avenue Bosquet and crossed the river. The driver turned right off the Étoile and dropped him off at the Hôtel Meurice. Spats arrived at eleven-thirty. Frank had anticipated the fellow's first question.

"Where is Julie?"

"She'll be here tomorrow. Please come in." Frank had turned on the TV. If the Brazilians loved their soap operas, the French were obsessed by literary talk shows. This one gave opinions on who would win the Prix Goncourt. As he passed the set, he raised the volume. "May I offer you something?" On the marble-topped coffee table, Frank had spread an assortment of cheeses: Brie, camembert, chèvre, boursin; and pastries: Napoleons, éclairs, tiny lemon tarts. And he had two bottles of wine, one red, Merlot, and one white, a Pouilly Fuissé.

"It is kind of you, but I shall have lunch later on at the Paul et France." Attila held up both palms and tilted his head. He smiled sheepishly.

"Well, before Julie comes tomorrow, I thought you could tell me today anything you heard about what happened to me."

"I heard very much. Everyone was talking about it." Spats sat on a yellow brocaded sofa. Frank was in a high-backed chair. He leaned forward to hear over the noise of the TV.

"Did the AVH know I was coming across the border?"

"Not at all, but the Soviets, the KGB have since complained to us. They wanted you back. There was some talk that they would charge you with murder."

"Nonsense."

"It took a call from Kadar to resolve things. He ordered Galos, the head of our service, to set you free."

"What about the Cooper case?"

"Yes. We learned that he was arrested, and my colleague from Montreal also, although he has been freed. He is back in Budapest. So is the wife of Cooper, Erzsébet Tokacs."

"She was Hungarian?" Frank was surprised.

"Yes, an AVH officer. She lived for a long time in England. Her father was a diplomat there."

"What about Cooper?"

"You had me looking for a man named Kadar. You are obsessed by Kadar, the president. If he farts, you people in the West believe Hungary is testing a nuclear weapon."

"Well, the reason is that the Hungarian translation of Cooper-Fassbinder is Kadar and..."

"In French it is *tonnelier*, one who makes barrels. But in Hungarian there is another translation of a *tonnelier*. Yes, it is Kadar, but it is also Pinter."

Spats went on to recount the story of Istvan Pinter's strange plan that led to his contrived escape.

"So it was his idea? And he was not really an AVH officer?" Frank asked.

"Not at all. He had been in the air force, but he was no longer able to fly, some kind of heart arrhythmia and he came up with this proposal to infiltrate the political opposition in Budapest. He said that he would then go to the West as a hero and would join the FBI. No one thought it would succeed. Then he was shot down over Lake Fertö. That was a simple miscalculation. His plan was supposed to be secret, and it was. But he was helped to get out of the prison by the AVH and the border guards and the helicopter patrol were diverted for a two-hour window. But he was late in taking off and he was shot down. The few people in Budapest who knew of the plan thought he had been killed."

"How did he survive?"

"That lake is very reedy, marshy. There was an Austrian in a little boat fishing in the high grass. He saw the whole thing. He pulled Pinter from the water. He was badly wounded in his hip and his face was smashed, but the man got him to Vienna. He had surgery, even plastic surgery. His hair had turned white from the shock. With that and the surgery his whole appearance was changed. The Austrians gave him documents with the German translation of his name, Fassbinder. The next time he was heard from, he was in New York. Then he got to Washington, not with the FBI, but with your agency."

"And we let him in the door."

"Everyone in the AVH who knew of the case was shocked. But then they decided to add an extra layer of security to the cover legend by having one of our agents who worked in the Austrian government destroy Pinter's records. In the worst case they believed that if the American authorities could trace him beyond Vienna, he still would be protected. They would discover only the original story, that Pinter was a defector who escaped across the border and in the West he was a hero. But obviously you did not get that far.

"But you knew none of this before?"

"Nothing at all, or almost nothing. What I knew, I told you. But now everyone knows. Tokacs gave us all the details we were missing."

"Julie will be fascinated by this."

Frank went on to debrief the Hungarian on other cases he had learned about in Paris. But it was hard to concentrate. After he had mentioned her name, all he could think about was Julie's answer. He was tempted to tell Spats about their engagement, but did not. One reason was that aside from the risk he and Spats had shared in Budapest, he had never really connected with this fellow. He didn't know why. Maybe it was because he had not been the one who recruited Spats, but he didn't think that was it. Still, Julie had recruited him and Frank knew that tomorrow she would do better than he had done. He was happy when the fellow left.

Frank didn't know what he would do with the food and wine. He went to the wastebasket and retrieved the wrappings and the bags he had thrown away and re-packed the stuff. He put the corks back in the wine bottles. When he was about to turn off the television, the literary show was interrupted for a news report. Frank stood and watched. A journalist from Canal 2 was sitting at a desk.

"...our reporter from Beirut."

"Hello, Raymond. I am standing at the scene of an enormous explosion at the Embassy of the United States of America. The embassy is located on the *corniche* in an exclusive section of the city that overlooks the sea." The camera panned along a roadway that ran beside the Mediterranean. People were running or wandering about, some dazed, others frantic. Fire trucks sat on the grounds of the building and outside the gate along the perimeter. "As you can see behind me, the devastation has been enormous..."

The camera refocused on the embassy, or what was left of it. The journalist was standing with a microphone about sixty yards in front of the cavernous, smoking, smoldering hole in the center of the multi-storied, horseshoe-shaped building.

"The attack took place at around 1:00 P.M. local time here in Beirut. Apparently, a suicide attack, it was carried out by one or two men who exploded a truck or car by driving into the center of the building. First reports are that at least thirty people have been killed, another eighty have been wounded. They include both Americans and Lebanese who were eating in the cafeteria, which is...was located in the center of the building, which sustained the greatest damage."

It took several moments for Frank to make the connection and realize the significance of what he was watching. He was transfixed by the horror.

"Julie." He said her name out loud.

"The center of the building has collapsed. That casualty figure is expected to rise. Also among those killed or wounded were Lebanese who were in the consular area waiting for visas. The embassy was on the avenue de Paris along the seafront. The President of Lebanon has arrived. And now...wait, please, here is someone."

The camera swung wildly and focused on a tall, gray-haired man in his late fifties. Blood covered one side of his forehead and he held a cloth to stanch the flow. The reporter spoke in English.

"Sir, what is your name?"

"Henry Reynolds."

"Are you with the embassy?"

"Yes. I am Deputy Chief of Mission."

"What can you tell us about this terrible occurrence?" Frank was glued to the set.

"What I can say is that it is a dreadful scene."

"And where were you when the attack took place?"

"I was in my office which is on the eighth floor next to the ambassador's office."

"And is the ambassador alive?"

"Yes. We used the staff of the American flag to pry the debris from on top of him."

Some people say that in the moment before death your whole life flashes before your eyes. For Francis Manion, dying at that moment would have been easy. Instead, he saw not his past, but the life he was condemned to live from that moment on. He dropped to his knees in front of the set. His hands covered both sides of his head. He pictured himself in a long gray twisting tunnel from which there was no escape and where pain and sadness awaited him at every turning. The tears flowed down his cheeks and his sobbing was convulsive. Suddenly, the figures on the screen shuddered and rippled. The image turned wavy and their voices were now disembodied, otherworldly. Frank heard Reynolds say, "We made our way down a back stair case."

Either the set had lost its horizontal hold, or the transmission signal from Beirut had been weakened. The distorted images continued to undulate. A thought came into Frank's head. He didn't realize it, but he choked out the words.

"A fun house mirror."

EPILOGUE

So, there it is. I gave you fair warning not to expect a happy ending. What else can I say? I can talk about the whole thing in intelligence terms. That, after all, is my profession. And if you look at it that way, what Bagatelle gave us provided the President with a tremendous advantage in his early dealings with the Soviets and for that reason we still consider the case a success.

But I also promised to tell you the story as I knew it and I've left some loose ends. If I haven't tied them up until now, it's because as I said at the start it took several more years for me to get all the details and many of them didn't come until after Bagatelle was killed in 1983.

When the FBI arrested Cooper/Fassbinder/Pinter, he used his one authorized phone call to give his wife a pre-arranged danger signal. She was in New York for a sexual assignation and she had Harold Blaney, who was also there and unwitting of her espionage, drive her to JFK, where she boarded a Canadian Air flight for Montreal. From there she went to Paris on Air France. An AVH officer met her at Charles de Gaulle and put her on a connecting Malev flight to Budapest. As Spats said, she was an AVH officer, one of the few women they had. Like Pinter, she was the child of a Hungarian diplomat and had spent several years in London when she was young. It was a clever choice of cover since British spouses are never run through a security check by the agency. Her English, while accented, was near perfect and when Pinter was unexpectedly hired by the agency, she was chosen specifically to join him in Washington. She's still living in Budapest, as far as we know still with Pinter, but like Brigitte Bardot, whom she resembled, she's lost her youthful allure.

Pinter himself never cooperated or broke under interrogation. What we learned about him we got from Spats. From the beginning Pinter's intention was to create a legend as a dissident, get to the West and infiltrate the FBI. He reasoned that if he went to prison and escaped, even if another prisoner eventually got out and came to the West, his story of opposition involvement would not be challenged. Nobody in the top ranks of the AVH thought it would work and the few who were aware of the operation considered Pinter to be a bit unstable, but his father had been a loyal party bigwig, so they agreed to let him try. He arranged to be arrested, to spend some time in the prison at Vac, and to stage his escape with AVH assistance. If anyone ever challenged him about how he got the helicopter, he was prepared to say like-minded friends in the air force had helped him. The plastic surgery to restore his facial structure left him unrecognizable to those he left behind and when the Austrians gave him walking around papers with (at his request) the German form of his name, Stefan Fassbinder, he decided for the sake of his legend to cut the ties to his Hungarian past so, as it turned out, much of his planning was unnecessary. He convalesced in Vienna. As soon as he was able, he walked into the American Embassy there claiming to be a refugee from Czechoslovakia. He requested and was granted political asylum under the Fassbinder name. He went to New York City, changed his name again to the American form, Cooper, then got a master's degree at SUNY, Binghamton in accounting. He became a naturalized citizen in 1975. He knew the FBI hired lawyers or accountants and he applied, but was rejected by the bureau, so he joined the CIA. The swinging sexual activity was a consequence of his personal proclivity, but also a way of making contacts with Americans who might be vulnerable to blackmail. It also gave him cover for meeting his AVH contact in New York.

For most of his time with the agency, Pinter was able to provide only the names and covers of some of our officers, but for the AVH that was more than they had expected. They immediately shared the names with the Soviets. Pinter came on Rzepnicki by chance and the Bagatelle compromise was icing on the cake. America, the land of opportunity!

Spats was unable to establish the final connection between Pinter and Rzepnicki and Bagatelle because shortly after he returned to Budapest from Paris he was arrested. In Frank Manion's absence, Tony Valletta set out to put down a dead drop for Spats in the Buda hills. He believed correctly that he was free of surveillance. What he didn't realize was that the Hungarians had put a transmitting beacon under the rear fender of his car and had no need to stay close. They plotted his route from a distance and drove it two minutes later. Tony had the package for Spats on his passenger seat. The car heater was on. It was a cool night and he tossed the package into the woods at an agreed on spot. The Hungarians had a heat-sensing device. It had adjusted to the ambient temperature in the woods and when they got to the spot Tony had chosen, the package glowed like an ember in their viewfinder. They staked out the site and that was it for Spats.

We found out about Rzepnicki and the fact that it was he who tipped Pinter off to Bagatelle by a fluke. That's often the way we discover things. Rzepnicki's wife, who was German, had read about the case in the papers. The name change from Pinter to Fassbinder to Cooper caught her attention and one day in good German fashion when she was washing all of her husband's clothing before she gave it to charity she came across Cooper's name and telephone number rolled up in a pair of socks. She called the FBI. They called us.

After the Berlin wall came down, the Hungarians proposed a swap: Spats for Pinter. We accepted with delight. Spats is now living in Milwaukee with a fixed income from the United States Government. He has also become a county official handling consumer affairs. He attends most of the classic car shows throughout the Midwest.

As for Patrick Kerrane, the Czechs, who are now very friendly, told us he never defected. He just ran off with about two hundred forty thousand dollars of our money. Well, it's true that technically it was money we had earmarked to be paid out to Kerrane's Czech agent, who, as we later discovered, was under Czech control the whole time as Kerrane had claimed. Mrs. Kerrane, his mother, died, but her son paid for her treatment and all medical bills. He probably paid off the bookies as well. We've had a recent report that Kerrane went to Ireland, so he's still fair game. We think he's somewhere in the Ring of Kerry. The FBI has circulated a computer-enhanced sketch of what he would look like today and we're hopeful of tracking him down, though given all of our other priorities, I'd have to admit he's low on the list and the chances of catching him are not great.

We passed some of Bagatelle's money to Justinha Marques. We rounded it off to $150,000. She wasn't entirely deserving of the payment. As Julie d'Andrade found out, within six months of Bagatelle's return to Moscow, she had taken up with a former Brazilian boy friend, something we never told Shurin. But we were conscious of the possibility that if her story ever got to the press, it would look a lot better for the agency if she revealed that we had been generous. It pays to advertise.

After only one year as chairman of the Communist Party of the Soviet Union, Yuriy Andropov died. He was replaced by Viktor Chernenko. Natasha Chernenko's family discovered that the new top man in the Soviet Union was a distant relative. They contacted him. Natasha was given a re-trial and it was discovered that she had acted in self-defense. She was actually decorated for having put an end to the life of a traitor. Natasha returned to Perm, where she became a party functionary until the communists were ousted from power.

I said I was speaking from an intelligence perspective. But of course there is the human element. The two are always intertwined. Sometimes we forget that.

Today, as you enter the main headquarters building of the CIA, if you look to the walls on your right and left, you will see rows of stars. They used to be gold, now they're sort of ochre. They represent the agency officers and personnel killed in the service of their country. Julie d'Andrade's star is one of them.

We didn't realize it at the time, but the taking of the hostages in Iran and the bombing of the embassy in Beirut were the beginning of a new era for the CIA and for the United States. They were the first attacks in a war that has brought us to 9/11 and to where we are today in the Middle East. Julie was one of the war's first casualties.

Frank Manion went through a rough stretch until the Bagatelle case was all sorted out. Harry O'Meara, the Raven, pecked and scratched and flapped his wings all over the place, but couldn't demonstrate that Frank had screwed it up. Frank spent a lot of his waking hours in Washington hooked up to a polygraph machine, but the Raven wouldn't believe the results that showed Frank was telling the truth. In the agency, some people accept the outcome of the polygraph only when it agrees with their preconceived notion of what happened. Over Harry's objections, Frank was assigned to other field stations, where he has done excellent work even with that cloud over his head. The Raven retired three years ago.

Eventually, of course, Frank was exonerated. I talked to him a lot throughout the ordeal. He told me that Julie had predicted her own death. Frank attended her funeral and met her family. Julie's grandmother told him that Julie told her she had seen it in the cards.

Frank Manion was aware of our unofficial motto: "And you shall know the truth, and the truth shall make you free." I never asked him at the end whether he felt free or not. I suspect that from the moment Julie was killed he never felt anything in the same way that he had when she was alive. What I do know is that when he overcame the opprobrium inflicted by our rigorous controls and, yes, sometime maliciousness and paranoia, the one person he cared about was not there to celebrate with him.

The counter-intelligence and security people, the Raven's colleagues and successors, make the case that Frank is thoroughly disillusioned (no surprise there) and therefore something of a security risk. They still keep their eye on him so they can be sure to catch him if he should topple over the edge of allegiance.

THE END

CPSIA information can be obtained at www.ICGtesting.com
Printed in the USA
BVOW011155171212

308423BV00009B/34/A

9 780741 427373